PARANOIA

VICTOR MARTINOVICH

PARANOIA

A NOVEL

Translated from the Russian by Diane Nemec Ignashev

Foreword by Timothy Snyder

NORTHWESTERN UNIVERSITY PRESS / EVANSTON, ILLINOIS

Northwestern University Press
www.nupress.northwestern.edu

Printed in the United States of America

10 9 8 7 6 5 4 3 2 1

Library of Congress Cataloging-in-Publication Data
Martinovich, V.
    [Paranoiia. English]
    Paranoia / Victor Martinovich ; translated from the Russian by Diane Nemec
Ignashev ; foreword by Timothy Snyder.
        p. cm.
    "Originally published in Russian in 2010 by AST (Moscow) and Astrel'-SPb
(Saint Petersburg)."
    ISBN 978-0-8101-2876-7 (pbk. : alk. paper)
    1. Authoritarianism—Fiction. 2. Emotions—Fiction. I. Nemec Ignashev,
Diane, 1951– II. Snyder, Timothy. III. Title.
PG2835.3.M38P3713 2013
891.735—dc23

                                                            2012038748

♾ The paper used in this publication meets the minimum requirements of the
American National Standard for Information Sciences—Permanence of Paper for
Printed Library Materials, ANSI Z39.48-1992.

All the events related herein are fictional:
the protagonists have never existed in any reality
other than that of the present text. Any unsanctioned comparisons
with historical figures or persons alive today may be qualified as a
criminal offense punishable under international and national law.
To avoid unintentionally committing acts prosecutable under
the Penal Code, the author—fully aware that, essentially,
he should never have written it in the first place—
enjoins readers not to read this book.

To lovely valkyries in dresses woven of stars who careen down the oncoming lane of life behind the steering wheels of enormous vehicles; to you who view the twinkle of lights behind tinted glass with a combination of fear and delight; to you who laugh at the fleetingness of the moment and know not the meaning of death, while headlights, those enormous, bright sheaves of light, those blindingly, painfully beautiful headlights . . . To you, to you, lovely valkyries . . . I dedicate this book.

CONTENTS

In the summertime, in the Belarusian capital of Minsk, young couples rent boats. They float, seemingly aimlessly, with the current of the Svislach River, until they find themselves under a bridge. Then they row, against the current, for as long as they can, hoping to find shelter from the sun and from prying eyes. The premise of Belarusian writer Victor Martinovich's Russian-language novel is that this is impossible. Once a police state such as today's Belarusian dictatorship is brought to perfection, someone is always watching. The young lovers are observing each other, whether they understand this or not. The only way to be safe in such a society is to abandon love, but true solitude courts paranoia.

At the beginning of the novel, the young writer Anatoly finds himself alone, his lover Lisa having disappeared from her apartment on Karl Marx Street. He leaves notes for her at the door, where they are duly intercepted and interpreted by the KGB.[1] These documents open the novel, inviting the reader to accept the perspective of the police. Anatoly then recalls a relationship that seems startling in its purity, or even naïveté: his last name, Nevinsky, means "innocent." In a café, a young man could greet a young woman by asking, "Have you been waiting long?" and get the reply "All my life." A love affair could proceed with such passion that the lovers don't even learn each other's names until they fight. The source of tension is Lisa's other man: Muraviov, the Minister of State Security, who controls the (obviously Belarusian) state, holds all the important offices, and can make people disappear.

Muraviov, not just a dictator but also a pianist, is not so much a Big Brother as a Big Lover; in *Paranoia* the conventions of ménage-à-trois are artfully overlain with those of dystopia. Lisa seems to be with child. But who is the father? Lisa seems to suggest to each man in turn that it is he. Then Lisa seems to have been murdered. Which of the two men did it? Muraviov claims not to know, but this seems unlikely; and of course he would hardly admit to such a thing. At first, Anatoly seeks Lisa and confronts Muraviov, but under interrogation he admits to the murder. Does his confession bear any resemblance to what actually happened? Or, in confessing to the deed, is Anatoly simply aiding the regime to cover up its latest killing? Are he and Muraviov, in some sense, in it together?

A young man who came of age as a journalist and political scientist during the dictatorship that Alexander Lukashenko has consolidated since his first election to the presidency in 1994, Martinovich raises again some of the essential themes of the East European dissident literature. The system is not simply the rulers, it is also the ruled.[2] Self-policing is more important than policing; lovers betray each other wittingly or unwittingly; we all betray ourselves in the end. In Anatoly, Martinovich portrays a writer who, while criticizing the aesthetics of totalitarianism, is drawn toward its power. Anatoly seems to want what Muraviov has. He describes at length the latte macchiato that Lisa drinks, an artifact of a lifestyle that is really only available within the system. He is disgusted but intrigued by her black automobile and its KGB plates. The writer encounters the state in the attractive medium of a young woman's body, or on the dignified platform of high culture. In the end, Anatoly confronts Muraviov after the Minister of State Security has performed Mozart's Piano Concerto no. 24.

The Belarus of the novel is different in some respects from the dictatorship of Alexander Lukashenko. But the challenge to the regime is obvious enough. Martinovich's novel was pulled from the shelves in Minsk after two days.

To travel to Belarus today is to make an acquaintance with the KGB. At the airport from which you depart for Minsk, a functionary, likely female and seemingly harmless, patrols the gate area. At a certain point she asks each passenger for his or her passport, although on what authority is a bit unclear. At the Minsk airport, as you depart Belarus, an obvious KGB functionary checks your documents one last time before you board the plane. Then he boards the plane with you. The KGB officer is probably accompanying a Belarusian official on a journey abroad, since Belarusians of any significance cannot travel without a political chaperone. But perhaps he is also watching you. As soon as you have that thought, you've entered the world of paranoia that is Martinovich's subject.

It is only in settings such as airports that you would notice the KGB at all, so of course you might also begin to wonder who is and who is not a KGB officer. For Belarusians, recognition almost always comes too late, as an arrest is already being made. As in the opening scene of Martinovich's novel, when letters are seized and read, the KGB have the right to enter any building at any time. Belarus's other and very numerous police forces, by contrast, are meant to be highly visible. The purpose of camouflage is to permit soldiers to fight unseen; when worn by riot police in Minsk, uniforms emphasize the threat. At street corners and on subway platforms stand interior ministry troops in dress uniforms, with batons or sidearms. This is all in addition to the ubiquitous uniformed city police. All of these security forces are effectively controlled by Lukashenko; the interior ministry and the KGB are under the purview of his son Viktar.[3]

Minsk is also full of soldiers and military officers. The officers wear outsized caps and ill-fitting uniforms, and always seem to be carrying briefcases. The soldiers wear red stars on their armbands, recalling a Soviet era that they are all too young to remember. They speak to each other in Russian, the dominant language of the country and the language of command of the Belarusian armed forces. About one civilian in forty-three in Belarus is serving today in the armed forces, a ratio that far exceeds any of its neighbors, and is among the highest in the world. The draft and the long term of service (two years) is a form of social control. Young people who seem as if they might pose a challenge to Lukashenko's regime are drafted early and sent to bases far from home.

The public space of Minsk, designed by Soviet authorities after the Germans destroyed the city during the Second World War, permits little solitude. Martinovich has Anatoly speak of a city made to order for the KGB, with long, broad avenues. Independence Square, an enormous plaza in the middle of the city, feels like a panopticon. Minsk is so clean that it makes Vienna look a bit dingy. Its streets are swept incessantly by uniformed sanitation men with besoms. Martinovich has his fictional Minsk decorated with sexy KGB billboards. There are in fact rotating signs alternatively commemorating the triumph of the Soviet Union in the Second World War and displaying women in lingerie. Most people in Minsk do not have cars and so cannot control their immediate visual environment. Many of the autos on the streets of Minsk are (judging from the plates) used by state functionaries. There seems to be no fleet, as such, but rather a collection of mismatched automobiles of German make, re-painted black after they were seized from the people who stole them the first time.

"They went home," writes Martinovich of his lovers at a certain point, "where else could they go?" In the center of Minsk, city blocks extend without a single bench. The message is unmistakable: when you have con-cluded your day's business, go back to your apartment. But home itself, as in the Soviet system of which Lukashenko's regime is a continuation, does not really constitute a private sphere in the Western sense. Although private property is recognized by law, ownership can be challenged on technicalities at any time. About four-fifths of workers are employed by the state, so almost no one has the independent capacity to pay rent or mortgage. Most state employees work on one-year contracts. If they show any sign of disobedience to the regime, they can be denied a means of existence by the discreet measure of nonrenewal. There are no indepen-dent trade unions or chambers of commerce.

Despite the solemn promises of rights in the Belarusian constitution, all that is not expressly permitted is forbidden. In order to do anything of a public nature, citizens must first announce what they are doing, and name the organization within which the action will take place. The action and the organization must be explicitly approved and registered in writing by the state. When authorities wish for an organization to disap-pear, they threaten the leaseholder until the group is expelled from its legal address, then prosecute members for illegally operating in a group without a legal address. The bugbear of "registration" amounts to an at-tempt at total social control. In December 2009, fifteen Belarusian citi-zens, dressed in red and white and wearing false beards, announced that they planned to spread Christmas cheer "as an unregistered association of Santa Clauses."[4] They were informed that if they did so they would be prosecuted. In May, riot police dispersed a small group marching for gay rights. In July 2010, several hundred young people commemorated a military anniversary with a public pillow fight. Riot police made several dozen arrests.

The pillow fight was a flash mob organized by students, using electronic means that the authorities have not quite mastered. In general, though, In-ternet and the university, the new and the traditional bastions of youthful rebellion, are far from safe. Internet cafés, scarce in any case, have to report their clients to the police. Only about 8 percent of the Belarusian population have access to the Internet, and only the government is allowed to maintain Internet domains. The universities, like public life in general, are penetrated by GONGOs: government-organized nongovernmental organizations. High school students are told that they must join Lukashenko's Youth Union if they wish to enter a university. Their professors must attend weekly ideological orientation sessions. All universities and schools, including private institutions, are under the direct control of the minister of education. The Academy of Sciences is under the personal control of the president.

Martinovich's protagonist Anatoly sees the regime's goal as "stability," or control. Aside from the domination of the public sphere and the isolation of citizens, Lukashenko's regime also pursues a third strategy, which may be called vegetation. Probably the closest historical analogue to Lukashenko's ideology is that of Marshal Pétain in Vichy France: an idealization of hearth and home, an unequal and cloying alliance with a powerful eastern neighbor, and a constant condemnation of outsiders. Lukashenko's ideal Belarus is an agrarian country. As he himself puts it, "I'm not like other presidents. There's a cow in me."[5] Lukashenko rules a country where agriculture is still collectivized and is himself a former collective farm director. This means that peasants are state employees who do not own the land, but have very little prospect of leaving it. The stagnation of the Belarusian countryside is elevated to political ideal.

The unofficial national motto is "Flower Belarus!"—but flowering is not really something that people do, it is something that plants do. Lukashenko's propaganda presents his own people, the Belarusians, as something less than a full political nation. They are rather an ethnic group, adorned in Soviet-era folk costume, somewhere amidst the cows and the flowers, mindful chiefly of food and shelter. Yet Lukashenko's denationalization campaign, far from being the primitivism of a country hack, has functioned for years as a clever strategy of foreign relations. In effect, Lukashenko has exported the national identity of his people to Russia, where Russian leaders nostalgic for empire were eager to believe that the two nations might one day reunite. In exchange, Belarus received very cheap supplies of Russian natural gas. Lukashenko has flattered Russian leaders from Yeltsin through Medvedev with rhetoric of inferiority: Russia, says Lukashenko, is Belarus's "mommy." He has also regularly agreed to various forms of economic union, and offered vague promises of political integration as well. None of these bilateral agreements was ever fully realized; Russian subsidies simply allowed Lukashenko to satisfy much of Belarusian society with a measure of economic security.[6]

For more than fifteen years, Belarusians have been told a story that is meant to justify this curious arrangement. Whereas most newly independent states celebrate national history, in post-Soviet Belarus the Lukashenko regime denies that there is much Belarusian history to celebrate. Lukashenko first returned Soviet-era books to Belarusian schools, then recruited his own former history teacher, Yakov Treshchenok, to write a new textbook. In this account, Belarusian political history is essentially coterminous with Soviet political history. Belarusians became politically conscious thanks to the Bolshevik Revolution, and prospered under the fraternal guidance of Moscow. Belarusians and Russians stood together during the German invasion. Happily, Soviet rule was restored after the war and even extended to the west, thus bringing the entire Belarusian folk under Soviet rule. Belarus is in a very special historical position: alone because almost no one outside the country recognizes the scale of the catastrophe of the German occupation, but drawn by this very suffering into a larger Soviet narrative of redemption through liberation by the Red Army.[7]

The truly overwhelming suffering of the Belarusian peoples during the war was exploited as Soviet counterpropaganda. In 1940, the Soviet NKVD murdered Polish officers at the west Russian forest Katyn. To confuse the issue, Soviet authorities chose a Belarusian village with a similar name, *Khatyn,* for a memorial site recalling settlements destroyed by the Germans. In April 2010, when Russian leaders decided to publicly commemorate the victims of Katyn together with Poles, Lukashenko's Belarus passed through a paroxysm of martyrdom jealousy. When the Polish president and ninety-five other people died in a plane crash on the way to Katyn, Lukashenko was the only leader of a neighboring country not to declare a day of mourning. Shortly after the crash, a Belarusian newspaper published articles claiming that Poland was somehow to blame for the mass murder Stalin ordered at Katyn.[8]

Similarly, the history of Belarusians as righteous wartime martyrs cannot accommodate the special character of the Holocaust. Just as Soviet historians used to reckon murdered Jews as Soviet citizens, Belarusian historians now reckon them as Belarusian citizens. This is true as far as it goes, but it overlooks the particularly murderous character of the German occupation for the Jews. Belarusians as a people suffered more than any other group in Europe—except for the Jews. Lukashenko's court historian rejects the reckoning of victims by ethnicity. Meanwhile, old Jewish quarters and synagogues are demolished. In 2010 a sewer line was dredged through a Jewish cemetery, uncovering human remains. Lukashenko calls himself an "Orthodox atheist," and his ideologists present Belarus as belonging to eastern Christian civilization. School texts have little on Catholics and almost nothing on Jews. Belarusian historians working in Belarus cannot revise these essentially Soviet positions. One dissertation on everyday life in Soviet Belarus between 1944 and 1953 was rejected (again, by Lukashenko's court historian) because it did not present Russia as Belarus's "birth mother."[9]

In fact, Belarusian political history is ancient and fascinating. The country for centuries was home to a number of varieties of eastern and western Christians, to Jews, and to Muslims. Adam Mickiewicz, the Polish national poet, was born in what is today Belarus, which he called Lithuania, in a town populated by Jews, not far from a mosque. The lands of today's Belarus lay at the center of the Grand Duchy of Lithuania, one of the largest states of medieval Europe. Boyars took part in the parliament of the Polish-Lithuanian Commonwealth, which the Grand Duchy established with Poland in the sixteenth century. The chancery language of the Grand Duchy was a Slavic language similar to Belarusian. Until the modern period, Belarusian history was quite distinct from Russian history. In a textbook for tenth graders, written (again) by Lukashenko's court historian, the institutions of half a millennium are treated as alien, while union with Russia is presented as destiny. This comes across clearly in the treatment of an uprising of 1863–64 in which some nobles and peasants fought against the Russian Empire. Rather than the Belarusian insurgents, the textbook celebrates the Russian official who had them hanged.[10]

Martinovich seems to prefer knowing references to contemporary Western culture than to Belarusian history; he invokes, for example, *The Matrix*. But his novel makes its most direct thrust at the Lukashenko regime by reference to that particular historical incident. The name of the Russian imperial official who carried out the executions was Mikhail Nikolaevich Muraviov. The name of the Belarusian dictator in *Paranoia* is Nikolai Mikhailovich Muraviov. The invocation of the Russian figure was a direct challenge, even if clear only to Belarusians, to the ideology of the Lukashenko regime. In Eastern Europe, the historical Muraviov is remembered as "the hangman." In the history textbook read by Belarusian tenth graders, Muraviov was "not only a 'hangman.' He was also a very talented administrator and organizer."[11] Martinovich's novel gives a sense of just how unpleasant that particular combination would be.

What is to be done? Martinovich's novel captures the economic emptiness of Belarusian state socialism, partially covered by the debt-financed atmospherics of Western-style consumerism. In Minsk you can buy trademark-violating Bela Cola, but also listen to audio commercials for Coca-Cola in subway cars. During the Cold War, the United States was able to leverage debt relief for creaky Communist regimes for political reforms. Belarus owes money, however, not only to Western countries and international institutions but also to Russia. The regime in Belarus will likely change when Russian leaders decide that the time has come to cut off the supply of cheap natural gas.

In December 2010, Lukashenko won the presidential elections for the fourth time. He can run for as many terms as he likes; as he admits himself, his regime fakes the results (though he claims that it fakes them downwards). This time the fraud was all too evident, perhaps even to Lukashenko himself; and he ordered violent suppression of the protests that followed the announcement of the results. He has intimated that he wishes to stay in power until his son Kolya is ready to succeed him—and Kolya is six years old. If Westerners wish for elections in Belarus to be free and fair, they will have to take part in the vote counting themselves. Otherwise, Lukashenko will simply respond to the demand for independent verification by inventing new GONGOs and having them confirm the official results.

Lukashenko's Belarus recalls nothing so much as the 1970s, when the dictator came of age in Soviet Belarus, on the collective farm, learning Soviet history. This is perhaps why Martinovich's novel renews the emphasis the anticommunist dissidents of that era placed upon individuality. As important as democratic procedures are, opponents of communism in Eastern Europe spoke more often of human rights. Without human rights, democracy can be, as they say in Eastern Europe, managed. And above all, to be free means to find that cool place under the bridge and remain there despite the current. Anatoly wants to look into the eyes of another person and see not fear but recognition. "I know, I know," he says, "I'm asking too much." But he's asking for the right thing.

Notes

1. In the novel the institution appears as the "Ministry of State Security" (MGB). I use here the familiar term "KGB," the Russian abbreviation for "Committee for State Security," which is how the institution is still known in today's Belarus.

2. Here the classic text is Václav Havel's essay "The Power of the Powerless" of 1979.

3. For good analyses see Kamil Kłysiński and Agata Wierzbowska-Miazga, "Changes in the Political Elite, Economy, and Society of Belarus," *OSW Studies,* no. 30 (2009); Elena Korosteleva, "Was There a Quiet Revolution? Belarus After the 2006 Presidential Election," *Journal of Communist and Transition Politics* 25, no. 2 (2009): 324–46.

4. For this and other incidents see U.S. Department of State, Bureau of Democracy, Human Rights, and Labor, *Country Report on Human Rights Practices: Belarus,* March 2010.

5. *Komsomol'skaia Pravda v Belorussii,* May 21, 2010, 2.

6. See Adam Eberhardt, *Gra Pozorów: Stosunki rosyjsko-białoruskie 1991–2008* (Warsaw: Polski Instytut Spraw Międzynarodowych, 2009).

7. This is a subject of my *Bloodlands: Europe Between Hitler and Stalin* (New York: Basic Books, 2010).

8. Vadim Elfimov, "O dvukh storonakh medaly," *7 Dnei,* May 29, 2010, 8.

9. See Hienadź Sahanowicz, "Losy białoruskiej historiografii: Od sowietyzacja do zachodiorusizmu nowego typu," *Studia białorutenistyczne,* no. 3 (2009): 103–43. One valuable dissertation on the extension of Soviet Belarus to the west was recently published abroad: Jan Szumski, *Sowietyzacja zachodniej Białorusi, 1944–1953* (Kraków: Arcana, 2010).

10. The predicaments of modern Belarusian national identity are a major subject of my *Reconstruction of Nations* (New Haven, Conn.: Yale University Press, 2002).

11. Treshchenok, Ia. I., A. A. Vorob'ëv, V. V. Volzhenkov, *Istoriia Belarusi s drevneishykh vremen do oktiabra 1917 goda* (Minsk: Adukatsiia i Vykhavanne, 2008), 191.

PREFACE
Diane Nemec Ignashev

Every translation project presents challenges, and *Paranoia* is no exception.

For a translator *Paranoia* is schizophrenic in more ways than are immediately apparent from the title. Schizophrenia is one of its strengths. Multiple personalities enhance its appeal for different readers, from political scientists to detective story fans who know nothing about Belarus or the Soviet Union or Russia. The novel's almost manic energy—another strength—reminds readers constantly that it was written by a young writer. *Paranoia* is smart, irreverent, hip. It also bursts with meta-artistic references that dazzle the reader with the spectacular range of the author's own tastes thinly camouflaged as his hero's. Schizophrenic and manic, *Paranoia* is not, however, chaotic. The madness of Anatoly's story is carefully orchestrated, not only by the Ministry of State Security (MGB). The novel's multiple narrative perspectives build on an intricately woven system of writing styles and voices. But precisely the qualities that should make *Paranoia* a compelling read complicated the process of rendering it in English. What follows is the short list of those qualities.

A Belarusian novel written by a Belarusian writer, *Paranoia* was first published in Russian and has yet to be translated in its entirety into Belarusian. (Perhaps Belarusians are still trying to untangle Martinovich's Russian?) Just as his protagonists came to know Akutagawa, Borges, Havel, and Hemingway through Russian translation, Martinovich chose Russian over Belarusian to connect with readers beyond the borders of his native country. While he flirts with other traditions, it is from Russian writers and artists that he borrows most heavily. The entire plot of *Paranoia*, for example, is neatly summarized in the eight lines of Pushkin's lyric masterpiece "I loved you once . . ." (Ya vas liubil . . .), which as a child Anatoly recited together with his Chukcha mentor, Yagerdyshka. Nevinsky's MGB code name "Gogol" links him and his story to Russia's nineteenth-century chronicler of phantasmal Saint Petersburg and originator of the concept of "laughter through tears." Like Nikolai Gogol's playful narrator in *The Overcoat,* Martinovich initially teases readers, situating his novel in a city easily recognized in references to real streets, places, and events, while refraining from naming the city outright. At the novel's end, however, Anatoly's situation hauntingly echoes the mad despair of Gogol's Popryshchin, the pathetic hero of *Notes of a Madman.* The ridiculous bureaucratese of the MGB field agents' reports traces its antecedents to the acerbic satires of Gogol's heirs in the second half of the nineteenth century, most notably to the work of Mikhail Saltykov-Shchedrin. Anatoly's incarceration bears unmistakable parallels to Ragin's in Chekhov's *Ward Six.* As Anatoly himself suggests, the novel's chess motifs—in both setting and plot structure—pay homage to *The Luzhin Defense,* an early novel of Vladimir Nabokov's, yet another model for Martinovich. Though a tower and not a basement, Anatoly and Lisa's hideaway among the flowers links them to Mikhail Bulgakov's *Master and Margarita.* For Martinovich Russian is more than natural language; Russian, not Belarusian, dominates the cultural universe of his creative world and this novel. "The medium is the message," Anatoly likes to quote Marshall McLuhan. Tasked with so many significations, Martinovich's Russian, not surprisingly, as medium is as stylized and deliberate as Anatoly himself with his "despondent raincoat, . . . haircut ('FREAKING GENIUS'), and . . . excessively mechanical—I preferred not to think about it—way [he] walked" (13).

The "anxiety of influences" coursing through Martinovich's narrative is as apparent in the translation as it is in the original. Like all of the writers named above—particularly Nabokov—Anatoly (and Martinovich with him) uses every opportunity to play with language, especially to pun. Some puns (alas, too few), like "Marx & Spencer Street" or the STIK-II (in Russian, LIPA-II) sealing device, were, as Anatoly's Rastafarian friend Dan might say, "no-brainers." Others—like Anatoly's play with the word *gorky* (in Russian the nom de plume of writer Aleksei Peshkov, Maksim Gorky, derived from the adjective "bitter") required direct interference in the text for it to make any sense to English-language readers. A particularly tricky pun was that of Lisa's name, which, with the stress shifted to the final syllable (*lisá*) means "fox," her MGB code name. Practicality was the deciding factor in the choice between available options: *lisá* tells the English reader nothing; "fox" illuminates Lisa's character and role. Yet another category of puns, some basic to plot development, had to be reformulated in order to be preserved at all. One of the more challenging puns was that of "redux" and "ducks" (in Russian, "days" [*sutki*] and "ducks" [*utki*]) in the graffiti Anatoly spots under the Trinity bridge. Russian has dozens of words that share the *-utki* endings of these two words, and in Russian the pun is so easy as to sound trite, which is appropriate to Lisa's character. But how many words in English could be construed as the word "ducks" partly obliterated by over-painting? Translation is a cruel looking glass that ruthlessly magnifies the excesses of the original. But excising the puns was not an option. To remove them would be to remove part of Anatoly. The same is true of the hero's problematic stutter, which intensifies as his situation worsens.

Like all satirical writing, *Paranoia* borders on parable, its genre suggested explicitly in the story-within-a-story of Anatoly's imaginary professor and his politically naive student. Tim Snyder correctly explicates the local origins of political realities underlying the satire, but the 1984 of Anatoly's "country whose name begins with B" can be found not only in Lukashenko's Belarus. Less out of fear of political repercussions than of narrowing the potential appeal of his novel for a broad spectrum of readers, Martinovich employed a number of literary techniques to liberate his work from the interpretive confines of one police state. Once again, his choices had significant implications for the translation. For example, he chose to refer to the Ministry of State Security not as the KGB, as it is known in Belarus. But in English MSS, the ministry's acronym in translation, not only lacks the connotations of "Big Brother" and the KGB, it suggests something entirely unrelated. For these reasons, this translation retains the acronym Martinovich invented in the original: MGB. Another question, raised in part by the novel's publication in Russian, involved the spellings of toponyms and other proper nouns: should we follow Martinovich's lead in using Russian spellings or revert to Belarusian? The solution was a hybrid, based on practicality, common sense, and consideration for a potentially already perplexed reader. Polish proper names are rendered using Polish spelling and diacritics. Belarusian spelling of most toponyms—particularly streets named after Belarusian heroes—was restored over the Russian original, if only to remind readers that events described in the novel, though obviously possible in Russia, are not set there. Names of metro stations, such as Oktiabrskaya or Frunzenskaya, on the other hand, echo the names of stations in Moscow and remind readers (as they do Minsk commuters) of Russian-Soviet presence in Belarus. Simple readability also was factored into the mix. Although awkward, "Yubileinaya" is the name of a real hotel in central Minsk, and to translate it as the "Jubilee Hotel" would be comparable to translating, for example, "La Quinta Inn." On the other hand, given the amount of time Anatoly spends roaming the streets, "Victors' Avenue" seemed preferable to the Belarusian "Prospekt Peramozhtsaw" or Russian "Prospekt Pobeditelei." Essentially, this translation relies on the kind of mixed naming employed by English-speaking expats living in cities like Minsk or Moscow. Some names have been translated because they are simply jumbles of letters otherwise; other names have not been translated because, for example, "Youth" will not help you locate a metro station called Molodyozhnaya, or "Goat Street"—ulitsa Kazlova. For transliteration a modified version of the Library of Congress system for romanizing Cyrillic has been used: soft and hard signs are not indicated; "soft vowels" are indicated by "i" or "y" preceding the phoneme, the choice dependent on position in a word; in masculine surnames "y" replaces "ii." The spelling of names of real historical figures conforms to the standards of *Merriam Webster's Biographical Dictionary* (1995).

The metric system of the original has been replaced with U.S. measurements. Somewhat unexpectedly, in the process of regularizing these seemingly insignificant details, yet another quality of the novel emerged, one also not without implication for how Russian- or English-language readers will approach the text. Despite Anatoly's experience abroad, the first- and third-person narrators of the novel associated with his character naively assume his international readership will be familiar with phenomena, not unlike systems of measurement, that are so basic to conceptualizing the realities of our respective cultures that it is difficult to conceive of them as not universal. In *Paranoia* Martinovich relies on readers to recognize things decidedly Soviet in origin, phenomena Anatoly's generation grew up with. But English-language readers have no comparable points of reference. Occasionally, as in Anatoly's description of the "City Day" rehearsal, such phenomena are described with enough detail that the basic idea comes across. More often, it does not. To do full justice to its referential system *Paranoia* should be accompanied by a multimedia glossary that would include the floor plan of a standard Soviet one-room (NB: not one-bedroom and not studio) apartment, images of high Stalinist architecture, of a Zhiguli car (preferably battered and of 1970s vintage), of a typical elderly female homeless person (like the one warming herself under Lisa's Lexus), of Felix Dzerzhinsky (the same photograph that hangs to this day in most KGB offices), and, for good measure, of tanks, rocket launchers, and APCs. It should also contain an aerial view of KGB headquarters in Minsk; reproductions of the paintings mentioned; a swatch of the Soviet institutional green paint Anatoly so despises; a short video of a Lexus (or similar gas-guzzler), siren blaring and blue light flashing as it herds other cars, particularly battered Zhigulis, to the side of the road; recordings of a Soviet (Belarusian or Russian) parade announcer against the background of the rumble of tanks, of the second movement of Mozart's Piano Concerto no. 24, and of the Chemical Brothers' hit "Believe." Even more appropriate would be a computer game that allows readers to manipulate Lisa's and Anatoly's routes and encounters in the city and beyond.

As I worked on this translation I occasionally wondered how the novel's hero, Anatoly Nevinsky, a young writer like Martinovich himself, would assess the results. Anatoly clearly is not enamored of translators who, in his words, have "raked over" his prose (24) and "couldn't figure out how to package" his puns (113). But Anatoly's translators did not have the assistance of the editorial staff at Northwestern University Press. To them, especially managing editor Anne Gendler and freelance copy editor Xenia Lisanevich, Victor Martinovich's translator expresses her sincere gratitude. They asked all the right questions, caught inconsistencies, trimmed sentences, straightened syntax, and suggested clever turns of phrase. Any infelicities that survived their triage should be attributed solely to the translator. To acquisitions editor Mike Levine I am grateful for having sent me the manuscript to consider. This translation was funded in part with a grant from the PEN Translation Fund (2011), for which I am also grateful.

Northfield, Minnesota – Moscow, Russia

PARANOIA

Protocol: Incoming Mail Perlustration

Surveillance site: Uninhabited apartment, 14 Karl Marx Street, Apt. 54

On 20 November at the surveillance site at the above-cited address an unidentified person perpetrated deposit of a standard legal-size paper envelope bearing neither mailing nor return address. Extraction of the contents of the envelope was accomplished using a portable STIK-II device; the envelope was found to contain one sheet of tri-folded (horizontal axis) A4 paper bearing laser-print text. 100X enlargement established the presence of residual printer micromarkings of a LaserJet printer, Serial No. HOj-233440PU-334543l, registered to the Quick & Reliable Print Copy Center, 75 Skrygan Street, License No. 34673, Owner: P. D. Komoniuk. Forensic investigators are gathering evidence at the copy center. Scrutiny of the printed text revealed the following content:

14 Karl Marx Street

Apartment 54

Dear tenant:

Your Central District General Repair and Upkeep Bureau (GRUB) extends its sincere apologies for its failure to respond in timely fashion to your request submitted from your kitchen, 18 November. The Central District GRUB would like to emphasize that its delayed response was conditioned not by any hesitation on our part regarding the merits of fulfilling our service obligations to you, but by the extraordinary sluggishness of our operations section and the dimwittedness of certain responsible individuals currently near the point of harming their person. As a gesture of apology, we invite you to visit our offices (recognizable by the chess figures on the door) tomorrow at 11:00 A.M. for the purpose of receiving a valuable gift from us.

The Central District GRUB with the Ministry of Communal and Residential Services takes this opportunity to assure you, the tenant of apartment 54 at 14 Karl Marx Street, of our sincere and undying love.

On completion of photocopying and examination, the letter, per instructions, was returned to the envelope, resealed using the portable STIK-II device, and restored to its position on the floor at its original location.

Commentary from the Analytical Section: No requests for service were received by the Central District GRUB on 18 November. Authorship of the above letter, as apparent from its production quality, should be attributed to a private individual. Recommendation: forward photocopy to Decoding Section.

MINISTRY OF STATE SECURITY

SECTION FIVE

POSTAL-INTERCEPTION DIVISION

Protocol: Incoming Mail Perlustration
Surveillance site: Uninhabited apartment, 14 Karl Marx Street, Apt. 54

On 22 November an envelope was inserted into the transom of the entranceway. The narrowness of the passage caused the letter to become lodged in the transom, its edges protruding beyond the frame. Extraction of the contents of the envelope, accomplished using a portable STIK-II device, revealed one sheet of A4 paper bearing printed text. Enlargement of the printout did not disclose security micromarkings, giving cause to surmise that the text of said letter was printed on a device not duly registered with the Ministry of Information. It is reasonable to assume that the letter was produced on a personal inkjet printer obtained for private use prior to the implementation of obligatory registration. Cited immediately below is the text of the note that, following examination, was resealed and returned to its original position:

> I'm anchored at the Dardanelles. Will be in dock tomorrow at 11:00 A.M.

Ditto: Advise forwarding photocopy to decoders.

Protocol: Incoming Mail Perlustration
Surveillance site: Uninhabited apartment, 14 Karl Marx Street, Apt. 54

On 27 November an unidentified person operating from the stair landing perpetrated forcible insertion through the doorjamb (6 in. beneath
the latch-plate) of a standard legal-size paper envelope bearing neither
mailing nor return address. Extraction of the envelope's contents was
accomplished using a STIK-II unsealing device; upon completion of examination of its contents, the letter was replaced on the floor at its original angle. The letter's text was executed using the handwritten method;
penmanship quality is uneven, with multiple strikethroughs, blots, and
erasures. The overall unsteady character of the handwriting would seem
to justify determination that the author produced the document under
dire emotional stress, was psychologically depressed, and suffered from
so-called grief:

> You don't answer my letters and don't show up for assignations. You've dis-
> appeared, just like everyone else who attempted to take him on (taking him
> on is like taking on atmospheric pressure, snow melting in the spring or, just
> the opposite, rivers freezing in November. Yes, that's just the right metaphor:
> irreversible, gradual, nightmarish freezing, and beyond the power of one, five,
> five hundred, or five thousand to thaw, whether by blowing or warming with
> the palms; instead, they could freeze to death themselves). What am I doing?
> Am I writing to you about him? No, no, no, I won't, I won't, I won't.
>
> I remember how careful you were when you contacted me that last time
> after those eight convulsive weeks during which we attempted to come to our
> senses (had we taken ourselves out of harm's way then, you wouldn't have
> disappeared now, but we couldn't restrain ourselves, we didn't come to our
> senses!). Yes, yes, I know. I'm acting like a troglodyte, slipping notes through
> the crack in your door: they'll track me down by my footprints, my scent, my
> fingerprints (I can't write letters to you wearing gloves); they'll sniff me out,
> and one night I'll wake to find a crowd of strangers in my room, dark, silent
> figures surrounding my bed. I've had this nightmare once already, once when
> I managed to fall asleep for an hour or two (I can't get a decent night's sleep
> these days).

You toyed with them as if they were puppies, wrapped them around your finger, allowing only me to see you. I can't do this. No, that's not it. I don't want to do this. I have no right. After all, when we parted that last time, everything was different. I talked to you, and you answered. Now all I hear in response is silence: the silence of emptiness, if emptiness can really be heard, sound negated, total zero, as if I were talking to myself. But to turn coward, to talk to myself, that would be the end. I told them that I came to you; I told them and didn't hide a thing, nothing. I pray only that you can still hear me.

I have no right to hide any longer, for—let's be honest with each other— your crime lay not in that you attempted to take them on. You, like me, never even challenged them. You were too lazy and too playful to take anyone on. Your crime lay not in that tiny secret of yours that I dare not commit to paper, even now. No, I, I was your crime. I. Precisely because of me, for my sake, you . . .

Alas! Our Garden of Eden turned out to be too close to their food-processing plant, and our wondrous creatures wound up ground into snacks to be sloshed down with beer in cars with tinted windows.

You know, though? I'm grateful to them. Yes, yes, grateful. If only for one thing: they don't leave traces. Grateful for the fact that no one has ever found any of his enemies, anywhere, under any circumstances. Not a one. And in this way they will remain forever alive: people do not live as long as his enemies will be waited for. First their wives will wait. Then their children. Then their grandchildren. I am grateful that I can now fold my hands, bury my face in them, squeeze my eyes shut, and tell myself that you're alive. That you're silent because I, I, not they, hurt you; I really did hurt you, and apologized, and chuckled as I composed that idiocy from the GRUB back then, in those first days when I still had the wherewithal to laugh.

But I still have hope. It's so good to start again from the beginning. "From the cob," as they say in Belarusian, the idiom conjuring visions of a delectable ear of corn with thousands of appetizing, untouched, virginal little bursts of sunshine which, once their harmony has been disturbed, must be gnawed to the end if only to avoid contemplating the exposed, defiled beginning, to finish it off and begin anew, from naught, from perfection. Perhaps (who knows?) his enemies can now gnaw the "cob" of life somewhere far away, knowing that for them there is no way back, that they have "vanished": even I have almost come to believe that twaddle. That they kidnapped themselves. I believe it for your sake, no, for my sake, for the sake of lending hope the space it needs to grow. I believe that you, and they, disappeared with no assistance from anyone, that you all also closed off your hearts to the past and flew from us forever. I believe, I believe, that you are alive. That you will read this letter as you pack your things behind thick doors through which I am destined never to pass. That you will reread it later, in the taxi, on your way to the airport. That a small shoot (an alstroemeria, a bird-of-paradise flower) will take root somewhere deep in the black, bitter sands of your wounded heart for you to water with your memories. That caring for this tiny shoot will help you live and make your coexistence with the bitter desert tolerable. Who knows? Perhaps one day this flower of forgiveness—precisely in it lies my hope—will bring your hand to write the word "Bear" once again. Everything else is not for their eyes. I utter this in a whisper while sealing the envelope, and I am certain that you can hear me.

Recommendation: consider initiating criminal prosecution for "slander" and "defamation of the Motherland and its government officials."

MINISTRY OF STATE SECURITY
SECTION FIVE

Conclusion
Based on Incoming Mail Perlustration Protocols for Surveillance site: uninhabited apartment, 14 Karl Marx Street, Apt. 54
Append documents herein to criminal case No. 12284/TE-12 (code names: Gogol and Fox). Restrict access.

Appendix I
Nevinsky, Anatoly Petrovich (Internet personal web-page profile): Born not far from the Arkticheskaya observation station above the Arctic Circle to a family of polar bears. (According to other sources, he fell from space as a meteorite.) In the Arctic, along with his mother's milk he absorbed a love for liberal values, the crunch of cucumbers, and the work of the Pre-Raphaelites.* Found by an Arctic expedition, he was brought to the B.S.S.R. for further study at the Academy of Science's Institute of

---

* The Pre-Raphaelite Brotherhood was a movement in English poetry, painting, and criticism during the second half of the nineteenth century counteracting the conventions of the Victorian epoch, of academic traditions, and of blind imitation of classical forms. Maintaining that painting had died along with Raphael, it espoused a return to the canons of the pre-Raphael period.

Potato Cultivation. Garnering strength from the other plants around him, he gnawed through the inch-thick bars of his cage and escaped. He was posted as a fugitive wanted by federal authorities, but quickly matured ideologically and physically, and changed beyond recognition. He began publishing an underground newspaper, which led to the collapse of the U.S.S.R. At present he is well known as a publicist, as a writer of prose fiction, and as a playwright. He is less well known (only to close friends) as a meteorite.

Evil tongues maintain that Nevinsky was born to an intellectual family under routine circumstances, the progeny of bipedal humans, and that he attended ordinary schools. On completing high school, with dreams of becoming an obscure teacher of Russian language and literature, he enrolled at the Philology Faculty of Belarus Lenin State University. Graduating with honors, he spent some time as an obscure teacher of the Russian language. But, to his surprise, he became an acclaimed phenomenon in Russophone letters, for which he was fired from his position at the school. He is the author of five collections of short stories and plays. His prose is distinguished by its irony, political savvy, and, at the same time, its lyricism. He is best known to readers at home for his collection of essays, *The Country Whose Name Begins with B,* and abroad for his collected articles on the post-Soviet era and its people, *Born from a Shovel of Poor Red Trash.* Several of his works have been made into films and translated into other languages.

PART ONE

WE

1

THERE WAS LIGHT, and then came darkness. My monitor went out, along with my desk lamp, and the enormous sun-drenched classroom—where an imaginary little man in a pullover, tie, and cute glasses paced back and forth, wringing his hands—began to melt. My fantasy world depended on electricity or, rather, on wires, fuses, and circuit breakers. A glitch in the electrical circuitry in our stairwell was all it took to hurt the innocent people I had not even finished creating before my monitor went blank. What was stranger was that along with the cozy light of the desk lamp that had been warming my shoulder, the bright summer light in the little man's classroom, which wouldn't have seemed to depend on electricity at all, also went out. That sunlight had been created by God in a world that existed solely in my imagination. Now the fragile creation, all of His mightiness in that world, had gone black because of some switches, wires, and fuses in this world.

For just a bit longer the little man stood in the middle of the class-room, talking to himself, or so it seemed, repeating over and over again the phrases "my favorite student" and "my very favorite." But without the shadow he no longer cast without the extinguished sun he could no longer exist, and I found myself alone among the cold, old-fashioned walls of my Stalin-era apartment. The urge to write had passed. The quiet was wonderful. A flashlight was in order. I went to find one, and lit the sole light I had: a still entirely phallophoric stub of a candle.

I saw myself reflected in the kitchen window. The image intrigued me: a man with a star in his hand stood behind every one of the stars in the heavens, an invisible apartment-owner wandering the heavens in search of a knife. Yes, I needed a knife, for the only way to restore the lights was to open the fuse box and flip the switches. Or wiggle the fuses. Or the chain. Or the electrons. Or the wave that is supposed to be electricity. In short, the fuse box contained three ebonite toggle-switches, one for each room, and you had to wring each of their necks before the wave would rise, the fuses return to their plugs, and my poor little man and I would have light again: I electric, and he sunshine.

The fuse box was closed, and one of the electricians had broken off the handle to keep handy residents from tinkering with their electric meters to set them to wind backwards, turning time back in the process. (The electric company was obsessed with time.) The slot in the fuse-box door was narrow, and the lock mechanism was hidden as deeply as the memory of a childhood trauma in the mind of a psychotic. This required an appropriate operating tool, one as tempered as Sigmund Freud's. The average nickel silver table knife would buckle like an object in a Salvador Dalí painting. I would have to get the knife with the wooden handle my father had made out of a two-millimeter piece of steel and polished with his hands and I continued to polish after him. That knife would have no problem slashing open the guts of the fuse box and probing the latch inside. But where was the latch?!

Finally, the fuse box swung open, the switches clicked stiffly, and light streamed from my doorway. I blew out the candle stub and went back to my desk to resume the miracle of creation. How little there was to do without electricity in this two-roomed tiny world with its flickering glimmers of candlelight on the wall! We are *Homo electricus:* pity McLuhan is no longer alive.* Having sat for a bit at my revivified desk, I realized that there was nothing to do here at home *with* electricity. As my mood slipped into the minor key of a spring evening spent alone, electricity drove me out into the night. Neither the sun-drenched classroom nor my little man in his pullover—Perhaps a bow tie would be better? No, professors in this country don't wear bow ties!—could distract me from myself. Actually, my little man was sad, because I was sad, and because spring evenings are so sad. It would be one o'clock in the morning before I would fall asleep, and here, among these walls, all you could think of, really, was that tea drunk alone has a different taste from tea drunk with someone else.

My appointment book contained a few freeze-dried remedies for loneliness, the ingredients consisting of a name and a combination of numbers to dial. The kind of remedies that end in a rush to put your clothes

* Herbert Marshall McLuhan (1911–1980) was a Canadian philosopher, philologist, professor of English literature, specialist in communication theory, and author of the notion of media as they extend social organization—famous for the phrase "The medium is the message."

back on. In a rush, because someone is waiting for you back home. Waiting and, perhaps, already undressing—the thought of which is particularly painful. No one has ever waited or waits for me at home. I can calmly disappear for hours on end and take a long, long time to get dressed. I know. I've told myself many times: people always get exactly what they want, what they aspire to, and not just in words. Voila! The only people waiting for me back home were the characters I had created and the words I still had not written, both of which needed me like God. That was OK, though, because spring had come, and the courtyard that inconspicuously opened out at the bottom of our stairwell greeted me with April, which had, unnoticed by me, turned into May. Over there to the right, in her usual spot, stood my Frau, in bad need of a wash to celebrate the end of winter. I really lied when I said that no one was waiting for me. I had my Frau, who needed me, if only to wash her, to fill her up, to drive her around town, and to look, as I exited the stairwell, at the bits of Bavarian sky in her circular trademark.

I didn't know where I was headed or why I was headed there, but for some reason I felt sad. The sadness I had wanted to transfer to the little man in the sun-drenched classroom remained with me, bottled up, unmitigated, without release. But no big deal, ol' man, no big deal. It's May, after all. I reached the end of the corridor of the little street leading from my apartment to Independence Avenue, our country's principal artery, which through some glaring oversight to this day does not yet bear his name. I found myself among well-dressed, apathetic passersby, who made me acutely aware of what I was searching for, what had driven me out of my apartment. I was looking for a pair of eyes, of course! I needed human eyes that would look at me, even if with indifference, but look at me, not at my clothes, at my despondent raincoat, at my haircut ("FREAKING GENIUS"), and not at the excessively mechanical—I preferred not to think about it—way I walked. No, at me. At this creature walking down the street, among other creatures, ready to love them and to look at them, really look at them, in the biblical sense, to notice them. Yes, I know, I know. I am asking for too much. This soon will pass.

In front of the Lianok linen store a Chinese girl stopped me and asked me to take her picture with her girlfriend, and as I attempted to frame them in the camera's viewfinder, she looked at me calmly and slowly, precisely as I needed to be looked at, just what I had been searching for. I pulled the camera away from my face and was ready to smile back at her. One smile would have been enough. I would have known that I was not alone in this city, that there was you, no matter who you might be, even if you didn't know a single word of my English—a simple exchange of smiles, two creatures communicating to each other that they understood each other. It would have been understandable why she looked at me that way: she was alone in this city of white-skinned oafs who thought they knew everything about people. I would have smiled back with just my eyes, handed her the camera, nodded to her and her girlfriend, and crawled back to my apartment to make myself some tea, think about her loneliness, and comfort myself with the thought that she was thinking about mine . . . But her look, the one I had interpreted as intended for me, shifted downward to the camera, now also aimed downward. She was looking not at me, but at the camera: she was looking at herself. Or, at the person the photograph was for. Not a drop of her soul had been apportioned for the person who had done her the favor of pushing the correct button and of handing her a digital image of her sincerity . . . directed at someone else. I was the one who had pushed the button. I was the one who had handed her the image! For a moment at the bus stop her inscrutable eyes (mere hints, mere half-shadows under the dark arches of her brows beneath her coquettish bangs) looked at me, and I decided that those eyes were cat-green, that I would run after the trolleybus whose doors had just closed; I would run to the next stop to utter just one word to those eyebrows: "Thank you." I needed nothing else. Honest! For everything else I had those remedies in my appointment book, each guaranteed to alleviate what hurt the most: that look. The trolleybus drove off, and her wandering gaze settled on a point in space behind me, behind me. I turned around and discovered the person for whom that gaze had been intended. Like a thief, I stalked off, embarrassed.

The Café Brigantine summer terrace had already spilled onto the sidewalk, but diners outside in the cold sat cocooned in blankets. Two girls, accessorized with glasses of red wine, shot a glance at me, but there was too much professionalism in their eyes for me to flatter myself. My head cold had not entirely subsided yet: fearful clouds of shivers coursed up and down my spine, as if my soul had goose bumps, while oncoming couples and schools of humans swam before my eyes like fish. To them I, too, was as exotic as cold-blooded tropical fish in an aquarium were for human beings: it was a kind of magic that worked both ways. Of course, you knew nothing, and would never learn anything about me, but I picked up your signal. The Antarctic of shivers down my spine intensified—I had not encountered a gaze capable of melting the ice—and probably I should have gone home to drink some tea laced with a good dose of raspberry-jam drowsiness, wrap myself in a blanket, and have a good sweat. But I kept on walking, as if heeding some call. Now I know that you were beckoning me, but at the moment I just ambled. On October Square, in front of the anti-utopian monstrosity of the Palace of the Republic, people lent their eyes to an enormous screen where he was talking about the country's internal and foreign enemies in a calm and sort of kindly way that made you feel the situation in the country was stable. For a while I had to walk with only people's backs to my eyes, wending my way through the crowd, hearing his inveigling words and sensing his paternal gaze, but his were unquestionably not eyes I wanted to peer into.

I thought about the eyes of the automobiles creeping down the avenue, the majority of which were, of course, insolent. There were lascivious eyes and evil eyes (my Frau's sharklike profile also, likely, evoked thoughts of a predatory nature, but she was in fact very kind and sweet), intrepid eyes and impetuous eyes, and the pathetic eyes of Soviet Zhigulis with their looks askance that spoke volumes as they peered out on the city from behind thick lenses in outdated frames. There were also terrifying eyes, half-hidden behind wire grates, with fog lights—the cars his people drove.

There were fewer people around now, and I realized immediately why: I had walked beyond the GUM State Department Store, decrepit from its attempts to restore socialism, and found myself in a part of town where I should not, just should not, be. There, right in front of me, bellowing Beethoven's Fifth Symphony, stood the Ministry of State Security (MGB), a complex of structures whose elegant façade looked out onto the avenue while its terrifying back walls faced side streets that buses with foreign tourists never entered. Stalin-era baroque: porticos, pilasters, bas-reliefs of hammers and sickles, Corinthian capitals with additional acanthus leaves draped downward in fecundity—the triumph of socialist realism in stone. This quarter of the city was crosshatched out of every map; at the residence, his residence, next door, uniformed guards were posted round the clock, and God forbid I slow down as I walk by, or, worse, pull out a camera. The colossal doors—there, in the center, set behind the columns, at the top of the stairs—were always closed: no one ever entered through the central entranceway. No one.

I hurriedly crossed to the other side of the street, having noticed that the little tower appended atop the roof of the right wing of the building and executed in a style slightly more controlled than the Stalin Empire style (Stalin rococo, was it?) glowed with soft light from within. Legends—our legends, legends born of nocturnal paranoia, of disappearing neighbors, of tales few and far between of "enemies" called in for interrogations, then released—these legends held that the tower had been added to the building by Lavrenty Tsanava, the almighty Belarus chairman of the Soviet NKVD. In calmer Soviet times people used to call it Tsanava's tower. Then *he* arrived on the scene, unified the country, and combined the country's security and militia forces into a single Ministry of State Security. Since then no one had any doubt to whom the tower belonged. Of course, he was sitting up there. And, because he never slept, the lights burned in the tower whole days on end. I don't know which is more terrifying: the abstract pronoun "he" or the surname "Muraviov," nowadays a common noun, or the fully loaded stripper clip of his combined titles: Head of State, Commander in Chief, Minister of State Security Nikolai Mikhailovich Muraviov. What are words like "military coup," "usurpation of power," or "arrests" alongside the simple, all-elucidating "Muraviov"? Muraviov! Yes. Muraviov. The minister who appointed presidents.

Generally speaking, one is not supposed to fear the Ministry of State Security. The more the lights burn in that little tower, the more the citizenry should stroll past it, look at it, and marvel at his diligence, his concern. But what if you were to blast it with a few rounds from a grenade-launcher? . . . Just then I heard the sound of steps behind me and I hastily quickened my step as a panicked thought flitted through my mind: did they now have the capability to wiretap thoughts? I ducked into the courtyard of a Stalin building topped with an old clock, came out on Marx Street, and quickly beat it out of that part of town. The footsteps from behind had been those of an ordinary passerby, fool!

I proceeded dutifully past the casino and bowed with patriarchal reverence before the building of the Philological Faculty, embellished with yet to be expunged graffiti: "I feel fuck," an unfortunate pun in contempt of grammar, a pun on the level of a trade school dropout. Too late: the bug—damn it!—had lodged itself in my brain, which now churned out a succession of Rubik's cube variations: "filled fuck," "fill faq," "filmed fuck" . . . Enough! Stop! Stop! I walked down Marx Street. No, not Karl. Nowadays the street is named after a different Marx, Marks & Spencer, for its glitzy, bright, self-aggrandizing, glossy capitalism, which coexisted quite harmoniously with—and even to the benefit of—the Ministry of State Security. That, though, wasn't important either. I was ready and willing to walk down a street named after Marks & Spencer if I could exist, if I could feel and sense that I, too, existed—existed as a living creature and not as a mannequin in a world of mannequins.

You had already opened two packets of sugar by the time I walked past the stately entrance of the Constitutional Court of the MGB. You had already poured their contents into the tall, curvaceous mug with its long, crane-like spoon. Like a spectator at a theater, you had made yourself comfortable, set your sights, and were ready and waiting for me to show up, distraught and driven by the incomprehensible expectation of you. Out of habit I noted the shingle outside the Chess Café with its enormous windows that revealed: the black-and-white interior; waiters dressed in old-fashioned costumes reminiscent of Nabokov's *The Luzhin Defense*— not the book, but the Hollywood version in which the characters wear outfits straight out of a Repin painting; customers actually playing chess in muted light at the far end of the room; you; several deliberately attired girls laughing at something on the screen of a lemon-colored laptop propped on the table in front of them; and a couple of balding gentlemen who had obviously devised some reason to laugh along with the girls and felt that the girls were laughing for their sake, but no—you! You! When I . . . I saw . . . You looked straight at me through the glass, unpretentiously and a bit ironically, as if to ask: how many wrong turns did it take you to get here? My search was over. Yes, yes, those were the eyes I had been searching for.

I won't say a word about your beauty, I swear. I don't think I even remember what you were wearing—something dark that accentuated your silhouette, your neck, your long fingers, all of these to frame your simple and kind gaze that laughed (so it seemed) at me; a gaze that while remaining perfectly stern, puritanical, and serious for others, said everything to me; the gaze with which you accompanied my glances and, when my eyes stopped on you, simply peered into the depths of my soul, into violet depths whose existence I had never even suspected. It wasn't enough that you peered into those depths in just that way, from beneath mocking brows made even darker by your light hair, you settled there. Without shifting your gaze, you brought the mug of ocher-and-white-layered liquid (a latte macchiato) to your lips and took a sip, the layers blending and swirling in a metaphor for what was going on inside me. I stood opposite you (a yard away? two yards?) on the other side of the glass, looking at you as if you were a photograph. Then your brows shot upward, as if rebuking me for my directness. You seemed to be saying to me: you fool, you can't just stand there and stare like that! What are you doing? You're making me uncomfortable! The ocher-colored solution in the tall mug hid your lips, but I thought you were smiling, smiling behind the mug, smiling at me. I knew that I was a person, a living creature, and not a mannequin, that in this city there was you, and you felt as I did, and you were looking this way, into my heart, while the street behind me pulled out of focus like a departing train gathering speed and racing off to Monte Carlo, Las Vegas, Syracuse, and New York. No one else was around, just me and your eyes and a host of supernumeraries who, as they walked by, brushed my shoulders, but could not brush my gaze, which no longer noticed the glass window. Yes, I was ready to head straight toward you, right through that frangible, transparent wall. The glass was thinner than the walls of the aquarium that had stood between me and those I had undressed and dressed before then. I was ready to step forward, had an earthquake not suddenly swept over your face, had you not looked down at the table. Your cell phone was lying there: an ordinary cell phone, emphatically ordinary and not to your liking, and, therefore, nothing special, just a phone, a means of communicating with someone. The cell phone was lugging itself across the table like a bug on its back. Someone was calling you, someone who could do that to your face. You picked up the phone and deprived me of your eyes by turning your back to me and . . . that was it! You covered your profile with your hand, covering the movement of your lips. The end was approaching. You got up with a jolt, and quickly—without looking at me!—headed for the exit nearby, two steps away, where you couldn't possibly make your way without our eyes meeting. But you turned away, and now I was looking at your shoulders underneath your raincoat and your hair gathered at the nape of your neck. Stepping quickly, you walked out, holding your phone—still open, but already lifeless—in your hand. Who was it who had called you? What had happened?

You succeeded in taking only five steps, because at step six stood a huge SUV, an enormous Lexus RX 470, parked illegally, right on the sidewalk, its body snow-white, like your face. The security alarm screeched shrilly as you circled the car from the left—you were headed for the driver's side! You were intending to drive that monstrous machine, but that . . . But how could that be? You had just been looking at me with the look I had been searching for. Of their own volition my legs carried me toward the giant SUV. I managed to take one, two, three steps, then stopped, because the white face of the Lexus was hidden behind the dark glasses of its windows. Your car was wearing sunglasses: but that can't be! It can't be! Take off the sunglasses! You don't need them! But you had already stuck the key into the ignition: rumbling its jet engine, the behemoth started up, its headlights came to life, and wild rap music echoed from inside the car as if from the center of the earth, as if over there, in Los Angeles, someone were throwing a mega-party and had turned the sound up so loud that the noise rumbled through the earth's core and came out on this side. You turned the wheels sharply, and with a growling, wild roar you peeled off the sidewalk, frightening the old homeless lady who had been camped there. Only after you had accelerated to a speed for which people in this city have their licenses revoked, only after your siren—not a normal automobile horn, but an official siren—had screamed insolently at a car (with the right-of-way) attempting to proceed down the main street, did I make the connection. The connection to what my eyes had seen while you were still walking toward the driver's side. Yes, yes. License plate number 2165 KE-7. The letters *KE* could mean but one thing. The license plate and the car belonged to the Ministry of State Security. It couldn't be otherwise. And, alas, the proof lay in the way you had been parked, in the way you drove, and in those awful tinted glasses on the snow-white face of your car. Who were you? Who? What were you doing with them? How did you get that car? Why were you driving it? Don't you know how obscene that was? You—with that face, those eyes, and those fingers!

I wandered home, trying to make sense of it all. Of course. She's the daughter of some MGB general. Hates her daddy, the murderer, with all her soul, but, hey, what can you do? She's not to blame for what her father does. But why did you take off so swiftly after that call? Why didn't you wave to me with your eyelashes to say good-bye? Had I offended you somehow? Had I stared at you too hard? Was it because of that? I spoke with her and spoke with her as I paced about my kitchen: the sole person who could help me was Dan. Of course, Dan would help me with her phone number. I'd call her tomorrow: it was too late to call a girl now. But not too late to call Dan. (Dan, it seems, never sleeps.) I'd call her and say "thanks for the look"; she and I would become friends; she would renounce her father, causing him to come to his senses, retire, and spend his days watering tomatoes with a hose at the dacha. And we would tease him by stepping on the hose and he'd say, "Why are you making fun of an old man?"

Dan was one of us, but happened to wind up with their information. Strictly speaking, he's not an MGB agent at all; he's a visual genius, an image-maker from God. They caught on to him thanks to the photo gags he had posted on the Internet, which poked fun not at the MGB even, but at other people's ads. With a single letter he turned the "Lada: most feted car on the road" ad into a caricature. His slogan, which ruined the Lada advertising campaign in the entire sales region, was "Lada: most fetid car on the road." The visuals—the pride of the Russian auto industry spinning its wheels in billowing mud—he left untouched. Strictly speaking, after the MGB measured his creative potential against their disappointment with the inventiveness of local talent, it concocted a criminal case against Dan for having raped a minor right on the steps of the school where she was a student and extradited him from Switzerland, where he had kept himself alive programming chemical research, and offered him a choice. He could conscientiously sit out ten years in prison—rather, not sit but stand, after what they did in prison with guys who had raped minors, which made sitting rather complicated—or embark on the road to rehabilitation and devote himself entirely to improving the image of the MGB. At least that was the way he told it. Dan's mouse deserved the credit for the poster that had turned public opinion of the MGB from one of contemptuous fear to legitimate fear. The MGB's last attempt at self-promotion in the graphic arts had been a photograph of a malicious enemy (an MGB agent posed as the enemy, since finding a sufficiently hostile mug among the civilian population had proved impossible) flanked on either side by grinning goons in leather coats. The goons were twisting the enemy's arms, and the enemy was obviously in pain. The slogan below read something like: "Enemies won't get away as long as they're hard at work at the MGB." The only conclusion to be drawn from the poster was that two mobsters had nabbed a third and were about to apply a hot iron to get him to spill where he'd hidden the cash.

Dan approached their ad campaign as an intellectual challenge requiring all the talent a man facing ten years in the can could muster. When I saw his work for the first time—an enormous poster hung right next to my apartment building—something inside me clicked. I spent the whole day thinking about how the work of state security agents was not as disgusting and dirty as I had allowed myself to misconstrue it. Ultimately, people who could stop crime before it happened, people who worked around-the-clock and who put themselves in harm's way were people we needed. And so on. Dan's brainchild consisted of a dark-blue background framing the face of a person who symbolized your average MGB "worker." One had to admit that Dan had done just as good a job selecting the face as the expression: a man with a halo of flaxen hair gazed at you with a look that was very open and trusting, but at the same time, seeming to know exactly where and over which periodicals you had masturbated as a child. His eyes gleamed with small Leninist beams. His lips were shaped in a half-smile—more Vermeer than Mona Lisa. His head was subtly illuminated from behind with a radiance easily taken for a halo. The man was dressed in a navy-blue suit with a gentlemanly Bordeaux-red necktie and a shirt of virginal whiteness. You got the impression that your father was looking at you. Or Jesus Christ. Or Batman. You could go to confession or take Communion in front of this poster. And the slogan, the slogan!

MINISTRY OF STATE SECURITY

WE SEE. WE HEAR. WE KNOW.

"Dan?"

"Yo!" His voice was hoarse as if after a cigarette. Dan could. Dan could do everything. He worked for the MGB.

"Dan, can you talk?" I asked once again, just in case, and the phrase mobilized him into action.

Having thought for a moment, he said, "Ah, Tol, I can talk now to the extent that I can, Tol, in principle talk, on the phone. You know what I'm saying, Tol?"

"Got it, Dan."

"What's up?"

"I need you to check out a license plate in your database. In their database, I mean. The plates are obviously MGB, ending *KE*..."

"MGB, for sure. Want me to check anything else?"

"Dan, Dan! Listen! I have to find out who the driver of that car is. Name, who the car's registered to, and, if possible, a telephone number. I really need to find this person. The number is 2165 KE-7."

"Your brother?" Dan's hoarse voice sounded guarded.

"More like my sister."

Humming something under his breath—the words "Africa," "Rasta-man," "Jamaica," and "Babylon" predominated—he tapped the keys of his keyboard. The wait dragged on.

"Tol, Tolyan, listen to me," he said. "Tolya, I've entered the numbers. There is no such car. Nothing. Not in the police database, not in the Vector special forces database, and not in the VIP section. There's no such license plate. Your sister's a mirage, man."

"Dan, I . . ."

"Tol!"

"Dan, I saw the plates, and the car was luxurious and not one you could hide, a Lexus RX 470. There's got to be only a couple of those cars in the entire city."

"Tolya."

"There's no way she was a mirage."

"Tol!!! I'm telling you: the car doesn't appear in any of the databases. I searched using three levels of access, the last two off-limits even for me: they can have my ass, by the way, for that. Those plate numbers don't appear either at the first level ('operations vehicles') or the second ('personal vehicles for management and special unit staff') or the third, the most secure, about which you don't need to know. There is no such car, got it? The plate numbers stop at 2164 KE-7, and pick up again at 2166 KE-7. Your plates aren't there. Think about that, Tolya. Those plates aren't even in the MGB database. Think, man."

Dan suddenly hung up. Redialing, I ascertained that his cell phone had been switched off. I understood. Of course, I understood. Your daddy is so high up the ladder that he had your plate numbers removed even from secret databases no one has access to except the MGB. His rank is probably no lower than head of one of the heavy-duty sections, like the Fifth. No, better not the Fifth. We don't need the Fifth. Anything but the Fifth. No such number exists. You don't exist. You came to me in a mirage. I made you up, spun you out of my feverish delirium, populated my Antarctica with you, scaring away the penguins. You came to me in a mirage.

What I had needed were human eyes, and you had appeared to me from a world where only people like you and me dwell, people fashioned from a single piece of marble. Yes, you have been hewn from marble, you are transluminous, and now so am I. You looked at me not as a statue, but as the pattern of swirls and veins deep inside the stone, for marble is translucent, as the great Italians who could perceive the slightest cracks in the depths of a stone knew. You appeared to me as a mirage and continue to appear to me. I am drawn to you with all my faults, my unpolishable bumps, my veins, and structural defects. You smiled, and the ice of Antarctica, which I had populated with you, melted. You cast a solar speck of light upon my mass, illuminating me for myself, flickered, and turned away. Now I must cast you out of my mind. No, not cast, but gather you in my arms, carry you out, and let you flit from my palms, so I might perceive your light in farewell and, illuminated for the last time by your crystal, squint my eyes tight: farewell! Let northern winds blow across my ice, let there be only penguins, only penguins and the white, untouched silence—it would be better that way both for you and for me: fly and don't look b . . .

[2]

ANATOLY WOKE ON HIS SIDE, and his hand, which had just held snow that seeped through his fingers, symbolizing there, in his dream, something connected to time—its fluidity, friability, rapidity, and irrevocability—was numb. He touched the lifeless extremity that had just held time in its fingers with his other palm, and the hand reacted with a piercing shot from the shoulder down: he would have to let it lie alongside his body and not touch it so the blood, instead of time, would flow through his veins.

The room, at the far end of which his sofa had parked itself behind a set of bookcases, had nothing in common with either a Gothic hall or a cave: the morning light illuminated it in all its prosaic homeyness, and for the umpteenth time it occurred to him that the word "remodeling" held a certain healthiness and cheer that stuck to you like wallpaper to the walls of life. His wallpaper, though, had come unglued and curled at the seams, and a draft swayed a spiderweb on the light fixture where a tiny spider dangled like a daring surfer. His connections to reality were contained in that curled wallpaper and in the web on the light fixture, owing to which he was forced to give TV interviews in cafés. Were the public to see the conditions in which his texts were born, they would be sorely disappointed. Of course, the reason that he pondered the spiderweb and the peeling, mummified wallpaper in the context of his connections with reality lay in his experience the evening before.

He recalled her glance, and this made him sad. As if now, besides inhalation and exhalation, his breathing had acquired yet another dimension that sent goose bumps of impatience through his body, goose bumps of desire to change something, and, were he more fixed to reality, that change would have taken the shape of remodeling. But in his case, with every third spiritual inhalation out of sync with his physical breathing, the text that yesterday had been simply an idea came increasingly closer to his throat.

This was wonderful, of course, for yesterday the absence of a finished text in his translator's email in-box had been cause for Anatoly to have a long telephone conversation in English with the editor of an American glossy magazine that had bought this text based on a four-sentence pitch. Both of them knew that this chance opportunity to spin-doctor Nevinsky's name, which far surpassed his modest reputation at home, had come about not because Anatoly's prose—especially after having been raked over in translation—held any real interest for anyone, but because the world was interested in Muraviov's name and the situation in the country he governed as the "last dictator in Europe." The German press agent who handled his work had once said, "What's distinctive about the present epoch is that nowadays anti-utopias can be based on entirely factual material. There's no more need to invent *1984*: just look around." In Anatoly's country, book plots that had been exhausted in Western Europe and the U.S. back in the sixteenth century still occurred. A measured, well-fed existence did not lend itself to Shakespearean passions. But where Anatoly came from, on any day one could read in the news about treachery and nobility, about feats of valor and of ignobility. Readers wanted to know how these people lived, what they felt, how they loved, and what they thought as they looked into the night sky, but the news was incapable of answering these questions, which is where Anatoly came in. The fact that he had never been interrogated by the MGB must have meant that his views of the night sky essentially coincided with the MGB's opinion of the night sky.

Inside his head the words were already spinning and weaving themselves together; the distraught little fellow in the sunlight-flooded classroom was already morphing from an ink-dot figure on a yellow background into nouns, adjectives, and verbs. All he had to do now was communicate all this correctly, without spilling, to the keys of the keyboard: drawing first the fluff of his disheveled hair, then his glasses in ridiculous frames that magnified his eyes three hundred times over, then his tenacious fingers, which he wrung and bent until they hurt. All he had to do now was set out the verbs—"sat down," "jumped up," "began to speak," "wiped," "quivered," "pounded," "died," "bounced," and "scratched"—in the right order. The melancholy that had sprung from yesterday evening helped Anatoly to do it all with the required degree of correctness and incorrectness, leaving his language lively, asymmetric, and illusory, the connections between his phrases for readers to draw themselves. The little man walked over to the desk from which his favorite student had argued with him, sat down at it, appreciating the angle, imagined himself the young man, and recalled their last disagreement in front of the entire class over Brutus's role in the Caesar affair: the boy was well-read and in addition to the Plutarch assigned for the seminar had read devil knows what else on his own, and kept referring to Suetonius, while the little man in the professorial sweater couldn't stand Suetonius. He didn't like him because he too frequently called things by their real name, which you must not do when writing history. Which you should not do at all. Ever. Better to do as Plutarch had. They argued, and the other students, of course, were on the side of the young loudmouth who blasphemed authorities. Very quickly and very predictably they jumped from Brutus and Caesar to the Ministry of State Security, and the student said "Muraviov." Then he said it again: "Muraviov." This alone sufficed for the professor to lose his chair: there were stoolies in the seminar and by the end of the break the dean who presided over ideological correctness would know everything. The professor knew that the dean would know, so he began shouting at the student, demanding that he not distort things. But during the break, after the class had ended, they both looked out into the courtyard through the classroom's enormous windows, windows streaked with dried rain, and they spoke to each other in a different tone of voice, like father and son. No one heard them, and the professor agreed, he agreed, but he implored the student to forgo in public all those monstrous comparisons with bloody antiquity: the truth would not suffer, and the student could continue his education. To this the student responded that it took but a single, the very first, act of treachery to make a scoundrel. He was, of course, correct. The professor placed his hand on the young man's shoulder as he thought about how, if he ever had a son, he would resemble his favorite student. Rather, if he ever had a son and he were able to raise him to be physically incapable of underhandedness, he would be proud of him. He almost admitted to the boy that he was right, that his professor was proud of him. But not aloud, never.

The problem was that, yes, his favorite student who used to sit on the left side in the third row from the top had been right, and the professor had been able to head the department all these years only because he had engaged in treachery, had kept silent, and had gagged those just beginning to speak, gagged them with the phrase "politics has no place in the classroom," although what was at issue was not politics but ancient history and the parallels that arose on their own when readings concerned Caligula or Nero, and you knew how Muraviov . . . No, no, one cannot talk about that. Ancient history should be banned from the curriculum and replaced with any other kind of history. Then everything would be clear-cut and logical. Then such monstrous questions would not arise in his classes, and he would not be forced to betray anyone. He touched the window at which he had spoken with the student: it bore blurred traces of the lines on his forehead and the jumbled grid of his hair. The professor had stood, leaning against this window, after being summoned to the dean's office and served a short, ridiculous ultimatum: by evening the next day one of them, either the student or the professor, would have to abandon these walls forever and with no possibility of reinstatement. The dean, with his puffy face and excessively large violet lips that seemed to hang from their own skin, informed him that the most appropriate reason to give for the expulsion would be academic truancy. His favorite student had already spent fifteen days behind bars for having uttered the word "Muraviov" during an even less appropriate argument. It had happened in winter. In hindsight, the student obviously had no intention of "committing himself to his studies." Just the opposite: he would continue speaking the word "Muraviov," and nothing would stop him. He would not be able to compensate for the classes in ancient history that he had missed. Therefore, the university could not allow him to continue his studies. No politics. Just academic progress. The professor could not remember whether the formulation was the dean's or if he had made it up while talking to himself in his empty (his wife had died seven years ago), tiny kitchen. What mattered was that he had convinced himself that the expulsion had nothing to do with politics and was based entirely on academic progress. That was why, after their telephone conversation, when the student rushed to his house to say good-bye and to return some books, the professor had been unwavering, had turned away, had insisted that the university had done nothing wrong. When the boy shouted at him that the university was the same cog in the system as tribune Helvius Cinna, author of the bill that allowed Caligula to take anyone's wife and do with her as he pleased to produce an heir, the professor only dropped the corners of his mouth as if insulted. He kept returning the student to his incomplete course work. He iterated century-and-a-half-old truisms: "If you just did some work, young man," "You should have worried about that earlier." Looking back, he realized now that he had sounded pathetic. His student cursed him—just that simply—called him a coward to his trembling face. Back in the kitchen he just kept stirring his tea with a spoon as if the sound had a transfixing, cumulative echo. The student was expelled, expelled with no right to reinstatement, and immediately drafted into the army. For the professor there was relief in this. It guaranteed that for a rather long time professor and student were certain not to run into each other. The student, as a fleeting face in a crowd, would not be around to remind him of what had happened. This put him at ease: eighteen months from then the arbitrariness of the phrase "academic deficiency" would have acquired the integrity of an expression that had predetermined destiny, and neither of them would remember, let alone argue about, what had happened. Perhaps they might begin to meet again and become friends in secret. The student, a sensitive young man, would be forgiving. He would understand that the professor simply had had no choice. However, just now, a second before he had entered this sunlight-filled lecture hall, the professor had been informed that his favorite student . . . His mother had called the dean's office, had asked for him, the professor, which meant that the student had not told her that he, the professor, had had him expelled . . . Had not told her, you see, because he held no grudge, had forgiven him, and did not himself believe it true. The mother had called and asked for him, not wanting to speak with anyone else except him; he had taken the phone, and she had sobbed to him about what had happened, as if the two of them—she and the professor— were the only people left on earth. Two bullets. One had shattered his spine, the other had punctured his lung. He never made it to the hospital. In his unit they said that the incident had occurred during automatic weapon practice, but, damn it, what automatic weapon practice could he have been at if he hadn't yet been sworn in. He had been killed, simply killed—drafted into the army to be killed, expelled from the university in order to be drafted and killed—shot by firing squad or beaten to death, it didn't matter. They had sealed the metal coffin before shipping it, but "something was rolling around inside," as if his head had been ripped off. The coffin was lighter than her son . . . Perhaps it wasn't her son inside . . . The professor said everything she expected to hear about how what was rolling around was probably a cap or something else, how it just seemed that the coffin was lighter. On—if not already over—the edge, the mother kept interrupting him, murmuring about how the coffin was made of thick steel, that she had tried to pick it open with a can opener, that she wanted to see her son, that she couldn't bury him without having closed his eyes. Her words conveyed such simple, primal horror that he no longer knew what to say, or how. Then someone, probably standing next to her, interceded and reasoned with her to calm down, and she did calm down, and stopped, thank God. He could not remember who hung up first. He knew only that the funeral was the next day, at noon, and that he could not attend the funeral because the word "Muraviov" was certain to be uttered there. And among those in attendance some would have come especially to hear how the word was uttered. But he must go to the funeral, because if he did not say good-bye to his student . . . If his student did not forgive him . . . There was already no forgiving him. He could not forgive himself that the boy had been killed, taken and deprived of life . . . That instead of debates, disputes, and shouts, his life had been cut short. Now he must be buried, although his mother wanted the coffin opened, which they wouldn't let happen, of course. Doing so would be a desecration, a profanation. Should he call and tell her not to do it? Obviously, they had delivered the student in a sealed iron box because inside there was nothing to look at, or that should be looked at . . . But the professor couldn't bring himself to think about his student in such terms. After all, he used to sit right there, at that desk, third row from the top on the left, and smile like a son when the professor repeated a joke he had invented seventeen years before, the one about Nero's mother. This was all just a barbarian remake of the New Testament parable where the real Teacher turns out to be the student, and he, the professor, fails the test. He must attend the funeral. He looked at the blackboard scribbled with lines and the words "academic deficiency," "inappropriate analogies," "I tried to get him to take it all back," "no politics," "the absence of makeup work." The professor understood that he—despite it all—was not to be blamed and really could not have done anything. But those streaks on the window? They were exactly like the rain they had seen together. He needed to remove his glasses—his vision was blurred; he couldn't see anything through them. Down below in the courtyard little boys scurried about . . . Anatoly felt the nouns, adjectives, and verbs forming into images that were becoming more difficult to control, and the images were forming into a plot, but maintaining the pulse of Life in that plot had become tiresome. Better finish it some other time. Three or four apt, substantial sentences plus the short phrase that would inevitably appear in the header of the journal edition—he had wanted it removed, but the editors would include it there and on the front cover—BASED ON A TRUE STORY—five words that would encourage people to buy the journal. The "true story" itself, a separate file on his computer's desktop, had been gathered from online news over the past month. Over that time the story's basic premises had remained unchanged: "university," "lecture hall," "disagreement over Muraviov," "expulsion," "army," "strange death." Life was more literary than literature.

His body still trembled with excitement. His words coursed through him like jolts of electricity, some striking on target precisely because they were so unpredictable, causing him to shudder, and concede, and agree that literature was more than just jotting down stories, it was physical energy.

He needed to take a walk, to get a breath of fresh air. What was more—and he had realized this just now, after hauling himself away from his keyboard: his plot had stumbled on her, on his dream that they . . . No, there was no pronoun "they," only the memory of those eyes, not a prayer of a chance that those eyes might enter the cognizable, conceivable realm of a union. Shivering, he hastily slid into his clothes. He had to rid himself of the power of the plot's words, to remove himself, so that later he would long to return to them. His excitement over what he had written metamorphosed into excitement over his experience yesterday. The professor's story poured itself into life just as the night before life had poured itself into a short story, lending a particular intensity to certain of its aspects.

Outside, everything glowed, flowed, and cawed. The rooks had arrived. Anatoly scampered to the gate out of the courtyard like a kitten, feeling like Savrasov, ready to take canvas in hand and layer it with dollops of spring's bright, transparent colors. The painting should have lots of azure: in the sky above, in the sky trapped in the trees' naked branches, in the sky in the puddles, and in the sky bounded by windows washed by the thaw. One of the birches struck him as particularly Savrasovian; all it lacked was a church in the background, but in place of the church . . .

The cheerful run of his thoughts faltered at the sight of the black Audi A8, which did not reflect the sky. It was parked in front of a distant stairwell entrance, its windows tinted; the letters on the license plate number, *KE,* quickly came into focus, its massive fender bore a short antenna for special communications, and the engine was switched off. Perhaps the driver lived in the stairwell and had swung home for breakfast, parking the car under the windows? No, this tinted limousine was docked here for the first time, docked here for purposes unknown. The solid tint of the windows made it impossible to tell whether anyone, even a driver, was inside. You couldn't just stand there and look at it: if they had come to arrest someone from that stairwell, stopping to look at it would provoke suspicion, and seeing how intently and fearfully Anatoly looked at their automobile, they might arrest him just for good measure—who knew what his relationship with the suspect was? The Audi simultaneously frightened and attracted him. Perhaps if he were to walk alongside it, his fears might dissipate. He might see numerous touching details: a scratch on the left fender, a branch stuck in the hubcap, a smeared blotch in the muddy streaks on the driver's-side door, meaning that the driver's trench coat must be hiding a ridiculous spot. The driver is upstairs eating cheese sandwiches, and his wife is cleaning his trench coat, scolding him for his carelessness . . . No, this car, like all their cars, had just been washed and waxed; you could iron white shirts on the hood without fear of adding to your wife's laundry pile, if, of course, these people had wives. There were no scratches, no dinks, and, of course, no broken branches in the hubcaps, nothing that might make this automobile ordinary. Instead, the corner of the windshield displayed the rectangle of a special pass, a dark band stretched diagonally across its undecipherable inscription, DUP 56–SPEC, followed by the slightly more comprehensible UN-RESTRICTED ACCESS. The black tinting obscured even the contours of the steering wheel. He should have just kept walking and not turned around like that. But he had turned around, and after rounding the corner of the building, looked back yet again. Thoughts that this time he'd gone too far with his writing drilled his brain. Would there be a summons, an interrogation, or, worse, criminal charges for "defamation of the Motherland

and government officials in the foreign mass media" (up to five years)? On account of the pathetic professor? Of course, he ought to write only about love, about infidelity, and avoid that black, predatory, frightening rot with its disgusting ability to materialize right next door, right in your backyard, should you even allude to it in your fantasies. But he couldn't. He didn't know how to reform himself, no matter how frightened he was at the moment.

The city, the springtime city with its rooks and Savrasovs, disappeared. He walked down the prison corridor of his paranoia—fearing, cowering, wondering whether he had already managed to do himself in; taking comfort in not having finished the story or sent it off; pondering how he probably ought to rewrite the whole thing, stop publishing abroad, and . . . He felt better already. Spring had done its job: the sun, the azure, and the moisture all around—not autumn's tired rainwater, but the life-saturated, life-bearing spring moisture that soaked the ground ready to burst forth in grass. It was a revolution of life, impossible to suppress or intimidate. The Audi was parked in the courtyard on some other assignment. Perhaps they were tracking down a criminal, a real criminal, not an enemy, or perhaps one mobster was visiting another. In any case, the last thing was to be afraid of their cars. If they came for you, you wouldn't have any options. And since he was already out on the avenue and they weren't right behind, it must mean that his short story was irrelevant. Besides, he'd already determined that their shared perspectives on the night sky overlapped.

The Audi receded farther and farther, and he thought about it again only as he descended into the blackness of underground crosswalks whose tile walls reminded him of torture chambers. His thoughts were interrupted by the word "chambers," which suggested intimate spaces. It was much too emotion-laden a word to designate tile in underground crosswalks. Like Savrasov's rooks, words once again led him into the warm regions of semantics, whence he was returned by the honk of an automobile horn.

People on café terraces sipped black dense liquid from cups white as seagulls, and while he really wanted coffee, he thought not about where he should sit, but about what to call the spring creatures who filled the terraces. "People" would be criminal. Something new was needed, like "spring-man," "sun-crawlers," or "thaw-sitters." Anatoly didn't think about where to sit because he knew exactly where he was going. It was as simple and unequivocal as the word "snow" and explained why he paid little attention to the inviting rattan armchairs and checkered cushions and plaid blankets tossed cozily over their backs that beckoned him to join the "thaw-sitters" for a cup of smooth cappuccino and to sprout under the sun along with the grass, the trees, the entire city. At the TsUM central department store he turned onto Lenin Street, walked past a small group of teenagers sprouting with the rest of the city as they drank beer on park benches, smiled again at the phrase "Constitutional Court of the MGB," and, accelerating his pace, headed down Marx & Spencer Street.

When precisely did he realize that she was waiting for him in yesterday's café, at the same table? Probably while still back at home, when the disheveled professor in sweater and glasses had still been nouns, adjectives, and verbs. She had upset his verbal harmony as she grew more prominent than the words emerging from under his fingers, until, in the middle of the professor's pacing, the phrase "got it, I'm on my way"—which had nothing at all to do with the plot—suddenly appeared on the screen. He hastily erased it, got dressed, and decided to finish the story later in three or four concise, weighty sentences. Like a watermark or certificate of the authenticity of his premonitions, her face appeared behind the enormous window of the café. She didn't look at him, continuing to stir her coffee slowly. The thought occurred to him that in his diptych *The Annunciation* (*Pushkin Museum of Fine Arts* album, in the hallway, second shelf, on the right), Alessandro di Mariano di Vanni Filipepi had endowed the face on the right with similar features. As his hand tugged the café door, as he nodded to the waiter lunging toward him, as he shook his head at the offer to seat him at the table with the wonderful view and soft leather sofa, as he moved step-by-step toward the table in what seemed an eternity, he invented one conversation-starter after another.

He could joke. He could tell her about the "thaw-sitters" and the heavenly azure in the trees. He could mention the artist with the funny surname Filipepi who had rendered her face in slightly inaccurate detail: in profile you could see a resemblance, but at a three-quarter angle you couldn't. His *Annunciation* ought to be ripped from the walls of the Pushkin Museum and (damn it!) dumped in the trash. In the eternity it took him to cross the floor, he could have written a humorous poem, something about a "Latte macchiato, stirred into a jumble, / Tiny grains of sugar gleaming in the sun. / Sat down at the table, with you, a total stranger, / The chairs around the table accommodating two." It could be done quite elegantly, like pulling a rabbit out of a hat, with a double somersault. Elegant and suave. Glowing from within, he, he . . . No matter how ridiculous, it would be delivered as it should, and received as it should. Instead—Attention!—he sat down next to her, not opposite, as people usually sit on dates that morph into hasty dressing. Not opposite, but next to her. He sat down as only he could sit down, neither quickly nor slowly. He sat down and with a particular intonation asked, asked, leaning toward her slightly, no longer looking her over because he already knew her by heart, every feature of her face:

"Been waiting long?"

Smiling into her latte macchiato, which indeed was in a jumble, but not yet sipped, just recently stirred:

"All my life."

They spoke about many things, discovering in each other that, yes, the voice was just what it should be, and it was OK to joke, but it was also OK not to joke, because everything made sense anyway. If one of them started to joke while the other was just finishing a joke, they laughed together at having invented something simultaneously. He penned his autograph in huge letters on a napkin, using the bowl of a spoon instead of a pen and macchiato instead of ink, and the autograph said it all: a long list of wishes, bits of advice, and even a last will and testament—"I ask that my aged Frau be disassembled into spare parts to be scattered from the roof of the National Library, taking care, of course, that no one is killed"—sealed with a flourished signature. She gave him her autograph as well, which he placed solemnly in his pocket, staining his trousers beyond rescue.

Spring smiled at them through the café's enormous windows. They began a game of table soccer, using a sugar packet scrunched into a ball. Her goal, marked off with a glass and a saucer, was too narrow, while his, set between a spoon and a piece of napkin, was too wide, but his little player, formed by index finger and middle finger, kept passing by her little player, and the score was six to zero in Anatoly's favor when the playing field was irreverently destroyed by a fastidious waiter. Anatoly ordered green tea— for some reason he already had macchiato on his lips—and they laughed constantly, although most often only with their eyes, only their eyes.

As it swung shut, the door of the café breathed such incredible spring air that they wondered why they were still sitting there, still inside. With animal—no, avian, even less rational—eagerness, like rooks, they flew in pursuit of the spring and, once arrived, perched themselves on a single branch with no intention of ever flying apart. On their way out Anatoly had attempted to pay the waiter for their combined tea-latte-macchiato, but the waiter had recoiled from the money, and the owner of the café, who all this time had been playing chess with someone with his back to the room, the owner, whose face resembled that of a chess piece, jumped up and fussily, fearfully waved him off: take money from people like you?! That was strange, very strange. He remembered her car, the license plates ending in *KE* and the letters *MGB* that flitted by off to the side, but all this seemed to have nothing to do with them. It was like a Gefest gas stove billboard on the roadside flashing by as you sped down the highway, the pale blossom of the flame on the faded ad causing you to question whether you had turned off the gas under the kettle: I think I turned it off, but maybe I didn't? For a while longer echoes of *KE-MGB, KE-MGB* pulsed in his head, then faded, faded, faded, before bumping up against a backdrop of heavenly azure. She was waving to him to notice how fast the clouds were floating through the sky. "Winds of change," she said.

She took him by the hand, and their touch was stunning—just half of their palms, a total of two and a half inches square, but as if something had begun to flow from her into him. Her palm was scorching hot, and . . . a palm to such a degree, such a palm . . . A girl's palm, a palm marked "she." And this made their touching a symbol for all touching on earth. If alphabet picture books contained a letter called happiness, their touch would be the illustration. For a while they listened to their own steps. Her touch had melded them into a complex unit that marched, stepped, went up, and came down in tandem. For the first time, his steps, her steps had acquired meaning. Everything was still in the offing. At her request, he sputtered the story of his life, noting to himself that she had heard nothing, not a word about him, which he thought was wonderful, for even if she felt that she knew who Anatoly Nevinsky was, he would show her a side of himself that would convince her immediately that, no, she did not know him! He had never known himself to be like this!

As they passed by the President's residence, he joked that in a state controlled by the Minister of State Security a president was as much an atavism as a constitutional court that was part of the structure of the MGB. Having laughed so hard just a moment ago at the circumstances of his birth north of the polar circle—the details of which he barely had enough time to invent as he narrated—she suddenly stopped laughing. Once again the letters *MGB* flashed by like the siren of a car with tinted windows traveling at high speeds. For a second it interrupted their breathing, and their four-armed, four-legged unit staggered and tripped out of sync. He understood that never again would he joke about the MGB in her presence. But she was already pulling at his sleeve, asking him to describe in more detail how he had evolved from meteorite to polar bear. Squinting with effort, he supplied more and more fresh details, described what it was like to spend long polar nights in a yurt, and told her how the Chukcha Yagerdyshka (from Lipskerovo, it seems), had taught him to drink vodka and schooled him in his letters, and about how the two of them had recited "I remember the wonderful moment" together.

The street turned to cobblestone. (The city had so little cobblestone it seemed designed for Muraviov's cortege: a city of straight avenues with flawless surfaces, he thought to himself, to himself.) The cobblestones carried them past the army tank with its erectile cannon and past the officers' club, where they deliberated what a polar bear's favorite food might be: if regular bears liked honey, what did polar bears like? The answer occurred to them both at once: sweetened condensed milk, of course! Because polar bears and condensed milk were both white. Where did polar bears get condensed milk? They stole it from polar observation stations!

Condensed milk put a damper on their conversation, and they deliberated the question while passing a long building that looked as if it had crawled uphill on all fours. The cobblestones led them to Gorky Park, next to which, Anatoly proposed, there must be a Sweet Park, and a Sour Park, and a Salty Park, for Gorky means *bitter* as well as referring to the writer. But she corrected him, saying that it wasn't a bitter park, or a Gorky park, but a "Bitter-give-us-something-sweet-to-take-the-bitterness-away" wedding park, where everyone shouted "Bitter" and "Sweet" to each other, and then kissed. At that moment they were on the tiny little bridge that leads into the depths of the park and under the trees. No one was around. At that moment they stood opposite each other, holding each other with both hands. It was as if he had just proposed to her, or with her comment on "bitter" and weddings she had proposed to him, and the trees, the water under the bridge, and the jackdaws were shouting "bitter." (The jackdaws' shouts were particularly distinct.) Slowly, he placed his palms on her shoulders, then on her hair, parting it like a curtain and, muffling all the shouts, blocking them out, barely touching, more symbolically than passionately . . . right on her open—suddenly she had needed air—lips. The kiss lasted but a second, but was enough to unnerve them both fatally: they were as unprepared for each other as a platoon of traffic police would be if sent to do crowd control. Stunned by what had happened, they emerged onto the park's stage; she even released his elbow from her palm, but quickly recovered and put it back. Speech was out of the question: their voices would be hoarse, and no matter what he said— be it "I . . . you" or something about fish soon to spawn—the words would come out pathetic and banal. No, they had to be silent; in these first few seconds, it seemed they should be silent for eternity. But eternity quickly passed. Harrumphing and clearing his throat, he more pointed out than spoke to her about the azure peeking through the naked branches above. She looked in the direction he pointed, while he looked at the branches and sky in her eyes. Reflected in her eyes, everything was more beautiful. Neither of them thought that they had spoken too soon or too hastily: everything came in its own time, everything between them would come in its own time, and everything else would come in its time. Now, though, they needed to talk. He asked about her life, but she only brushed his questions off. He sensed it was better not to ask again. The speeding car with the tinted windows had made one thing clear: better to keep mum about life and the past. They had been cut from the same piece of marble, and they were made for each other. But they had only just realized this, which meant that they needed to talk about the present and the future. In the present ducks swam about the landscaped creek that flowed through the park. "Oh, look at the little ducks!" she chirped. In their own language the ducks quacked back, "Oh, look at the people!" The ducks might have waddled toward them, but seeing that the bipeds had no food, they responded to the couple's selfless tenderness by pragmatically showing their quivering back ends. She was devastated; he stroked her hair and promised to shoot them all with his slingshot, fry them, half-eat them, then restore them to life and force them to ask for forgiveness. She remained inconsolable and solemnly swore to make ducks the symbol of treachery, infidelity, and greedy self-interest: "He abandoned her and their two children, as only a duck would."

The people walking toward them no longer balked; it seemed that they knew all about them and smiled—sympathetically, inwardly, as if reminded of themselves. Looking at them at that moment, you couldn't help but smile. The path, which wound without rhyme or reason through Gorky Park, away from the traitorous ducks, led to a clearing near a wharf, where a retired, half-sunken diesel boat groaned in old age at its own misfortune. Its fate had been sealed. In minimal time, with the legendary daring of French corsairs seizing a Spanish merchant ship, they captured the diesel boat. Anatoly ran up to the gap in the granite guard wall just opposite the boat's entrance. The gap was shamefacedly cordoned off with a rope, but the rope could not stop the corsair. He removed the rope from the nail that had harbored it and stepped onto the deck. She, though, was afraid and looked at the icy water below in terror, saying that only a duck would be so mean as to disappear into that boat. Her fears were realized when, finally, through coaxing, vows, and promises, he got her to step (more like "jump") onto the deck, and the nail denuded of its rope left a long gash in her raincoat. Anatoly promised to sew it for her. That was the first time she called him Bear.

The boat was dark inside, with so many discarded condoms scattered about the floor that both of them felt awkward. The condoms resembled beached jellyfish, and their numbers suggested an ecological disaster, but after giving it some thought he decided not to joke about this either. Besides, just running your eyes over this crumpled, hardened, dried-up mess was awkward, awkward. Trying not to step on the dull white jelly-fish corpses, they made their way to the passenger area where someone quite recently (just this past winter) had built a campfire in the middle of the floor. They looked inside the impressive nautical door made from heavy metal, with rivets and a round thick glass window. Behind the door a ladder disappeared into the water at its fourth rung; the rungs, over-grown with seaweed that crept even farther below—where visibility was nil—held something so romantic that they both momentarily stopped dead in their tracks, while reflected ripples on the water's surface illumi-nated their faces. Spurred by the instincts of a corsair, Anatoly dragged her on, while she timidly inquired over his shoulder what it was they were looking for, to which he, laughing heartily, responded, "For treasure, of course." They found the treasure in a tiny room just behind the passenger area. The little room had none of the ocher-colored wooden panels of the seating area, and no oval windows that promised speed and spray. Here everything was Spartan, monotone, painted in businesslike salad-green and populated with gadgets long ago obsolete, as was apparent, most of all, from the font used in their labels. But, and this time they both gasped together as soon as they caught sight of it, there, in the center of the tiny cabin, unharmed—owing to the vandals' sentimental memories of childhood? . . . There, in the middle of the cabin, stood a real captain's wheel. The real thing. Just as the two of them would have imagined it: made of painted metal with wooden handles polished to a luster. "Oh," said Anatoly. "Oooo!" said she, his captive.

They sailed off. Rocking sedately, they inched past the Dardanelles and the Pyrenees. "Approaching the Bosporus," he reported laconically. "Full steam ahead," she shouted. You couldn't tell which of them was the captain: it looked as if they were both captains—he of the left half, and she of the right. The pilot room was raised above the level of the passenger area and directly in front of the wheel was a not-too-large window that had once made it possible to follow the sea-lane, but, after ten winters out of commission, the glass had clouded to milky-white opacity, which made it possible to follow nothing. But they really didn't need to see the sea-lane; they didn't need the Svislach River. Anatoly asked her to look to the right at the profile of the Great Sphinx. From the Nile they somehow made their way up the Ganges. From there they went directly to the Mississippi, where he sang her songs of black America, and she responded with quotations from Mark Twain. He gave the wheel a swashbuckling spin to the right, and the mysterious Amazon opened out before them: not the tame stream shown on the Discovery Channel, but the mighty river you can read about in dog-eared old volumes from the Library of Adventure and Fantasy series. She shouted, "Watch out for the pelican!" "They're duckbilled. They're all duckbilled!" he shouted back and drove the boat right over the pelican. She forwarded a complaint to the United Nations, so he set sail to New York to clear up the matter of duckbilled animals at the UN, but detoured into the Rhine, proposing they pause to admire the Cologne Dome, where he described the view in great detail as she listened, eyes wide open to his fantasies. They completed their round-the-world cruise, establishing an all-time world record for diesel boats—approximately forty minutes. Exiting the pilot room, rocking from weariness, they agreed that it had certainly been worth the torn raincoat. Jumping back onto the sidewalk, they embraced—without ceremony, like sailors on the *Cheliuskin*—and calm, proud, and close to each other, they headed out of the park.

Their need for the outdoors had passed. Having the whole world put at their disposal, they had played till they could play no more. But the city kept slipping them even more sights: the monument to Gorky, whose resemblance to a sphinx attracted Anatoly's attention; the Parthenon, which turned out to be no more than an arch over the entrance to the park, its sickles and hammers alluding to the Athens in whose honor it had been erected; the Eiffel Tower of the TV tower protruding above the buildings. They had seen all this already, and none of it was what they needed. They listened to the jackdaws' cries of "bitter!" but no longer felt awkward; they listened as would lovers who had decided to legalize their relationship ten years after they had first met. It wasn't for jackdaws to decide when "bitter" and when not.

Having passed under the first bridge, under Independence Avenue, they leaned over the granite guard wall and stared into the water. The ducks swam up to them immediately and didn't leave, even after seeing that there was no food for them. She rehabilitated ducks, saying that not all ducks were foul . . . The water, until just recently under ice and not yet having relearned how to flow, reflected the cathedral off in the distance and the Palace of the Republic. They, too, wanted to be reflected in it, but that would require leaning too far over the guard wall. (As it was, Anatoly's feet were off the ground, but his face was still not reflected in the water's smooth surface, which led him to propose that during their round-the-world cruise they must have become invisible.) They continued walking. Runners dressed in solar-reflective spandex passed them by. Most of the runners were very old, but a few comparatively young ones could be seen among them, and he and she decided that runners grew younger as they ran (the more laps—the more years slipped away), and that this place was particularly charmed: ten years off per lap. They also agreed that now that they had each other, they must live a long, long time, and they raced the two hundred yards to the nearest intersection. (Anatoly took a hopeless lead because, bear that he was, he had not allowed her a head start.) Passing under the enormous lindens that accompanied the Svislach on its way to the Trinity district, in unhurried conversation they arrived at the conclusion that for ordinary runners the place had a graduated effect—ten years per lap—but for runners in love the effect was equalizing. Now both of them were eighteen years old, and it was not at all important how old they had been before their sprint. Anatoly insisted that the winner of the two-hundred-yard dash deserved a prize, for example, an extra half-year of youth, but instead of a prize he got a rather hefty punch in the liver. He promised to report her to the UN for cruel treatment of polar bears.

By this time the Trinity district bridge stretched its wings overhead. It was evening: they had spent the whole day together. Lights went on in the high-rise apartment buildings far across the river, while streetlamps cast lunar paths along the water's surface, and the hustle and bustle of the city faded. Here, under the bridge, there was no one and nothing, just the rumble of traffic above. But, if you stood close to each other just so, you quickly forgot that the rumble came from cars. Rather, it seemed as if the heavens were rumbling, rumbling a tune. They looked at the city as if into the flickering coals of a campfire. They no longer spoke, but whispered, their whispers seeming louder than speech. More important, whispering produced the right timbre of voice.

The cold set in, and they needed to go inside to warm up, so, of course, they went home: where else could they go? After the Pyrenees and the Sphinx, after the ducks and the pelicans, and after the runners, how could they possibly just go their separate ways? Now they were invisible, reflected not even in the river. But they were reflected in the puddles, and in these reflections her head lay on his shoulder, and her hair tickled his chin, and, well, how could they part now? How could they part if they now cast four shadows in the streetlight, if the moon shone like that up above, and if her raincoat was torn? She led him off in the direction of Marx & Spencer Street, and he noticed how over the course of the day everything had changed: everywhere they were surrounded by eyes, the kind that peer deep inside you. Couples peered at them, as did families with children, and only rare lone individuals wrapped in scarves and hiding their frozen hands deeper in their pockets jabbed them with icy, piercing stares. Anatoly realized now that yesterday the problem had been with him, with him alone, and not with those around him. He had been one of those troubled loners, demanding love and attention, demanding that the person inside him be seen as a live, thinking, and suffering creature, but unworthy of all this. Now all that seemed unnecessary, and because he was being regarded just as he needed to be, he must have changed, he must have become more human, he was both attracting and emanating warmth. He attempted to convey all this to her, but couldn't, stammered, and just thanked her for her eyes, then added that in a person's eyes one could see all the meanness and kindness of which they were capable. Her eyes had wakened his eyes, which had been looking the wrong way in the wrong places . . . By this time they had already turned into the courtyard directly opposite the Chess Café and approached an unremarkable doorway and ascended to the third floor up a flight of stairs that seemed long enough to stretch to the fifth. She extracted an enormous ring of keys—why so many?—out of her bag, and took a while to turn them all in the steel door, even though she worked with the same speed as he had when he had spun the pilot's wheel on the boat. That, thought Anatoly, was wonderful, for it meant that her MGB daddy was not at home, and he, Anatoly, wouldn't have to sidle into her room with a forced smile, trying not to have to say hello, not to touch that extended hand . . .

With a picturesque gesture and looking like an elf-princess, she stepped back and invited him into her fairy-tale forest. The entrance hall, which allowed for the chance eyes of neighbors, plumbers, and communal services workers, of all those who shouldn't be allowed past the threshold, was restrained, designed simply, as if from a picture in a deluxe interior design magazine. Rococo intermingled with moderne in a subtle combination that had required not only bunches of good taste, but heaps of money. There was a small hassock on which one was supposed to sit—on your rear end, what blasphemy!—while taking off or putting on your shoes. The hassock—where Gaudi tangoed with the Palace of Versailles—had gigantic lilies hand-carved on its legs, while the asymmetric peony rising from behind in an explosion of splayed branches turned out to be a shoehorn one wanted to place under glass and not touch, especially with one's feet. (One of his socks was inside out, which made his foot look like a small catfish, and the other sock had a glaring hole—right where you couldn't possibly hide it—from which his toenail stuck out its tongue.) The entrance hall ended in a double-hinged door with stained-glass windows depicting something winding, vegetative, vine-like (art nouveau), and he had a hole in his sock. The stained-glass door quickly swung open: she did all this without a hint of boastfulness and with an obvious desire to keep the excursion maximally short and thereby exclude any possibility of ooh-ing and ah-ing. The light in the living room turned itself on, and it was here that—despite having tried hard to contain himself, although he knew she wanted no compliments, no compliments whatsoever—he let out an "ooh" of surprise. Behind the stained-glass window was a palace. Modest, not the most extravagant, here and there even spartan, with none of the excesses of Rastrellian baroque, but a palace nevertheless. The furnishings consisted of an oval table with a vase of luxuriant fresh flowers, armchairs carelessly set around the table, and a mirror in a thin, vine-like frame—all of it eighteenth-century, continuing the French motif begun in the entranceway. The furniture was white with the slightest hint of gold, the walls white with golden vignettes, and the marble floor was partly covered with a rug, also yellowish white. Even the light fixture—apparently solid crystal without a single piece of metal and extending from the sixteen-foot ceiling almost to the surface of the table and probably weighing a ton—seemed opalescent white. Near the window, treated with floor-length silk curtains, stood a varnished grand piano, obviously from the century before last, and wasn't it amazing that they had made such cloud-white instruments so long ago?

She stood there, in the middle of the room, at a loss what to do with it all now, how to integrate the two of them into this interior. A good copy (or, perhaps, the original?) of Alessandro Magnasco's *Bacchanalian Scene* hung on the wall. Anatoly urgently needed a bathroom to turn his sock right side out and to recover a bit; he asked with his eyebrows alone, and she waved in the direction of the corridor leading from the living room off to the right, as if she didn't quite remember how to find the bathroom. He walked for a long time, here and there managing to turn on lights and peeking into pastel blue, pink, and ocher rooms where beds, desks, and libraries stood untouched. He walked through rooms a bit smaller; he saw the kitchen—an ordinary contemporary kitchen with dark-blue polyvinyl cabinets that looked like a moment of madness in this mosaic among all the French words surrounding it. Doors off to the side led to new corridors, but finally, he found it—brass fixtures and a bathtub right in the center of the room. He quickly adjusted his socks, splashed his face with ice-cold water, and whispered to the mirror, "Holy shit! Holy fucking shit!"

What really bothered him was something altogether different: who was she and how had she acquired this palace tucked away inside an ordinary Stalin-era building? But not knowing whom or how to ask, or whether he should ask at all, he simply dowsed his face a second time with icy water, smoothed his hair with his hand, and walked out. The way back was easier to find: he'd left the lights on in some places and all the relevant doors were cracked open. She was sitting with her back to him, a bit too casually to look natural. He entered with such an inquisitive glance that she volunteered, "A communal apartment used to occupy the entire floor. The residents were bought out, and it was remodeled as a single apartment." She didn't care to say any more about the apartment, and he attempted to restore their mood by jesting about the hole in his sock and his disheveled appearance, comparing himself to the shadow of Hamlet's father coming to the wrong palace to look for Hamlet's father's son. But—he noted with alarm—she was already reacting more coolly, laughing less readily, and, when he, still attempting to revive and reanimate the situation, strutted over to the grand piano, opened the cover, and began to pick out with one finger the sole melody he knew ("Chopsticks"), her demeanor changed entirely. It was terrifying to see her like this. He leaped toward her and, mugging like a bear, begged her to help him play "Chopsticks," because bears like "Chopsticks," and she brightened, softening at the word "bear," and she banged on the keys along with him, embellishing the basic melody with unexpected improvisations from the classics. She played with a trace of excitement, and they ended with a bear hug, on the floor, laughing as he gratefully licked her hand while she patted him on the back of his head, and everything was good again.

Then suddenly, as if she had been struck, she froze, in such a way that he froze too, sensing that now, precisely in this way, as if during a sudden attack in combat, one was supposed to pull oneself together, fall silent, and be just ears and eyes. She lay there motionless, and he already knew what the problem was. Somewhere her cell phone was ringing. All of this was because of the cell phone, precisely because of the cell phone. She jumped up, ran out to the entrance hall, and returned with the ringing phone without picking up, without picking up the call, attempting to clasp the phone between her palms so it was not so loud, holding it with extended arms as if it were a poisonous reptile, a snake, a . . . The phone rang and rang, and she looked at Anatoly and begged him to help: the ring of the phone was like the strike of a clock at midnight, the carriage was about to turn into a pumpkin, and the bear would have to go search for the crystal slipper!

"Answer it, just answer it! There are no phone calls you need to fear like that," he said to himself, and, seeing her fright, he iterated aloud, "Answer it! Answer it! I'll go out into the hallway. It's no problem. You can talk!" She began to shake her head quickly back and forth, while still holding the phone, and uttered:

"That's it!"

"What's it? What?" Anatoly tried to get her to release the pent-up words. "What happened? Who was that who called? Do you want me to answer? What should I say?"

"That's it!" she repeated in response, prodding him toward the door as she walked with him, imploring, "That's it!"

It sounded like a request for him to leave—immediately, immediately.

"Do you want me to leave?" Anatoly asked. "I'll leave, take a walk for half an hour and come back, OK?"

"Leave now!" she exploded. "Leave immediately! And never come back here again, you hear? Don't you dare come here anymore. Get out! Forget you ever met me! Otherwise it's all over, you understand? Over! Get out!"

"You're throwing me out?" He attempted to sound insulted but it came out wrong, and he could see that she was in no condition to hurt anyone else.

"You fool! Leave! *Basta!* Don't you get it? You have no idea! Leave! And! . . . Don't you ever! . . . Dare! . . . Come back here again!"

He was already outside the door. She looked at him, and her eyes shone— from fear, perhaps, or perhaps because it really was forever—but he just couldn't believe that this was forever, that she was shouting, "Farewell! Farewell!" as the phone continued to screech, and "farewell!" is not "good-bye," which meant that he would never meet his . . . his . . . He didn't even know her name! They had become so close, they had traveled round the world together, she had called him Bear, and he had switched to the familiar "you," and nothing was more intimate than that "you." The door was already closing shut, cutting off her face, when he yelled, "What's your name?"

Muffled because of the already almost-shut door, as if from Hades, came "Elisaveta."

"Anatoly," he answered the closed door, and hadn't he already told her his name was Anatoly when he was talking about himself in the third person? "At this point Anatoly ate his way through the bars of the grating . . ." So it was clear that he was Anatoly . . . How strange it was to think that they had been acquainted for only one day! He pressed his ear to the door in hopes of hearing her voice, no, not even that, in hopes of hearing her steps, her laugh, for the door to swing wide open and for her to say that she had played a joke on him. No, her terror had been too real. There could be no joking with that kind of terror. God, what was going on?

Third floor. Apartment 54. Karl Marx Street. He would find her name by her address, look up her phone number, and call her every day. She had forbidden him to return, but he would call. She had been frightened. For him or for herself? Anatoly didn't want to leave the landing. He feared the irrevocability of leaving. He also feared that the fear and sadness elicited by that phone call would play itself out, as in a Hollywood film, in a slow leap from the third floor, which, because of the sixteen-foot ceilings, was more like the fifth floor. Just at the moment he walked out of the stairwell, she would appear on the balcony of her splendid palace and soar into the starry night, her flight culminating at his feet. By the way, where were her windows? Still standing near the stairwell door, he looked up and found the third floor, where muted light glowed here and there. He quickly realized that the apartment might extend to the very end of the building and even round the corner, and, who knows, maybe it was two-storied. Maybe the entire building was all her apartment, totally evacuated.

He meandered toward home, encountering few people still on the streets—"people," "people," rhyming in his head with "steeple," then "staple," then "playful," as a way not to think about her. He would find her anyway: by phone, by post, by prayer, by word of mouth . . . It became somewhat difficult to continue his word games while looking at the monolithic Audi A8 that stood in the same place it had startled him the last time, in his courtyard. No apartment search, no field interrogation under torture could last that long. Why was that car here? Who had it come for? He lost the rhythm of his fast gait, which had been so conducive to his rhyming-and-timing ("by phone, by word of mouth, by breaking out"). With leaden steps he approached the raven Black Maria.

The Audi was so out of place here among the native chestnuts, like a gallows in a children's playground. As if you looked out your window one morning and discovered next to the lopsided carousel and the half-sunken slide a scaffold with a noose dangling in the wind. Everything else was as usual: neighbors strolling, pensioners sitting on benches, and everyone afraid to stop alongside or rest their gaze on the car, as if suddenly that might seem suspicious, or that might get you . . .

He walked over to the Audi and looked inside the windows, black and opaque as metal. He had hoped to catch some sort of movement, some flash of an antitheft system (as if that car needed an antitheft system), but all he saw was himself, and it occurred to him that the sight of your own reflection in glass behind which you were attempting to find something rational to explain your gut fears was a fine metaphor for paranoia. His paranoia was rising in waves from somewhere in his stomach, his common sense telling it: "There's nothing to fear, the car could have come for anyone." Or, "If they were following you, they would have parked right in front of your entrance." His "I" was already churning, already whispering, already beckoning him to get the hell out of there and not stop, but he controlled himself. Then, just at the moment when he had convinced himself that the car's doors were not going to open and no one was going to push him inside . . . Just when the absence of any discernible movement in the car's depths had assured him that no one was inside, that the vehicle was deserted . . . Just when he was about to walk away . . . At that very second, confirming his horrifying suspicion that while he had been peering into the blackness behind the window, someone, or . . . or something (he shuddered) had been watching him from inside, studying him with birdlike (raven) eyes, just as he had been examining his reflection and thinking about his paranoia . . . In short, he already couldn't remember what had happened first: had the motor, detonated by the ignition, turned over first or had the blinding xenon headlights turned on first? With the sleekness of a cobra the car turned its wheels and slithered off. Making an unnecessary circle through the courtyard, on the lookout, on the lookout for its prey—the circle of a predator, unhurried and ready to lunge—making this circle, the Audi picked up speed, picked up speed and disappeared.

Anatoly was already running homeward, choking from fear: had they been waiting for him? Had they left only when they were sure he had arrived? What was going on? What had he done wrong? The faster he bounded up the steps, the worse it got, movement seeming to impel the oppressive feeling, to exacerbate it. Only at home, after closing the metal door behind him, after turning on the lights and checking all the rooms, did he sink into an armchair and try to calm himself. It was a misunderstanding. Of course, a silly misunderstanding. The officer was your usual MGB scum, and had probably had a good laugh watching Anatoly circle the car. The main thing was not to say "they": that was what he'd once been told by Dan, who before going to work for them—no, not for them, for the MGB, for the Ministry of State Security—had been so spooked that he almost wound up in the psych ward. "They" were an ordinary department, not an omnipotent force, and should be called by their name, for God had given each of us a name, and only the demons of our fears were nameless and numberless. "They" were the Ministry of State Security, and even if the Ministry of State Security had been following Anatoly, there could be a rational explanation why. There was nothing terrible in all this for Anatoly, no reason why he should be sitting like this, pressed into his armchair. Reason calmed him, but inside he was still in shreds, still shuddering, and thrice he approached the window and surveyed the courtyard (the car wasn't there), once again paced about his rooms, then called Dan, hoping to talk to him about nothing in particular, which always calmed him. But Dan couldn't be reached, and the turmoil in his soul was settling, settling into a dull calm.

They had just, hands joined, jumped on their boat. She had just, head tossed back, burst into laughter when he asked her why she had blond hair when she wasn't a blond, when that screeching ring, which he'd first taken for a streetcar bell, had resounded from that dark, resonating world. For a second he thought that the sound that had so frightened her might simply be the sound of her alarm clock, that she had awakened to a different reality, and that was why she had turned him out, why she had said that they would never meet again. This interpretation was so attractive, so elucidating, that he would have remained with it, were it not for the second, this time unmistakable trill of a telephone—the gray, Soviet-style, dial phone standing in his kitchen—that yanked him irreversibly out of his dream, melting his sweet conjecture that she had been awakened by a phone call or an alarm clock from another reality. The very place where that conjecture could exist had disappeared. The clock near the sofa read 4:32. Tiny hammers pounded inside his head, first hard and slow, then accelerating: there was nothing more terrifying than a phone call at 4:30 in the morning. "A Black Maria!" His thoughts had returned to the car, and he managed to entertain the thought that "they" always arrived at night to conduct searches, but it wasn't the doorbell that rang, it was the phone, and suppressing his wee-hours-of-the-night disquiet, he picked up the receiver.

"Hello, is this the Nurmambekovs'?" asked a taunting male voice.

It was obviously not the Nurmambekovs' apartment. What he would have said was, "You've got the wrong number," and just gone off to sleep, if it were . . . if it were so simple. But he had made up the comical Nurmambekovs. Gagging with laughter, he had dictated the name syllable by syllable, thinking it was impossible to spit the name out in one stream. He had dictated it to his school friend Grizzly, while Grizzly, chuckling along with him, had written it down and practiced pronouncing it: "Numbambe . . . Nurmabme . . ." The taunting sarcastic voice on the phone had spit it out without a trip or slip of the tongue. In school he and Grizzly used to make air guns out of ordinary pen barrels and covered the entire periodic table on the wall with spitballs, which they subsequently, after a visit to the principal's office, had to wash off. During his studies at the Presidential Academy of Public Administration Grizzly, still floppy-eared, had turned into Sergei, his neck bobbing in the collar of his shirt like the country's foreign policy at the time. A year ago, when they accidentally met on the street, Sergei introduced himself as Sergei Petrovich, and Anatoly discovered with surprise that those impossible ears now lay flat against the sides of his prematurely balding head. Sergei Petrovich extended his business card—United Secretariat for State Administration, vice-somebody of something—and said that he read him and, with a slight twinge at the corner of his eyes, that he made him laugh. Predictably, they wound up, as they always had as students, despite the differences between their educational institutions and opinions, in an underground bar called the Don Quixote, at a table filled with empty beer glasses. Sergei Petrovich, who had reverted to Grizzly, reiterated that he had read everything, although he didn't keep it at home ("not allowed") and that it had made him laugh. Not just laugh, but laugh "till he crapped in his pants." Interrupting the flow of their beer blather for a second, he sobered and said, "You know, Tolyan, that scribbling of yours can get you into some deep shit. Up to your ears. If anything, I'll know about it well in advance, man. 'Cause it's my job to know. You understand, though, that I won't be able to warn you directly. 'Cause if a guy's in deep shit, then anyone who tries to warn him is also in deep shit. Here's the plan. Someone will call you for me, as if they dialed the wrong number. And tell you you're in deep shit. That is, not you, but the person he's supposedly calling. You can decide then what conclusions to draw. Just one thing: don't go looking for me, or you'll burn a hole, damn it, in my brilliant career." After that he began to fantasize who the caller should ask for on the phone—Susanna or Vasisualy—and had a good laugh. Anatoly noted that since Grizzly had started working there, his sense of humor had changed. Anatoly proposed that the name sound more or less plausible and jotted down "the Nurmambekovs," and Sergei folded the slip of paper and stuck it in his wallet, and started explaining again about how he read and laughed, and again that someone would call and say nothing of any relevance.

"They'll just say 'Itzak,' for example. You don't say that you're not Itzak. You, ah, just mumble something, so the guy can deliver his message. Just mumble something indistinct. And he'll say, 'Itzak, you got problems.' And hang up. Then you think about where you fucked up. Got it? I'm not going to repeat this."

After that Grizzly, naturally, took his pen apart and shot spitballs at the waiters, but when it was time for them to go their separate ways he suddenly sobered up and said that he would walk out first because he and Anatoly shouldn't be seen together (don't keep the stuff at home, no way). And just now someone on the phone had asked whether it was the Nurmambekovs' apartment. The voice was young, obviously that of one of Grizzly's underlings, and, judging by the noise, he had called from a phone booth. Anatoly had blurted "no," instead of something unspecific, but a year had passed since they had agreed on this plan, and he could have forgotten. The voice on the other end of the line was already saying something, disregarding the "no" and the nonexistent Nurmambekovs.

"Vanya, Aunt Aliya told me to tell you that you started some business yesterday that you need to drop. You got that, Vanechka? Hello? Hello?"

"What business? What the devil business?" thought Anatoly, and Anatoly could think of nothing because his business yesterday had been of a particularly personal nature. The envoy from Aunt Aliya hung up, and just at that moment Anatoly remembered. Of course! His short story. It was too heavy-handed and too obviously about them. About all those scum in Audi A8s. But how had they got wind of his short story? Until yesterday morning it had existed only in his imagination. He hadn't used his computer to connect to the Internet (here he put his thoughts on hold and checked: yes, both cables—the phone line and the apartment's cable connection—were just hanging there, disconnected). How had they found out about the story? Could someone possibly have managed to mess with his computer, download, read, and turn in a report within the space of his stroll? A special committee of men in black had met and scratched the shaved backs of their heads and deliberated whether or not to allow it? And had decided that no, it wasn't a good idea. It contained too much about real life in it. Too much about what really goes on. Too much of everything that it all and always swung on—fear and petty deceit. And . . . and what now? How had Grizzly found out about it? Had they called him and said, you're in contact with Anatoly, call him and wag a finger at him? But he had gone out of his way to code everything and devised the Nurmambekovs precisely so they wouldn't know about their connection. What to make of it all, then? Either his, Anatoly's, problem was bigger than that. Or they had already set the gears in action, so to speak. Over a story that wasn't finished yet? And Grizzly would certainly have heard about it because it was his job to know. But why had they decided to break into his computer yesterday, when the story had already been written? No, it wasn't finished. How had they figured out (by the look in his eyes?) that he had written something? Or did they visit his apartment daily to check out all new Word documents? He goes out for coffee, and they close in, download, and read. WE SEE. WE HEAR. WE KNOW.

Again, suffocating waves of "they" rose and swept over him. His paranoia, now concrete, was related to a case whose gears were already grinding. That Audi under the window had been no accident—maybe they ("they") had been tracking his entrance into the courtyard while the operations group was scanning his hard drive. All of it really did make a certain sense (albeit lame, wounded, and sick): the stairwell had only one entrance, the courtyard was fenced in, with a gate at one end only, precisely where they had been parked.

His common sense protested, screamed even, that you can't get arrested for a literary text, and that you got slapped with "defamation of the state" only for interviews and articles. But his body, shivering with nervous fever, had already turned on the computer. A criminal case. "Tolyan, that scribbling of yours can get you into some deep shit. Up to your ears," he thought. Then thought some more: "Why, given all the sleaziness of that 'service' of yours, don't you wind up 'in some deep shit,' Grizzly? While I, with my 'scribbling,' as you called it, with my make-believe heroes woven from late-night strolls and alien looks, with that disturbed, lonely professor of mine and his favorite student who can't understand that antiquity is in the past, while the present is gray, boring, mean, and satiated, filled with the likes of you, Grizzly . . . Why am I considered by you all to be the enemy? Your head is stuffed with enough complaints about this system, Grizzly, to justify three firing squads. But the cars are parked under my windows, and I get the phone calls at 4:30 in the morning. Why, Grizzly?"

If that was protestation, it was under siege, encircled on all sides by thugs with revolvers. Sweat froze his armpits as his cursor danced to the file he wanted, dragged it into the trash, the sole copy. You, Bulgakov, were wrong: manuscripts do burn, permanently! A criminal investigation. Two more clicks of the cursor—"Empty trash." Choke on it, you freaks. All that was left was to clear his memory and brain of the plot, of those so auspiciously devised phrases, and not regret, not regret, not regret!

⌊3⌉

EIGHT WEEKS PASSED. Eight. Enough time to forget just about anyone. Eight. Eight weeks. Eight more weeks until autumn. We met in the
spring, and now it's summer, and eight weeks from now it will be autumn.
Eight, wait—they rhyme! All day outside his window the leaves in the
trees—one more reminder that spring had grown into summer—rustled
with the sounds of radio interference. Now, however, it was quiet. The
poplars held silent in quiet fear as they awaited an evening thunderstorm
and exhaled the heat they had stored up over the course of a day casting
shadows.

Time is the best healer not because it blurs and obliterates people—
who ought to be forgotten. We resurrect these people and find places for
them somewhere in our hearts, feed them with our memories, and nur-
ture them into brightly colored pocket-sized manikins having nothing in
common with the living who preceded them. And we love these manikins
until someone else, someone live, comes along. No, time is the best healer
precisely because it brings us to accept more new someone elses, new,
living someones. They open their mouths, stick out their tongues, say,
"Ah-ah-ah," and we acknowledge that without us there's no healing their
sore throats. The manikins melt to be replaced by the new someones—
live, warm, and though capricious and imperfect, so much better than the
someone who had been and incomparably better than the manikin.

Over those eight wait-for-autumn weeks, time did nothing to help. It
brought no new patients with sore throats, not even an exciting silhouette
at the wheel of the car in the next lane, a graceful neck, a bared shoulder. That is, there were more than enough silhouettes, and we exchanged
looks, and they even smiled at me—my Frau is an eye-catcher. But a split
second before the moment when your soul seems to depart you to alight
on the passenger's seat alongside her, when you begin to do silly things, for
example, racing with the owner of the graceful neck and bared shoulder,

ignoring all the colors of the rainbow exuded by the stoplight—exactly one split second before that moment someone or something would place a hand over my eyes and—I curse you, time, best of healers!—whisper in my ear: "That girl, behind the wheel. She looks like *her* behind the wheel. She, too, is somewhere, behind the wheel. Listening to her rap music and parking on sidewalks." When the hand over my eyes withdrew, the one with the bared shoulder had already driven off, and there I was, hurtling down the rails of my memories. And so it was, eight long weeks.

What did I do during this time? Well, I acquired the disgusting habit of talking to myself. To her, that is. I told her about everything I saw. The pensioner in bizarre brass-framed emerald glasses, and the pink Lincoln, and the posters for the Andy Warhol exhibit—all of this was turned into words prefaced by "Lisa": "Lisa, today I saw an old guy in green glasses who looked like a gnome." That was my way, probably, of tucking her into the space of my rib cage, the door to which was open—she could leave at any time, but, to be honest, she never entered. I talked to her, which was better than engaging in self-satisfaction, foundering in a sea of memories only to float out into an ocean of fantasies.

I couldn't manage to forget her, forget you—I don't know how to talk about you, in the third person or the second. It was as if we were online with each other. No matter what I did, she was with me, somewhere with me. The first few weeks I honestly tried to write and did a good job torturing myself in the process, but nothing came of it: pronouns slipped from my hands like minnows, language seemed to have acquired life-forms that devoured everything that had come before, everything that was familiar. You became my principal reader, and I strove constantly to bend my sentences to address you, then, when I reread it, realized that it was all wrong, that that was no way to write. I honestly attempted to restore the story murdered by my cowardice, restore it for myself, to bury it in password-protected archives, hide it in my mailbox, but it was as if language took its revenge on me for my betrayal, and phrases I remembered and thought would be easy to restore wouldn't stick. I realized that this damnation, this plot, would remain forever in that better, luminous world where destroyed files go.

I did a search on her apartment, and was somewhat ashamed of what I found out: it was registered to Elisaveta Supranovich, place of birth—Kobryn. Using my security, police, communal service, and even university connections I was able to find out not all that much: parents had died at a young age, raised by her granny in Kobryn, Elisaveta Supranovich had graduated from the foreign language institute. That was it. After graduation—nothing, no mentions whatsoever anywhere. Where she worked, what she did—all unknown.

Of course, I hung out beneath your windows, which embarrasses me probably most of all. Hung out like a spy, like an MGB flatfoot, comparing myself in vain to a minstrel or goliard: I had no mandolin and hardly any intention of singing. I wanted to know when you would arrive home so I could—totally accidentally, dropping my shopping bag of milk and eggs—meet you the next day in the archway at the entrance to your courtyard. But you never showed up at your place, and it hurt me to think at whose house you could be spending the night all these eight weeks. Admittedly, you might have a night job or have left for a two-month vacation. And, at the end of the day, spying is not polite.

Apparently having come to the same conclusion, the Audi A8 never again appeared beneath my windows. And—now here's a real symptom of paranoia—I very quickly, within two days, completely forgot about what it was that had forced me to shudder in horror. The stimulus had disappeared, and Pavlov's dog stopped salivating and doing whatever else Pavlov's dogs did.

Her name is Elisaveta, a tremulous, mellifluent name resembling the fairy-tale melody of a music box made by a Belgian artisan back in the days when things were very beautiful. A music box capable of imparting dreamlike languor even to a lilting little aria from Mozart's *Don Giovanni* to produce "E-lis-a-vet-a." "Lisa" was in my ears constantly, tucked between one letter in front and four behind. None of this resembled parting forever. We were both sure that we would meet again and were just procrastinating (why?). I need only drop the corners of my mouth and she—apparently herself unable to endure our silence—would give me a sign to confirm that she did not believe I was serious in my desire to forget her.

Once, for example, at the Chess Café, at the same table where we had played table soccer, a can of condensed milk suddenly appeared next to my cup of green tea. In response to my attempts to find out who, who and when, the waiter just widened his eyes and swore that he had put it there by accident on his way to the kitchen to give it to the chef to add to the tiramisu. But somewhere behind his frightened face hid another, mischievous face, and if I were to burst out laughing, he would, too, with that other face, burst out laughing and tell me about how you had been there, how and when. But I got worked up, he became confused, and it occurred to him that perhaps this can might be more than just a mischievous trick. I pulled myself together and attempted a smile. (Just try smiling where we are concerned!) But he had already escaped to the kitchen with my can, a can of treats for a polar bear. I took off after him, grabbed him by the back of his collar, and shouted that the can had been for me, and he gave it back. Back home, every milligram of the condensed milk was filtered, every millimeter of the label was studied under a magnifying glass, in hopes of finding some clue or message, but *the medium is the message* (McLuhan again!). The can was both the clue and the message.

Another time, at the end of the fifth week, near the bridge to the Trinity district, our bridge, the bridge under which we had watched the smoldering coals of the city, a billboard announced HONEY BEAST, written out in huge golden letters: what an unmistakable sign, thank you! When I came closer, I could see the illustration: one young man with a cup of green tea was pushing a bowl of sugar to the side, while another was pouring sticky, gooey honey into his cup. Grinning, he looked to his right (there, in the Chess Café, you had sat to my right!). The text, which I had mistakenly thought was a direct reference to me, read HONEY'S BEST! Just below, in tiny letters, was the name of the company, HoneyEast, a wholesale honey distributor, which (I checked) had never, of course, existed. At the state ad agency they just shrugged, saying that a photo-ready sketch had arrived by email, the order had been paid by money transfer, and they, of course, would not tell me the name on the account. I didn't know whether to believe them. Perhaps you had sat alongside as the graphic designer, tongue between teeth, sculpted that HONEY BEAST on the computer as you corrected the work. But that wasn't the point. The point was that I knew that you were with me, that not everything was over, that our separation was not forever, and that we would surely see each other again.

Outside my window came the first distant roll of thunder, and the first flickering flashes of lightning. The poplars had had good reason to sweat in fear! The silent trees had been saying that a thunderstorm was inevitable, that it was on its way, that all windows should be closed and all plugs pulled out of their sockets, and that it was time to go to bed, because tomorrow (tomorrow!) we would meet: of that I was certain.

Today, walking under the bridge—idleness frequently takes me outside for long walks, although in the past I used to walk mostly around the center of town, looking for plots and listening for the right words in the rhythm of my steps . . . Right, as I was walking under the bridge (I'll add only that my routes these days have changed radically, and I now walk down abstract streets; among the three-story buildings on Communist Street, ferreting out ways to turn in the direction of our triangle—Marx, Trinity, and Gorky Park) . . . Right, strolling under the bridge, I discovered a little man in an orange coat vigorously eradicating graffiti done in your hand. The back of his coat bore the acronym MINCOMMSERVORG. The little orange man was from the same public services organization that trims trees, sweeps courtyards, removes anti-Muraviov fliers, and paints over graffiti, the punishment for which (did you know this?) is up to five years in prison. The little orange man had begun painting over the graffiti, starting at the end and obstructing the middle with his body, so it was hard to figure out . . . Generally, you're not supposed to stop and watch, because the MGB could be at work here collecting evidence against the vandal who had damaged city property, but not a soul was around. The graffiti had been written with ocher-colored spray paint. The letters *dux* appeared from behind the orange fellow, and there were no other possibilities: I almost shoved him out of the way to stare at the wall, and I must have looked professional enough because he didn't object, just moved aside. It read: "redux memorial for those disappeared. Tomorrow at . . ." the ending, so critical, having already been painted over. You had done everything correctly: notices of "memorials" often appeared on distant bridges and fences far from the center of town. Those still alive and still at liberty photographed them and sent them to the West, so the West imagined that a mass national resistance movement existed, while the MGB infallibly tracked down the graffiti artists through traces left at the scene of the crime, by email addresses, and by God—no, devil!—Devil knows how else!—and put them in prison. With each year the number of graffiti diminished. If you saw this kind of graffiti, you were supposed to place a lighted candle in the window at the time indicated to show that you remembered. But no one did that, of course, out of fear, although to put a candle in the window at a particular time was not in itself a crime.

The word "redux" was written very strangely, with the letters *e* and *d* separated by a colon cramped between the two syllables. Of course, it had occurred to the MGB that the graffiti artist, having pulled out his spray paint and written the *re*, had been spooked by something, stopped in the middle of a letter perhaps, took off, and returned later to pick up where he had left off, leaving the dots that would communicate to discerning eyes his moment of weakness. I immediately read it as intended: instead of "re:dux," I saw "dux," our ducks, our traitorous ugly ducklings, "duck-fuck," "ducks-redux." But you had not considered the most important thing, and now, back in their special institutes and analytical groups, they were racking their brains over a nuance: memorial days for dissidents always occurred on the sixteenth day of whatever month, on the day when his principal enemies—Sierakowski, Wróblewski, and Dąbrowski—had disappeared. Enemies who had either kidnapped themselves or been killed: it didn't matter. But today . . . What was the date today? July 1! So easy to remember: July 1! Tomorrow would be July 2, which meant that for lack of anyone to remember, no "memorial day" was planned for tomorrow. Silly thing, you likely hadn't known what all these "memorial days" were about when you'd looked for a word with "ducks" in it for me. I had come by this way yesterday, and the wall had been clean, which meant that the graffiti could have appeared only today. Of course! How else? If it had appeared any earlier, it would have been eradicated and painted over: in this city graffiti never survives more than two hours. The only thing left to figure out was at what time. What was under that fresh layer of gray paint? Here and there some numbers could be made out, but they were largely illegible. Without giving it a second thought, I asked, realizing that I was taking a risk, but the MINCOMMSERVORG guy had let me read the stuff about the "days." "What came after that?" Smirking contemptuously and screwing up his eyes, either in mockery or with opprobrium, he asked in response, "Who's asking?" Attempting to reproduce their intonations—although I'd never heard them—businesslike, with a suggestion of possible violence, I said, "Somebody." Immediately any suggestion of a smirk vanished from the orange guy's face, he looked at me with contemptuous repugnance, turned back toward the wall, and bawled unnaturally, "If I got my hands on the person who wrote this, I'd pull his arms off. The fucking grant-suckers. Four forty-five." "Nothing else?" I clarified, but he no longer turned around, demonstrating at once both his contempt for and fear of "somebodies."

Naturally, even if he hadn't told me, I still would have waited for you there by our ducks, waited from early morning on, for days on end, by our ducks, until you showed up. Polar bears love condensed milk. What do Elisavetas like? Why hadn't I asked? Music boxes? No, more likely, melodies, mellifluous music, like her name. I needed to come to the ducks with pockets full of music, with handfuls of notes, and feed them to you, removing the wrappers from the notes myself. I could already picture what these wrappers on musical notes—delicious, chocolate notes—looked like, but this was a dream, a dream.

The crowds began at the gate to our courtyard. It was as if people from all over the country had gathered in the poor little center of the city, on the quiet little patch of land where my Stalin-era building had sprouted. Strange things had been happening since morning: in place of the cats that usually dotted the courtyard like scattered chess pieces and in their diurnal half-sleep always faced one another, ready to break into warlike howling at any challenger daring to cross those boundaries of cat territory invisible to the human eye . . . Instead of these squinting wineskins, people with sleeping pads or just old bedcovers, with sacks of food and cases of alcohol, were camped out under the poplars. They spread themselves out on the playground and under the clotheslines; they sat on the ground, cut piles of tomatoes and cucumbers, and poured out vodka into little plastic cups. As they did this, the cats, hiding under the cars, having acknowledged in amazement that these enormous, heavy, smelly bipeds could not be driven away merely with aggressive howls, were retreating in disgust, when one of the picnickers offered them a piece of lunch meat sweaty from too many hours unrefrigerated in its cellophane wrapper. It was as if the entire country were holding a wake and had gathered to commemorate the dead in my courtyard, overflowing into the entire center of town.

I carefully picked my way past those who had already introduced themselves and moved their blankets and mats together to create a large table—the cats observed this consolidation of territory with amazement, further convinced of their sterile superiority to this biped, chaotic race. I politely refused an unexpectedly extended plastic cup, allowed a war veteran decorated with medals to hug me, and remembered. Of course. Today is July 2. Dress rehearsal day. How could I have forgotten? She had set our rendezvous for today precisely because there would be a crowd at "the ducks" and the casual observer would be unlikely to pick us out in this motley, drunken crowd of out-of-towners. It was dress rehearsal, the day before City Day. At one time City Day, July 3, the day we celebrated the city's liberation from Nazi troops, had been a major event for these people, a celebration with a military parade, a gala concert, and a fireworks display. But Muraviov felt too much disgust for this happy, potato-faced constituency to mix his celebrations with theirs. So it came to be that for the people they held a "dress rehearsal" or, as the posters read, DRESS RE-HEARSAL, with real fireworks, a nighttime parade of military technology, and a concert. Then, on the next day, cordoned-off celebrations were held for Muraviov, members of the MGB holding special passes, the President's administration, and members of the government. Nobody knew precisely what took place there on City Day: for at least ten years "dress rehearsals" had in no way coincided with the "rehearsed" performance. Inhabitants of houses near the reviewing stands, who were forbidden under threat of sniper fire even to come close to their windows, told of horrendously loud organ music, of Chinese dragons flying through the air, and of French cinema classics projected onto the walls of the nearby high-rise buildings so the "screen" for one special spectator stretched more than a third of a mile. I would have liked to have seen his face as he watched all this. One thing was certain: there were no fireworks displays, no circus acrobats or ski jumpers, and no Alla Pugacheva at Muraviov's celebrations. If you were to tell this to any of these hearty, stocky men in short-sleeved white dress shirts, they would not have believed you; they were drinking now, warming up for the incredible miracle of the fireworks display, raising toasts "to him," celebrating their camaraderie, sitting *him* down at every table, pouring *him* a glass, offering *him* snacks.

Each year on the day before dress rehearsal I tried to leave town—the event struck me as a monstrous lie. But jostling my way through crowds in the direction of Gorky Park, I saw only happy faces. I understood that here, too, Muraviov had done everything right: this kind of celebration was precisely what these people needed. Nearby, a large group of young people were drinking vodka, passing the bottle from hand to hand as they walked, and wrapping, wrapping themselves in the green-and-red national flag. Behind one of its folds a couple was kissing and rolling on the ground, under the others' feet, oblivious to everything. People stepped over the half-dressed and drunk couple and paid them no heed, because who knew what you might see at dress rehearsal on the night vodka sold for half-price in all the stores, and the police were forbidden from touching the drunks or breaking up fights. Suddenly, someone grabbed me by the hand and pulled me somewhere off to the side in the direction opposite where I was headed. I was in a human dance chain winding through the human masses, singing something patriotic. A red-haired imp wrapped in a short little glittering stretch dress had already attached herself to my free arm and was smiling right at me. (God, why can't I be as simple as they are?) I linked her arm with the one that had pulled me into the chain and blew her a kiss, although she had already turned the other way. Trash crunched underfoot, and a massive fistfight was in progress up ahead: someone had said something the wrong way or, more likely, taken something the wrong way. Girls were squealing, and in the dust and melee only bright patches of blood, looking so heroic on white shirts, stood out. The police detachment standing about two hundred yards away did not interfere, of course. Each of them, perhaps, had an invitation to tomorrow's real celebration, and who wanted to show up black-and-blue for having been overzealous keeping the peace during the rehearsal? The human crowd changed the lay of the avenue, and I lost my orientation: here and there singers moved about on stages, looking a bit more apathetic to what was happening than a concert allowed. But the spectators—red in the face and reeling, saliva running down their chins—forgave all. Here in the center of town no one sat—there wasn't room. Everyone stood, walked, and danced, and drank while walking, saying things to chance passersby—like that man with the helmet of black Bashkir hair trimmed to resemble a hat. Slipping into some Asian language, he told me about our hero-city and called me Andrei, then, dumbstruck for a moment, he peered at me and asked me where Andrei was and ran back to look for his Andrei. All I wanted to do was to get out of there, just get out. To change my habitat, to swim from the salty waters of the crowd into our fresh water. The landscaped creek with the ducks lay straight ahead, as did the bridge where you had chirped while looking at the ducks, but all of this was sown with bodies clinking glasses, ain'ting, and wuzzing. Disconcerted by what was happening, the ducks had either flown off for warmer climes or stuffed themselves full of lunch meat (sweaty from too many hours unrefrigerated in its cellophane wrapping) to the point where they couldn't float anymore and had sunk like stones to the bottom. I looked insufficiently alien to my surroundings, not alien or polar bear enough, because people kept coming up to me. I did everything I could to make them understand that they had the wrong person, that I had not come for the dress rehearsal, not to their dress rehearsal, and a man with a mustache—wearing not a short-sleeved white shirt (what a miracle!) but a real military blue-and-white striped undershirt—who had just a couple of minutes ago somnambulistically danced right in the center of the landscaped pond, a bottle of vodka in one hand and a chunk of bread in the other, danced in a pose that made him look like Picasso's *Girl on a Ball,* asked me, "Where will the fireworks be?" Before I could figure out that not to answer him at all would be rude, that I had to answer him, his friend, who had just been groping the bottom of the pond trying to catch goldfish (to go with his vodka?) answered for me: "Everywhere!"

Here you could see it all: an eight-year-old drinking beer out of his father's bottle, an elderly woman in her Sunday best walking her pug, three high school girls posing for a fourth, T-shirts raised to expose their breasts. Here you could see everything, except her, although a half-hour, an hour, and an hour and a quarter had already passed since our appointed time. I was beginning to doubt the meaning of "dux," to think that perhaps it really was "redux" and that our ducks had nothing to do with it. A few instants later, two nimble hands covered my eyes from behind. Without your raincoat, without your high-heeled boots, dressed in a T-shirt and jeans, you looked like a miniature doll, much more miniature than I remembered you, but with a particular kind of petiteness: everything that was important about you—for example, the fingers I so loved, your eyebrows, your lips—were all the right size. Your face was just a bit long, with dimples on your cheeks. My hands locked on your folded wings, and we stood there, rocking back and forth, feeling no pity for the goldfish already skewered on pocketknife-hewn skewers and being carried to a miniature campfire. Over the past eight weeks I had thought about the first words I would say to you when we met, and you, I'm sure, had prepared something eloquent in your head as well, but, forgive me, I wouldn't be a polar bear had I not improvised:

"You're late. It's six already."

To which you sniffed:

"So I was supposed to show up early, huh? Build you a yurt? Paint northern lights on the trees?"

To which I huffed:

"But the wall read 'quarter to five'!"

To which you, pressing up against me again, said tenderly, now, with no suggestion of bickering:

"The wall, Bear, read '6:00 P.M.' Plus the clue about the ducks."

A few more seconds passed in convulsive embraces before it dawned on me: "Right, the MINCOMMSERVORG guy! He pulled a fast one on a 'somebody'!" You felt me shake with laughter, stepped back, and asked what was wrong. I explained:

"The guy who was painting over your graffiti had managed to cover over the time, and when I hinted to him that I, uh, was from the 'services' and asked him what time had been there, he told me four forty-five. What a friend! Amazing they haven't locked him up yet! Perhaps you hired him to paint over the graffiti? I was already beginning to doubt, by the way, whether I'd got your signal right."

"Serves you right! You should have arrived earlier! If you'd come to the bridge on time, no one would have painted over anything yet."

"How was I to know? You're lucky I was there at all. You could have found yourself in this wonderful company eating barbecued goldfish with those wonderful gentlemen in the striped undershirts."

To which you said seriously:

"You can't really believe that you happened to be at that bridge by accident?"

And I:

"I don't know what you're getting at. We hadn't agreed that I would check out the bridge every night. Or had I missed something?"

To which you answered, putting your hand on my chest:

"You fool! I had written and told you to come. And you heard me and went there and read everything as you were supposed to. If only clumsy bears could walk a little faster." She twisted my ear in reproach, and I growled with pleasure.

We headed off, we set off, both of us heady and set, set and touched, touched by each other's hands. I led in the direction of civilian quiet streets detoured by the dress rehearsal, while you pulled me toward the thick of the crowd, straight down the poster-lined—EVERYONE IN THE COUNTRY TO REHEARSAL!—path toward Victors' Avenue, where the crowd was its densest and drunkest at the Stela to National Heroes. All of my questions were forgotten, tangled in your hair, and how would I have asked them? It was too noisy, your ears were not meant for shouting, and I was prepared only to whisper in them. The crowd pressed us up against each other, and while back in Gorky Park we had walked palm to palm, by the time we got to the top of Victors' Avenue we were pressed together and inter-twined so the crowd wouldn't break us apart. I no longer had any desire to extract myself. Having found my other half, I was assured that our species was adapted to their salty water, that we could breathe even if submerged in beer if together, if our fins flapped and gills moved in tandem.

At the Yubileinaya Hotel, the single place foreigners were allowed to stay, the windows were swung wide open, a guest from beyond the seas in each, all of them too frightened to go downstairs yet at the same time too stunned to sit in the bar and wait out this invasion of Martians—at this hotel, next to the disfigured parking lot with its capsized and burned-out trash bins, something swept over the two of us, and we tried to stop and to embrace but couldn't: we were being pushed from behind, prodded farther and farther, closer and closer to the stela with its infernal scarlet lighting, its bayonet already in sight above the sea of heads. For a second it was terrifying that this measured, robot-like propulsion of humans might not release us at all, that at a slow (one step per heartbeat) pace we would make our way to the viewing stands, watch the evening parade and nighttime concert, then be turned about face and with the same prodding at our backs sent on to the train station with everyone else, just as slowly, eventually to be delivered to the train: a single long train that would take these people back home to their bedroom communities on the outskirts of my city, home to their sleepy little towns that also suffered from hangovers, and we would be pushed out (rather, squeezed out) at some whistle-stop called Mile 605, where we would understand what had been predetermined for us, right here, predetermined by the people themselves. I would build a hut, and you would grow gherkins. We'd be happy as rabbits, as a leaf of cabbage, as yeast dough. The same thought, apparently, had occurred to you, or you had overheard what I was thinking, because you smiled at the persistence of the human mass pressing us forward like hamburger out of a meat grinder. The air shook with the drumrolls of military marches. The voice of the announcer— lifted straight from official Soviet propaganda of the stagnation period— a voice amplified many times over and present everywhere (behind, up ahead, along the sides), a voice that canceled itself out with its meandering echo, informed us of "roll-out deployment time," which I visualized as a rocket wrapped in cellophane and people fussing to unwrap it as soon as possible, of "strike radius," and of "salvo fire installations," all of which had no place in our world yet tore into it like thermonuclear bombs. And there was no place else to go: the masses up ahead held us back like a prison wall that had run up against the prison walls of the masses ahead of them—solid backs and backs of heads, a monolith of backs of heads, a baked pudding of backs across which we, like a teaspoon of jam, slid as we attempted to make our way to the middle of the confection. As if especially to enhance the solemnity of the parade, the darkness all around had already thickened, and you pulled me off to the side onto a small rise, where it was quieter, cleaner, and less crowded. We plopped ourselves on the ground, and I removed from my back a piece of beer bottle that had not made much of a scratch and said: "Shrapnel wound," and you—miracle of miracles—heard what I said! We could have a conversation here! You let out a long tirade about the vehicles crawling down the avenue weighted down with sixty-five-foot strategic rockets; you outfitted the parade with alternative commentaries, for example, about "a column of young patriots whose hats were not sufficiently ingrown into their scalps yet, so, comrades, let's show the weather our thanks for this quiet, windless night! About the pride of our antiaircraft defense system— the Shilka ZSU-23-4—with its updated version, the Shilka-Up-the-Ass (abbreviated as Shilka-UA); about the BM-21 Doomed City multiple-rocket launcher. About our principal strategic weapon, to wit, the voice of the announcer himself, capable of turning rusty Soviet technology into a daunting response to potential aggressors. Only when the tanks rolled out onto the street, damaging the asphalt with their caterpillar treads, when they stopped right in front of the viewing stands and bellowed blanks out of their cannons so loud that, screaming, you pressed yourself against me, only then did you and I both find it all no longer funny, but frightening. The crowd, on the other hand, showered with clouds of gunpowder ash, was roaring with its hundreds of thousands of larynxes, ready for anything, ready to spread like a black avalanche and suffocate, rend, and rape. The crowd, having smelled gunpowder, was like war itself, while the tanks with their caterpillar tracks on the asphalt on the rise just above us sent tremors through the earth: the earth was terrified, we were unable to console it with our bodies, and I thought, how fortunate it was for us that we had moved off to the side, for otherwise they surely would have sensed the enemies, snakes, and spies within us—sensed it by the way our eyes didn't gleam, our throats didn't yell, and our hands were not clenched into fists or raised above our heads. They would have ripped us to shreds. These tanks driving through the nocturnal city held, without doubt, something mystic, something larger than a mere holiday for the people, as if a valkyrie, a blood demon, flew above each of them. I attempted to formulate this thought into words:

"Stop shaking, Comrade Commander in Chief! You're scaring the earth, which because of you trembles as well. Better your nervous jeering than this cowardly trembling!" To Lisa I said, "You know, it was the first time I'd ever experienced such a rush of energy. It's just not there when you watch on TV. Did you feel it, too?"

She nodded, burying her face in my shoulder. I continued:

"It's as if all these armored vehicles held the answer to the question of what our wonderful country is, of how to this day it still preserves its sense of well-being. The answer lies in tanks, not in the economy. We have neither oil, nor gas, nor normal manufacturing—nothing but imitations, an attempt to sculpt a microwave oven from sketches stolen from Samsung. The GNP is on the rise, there's not a hint of inflation, salaries comparable to those in Europe, pensions in excess of those in Russia, which has both oil and gas and some industry—gas and oil for the most part, of course. You watch all these rockets and soldiers, you hear the Soviet military marches, and you feel it, don't you! It makes you shiver, doesn't it! The state's vitality is not solely a question of economics! Everything is determined at very subtle levels—for example, at the level of the crowd's roar, of tanks in the city. What can the economics of hard-currency exchange rates explain, for example? On a superficial level, sure, something, but if you dig deeper into all of those correlations, you'll be frustrated. The price of oil, the GNP, and gold-currency supplies. How is the price of oil determined? Why does it soar, then crash? What will it be a month from now? These are all nuances. Not a single economist can predict a frigging thing. They said that in ten years everything would go to the dogs, and what? It just gets stronger!

"What difference does it make, in the long run, how many televisions are manufactured and sold, if Muraviov sets the price of vodka? Maybe somewhere in the U.S. someone would not follow orders and set some other price, but not here, not here. For as long as there are parades like this, there will always be enough vodka, because people work like robots and are afraid of landing in prison cells. Where does that fit in *Economics*? Or in *Kapital*? The state is more than just money . . . The state is energy. A ruler can opt for low energy—human rights, democracy—and money will have consistent value, and the laws by which inflation occurs will be consistent. Or it can concoct a dictatorship. Then both money and inflation will operate differently. Of course, there are African dictatorships where a dollar is worth three billion tugriks, but that's out of inanity. No, not so, out of an inability to control outlays of energy. Why did the Soviet Union fall apart, after all? There were parades, everybody shouted in chorus, rockets were produced. Everything was good. There were enough sausages and black-and-white TVs for everyone. Then suddenly against this background—kaboom!—human rights were brought up, dissidents were allowed to return, and Stalinist repression was condemned. But repression was precisely what propped it all up! The spirits floating above the tanks busted their brains. They gave up and flew away. Where? Here! Here is where they flew to! The Evil Empire fell apart, and democracy and parades like this are mutually exclusive. These very tanks . . . through a citadel of democracy, with land mines . . . ? But in this country we have precisely the monolithic stability of tanks: the MGB, dissidents, the whole Soviet ball of wax. In this regard, those who have disappeared are as important as zero-percent interest rates or investments in innovative technologies. Spirits need victims, human sacrifices—there you have it. Those Soviet military marches are also important: they invoke the spirits. Perhaps these marches are much older than we think: listen to the primitive beats, as if a shaman were striking a drum: no rhythm, just boom, boom . . ."

You weren't listening: I had launched in on politics again. First, you rubbed your head back and forth against my chest, resting your miniature profile more comfortably on your bear's belly. Then, you turned your face toward the rituals near the stela, and I could see only the back of your head, the obstreperous nape of a naughty girl. There was no way for me to determine how you felt about what you heard. We keep running up against politics. I shouldn't talk about it, just not talk about it. But watching as your head rose and fell with my breathing, as it turned slightly each time, turned as if to indicate a point out there in front of us, a point on which your gaze was firmly fixed, I felt something, that something . . .

"Something wrong?"

"Look," you said quietly, intimately, without the intonations of a public speaker with which I had waxed on about energy and spirits. "See that guy in the Hawaiian shirt?"

I saw a large man sitting half-turned toward us about sixty feet down the slope, trying to feel us out with the back of his head and all of his ears, to turn around, and occasionally he would turn around, casting a brief glance at us. His short fair hair barely covered the pink flesh of his head. His shirt was impossible, as if he were attempting to cover up his mission, as if . . . Alongside him lay a newspaper rolled into a tube. Who in the world needed a newspaper at this dress rehearsal?

"Yes," I said, not changing my pose. "I see him. Oh, I see him!"

"You wouldn't happen to be a secret conspirator? An underground terrorist? Have flatfoots ever followed you before?"

"No. Never!"

"Well, congratulations! They are now. I noticed that little boar back in the park. It's not often you see a man talking to his newspaper. What did you do? Fess up."

"Listen, there's no reason they should be trailing me."

"Right."

"It doesn't occur to you that he might be following you?"

"It's easy enough to check. But let's not. He . . ." You suddenly raised your head and turned toward me, but I couldn't decipher the expression in your eyes—whether they burned with excitement or fury. You seemed to be pleased that we were being followed. "He, he promised me" (you emphasized the word "promised") "that no one would ever follow me. I trust him on this. If we were to go in separate directions now, that bloodhound would traipse after you, but . . . But we're not going to run off our separate ways just because of some go-for major. You ready?"

"For what?"

"Ready?"

"Ready, I guess."

"On the count of three we jump up and run. Follow me. Don't lag behind. You're in charge of the rear. You look behind to see if he's taken off after us. One, two . . ."

Not waiting for "three," you jumped up, softly. (I marveled particularly at your ability to move quickly but smoothly, like a cat—you're a member of the cat family, for certain.) While I was still jerking and yanking myself up, you had torn off about ten yards ahead. I had to run till my tendons cracked to catch up with you. You ran off somewhere into the courtyards of identical brick high-rise apartment buildings, the same ones, legend had it, that Muraviov projected his French movies on. Catching up with you, I looked back and saw that the albino had stood up and was following us with a quick step, walking and talking with his rolled-up newspaper. He couldn't possibly catch up with us given his pace. Then—a cracking sound came from my elbow, my ribs, and—oh, how it hurt!—I hit my head against the sidewalk: I had tripped on the curb while running and looking backward. Everything went black. I couldn't see anything. Something warm was trickling down the side of my head: had they shot me? You were pulling me up, propping me on your shoulder, and the two of us, like a wounded four-legged beast, hobbled forward. Slowly, as in a movie theater when they turn the lights on, my sight returned. I could already run on my own, were it not for the sharp pain in my side. In the meantime that red-haired, buzz-cut asshole had picked up incredible speed, given his two-hundred-and-twenty-five-pound weight. He was less than a hundred yards behind us. Though he resembled a fat clodhopper, a caricature of an American in Hawaii for his annual vacation, the shirt must conceal solid muscle. He was making tracks behind us, like a tank. It even seemed as if the earth shook beneath him, and—to be honest, no beating round the bush—the bison could kill me with his bare hands, break my neck with a single turn. What did he want from us? Perhaps we ought to stop, stop, stop . . . as I had just now . . . Stop and turn toward him and, bending to catch my breath faster, approach him and ask what he wants. But you had already come back for me. You, your face no longer burning with excitement, no longer furious, but scared, and your shout, plain and in a single breath: "Shiiiiiiit!"

A short rap on the shoulder, and I understood, understood immediately, that we had to keep running. Now he was only about fifty yards behind us. I saw what that rap on the shoulder had meant: you were telling me that something bulged prominently under that shirt, from his shoulder down, covered over by that too loose-fitting shirt. Now, when that tank was at full speed, the shirt stuck to his body and, yes, there was a holster, and devil knows what he was trying to do with the pistol inside it, and your "Shiiiiiiit!" meant we had to run, that we didn't know his intentions and, therefore—full steam ahead. Judging by the intonation of that "Shiiiiiiit!" there wasn't far to go, not far to go to whatever, some haven. Once again, on legs turned to mush, on stiff stilts that refused to bend, as fast as I could behind you . . . But something was tipping me over, my legs were already exhausted, my entire face in saliva—a long time had passed since I'd last run—and you were already far ahead. I knew you wouldn't abandon me, but still, you were so far ahead! With the last strength I had I tore off, already (I'll admit honestly) having given up, already ready—all right, devil take 'em—to take the bullet, to engage in what was certain to be a fatal fight for me. I was slowing my pace, when in the depths of the courtyard I heard the loud screech of an opening door: there was the car; you were already turning the key in the ignition, pumping, hysterically pumping the still dead gas pedal to the floor, and the SUV—jet-black and even more enormous than that snow-white Lexus RX—lunged forward, and with the wallop of a tank the open door on the passenger side rammed a squealy car in the lot, smashed it from trunk to hood, and then slammed shut, almost lopping off my hand in the process.

We picked up speed (you drove extremely recklessly, and very fast), sideswiped a couple of trash containers, raked over a motorcycle with its ass sticking out onto the street, dragged it, then dumped it against another car in the courtyard, while antitheft alarms screeched everywhere, and the speedometer read fifty as we drove through the narrow, car-lined courtyard, when something jerked us up—you had hit the curb with your wheel—then dropped us back down with a slight swerve, and the courtyard, long as a corridor in a morgue, ended at an intersection where—clear and unambiguous—a stoplight burned in our direction and, about half a block away, stood a traffic cop in a salad-green vest, one of the multitude who always secured the parade. You ran the red light right into the path of not one, but a whole stream, of cars, pressed something under the steering wheel, and the SUV belted out the sound of a siren. The traffic cop could only bust his buttons at such impudence—you were flying straight at him so even he had to retreat to the sidewalk. Up went his hand with the baton: he was flagging us down, and when you didn't stop, he would jump in his car and take off after us flashing his red lights, and if we still didn't stop (and we weren't going to stop!) he would shoot his service gun at our tires, which, considering our speed, would stop us dead in our tracks, causing the car to roll on its side, and . . . What the hell was he doing?

His hand continued creeping upward and had already reached his chest, then his shoulder, where the baton slipped out of his hand and swung on its lanyard from his elbow, while his hand continued its climb upward, and—no way!—he touched the edge of his visor in a salute. We'd just run a red light, and he was saluting you, us! You drove up the center of the street, one hundred miles an hour inside the city limits, brazenly flashing your brights at law-abiding little cars creeping down their kiddy-lanes, plowing them off to the sides where they clung to the curbs on both sides, yielding the road to that roaring black monster with the tinted windows, and we, we, were in that car. Victors' Avenue ended, and barely reducing your speed, you pulled out onto the ring road, then onto the

Grodna highway. We were leaving town? We had decided to dash across the border? The European Union was eighty miles away, I had my passport with me, and the terror of our initial drive had passed. Needing to ask something ironic, I managed:

"Don't tell me: we're escaping by way of the ice in the Bay of Finland to Germany? And when we come back, we'll lead a revolution?"

You, though, were in no mood to joke. Helplessly weaving across lanes, shuddering whenever the highway took another bend, you were riveted to the road and said hoarsely:

"We're going to Tarasova. I have a house there. No one is following us."

To verify this, one need only look in the rear mirror: not a single car in the sparse stream of traffic on the Grodna highway even attempted our mad speed. With a casual flick you touched a button, and the speakers screeched over-the-top, bestial sounds from somewhere underfoot, radiating such vibrations through the car's iron surface that even if you plugged your ears you could hear it with your diaphragm. The giant subwoofers heaved, and the unreal, otherworldly tune—something like explosives dragged across a grater or the roar of thunder—was deafening. The Chemical Brothers. The best music ever for all-stops-out nighttime driving. We sailed down the left lane: not a single creature in the world could catch us, and the voice that seemed to be coming from inside me, and from inside you, sang—no, shouted, shouted at the top of its lungs: *I needed to believe!* As long as the melody pumped out its sounds, as long as The Chemicals heaved through the subwoofers of that terrifying car, nothing could terrify us, and we would never die. *I needed to believe!* Louder and louder, gas pedal on the floor, not even the roar of the enormous five-liter engine could be heard. Up ahead were just two dots of light, the lights of oncoming cars, and then the quick flash of the rear lights of ordinary mortals, while we, two gods, sang to this powerful, exciting, bellowing roar, as if riding on a heavenly chariot, *I needed to believe!*

Zeus's car, Zeus's music, lightning in my hands, oncoming headlights reflected in your eyes, and we danced, bouncing up and down on the seats: we had just escaped pursuit, mortal danger—come on, be honest, they almost shot us (who knows who or for what reason)—and that red-headed dick-bison turned out to be a frighteningly fast runner! But now we were tearing through the night, the (turbine-driven, I'd bet) engine at 4500 rpm and one and a half tons of metal slashing through the night like a bullet. We feared no one, and no one would dare to catch us as long as this melody played, and, if it suddenly came for us to die right at this moment, it wouldn't be terrible at all, for the main thing was *I needed to believe! I needed to believe!* continued to roar. I couldn't decide: was the night like this because The Chemicals were roaring, or were The Chemicals putting out like that because of the night, the road, and the speed? Either way, the song was like a war whoop, like the incantation of a berserker; the song was also us, our confidence that no one could do anything to us. Our license plates ended in *KE,* cops saluted us, and if suddenly a helicopter with snipers should appear above, we would simply crank up the volume, and all those scum would come crashing down from the skies at the beck of our will. *I needed to believe!* I, too, wanted to believe, to believe in you, to believe in myself, and I did believe! In everything, for real! I had no idea who you were or what you were, but I couldn't take my eyes off your shoulder as it moved rhythmically to the beat in the twilight of our roaring tiger. They were chasing us because of you, but we had escaped their pursuit and were sailing off to somewhere in Tarasova, and Tarasova, as everyone knows, is the local equivalent of Moscow's Rubliov highway area, even more elite than the Rubliov area, because the people who live along the Rubliov highway are oligarchs but not the ones who milk them—the ones who milk them have their dachas in unremarkable places the names of which no one knows; Tarasova is where those who do the milking live, those for whom all is allowed, those who have special numbered license plates: members of the Party and of the administration. Any businessman with a four-story palace like theirs would instantly be dispossessed into a dissident.

I hadn't been here for a long time: the tiny village now looked more like Switzerland, with the one difference that in a structure built for five to seven Swiss families lived one modest deputy chief of the MGB administration. All the buildings were strictly set out by rank: you could tell who was higher-ranked and who was subordinate: the roofs were all more or less flat, allowing for advancement in rank, and freshly added floors indicated recent promotions up the service ladder. The light in the windows was so cozy, so benign, that I would never have thought . . . But I thought now, for sure, about who each of these palaces belonged to, which of them you lived in, and in what capacity.

But Tarasova was behind us. I turned toward you inquisitively, but you just motioned with your cheek for me to be patient, and I imagined how you would drive another half-mile or so, make a U-turn, then pick up speed and ram the gates of that house, the last one in the village, smashing them to pieces and parking on the front lawn. I'm sorry, but that would have coincided entirely with your driving style. Instead, we continued driving deeper and deeper into the forest. A solid fence constructed of sixteen-foot concrete blocks appeared on the right, most likely it was some gigantic military base, because we had been driving (at your clip) about ten minutes, and only now had I noticed spotlights on the fence every thirty feet or so, a camera under each spotlight, and alongside each camera near the bottom a fish-eye mirror that increased the observation angle and excluded blind spots. Several rows of barbed wire topped the fence. More security than at a prison. What kind of place was this? Up ahead several lonely streetlamps illuminated NO ENTRY signs to the right and to the left on the shoulder of the road, but you, of course, stepped on the gas (revocation of license for two and a half years and a fine of nine hundred dollars, by the way). The road was in good condition—a wide road with an ideal surface and markings (strange for such an out-of-the-way place)—that culminated in a tidy little dead end, where you turned and drove right up to the gates, each of which, intensifying the similarity to a military base, bore huge red stars. But no signs, no signs.

You pressed something tucked in your jeans, and the gates began to open, revealing virgin forest and a narrow, gravel-covered little road through the trees. We moved forward, and five minutes hadn't passed when our headlights lit up a good copy of the tsar's palace in Pavlovsk outside Saint Petersburg, with its touching weathervane on top. The palace was dark—not a soul around. As I slowly recovered from the shock of what I had seen, you slammed your car door and jumped from the side panel—you really did have to jump. My door wouldn't open: I struggled with it unsuccessfully, moving the chrome handle this way and that, thinking that you had locked me inside the car for a reason, like a disobedient child, like a hostage, but then I remembered how the door had hit the car in the courtyard when we were taking off and realized that it must be jammed. It was silly to expect you to come back and assist your bear—you were already busy picking at the door to the palace, kissing it (no, just putting your eye up to the scanner). I scrambled over the platform around the gearbox (which looked like a pool of mercury), climbed out on the driver's side, and examined the passenger door as you looked on disapprovingly: there were a few shallow dents and a slight jam. The Zhiguli had been totaled!

The lights had already switched on in the house, illustrating the indifference in the phrase "the insurance will cover it." The entire scene—a man sighing over a dented Porsche Cayenne, and a woman walking to the house without even glancing at the car—what a great plot for an insurance company commercial, right, Dan?

Only part of the entrance hall was illuminated—the part needed to make your way along the tiny corridor, noting for yourself something elusively Chekhovian in all these interiors: this little room, for example, with its precious striped armchairs and lacking only a lace doily with a dish of jam next to it, a carafe of liqueur (yes, you know, from cranberries, yes). You impatiently clanked some glasses up ahead to remind me that this was no excursion. The kitchen, like the one on Karl Marx Street, was set behind a blank door and done in a style strikingly different from the style of the interior as a whole. Yes, I reasoned, a space for the hired help: where the cook worked, where she brewed her master his coffee, made him something to eat. Now all the pieces fell together: you weren't anyone's daughter, you were just a housekeeper for some top-ranked— the size of the residence and its location dampened any desire to think about how top-ranked—officer of the MGB, a member of *his* inner circle. That explained the cars with the special license plates, which you treated, of course, far too casually; that explained why you wanted to forget me. With that scribbling of mine, no one was going to pat you on the head for getting involved with the likes of such a—what would you call us?— partner!

"I like it better here: it's more human." You sat on a regular wooden chair, moved a glass of blood in my direction, and took a sip from yours. No, not blood. Tomato juice. With vodka.

"As you can imagine, I have a lot of questions."

"Ask." You looked tired. We needed to embrace. And to continue the conversation close up, the way we were used to, in half-whispers, I even leaned toward you, then caught myself. No. Not that way. First we needed to talk. We needed to make sense of all this.

"For example. The car. Last time you were driving a Lexus RX. This time a Porsche Cayenne. You . . ."

I didn't know what I was trying to ask. The situation offered such a broad selection of questions that I didn't know what to ask about.

"Do you crash them all?" I turned them into a joke, not very successfully, nervously, hee-hawing like an animal.

"I forgot that I had been in the Lexus. The Lexus is in the special garage in Uruchcha. It's all right. Is that all you wanted to ask? What happened to the car?"

I made an idiotic face to say that I needed help.

"All right. Let's be straight."

"Let's."

"Those really aren't your cars, right?"

"The cars are mine. That's two of them. There are five more. All different. Including two sports cars, but I like the SUVs. I feel more secure in them. No jerk is going to cut me off."

You become crude when you speak about cars, but I was thinking about something else. To tell the truth, I didn't believe you, and I dared a smirk when you said that they were all yours, and the smirk was most impolite, probably. You dug around in your handbag and tossed on the table a wallet somewhat larger than usual and filled with car papers, and I permitted myself to thumb through all the vehicle registration cards: a BMW Z4, a Porsche Cayenne, a Land Rover—all with license plates ending in *KE,* and all with "Elisaveta Supranovich" on the owner line. One helluva cook!

"This house and the apartment are yours as well?"

"Anatoly." You were very serious, while the vodka, because I was unaccustomed to it, had gone straight to my head. "Anatoly, I want you to understand once and for all and never to ask such questions again. I am the owner of this house, of three apartments in the capital, of six houses on the ring road, and of three in other regions. I also have real estate outside the country: in Italy, Germany, France, and even in Latin America. My total worth is—I'm not entirely sure—more than a billion dollars. Can we put the topic of real estate to rest now?"

Stunned, I shook my head and tried to control my lips. I understood that if those two turncoats parted into a smile, you would dump the deeds for the residences in front of me, and that asking any more questions would be thoroughly rude: we had been talking about license plates, not even cars, about . . . how the devil, how in the world, . . . I still didn't understand a thing!

"Where did you get all this?"

You answered. There turned out to be much more vodka in the juice than I had thought. The kitchen began to spin, accelerating with each sentence you spoke.

"All these things are presents from Nikolai Mikhailovich Muraviov. Head of the MGB. The head of state. On paper he owns nothing in this country; the only thing that's registered to him is the two-room apartment in Malinovka where he used to live before . . . Well, you know. All these houses and cars are his. But they're registered to me. I am their legal owner on paper, although I don't pay for the gas, or for the electricity. All that gets taken care of somehow. I also have a Trustbank credit card with unlimited credit and underwritten by the strategic gold reserves, but it's entirely useless because in the stores that carry the things I like they already know me and give me whatever I want without charge."

You looked at me intently, and when I looked in your eyes like that, deeply and more deeply, anchoring myself to them, the room didn't spin as much, and I was still capable of understanding.

"So, Anatoly. That's the story."

Because the question had already been asked by my eyes, by an unraveling me . . .

"Nikolai Mikhailovich gave me all this as a gift. Because. Because he and I . . . He and I are close in a certain way. You understand?"

Yes, I understood all right, understood who you were and what you were, understood that I had drunk juice with vodka bought with his money, understood that he . . . That you . . . I understood why you had such a large, heavy ring of keys that took up half your purse . . . And, of course, I understood that with the aid of the unfortunate, comical Nurmambekovs Grizzly had tried to warn me not at all about the pathetic short story I had been writing and destroyed, the short story that no one knew anything about. I understood that I had become involved with a person, with whom . . . For whom . . . I understood why you had asked me to forget you and had tried yourself to forget but couldn't, and had arranged for us to meet, although what needed to be done was precisely to forget, that forgetting would be better for you and for me. Because he was not the kind of person who . . . I understood the meaning of your words about his promise that no one would ever follow you: they were following me. We had met, and now we were probably being watched through hidden cameras: were there any of them here? Did he ever come here? Of course, he did! And sat with her here in this tiny kitchen for the servants, and guzzled vodka, and perhaps right now I was sitting in his seat. I shouldn't stay here any longer, not a second longer, not a second longer.

It wasn't ours, wasn't ours. It was cursed and black: here the tomato juice had such an ominous look to it that I wouldn't, wouldn't, pour any more of it into my body. We had to get away from here, far, far away!

We rented a little apartment, a tiny one like the one we had dreamed about, in a neighborhood near one of the train stations. It was in a high-rise building resembling a tower and surrounded on all sides by trees and smaller houses, like a commander who had collected his squad around him—not for battle, but for a bivouac. The sidewalks that wound around the five-story buildings were lined by lawns with alstroemeria, strelitzia, anemone, orchids, and camellias—that's what we called them, not being able to differentiate these flowering, big-eyed, bumpy, and at times indecently opened buds and blossoms. Occasionally I managed unnoticed to twist off one of their heads and adorned your hair with it. No sooner had we entered the stairwell than you called me Bear and said that I knew only how to trample beauty. We rode up in the elevator, when it worked, and I looked at you and stroked your hands or, unable to contain ourselves, like two butterflies trying not to dust the other with pollen, we embraced and just stood there, needing nothing else, as your body breathed under my fingers. The door had opened long ago, and someone was coughing—a bit bewildered, but not angry—outside the elevator door.

We entered our apartment solemnly, we walked through it as if to an altar, with bated breath: it was our first house, our first shelter, our first place, and the entrance hall was decorated with antlers, and directly opposite was a little shelf with a telephone whose line had been cut. The owner thought that if she cut the line, we wouldn't be able to skip out after having spent a couple of days on the phone with Paraguay or Colombia or Venezuela. But we knew: the phone's lost tail signified that this little apartment was our world, and we needed no one else and no calls. The corridor leading to the kitchen culminated in a phantasmal dead end, a walk-through wall, a curtain of reeds on which in Mao's days something elusive and Chinese had been painted, but over time the paint had worn off. (You would play by wrapping yourself in these scatterable curtains that hardly covered your nakedness, pretending to be a bride.) The ceiling lights, the clumsy dripping faucet, the ceramic boot full of burned matches, the range hood with its broken clock, the kitchen cupboards with bay leaves, coriander, and black pepper ready at any moment to help us boil up *pelmeni* meat dumplings, the ZIL refrigerator that looked like part of the inside of a Pobeda automobile, with a door handle that looked as if it came straight out of a car, a ticking clock, and the windows with a window leaf that—considering its age—one was tempted to call a transom: all of it as sweetly antediluvian as the REGIONAL FOOD STORE sign on the lopsided grocery store at the entrance to our courtyard.

Our tower, like the thickets of alstroemeria around it, was a paradise, and we had nothing against the Regional Food Store adjoined to our heavenly gates. We walked through the courtyard to the squawking of the train station's loudspeakers; here, under the anemones, we realized that once again we had accidentally filched a red shopping basket from the food store instead of leaving it at the exit, and at the moment, the basket contained mostly wrappers from chocolate bars you had gobbled down with phenomenal speed. We left the basket at our door to be able to carry it off once again and return it to the stack of other baskets nested one inside the other alongside the grocery section called *bakaleia*—a forgotten Turkic word whose meaning was hardly made any clearer by such familiar items as buckwheat, rice, and millet. We would sit opposite each other, and I would put on the tea, as if we had any use for it our first days there, and we simply breathed the same air, studying each other's face with our palms, wrists, cheeks, while down below, under us, the trees rustled with the sound of breaking surf, and we floated above them in our tower. Autumn was approaching, and for some reason that frightened us both.

The lines on our palms began to move. I could make out myself in your life line, and you in mine, and often, often, very often I would hold you by the hand and not let go, because I believed that way my features would leave their imprint on your fate, while the lines on your hand would be reflected on my palm, and our fates and our lives would be so intertwined that we would become mutual reflections, with a single mold for both our destinies. In the meantime, the kettle boiled dry and blackened, charred by the heat, and the boys in the courtyard played soccer, and the average temperature in August was seventy-one degrees.

Appendix 2

Muraviov Nikolai Mikhailovich (material from a free Internet encyclopedia)—Minister of State Security, Supreme Commander in Chief, guarantor of the constitution and laws.

Born in Moscow to a military family. His father was the supply officer for Soviet troops quartered in Dresden (GDR). In the GDR Muraviov attended a school for the children of the supreme command and studied German and French. After his family's return to the U.S.S.R., he was placed in a special music school, where he studied for five years. According to his teachers, he made particular progress in piano and had great potential to become a concert pianist, which he chose not to pursue.

Following his term of service in the army he graduated from the Military Commanders' Training School, later serving at the rank of lieutenant in Afghanistan, where he received a contusion and a light wound. After the dissolution of the U.S.S.R., he left military service and actively participated in political life, supporting the so-called power clan, which accomplished the establishment of statehood through an event that propaganda calls "restoring order" and the opposition a "military coup." While serving in the secretariat of the Security Council, he successfully played the rivalry between the KGB and the Ministry of Internal Affairs (MVD), systematically weakening key representatives of both conflicting organizations. Finally, after officially criticizing the ineffectiveness of the old organizations, he achieved unification of the two in a single entity, into which he integrated border troops, the Security Council, and military espionage. He called the new organization the Ministry of State Security (MGB). Those who dared to joke about this, the writer Nevinsky in particular, interpreted the acronym as "Muraviov's State Security."

He averted a so-called velvet minirevolution. Its three key figures—the self-proclaimed head of parliament Zygmunt Sierakowski, the self-proclaimed prime minister Walery Wróblewski, and presidential candidate Jarosław Dąbrowski—disappeared one November night during a drinking party at Sierakowski's state summer residence. According to official sources, they "abducted" themselves so as to cast a shadow on Muraviov, regroup their forces, and organize a new "revolution." According to other sources, all three were assassinated by one of the special sections of the MGB.

Muraviov asserts that at the moment of their disappearance he was practicing Chopin piano nocturnes. At the press conference in response to a journalist who asked where Muraviov had been on the night of the disappearance, he offered to play Chopin nocturnes for him personally, after which the journalist hastily left the country. He currently resides in Norway.

During the presentation of the icon of Archangel Michael, the patriarchal exarch publicly called Muraviov "an executioner and a cannibal," after which he was removed from his post by the Church and has not been seen since. According to official sources he became a hermit in the monastery in the village of Zhirovichi.

Muraviov is currently married. His son attends school in London.

PART TWO

THEY

Protocol: Audio Documentation
Surveillance site: Private residence, 16 Serafimovich Street, Apt. 7

2 September
Senior Operations Officer E. P. Tsupik

Surveillance objects Gogol and Fox appeared at 1836 and opened the apartment with a key. At 1845 they proceeded to the bedroom (Microphone 1), from which sounds of a bestial, passionate nature emerged. At 1900 a conversation began.

[*Microphone 1*]

GOGOL: We're breathing in cadence.

FOX: Left, left!

GOGOL: You inhale, and I'll exhale. That's it. Right.

FOX: It's so quiet. Was it always so quiet here? So intimately quiet? We can probably be heard.

GOGOL: Who would want to listen to us? Let's turn on the light.

FOX: No, no, don't. When the light's on, I feel as if I'm being watched, but when it's dark, it's just you and I.

GOGOL: Your nose is hot.

FOX: Your lips are dry.

GOGOL: Dry lips. Like tree bark?

FOX: More like sand at the surf line where a wave crashes, then recedes ever so lazily, leaving the sand to whiten, sun-dry, as the wave comes rolling, rolling back, and the sand . . .

[*The surveillance objects produce the sound of a loud puckered kiss.*]

GOGOL: I'm standing in the middle of a damp meadow touched by dew. Overhead is a primordial sky—ultraviolet, with whitish feathers. This is the beginning of the world, of you and me, just molded from clay, first me, then you. Dew is everywhere, like droplets of sky, wetting our feet with a light, blessed moistness. Close your eyes, and I'll show you this meadow.

Fox: Take me there. I see a rainbow.

GOGOL: It just rained. The moisture isn't dew, but drops of rain. The air makes breathing pure delight. If you're ever sad, let's meet in this meadow. In this place, at the end of the rainbow.

Fox: At the end of the rainbow. I'll remember that.

[*The text transcribed below appears to describe sensations of a delusional nature that accompanied Gogol's so-called orgasm.*]

GOGOL: As we chased the rainbow, I saw a certain presence in the distance. An alluring beauty, at first just a hint, like a cloud over the distant horizon in an unfamiliar place, you know, like when you can't tell where the sky ends and the land begins, what is snowy peak and what weather front, but as you draw nearer and nearer, you begin to make out a pillow of the cloud's illuminated top half from its darkish blue-black underbelly that has already spewed forth its rain, and the rainbow, our rainbow, in the place where beams of sunlight fall on slanted lines of rain. I flew toward it. I perceived its melody of multicolored notes. Each blossom of color burst inside me, moving me forward. But I couldn't keep up. I couldn't keep up with those blossoming bursts of color, and their stems broke and collapsed. It grew warm, I became thirsty, and I thought my goal was to run as far as the rainbow to see its arch above me. I reached for the rainbow, but it hung in one place as if nailed to the sky, and my path was strewn with the fallen petals of flowers scorched by the heat. Then suddenly I realized that the point wasn't to catch it, but to catch its meaning, and when what happened to us happened I had the feeling that I had understood what it was like to be a rainbow. All the colors and all the flowers, all light and all heavenly bodies, streamed through me.

Fox: Want me to stream you a heavenly body, do you?

GOGOL: How aggressively unromantic you are. Oops. Looks like we've got a problem!

Fox: What?

GOGOL: Uh, you see, to put it in your aggressively unromantic terms: at a certain moment our protected sex suddenly became unprotected. It turns out. See? I didn't even feel anything.

Fox: Me neither.

GOGOL: There are two ways out of the situation. At the pharmacy . . .

FOX: No.

GOGOL: It's harmless.

FOX: No.

GOGOL: Then we'll just have to hope that you weren't ovulating . . . Sh-i-i-i-t! That hurt! I fell on my ass.

FOX: In decent homes, Bear, people get thrown out of bed for using the word "ovulation." This is a decent home.

GOGOL: I, by the way, fell on my ass!

[*Pause*]

I'm going to bite you.

FOX: Just try!

GOGOL: Damn, what are you yanking around for?

FOX: The bedcover's ripped.

GOGOL: You ripped it when you pulled it!

FOX: Why are you always ripping things?

GOGOL: Back there in the park you got caught on the nail by yourself!

FOX: All right. Next time we meet we'll bring a needle and thread and do some darning.

GOGOL: I don't know how.

FOX: You'll learn how. You learned how to talk, didn't you, clumsy hulk of a bear!

GOGOL: All right, all right!

[*Pause*]

Listen. You have fifty words. Describe this morning. Imagine that you're writing a short story, and you need to describe the heroine's morning. So that it's specific enough, but not overloaded with details. As if in passing. First her morning, then she meets her lover, then the two of them are discovered and murdered.

FOX: Fool.

GOGOL: No, romantic!

FOX: That kind of romanticism became obsolete roughly during the reign of Friedrich Wilhelm I.

GOGOL: Don't try to squirm out of it.

FOX: Is fifty words a lot?

GOGOL: A short paragraph. Five sentences.

Fox: She woke and brushed her teeth.

Gogol: I'm getting dressed and going to live with Friedrich Wilhelm. At least he was a romantic.

Fox: The bright light in her eyes wakened her . . .

Gogol: How about something a bit more sincere? Not necessarily cohesive. But real? Huh? Or are you really Ivan Melezh?

Fox: Who?

Gogol: Well, Vasily Shukshin.

Fox: Leave Shukshin alone. You've got a long way to go before you're Shukshin. All right. Such a good dream, so much light, a Carrollesque garden . . . I'm walking, and giggling, then comes a breath of reality, an awakening, and a slight aftertaste of sorrow in my mouth. I'm sad, with the sadness that comes when you're brushing your teeth and searching in your eyes reflected in the mirror for the echoes of your laughter, and not finding it, look long and hard at a glass of juice . . .

Gogol: That's already too many words. Not just awakening, but the whole morning, please.

[*Pause*]

One more strike, Elisaveta, and I will begin to hit back. I'm going to have a black-and-blue mark!

Fox: OK. Curtains rustled by the wind make it possible for the wind to exist. A chill breathes through them—the first, still premature, whisper of autumn. The shimmer of the sun on the side of the coffeepot, and my conversations with a glass of juice in which you're hidden, deep inside. A light rustle across the wood floor . . . Oh, right, those are my feet. Hello, morning! Do I pass?

Gogol: Pass. Just barely.

Fox: Fool.

Gogol: Listen.

Fox: What?

Gogol: You didn't see the candlelighter, did you? The one shaped like a torch.

Fox: No, not really. Not since we moved in here.

Gogol: I took a long time picking it out. They had another one shaped like a little devil, but I decided that we didn't need any devils.

Fox: What is it? What are you thinking about?

Gogol: Nothing.

Fox: Well?

GOGOL: Just about the lighter.

Fox: Forget about it.

GOGOL: Sometimes things disappear at home, too. Not very important things, but like . . . Gadgets. A postcard from somebody. Or a shoehorn. It's a weird kind of awareness. An awareness of some sort of presence. As if someone were constantly with you, living in your home. Or just observing your life. You eat, and sleep, and read books, and don't think anything of it, except the chair sometimes turns up where it shouldn't be. Or the dirty fork in the sink is not in the same position as where you left it. Or the shoehorn has disappeared. Or the candlelighter.

Fox: You probably just threw it out. No one's living with us. No one's stalking you. I can tell you for a fact that living with you is impossible. You rip bedcovers and use foul language. I'm the only one, my burly bear, able to put up with you.

GOGOL: You're right on that count.

Fox: Are you asleep?

GOGOL: Huh?

Fox: I'm going, my dear. See you soon.

MINISTRY OF STATE SECURITY

Protocol: Audio Documentation
Surveillance site: Private residence, 16 Serafimovich Street, Apt. 7

9 September
Senior Operations Officer L. L. Skrygan

Surveillance objects Gogol and Fox met at 1900: Gogol had arrived at the apartment at approximately 1630 and opened the door with his key; surveillance object Fox appeared at 1900.

Until 2107 they gave themselves over to carnal pleasures (Microphone 1), then had a conversation that made little sense as they discussed their recent intercourse. At 2130 they initiated an encoded conversation, the contents of which may be of interest to Section Five's External Control and Surveillance Command. Potentially, the material of this conversation may facilitate reconnaissance of external contacts.

Fox: So give me a meeting time, my love.

GOGOL: Let's meet in the kitchen in ten minutes. Next to the range vent. Better make that in twenty minutes. Let's lie around for a bit more.

FOX: No, seriously. Sometime in the future a situation might arise when we wouldn't be able to communicate openly.

GOGOL: Then we'll openly not communicate.

FOX: Well, just assume that we're both being bugged. And we have only enough time for one call on the phone. That someone's chasing us. And that we urgently need to agree on a place to meet that only the two of us would identify. Well, for example, instead of saying "in the kitchen," we say, "at the post-solar clock," understand?

GOGOL: You'll find a way, without advance arrangements. Like with the bear, when you thought up that "honey beast"!

FOX: But just in case.

GOGOL: OK. Let's meet where you and I navigated the Dardanelles. [*Section Five, External Control and Surveillance Command—Comment: location not identified*]

FOX: Right! Excellent! Let's meet where I was drinking the macchiato that first day we met. [*Section Five, External Control and Surveillance Command—Comment: possibly a reference to the Chess Café, 36 Marx Street*]

GOGOL: It seems to me that you have the disgusting habit of drinking macchiatos in one and the same place, so that won't work, they'll figure it out.

FOX: Let's meet where the tanks were firing. [*Section Five, External Control and Surveillance Division—Comment: location not identified*]

GOGOL: That's much better, although they can still figure it out.

FOX: The longer we're together, the more secret places we'll have that only we'll know about. We'll be able to set up rendezvous at places the flatfoots will never find, no matter how hard they scratch their heads.

At 2200 the surveillance objects relocated to the kitchen (Microphone 3), where they discussed plans to emigrate (the idea was Fox's), subsequently agreeing that emigration was not for them. Gogol spoke of an official who had been arrested—Zheludev? Debezhev? (inaudible)—without whom things "would get worse." They wanted to buy a vase for flowers (check: possible drop). They left at 2300, locked the door with a key, and did not reappear at the observed site.

As instructed, I am forwarding a complete transcript of the 16 September meeting between surveillance objects Gogol and Fox. The transcript is provided without time-keying. The surveillance objects appeared at the apartment at 1730 and opened the door with a key. In total the meeting at the surveillance site, a private residence at 16 Serafimovich, Apt. 7, lasted 45 minutes, the larger part of which time the surveillance objects engaged in intercourse of the corporeal variety. Consequently, a significant portion of their remarks is not reproducible, consisting largely of interjections, grunts, and groans that are both undecodable and untranscribable. Over the course of their rendezvous at the surveillance site there occurred no transfer of information comprised of state secrets or related to the overall social and political situation.

MINISTRY OF STATE SECURITY

SECTION FIVE

AUDIO-DOCUMENTATION COMMAND

COLONEL SOKOLOV, HEAD

[Entrance Hall (Microphone 2)]

Fox: You didn't lock the door.
Gogol: Right, right . . .
Fox: Two key turns.
Gogol: What's with you today?
Fox: I've got that nasty feeling again that I'm being tailed.
Gogol: You saw someone?
Fox: I felt someone. Not today, all right, love?

[Bedroom (Microphone 1)]

Gogol: Certainly not today! Lift, please, right here.
Fox: I'm serious.
Gogol: I'm just as serious! We're not going to, no way! Here, closer. Uh-huh, let me pull off . . .

Fox: Stop. What are you doing? O-oh.

[*For the next nearly 5 minutes rubbing and slapping sounds were audible, their origins difficult to establish.*]

Gogol: Now I'd really like to put you on your side and, that's right, from here.

[*Subject Fox groans.*]

Gogol: Let's not rush. No rushing. I'm going to touch you here.
Fox: Yes, harder right here.
Gogol: My God, you're as taut as a string.
Fox: Don't stop. Keep moving like that and don't stop. Don't st-ah-ah-ah-ah-ah-ah-ah-p.

[*Microphone 1 is silent for some time.*]

Gogol: Do you think it would be criminal for us to rest on our accomplishments?
Fox: Darling, just hug me . . . like that, hard . . . Press me to your chest. Let's just stay like this together for a while.
Gogol: I'll hug you and kiss you. Right here in this little indentation . . . You know, my nose fits inside here when we do that. A kiss to you for that. And what's this?
Fox: Maybe, I could . . . you . . . right here, at the same time?
Gogol: Going down . . . Here, in the foothills a herd of wild rams grazes, and grapes grow, and here . . .
Fox: O Lord!
Gogol: And here, on the plateau of our little tummy hides the tiny little lake of a navel.
Fox: Lower, lower! Your stubble! Oh, no, don't you dare. Lord, what are you doing down there?
Gogol: Could we just do this?
Fox: Like that, yes?
Gogol: Arch your back a bit. Right, right, like that. We'll do it like this . . .
Fox: Uh-huh, like that . . . Yes . . . Ouch, that hurts a bit. Not like that . . . Ah, oh . . . Don't stop . . . There, yes . . .

[*Transcriber's notation: loud, uncontrolled sounds indicate ensuing coitus climaxing in orgasm.*]

Fox: Did you duh-duh-duh-DUH-duh-DUH?

Gogol: Me? Uh-huh! And you? Did you?

Fox: Yes, right at the very end, but very deep and even now, when you do that . . . See? It makes me shiver.

Gogol: Yes! Yes!

[*Gogol emits loud, jubilant sounds to the melody of the "Marseillaise."*]

Gogol: "*Allons enfants de la Patrie, / Le jour de gloire est arrive.*"

Fox: There's an *é*: it's *arrivé,* you bear!

Gogol: Don't interrupt! "*Aux armes citoyens! Formez vos bataillons! / Marchons, marchons, / Qu'un sang impur . . . !*"

[*Fox sings under her breath, correcting his errors.*]

Gogol: It was like that, like "*Allons enfants de la Patrie.*"

Fox: Oh, I don't know how to describe things like that. I can breathe. It was like breathing again. After a long period of suffocation.

Gogol: Breathe, my sweet. I am your lungs. Let's breathe together.

[*Transcriber's notation: 12 minutes passed.*]

Gogol: A golden autumn. How do you know when autumn's on the way?

Fox: It starts to get cold.

Gogol: The leaves. The fallen leaves begin to rush along the paths. It begins in August, but by September there are even more leaves, along with that funereal smoke everywhere: the private sector raking its leaves into mounds and burning them. Golden autumn. A time when I wander and think about how the gold comes not from the leaves, but from the light. Have you ever noticed how golden the light is? Golden . . . Listen, perhaps the phrase is not the adjective "golden" plus noun, but the participle "gilded"—"gilded autumn." Autumn not only golden, but coated in gold to cover us over with its dome and protect us from winter. Instead, though, its gold "leaf" flakes apart, the leaves fall, cars drive over them, yard-keepers burn them, and soon there's nothing left but bare branches, and the first snow . . . What happened? What's wrong? You look petrified!

Fox: My sweet . . . my sweet . . . I'm worried. I don't know why, but I'm terrified. While we were . . . being intimate, I momentarily forgot, but now it's as if the beautiful melody of our being together is being drowned out by the sound of someone banging out Alla Pugacheva tunes on a piano on the floor just above. And this second, terrifying melody—still barely audible through the ceiling—is gradually growing louder, frightening away . . .

GOGOL: Calm down, my dear . . . We're together . . .

FOX: Sweetheart, would it be all right if I left now?

GOGOL: What's happening to us? Let me hold you a little tighter. It'll pass. Just lie there like that . . .

FOX: I'm terrified, terrified, and when you embrace me I become terrified for you too. I'm going. I'm not asking, I'm just leaving, OK!

[Entrance Hall (Microphone 2)]

GOGOL: It'll pass. Just remember our meadow with the rainbow.

Resolution of Minister of State Security, N. M. Muraviov:
"Documentation thorough. None additional required."

MINISTRY OF STATE SECURITY

Protocol: Audio Documentation
Surveillance site: Private residence, 16 Serafimovich Street, Apt. 7

23 September
Operations Officer Second Lieutenant P. D. Movseisiuk

The apartment was equipped for listening by 0900. The surveillance objects appeared at 1700. First they satisfied their erotic needs: object Fox climaxed twice, object Gogol once. During their intimate sexual encounter no conversations took place between them per se; for the most part they discussed sexual positions and the course of their erotic actions. On completion of their sexual procedures they relocated to Microphone 3, where they began discussing a certain third person.

[Microphone 3]

GOGOL: So, tell me, how did you meet him?

FOX: Why are you doing this?

GOGOL: Really, tell me. I don't know, after all, and will never find out otherwise.

FOX: I . . . No, I shouldn't!

GOGOL: Look: he's not a constant, I hope, but a transitional phase in your life. And in order to make him transitional, because for me he'll be a constant as long as I don't know how he came to be with you . . . That is, in order to make him transitional, you need to tell me. That way I'll know that he wasn't always around. Then I can believe that he won't always be around.

FOX: No.

GOGOL: Are you protecting your past with him?

FOX: I'm not going to tell you anything. That's the last word.

GOGOL: A confession. Let's think about it as a confession!

FOX: You don't confess to a holy father what concerns him personally.

GOGOL: Just the opposite! Holy fathers are obligated to hear such confessions. To forgive sins.

FOX: You're not a holy father. Holy fathers are forbidden to marry.

GOGOL: Not in the Russian Orthodox Church.

FOX: I'm a Catholic. Our holy fathers are forbidden to marry or fall in love.

GOGOL: So that they might love all people. You know that! Not one person, but all people!

FOX: So that they might love all people—you've got that right. Love everyone and hate no one. If you love one person, you hate those who hurt her.

GOGOL: Has he hurt you?

FOX: You hurt me. As you did just now, when you asked me about him. Don't.

GOGOL: Do you love him?

FOX: Don't.

GOGOL: I don't understand how you can love a cannibal. Does it turn you on? Do you want me to kill someone?

FOX: Calm down!

GOGOL: Right!

FOX: Here are my hands. They hold our meadow and our rainbow. Love, this is us.

GOGOL: Sorry, sorry. Listen, though, I really don't understand . . . You don't know who he is? Should I tell you about my meeting with Sierakowski's widow? A kind, gaunt little woman with tear-reddened eyes and hair that turned gray within a month? You want to hear about it?

FOX: I don't know who Sierakowski is.

GOGOL: He's the enemy disappeared. He was, then he disappeared. Curious, isn't it? Language doesn't have a part of speech to designate that kind of irretrievability. Language knows what to do when a person is murdered; it has a whole slew of nouns appropriate to that situation—corpse, widow, mourning. But what if the person simply disappeared? Here language can only shrug its shoulders. Language isn't prepared. In language letters don't just drop off the face of the earth. I called around to get her telephone number, because I felt that I had to see her, to support her, but I didn't know how to refer to her: as Sierakowski's widow? He hadn't been killed; he had disappeared! A linguistic conundrum. Just imagine: he was supposed to return one frosty morning, but didn't. Then didn't return in the afternoon. Or in the evening. When I met with her, six months had already passed, and it was clear to everyone what had happened, but she continued to wait for him and kept asking me during our conversation whether it was possible that he could still be alive. I understood that I was supposed to answer that it was, that perhaps, that certainly he would come back.

FOX: I don't want to hear about all that.

GOGOL: You didn't know, did you? That's not what attracted you to him?

FOX: My love, I'm asking you, please don't!

GOGOL: I'm sorry, but I can't not think about him or about the two of you. So, tell me, that bestial strength, that threat in him, those clenched teeth, that fist shaking at the TV cameras—do you like that? That crimson beret? The military posture?

FOX: Listen to me carefully. This is important, and it's all I am going to tell you about him. He never shows me his bestial side. He was able to . . . to enchant me, to put it lightly. He is a wonderful pianist. His French, the flowers, conversations about cinema. I've never seen him in his crimson beret or in his camouflage uniform. That's not him at all. Elegant ties, cuff links that he removes before he begins to play and places on the top of the piano, and a scintillating gentleness. He's calm and quiet. His voice is not at all like what you hear on television. Enough! Here's the point: what I loved in him was not him. When he waves from the grandstand, which is terrifying—brrrr!!! I think that in him I was looking for you. Everything that exists in him as a suggestion or as mixed up with the devil knows what else—you have in just the right quantities. Why didn't you show up earlier? You, the real one.

GOGOL: Of everything you said the main thing was that he "never shows" this side. Present tense, you used the present tense. He's real for you; he's in the present tense.

Fox: Stop that. You're in my present tense.

GOGOL: How much of a present tense will we have? A half-hour? Who'll be in the present tense after that? Who in the past tense? What are you planning to tell him about me? Never mind, I know: nothing! Because I don't exist. Not with you. I am a mirage. For you I am someone who's disappeared!

Fox: Stop it.

GOGOL: There's more. When you compare me with him, keep in mind one thing, please. I never killed anyone. Remember that. So the comparison . . .

Fox: You misunderstood me.

GOGOL: I was listening very carefully.

Fox: You were listening with your ears!

GOGOL: I was listening with everything I could listen with.

Fox: You were the one who brought this up.

GOGOL: Yes, yes, I know.

Fox: There was no need to, none at all. I don't interrogate you about who you were with before me; I don't go poking around in your past . . .

GOGOL: What are you getting at?

Fox: You never loved anyone before me?

GOGOL: No. Never! I swear to you that everything that came before us is a white background, a flicker of smiles and eyes, the boot-up screen of a computer. I remember the stickiness of saliva, the doughy pliability of flesh, and shocks of hair. I remember eyes and noses that became stupid and bovine when I drew close enough to kiss them. Passive submissiveness, cellophane bags, not human beings. Like someone else's lipstick on your cheek. If it's still there, someone had kissed you. As soon as you wipe it off, nothing had happened. I could have lived my whole life that way, could have had even more cellophane bags to pump life into, so their kisses would then be wiped away by the back of the hand of my other I. There was nothing: not love, not lovemaking, not even life itself. Just my heart, in a vacuum.

Fox: Silly boy, there never was any vacuum: I was always at your side. I saw you in other people and loved them for your sake.

GOGOL: That wasn't me.

FOX: You.

GOGOL: Enough. See you soon. Take the trash with you.

MINISTRY OF STATE SECURITY

Search Protocol
Surveillance site: Private residence, 16 Serafimovich Street, Apt. 7
Section Five
Operations Group
P. Zharikhin, Head

Investigative procedures were carried out at 0900, 25 September, the distraction group covering the stairwell entrance and the neighbors. The inspection was conducted according to Procedure 6: Polaroid snapshots were used to establish original positions of objects, to which they were replaced as indicated in the snapshots following the inspection.

The surveillance site consists of a 21 ft. long entrance hall, a 10 x 12 ft. living room–bedroom, an 11 x 6 ft. kitchen, and an 8 x 6 ft. combined toilet and bath. Since the last inspection (conducted during the installation of audio-monitoring devices), the following changes have occurred. (For prior description of the premises consult the protocol of the first inspection).

The antler coatrack in the entrance hall now bears a man's gray raincoat, the pockets of which revealed: one metro token, one broken lighter, one used opera ticket, and a sheet of A4 paper bearing numerous cryptograms and folded multiple times (photocopy attached). Cryptographic analysis established that the handwriting belonged to Gogol. The top center of the document bears the title "Our World" surrounded by a wreath of manuscript-style curlicues in the shape of latte macchiato mugs. In the center of the page there is a distorted map of W. Europe with arrows labeled, respectively: the Bosporus Strait, the Dardanelles, and Elizabeth's Palace (in Great Britain). In the region of Egypt an attempt was made to sketch Fox in the shape of the Great Sphinx. Beneath that, a pictogram titled "Our Boat" attempts to render a standard Strela diesel boat. At the boat's helm is a poorly drawn figure in a captain's uniform with an arrow indicating "Captain Nevinsky." Along the edges of the sheet is a pictogram titled "Our Universe": Gogol in a space suit dragging Fox across a starry sky. The drawing has no artistic value; possible political significance is being investigated by the decoding group.

Above the antler-shaped coatrack hangs a poster with the words ABANDON ALL COATS YE WHO ENTER HERE written in Gothic script.

Alongside the shoe cabinet lies a wall rug of the national coat of arms. Expert analysis indicates that the rug is used to wipe feet (consider raising criminal charges for the desecration of national symbols).

In the SW corner of the entrance hall a Rafaello candy wrapper bearing Fox's fingerprints and rolled into a 2 in. ball was found behind a cabinet.

In the living room–bedroom linen chest were two sets of bedding (one pillow) and an opened packet of Durex condoms, with one condom missing. The 60W lightbulb in the ceiling fixture had been replaced by a 40W lightbulb, presumably with the object of creating an intimate atmosphere.

One of the violets on the wallpaper above the bed has been traced with blue ballpoint ink, with a .3 in. color photograph cutout of Fox's face appliquéd (using a glue stick) in the middle.

Examination of the bedding on the bed revealed a 10 in. rip in the duvet cover along the perimeter of the decorative hole in the middle through which the blanket is inserted. The tear is darned with crude, uneven stitches in white thread spelling LISABYE.

On the Czech bookshelf over the bed the following books have been added: Orhan Pamuk, *The Black Book;* Milan Kundera, *The Book of Laughter and Forgetting;* Pierre Bourdieu, *L'opinion publique n'existe pas* (a collection of essays in French); Gabriel García Márquez, *The General in His Labyrinth;* Aleksandr Solzhenitsyn, *The Oak and the Calf.*

In the cabinet behind the toilet in the bathroom 3 rolls of toilet paper (184 ft.), with a picture of a kitten chasing a butterfly on the label (Dobrush paper mill) were discovered stacked one atop the other. A toilet brush has appeared for removing remnants of excrement from the toilet basin (correction: verification has established that the toilet brush was there originally, but erroneously not included in the preceding general inventory).

On the glass shelf above the bathtub to the right of the faucet there are now: Camay soap, Aquafresh toothpaste, Head and Shoulders shampoo, and a Gillette shaving kit with three extra razors in the organizer base. Extraction of the razors revealed a secret cache, inside which a note (cryptographers' conclusion: Fox's handwriting) was hidden. Presumably, it was left by Fox to be discovered accidentally by Gogol as he worked his way through razors and naturally required a new shaving head. The note reads as follows:

The Elisavetalogue

1. Thou shall not kill Elisaveta, no matter how much she gets on your nerves.
2. Love Elisaveta as you would love yourself.
3. Thou shall not covet thy neighbor's Elisaveta.
4. Thou shall not be proud over Elisaveta.
5. Thou shall not lie to Elisaveta, or else you'll get a punch in the liver.
6. Thou shall not commit adultery against Elisaveta, for if thou dost, terrible will be the wrath of the Lord.
7. Thou shall not curse before Elisaveta, for she can outcurse anyone and everyone.
8. Buy Elisaveta flowers, for theirs is the Kingdom of Heaven.
9. Be fruitful and multiply with Elisaveta.
10. Sing praise to Elisaveta or face the consequences.

The kitchen cabinet over the stove contains two packages of tea (black and green), a package of coffee, and a box of sugar. The freezer compartment of the refrigerator contains a package with seven *pelmeni* meat dumplings (the freshness date for which expired fifteen days ago).

One of the soup bowls has written on it with indelible marker LIZ YOUR BOWL CLEAN, while a second soup bowl reads PAPA BEAR.

A used red candle 3 in. in diameter stands on the table inside a sectioned circle drawn on the tabletop with indelible marker; the candle is labeled POST-SOLAR CLOCK.

On a small table near the stove stands a faceted glass vase (Neman glass factory). The trash bin contains a bouquet of wilted irises. For a detailed inventory of discarded refuse consult the appendix to volume II of the case record.

On the hook near the door into the kitchen, beside a waffle-weave kitchen towel, hangs a silk napkin bearing a picture of a bear cub (made in China). Embroidered on the napkin with red thread: TOLYA WANTS MORE (Fox?).

A dark-blue slipper (size 12 male, Belvest shoe factory) was found under the padded corner sectional bench in the kitchen. The second slipper (in very dusty condition) was located atop the clothes cabinet in the corridor. (It has been proposed—by Senior Operations Officer E. Tsupik—that the couple used the slippers to throw at each other during their love games.)

Overall, the apartment creates the impression of being tidy, with no indications of having become a hellhole.

During the inspection, power supplies for the portable auditory monitors were replaced, and the system tested and adjusted to improve audio quality.

Psychotropic and/or narcotic substances were not uncovered during the search of personal items and of the premises, as a result of which (in accordance with Section Five Procedural Directive No. 576), a 1.2 in. x 3 in. packet containing 3 g of powdered heroin was planted in the gap between the 6th and 7th floorboards in the living room–bedroom. The packet dropped .8 in. beneath the boards. Removal of the floorboards is not required for recovery.

An interview with a representative of Section Five's Special Operations Group, Senior Operations Officer E. P. Tsupik, published in the newspaper *SB* 27 September. (Details of the present case were suppressed in the interview per Procedural Directive No. 165—"On Press Releases"—attached.)

A Visit to the MGB

Our feelings about the Ministry of State Security vary. Many fear it; those whose consciences are not clean despise it. But who is today's security officer, that manual laborer hard at work in daily service to preserve the stability of our country? Senior Operations Officer Evgeny Petrovich Tsupik of the MGB met with our journalist, Valentina Pankratova, right on the porch of his hospitable green house in the village of Tarasova. The family's darling red dog barked amiably, Mrs. Tsupik baked pies, and even the sun shone over the house with a particularly agreeable light.

The hero of our report told us that real boletus mushrooms grow on his lot: "I am a hard-core mushroom hunter, and when I need to mull over service assignments I like to go for walks in the woods. Your nerves unwind immediately, and you're reminded that no matter how complex and dangerous your work, you're doing it so the woods continue to be completely silent, so the mushrooms might grow undisturbed, and so the birches might overflow with sap. So that air-raid sirens of a new war would never sound, so the boots of Hitler's soldiers would never trample the moss. Generally, I clean the mushrooms in front of the house just after I've picked them. As a result, a whole ring of porcini mushrooms has popped up here. We watch them grow and cultivate them."

In the meantime, Evgeny's winsome wife calls us back home: "The food will get cold before you finish talking," she jestingly chides her husband, and one can sense that no matter how strict the MGB operations officer is with criminals, at home he is no despot, but a good, kind, responsive husband.

As his wife sets out before us cabbage pie, egg pie, and a sweet pie with cinnamon, Evgeny Petrovich seats his children on his lap: he has two, both boys, aged seven and ten. Their jaws dropping, the boys listen to the story of a recent shoot-out in which their father took out two spies: there's no doubt who these boys will grow up to become.

"People say many things about Section Five," I tell him, fearing, of course, a sharp response, if not something worse (it's the MGB, after all). "It's almost as if you were political sleuths, kidnapping people and whatnot."

Evgeny Petrovich laughs heartily. "Yes, Sierakowski's buried right here in this garden. I did him in myself with a shovel. Ha-ha-ha! You want me to dig him up and show him to you?" I go along with his game, and we spend some time digging in the garden, but all we find are potatoes that haven't been dug out yet. "Well, as you can see for yourself, the MGB has no connection with kidnappings," he continues. "As for us playing politics, the people in our field of vision are all ordinary bandits. Are we now supposed to stop catching criminals?"

Evgeny Petrovich points to the sprouted potato found at the spot where we were looking for Sierakowski. "This vegetable here had the potential to feed a human being. It could have grown leaves and become compost to lend life to yet other plants. In order for that to happen, it had to be harvested, sorted, eaten, or planted. This one wasn't planted, so it's going to the trash heap. At the MGB we don't just 'plant' people away. We provide a future for those for whom there would be none without us."

In the meantime, the sun is setting, and the entire Tsupik family has gathered in the fireplace room. The logs crackle cozily in the hearth. The eyes of Feliks Dzerzhinsky shine in the portrait of him on the wall. Dad is telling his sons about how, not long ago, the vigilance of one of the listeners in operations made it possible to prevent a terrorist act. As a woman, I envy his wife: with him for a husband you feel protected. In the meantime, Tsupik is reading Esenin (unfortunately, I don't remember exactly what). Outside, night is finally approaching, and the light in the fireplace reminds one of the warm glow of a campfire. "Eh, let's remember what it was like to be young." Evgeny Petrovich waves his hand, and the exquisite wood of a six-stringed instrument comes to life. "You tenderly embrace the curves of your guitar," he sings with his wife as they rock back and forth in unison, holding hands. Ah! If only the spies and the enemies he so assuredly foils on a daily basis could see him now!

Afterward, we all go upstairs to the roof, and the starry sky comes to life above us. "When I look at the sky, I never cease to be amazed by the limitlessness of the universe," Evgeny Petrovich says. "Nowhere else except beneath this beauty can you sense how enormously insignificant you are. And when you acknowledge the billions of probabilities, you can't possibly believe that we are alone. Of course, somewhere out there someone is watching us. And if the stars are capable of surveillance, then that means that we're also allowed to watch."

I leave the Tsupiks' with a full bag of treats: pies, buns, and even honey from their private apiary. Glancing at the streetlights that so resemble stars floating by outside the car window, I am calm, for I know that the right people are watching me.

MINISTRY OF STATE SECURITY

Protocol: Audio Documentation
Surveillance site: Private residence, 16 Serafimovich Street, Apt. 7

30 September
Senior Lieutenant P. Grabar

The surveillance objects penetrated the surveillance site, opening the door with a key, at 1707. In the entrance hall (Microphone 2) they had a conversation about Serafimovich, vocalizing their conjectures as to who he might have been: Gogol thought he might be a partisan commissar who had died and gone to heaven, to the seraphim; Fox thought that he was a Party figure whose ancestry stemmed back to Saint Seraphim of Sarov. Gogol invited Fox to Microphone 3 (the kitchen), to drink some "chickatee." During preparations it became clear from the conversation (Gogol: "How black and fine it is!") that they were talking about tea and not a bird. The concept underlying the pun has not been explicated, but there were no indications that the speaker intended perverse connotations. It is possible that such behavior was dictated by ordinary silliness. While drinking the tea—judging by sucking and puckering sounds emitted by the objects—they began to kiss, after which they began mating. The sound of a falling chair and characteristic remarks (Fox: "Oops, I'm slipping off. Let me hitch myself up a bit.") suggest that Gogol had situated Fox on the kitchen table (sketch attached). In the process of mating they decided to relocate to the living room–bedroom (Microphone 1), where they mated another 45 minutes.

Subsequently Gogol lay and made bellowing sounds with his lips, nose, and other respiratory organs, imitating either a steam engine or a boat. With the help of these sounds not formed into words Gogol seemed to be attempting to convey a certain aspect of his condition, as evidenced by ensuing turns of speech, such as: "First it was like 'oo-oo-oo.' Then, when we started to pick up speed, it was more like 'oo-oo-oo-eh-eh-eh.'" Or, "We fell into this rhythm and it was 'eh-eh-eh-ah-ah-ah.'" Fox conducted herself as if Gogol's speech behavior were fully intelligible and generally conformed to that of a normal human. Thus, after the second "like oo-oo-oo-eh-eh-eh," she inquired whether it had not been more pectoral—"oo-oo-oo-oo-eh-eh-eh-eh-yah-yah-yah-yah," and he agreed that indeed it had been. The possibility cannot be ruled out that the surveillance objects were communicating by way of a certain code language, having previously agreed on the meaning of the various sound combinations. Also not to be ruled out is that this fragment of their conversation took place under the influence of hallucinogens. (In the surveillance objects' discussions the narcotics term "ecstasy" figured more than once.) Ten minutes later the conversation became more matter-of-fact.

Fox: So do you think they've found out about us? Can they be listening to us now?

Gogol: I don't care. Really. I just don't care.

Fox: All our groaning, all our little words, everything that's supposed to be just between us?

Gogol: I swear to you, it doesn't matter. But I do think that they are probably listening.

Fox: But how did they find out? You rented the apartment through Boris, right?

Gogol: You know, if you want to get totally paranoid about it, you'll wind up concluding that the first person who could have called them was

Boris. The whole premise—that a friend's relative needed an apartment but couldn't rent it herself—sounds like a good reason to call them, don't you think? But I doubt that Boris turned us in. I basically don't want to think at all about why they're listening to us.

Fox: I go to the hairdresser's once or twice a week. The fact that when I enter the stairwell where the salon is I go past the door and up the stairs to the apartment we've rented is hardly apparent. In order to establish where I'm going they would have to keep track of the people in the salon, and I've never seen anyone suspicious there.

Gogol: A nice theory. But it works only if you exclude the possibility that those stylists have epaulets under their outfits. Listen. Once or twice a week you and I show up in the same place. One time, maybe twice, I managed to shake my tail by cutting through stairwells with back and front doorways, that is, if they weren't baiting me, letting me think I'd lost them . . . But I've got the sense these days that they're not following me right now, but that can also be interpreted as direct proof that they've discovered our den and bugged it. Most likely, they've figured out that our paths cross in the area of Serafimovich Street. Everything else depends on what Comrade Muraviov personally decides.

Fox: Do you think that they've been here? Touched . . . our bed? Seen our . . . silly games? People in gray suits, sweaters, and lace-up shoes? Intruders who stink with the smell of bad eau de cologne?

Gogol: Let's not exclude that possibility.

Fox: And he . . . He was here?

Gogol: I don't know. Maybe they're not listening to us, silly! Don't move away. Come sit by me.

Fox: They hear our secret names, they know that you're "Bear," and they listen to us messing around and talking about our orgasms?

Gogol: Don't worry, my little one. There's no one here. The MGB is a bunch of pederasts. You listening? If they were nearby, they would obviously object to that statement, my love. Don't get worked up.

Fox: I'm cold.

Gogol: You can't be cold . . . Don't be afraid, you hear, don't be afraid! Listen, just listen to me: I don't believe the MGB really even exists at all . . .

Fox: Uh-huh. How's that?

Gogol: Calm down, and listen. Just imagine that there really is an agency with its own goals, with its own circle of interests, and that they keep the peace. There's an agency like that in every country. And normal, everyday people—like the agent the newspaper wrote about—work there. All right, so they hunt for people and even do wiretaps. Everyday people. With families with children who sing songs and play the guitar and look up at the stars. What's there to be afraid of? That dark, clammy sensation we're drowning in now, Lisa, has no connection with them. We're the ones producing the sensation. Sure, they have government-issued Makarov pistols, good salaries, pension funds, and housing. Sure, their windshields are tinted, and their ugly mugs are attentive. But they're not terrifying. They're everyday people. So what if they listen to what we say about our orgasms? Or that they write down how you push me out of bed? So? Is that serious work?

That they seem terrifying and omnipresent is all the product of our paranoia. If we stop fearing them, they'll stop being fearsome. What danger can we be in? What's the maximum? What? Prison? They'll plant narcotics and put us in prison? So? We're afraid of that? Afraid that they'll feed us cabbage soup and lock us up in cells with slop buckets?

No, we're shaking because they—oh what a terrible pronoun!—because they know everything. Because they can deprive us of our very selves. Because just by narrowing their lips during an interrogation they can crush us. Because they see right through us and know what we'll say next. But they're normal family people who think about how they can buy themselves a new set of wheels or slip away early from work to be with their wife. Without our fear, without these clammy waves of . . .

Fox: But I'm terrified.

Gogol: That's not the result of their work. That's your paranoia. Drive it out of yourself, and there'll be nothing to threaten us!

Fox: There's only one argument contra. Sierakowski, who you talked about. It wasn't my paranoia that kidnapped him.

Gogol: Listen, Zygmunt Sierakowski, Walery Wróblewski, and Jarosław Dąbrowski are . . . That's very complex. They . . . were romantics and idealists. And fools, of course, is what they were. Like the Decembrists, they tried to forge happiness on earth with their bare hands. A butterfly versus a tank . . . They would have done better to study the history of the Grand Duchy of Lithuania. I'll tell you one thing: there was no need to kidnap them. Their plot was utopian, a romantic dream that only they believed in. Shush at them like at children and they'd scatter . . . That's why I don't know what happened to them and what the MGB has to do with them. I don't know. It's a very strange affair. That's all.

Fox: That's all? You spoke to the widow of one of them. The widow. He no longer exists, but she does. Nothing makes sense, but he's gone. He's not with her. I'm terrified. I can see that you're terrified too. They can hear you. Don't do that, don't. Maybe I'll get dressed?

Gogol: You're afraid that they're going to hear you naked? Achtung! Elisaveta is putting on her panties. They're stretching tautly over her tiny bottom!

Fox: Stop that, Bear!

Gogol: Elisaveta is pulling on her bra! Oops, one breast has fallen out!

Fox: Come on, stop it!

Gogol: We continue our report for the officers on listening duty, whose burden today has ripped them from the arms of their wives and children and cast them in the abyss of counterintelligence. Her blouse is buttoned and tucked in, but if only you could see, my medal-bearing friends, the view from behind! Oh-oh, the subject is departing! The subject has locked herself in the bathroom! Now, my friends, I understand completely what a difficult job you have: I can't see a damn thing, but those muffled sounds made by her tight bottom squeezing into those jeans is driving me crazy! What a difficult assignment you have, my friends!

[*Microphone 2*]

Fox: Hush, you bushy bear!

The surveillance objects hurriedly dressed and abandoned the surveillance site. On leaving Gogol shouted: "Don't get bored, Comrade Officer!"

MINISTRY OF STATE SECURITY

Protocol: Audio Documentation
Surveillance site: Private residence, 16 Serafimovich Street, Apt. 7

4 October
MGB Second Lieutenant A. M. Gevorkian

Having appeared at the site at 1600, Gogol (who opened the door with his key) spent a long time in the kitchen: judging by the noises, he was preparing dinner. Fox arrived at 1900, and they proceeded to Microphone 3, to eat. After dinner they withdrew to the living room–bedroom (Microphone 1), where they made love. After that they had a private conversation of an intimate nature and talked about things having no informational value or relation to the current social-political situation. In particular, they recollected their childhoods. In view of the absence of any reason to document this information, these conversations—of interest only to the two of them—are not included. After that the subjects fell asleep and slept the night through at the surveillance site. At 0835 Gogol woke, banged around in the kitchen, then, after dropping in on Fox in the living room–bedroom for a second, he left the site without having wakened her. Fox left the site at 1000.

NB: This protocol is being returned to the Audio-Documentation Command with instructions to "Redo the decryption."

Revised Transcript of Audio Documentation
Surveillance site: Private residence, 16 Serafimovich Street, Apt. 7

4 October
Senior Operations Officer E. P. Tsupik

Gogol met Fox near Microphone 2 with the words, "The pineapple chicken is over there." After eating, they proceeded to Microphone 1, where for nearly an hour the surveillance objects emitted sounds of a passionate, bestial nature. Conversation was initiated by Gogol.

GOGOL: Tell me about your childhood.

Fox: I grew up in the city of Kobryn, in the shadow of a Ferris wheel. It was the principal structure in Kobryn, towering high above the town, like a city council building over an old European burg. To this day it still seems as if life in Kobryn were in some secret way controlled from the Ferris wheel, which stood out like a spider's silhouette against the setting sun. I graduated from high school in Kobryn and left for Minsk to take entrance examinations. That's where my childhood ended.

GOGOL: I'm not asking you to fill out a form. So what in your childhood stands out in your mind most of all? What *image* comes to mind when you hear the word "childhood"?

Fox: [*After a long silence*] Our house had three stories and was made of wood. It housed five families. That type of building was built right after the war. It was nested in a briar patch, with a meadow full of tiny roses out front. My grandmother used to water and trim them. Once I even saw a real live hedgehog there: he scampered across the grass like a dog, and looked so unlike the pictures of hedgehogs in our school primers that even back then I began to suspect that the adult world was one big lie.

GOGOL: Are you saying that the world of childhood invented by adults is a lie?

FOX: No. It's the adult world that's a lie, not a child's. I have no complaints about my childhood. Our house stood on a clay bluff with a dried-up stream in the ravine below, a ravine overgrown with stinging nettles . . . Once someone abandoned an old bus in the ravine, and literally overnight everything of any use had been stolen from the bus: wheels, engine, radiator. All that remained were the shell, a steering wheel, and rows of switches. I literally moved in to live there. I remember how the door opened with a lever that I could barely reach and that the middle of the dashboard housed an enormous speedometer the size of my face— its arrow moved when I revved my jet engines. I don't remember now whether I actually took off in it . . . I invited very few people to ride with me: our old pensioner neighbor who always wore a brown suit, stood up straight, and was very kind, till the day that he died. My mother and father whom even then I barely remembered. A little girl from the house next door who couldn't walk—something was wrong with her legs. She would sit at the window and constantly look down as I picked roses and used them to spell out the words "mama" and "papa" in front of her—two paired words that were never really mine.

The dashboard also housed two round convex switches, one red and the other green. When the sun fell on them, they would light up with ruby and emerald hues that I saw only later in Chagall paintings. After a winter in the ravine, the bus's roof caved in, and it was damp and uncomfortable inside. Also, someone had unscrewed the steering wheel for no real reason, and it just lay there on the floor helpless, like an animal struck by a car. I continued to drive the bus for a while, but it got harder to do, as if my imagination had petrified. The switches no longer shone with the same gem-like radiance, and someone had broken the glass of the speedometer and pulled off the arrow. The adult world, with real cars and real flying, turned out to be a complete counterfeit . . . Your turn.

GOGOL: Tell you about my childhood?

FOX: What's the first thing that comes to your mind when you hear the word "childhood"?

GOGOL: Let me think. The inky dark blue of night . . .

Fox: Inky dark blue? What does that mean?

GOGOL: That's like looking into an inkwell against the light.

Fox: An inkwell? Is that a hole in the ground filled with ink? A cartridge for a printer? Technological advancements have made the metaphor a bit stale.

GOGOL: All right, the dark-blue—like the background of the Internet Explorer icon—blue of night . . .

Fox: Enough joking already. I won't interrupt anymore.

GOGOL: The inkwell blackness of the night, with the crystal of constellations overhead, and Mama—my enormous, warm mother—offering me her hot, life-filled nipple filled with dreamy milk, but the nipple has to be cleared of the icy crust and frozen fur that has covered it over. You work away at it with your moist nose and are burning with impatience, and freezing, and shivering. A bit later—comes diving through ice holes, and the tremulous flapping of a chewed fish in your mouth, and the phosphorescent—as if drawn on a computer—aurora polaris overhead, and, most important of all, consciousness of the fact that no matter how long life will last, there will always be enough fish in the sea and light up above . . . What the f—— are you doing?

Fox: Anatoly Nevinsky: born to a family of polar bears, trained to interact with ladies at the Institute of Potato Cultivation! I was honest with you! I was totally sincere! Squeaky sincere!

GOGOL: And I never pushed you off the bed.

Fox: Come on, Bear, tell. No funny business. Seriously!

GOGOL: The sun dances across enormous floorboards. A sleepy noon, Mama's cooking in the kitchen, and it's so quiet, so, so quiet at home that I hear the pieces of dust rubbing against each other in the sun. No, not rubbing, rather, crashing into each other with the slightest sound of glass against glass. I am lying on the floor in a ring of sunshine, entirely encircled by it, embraced by it, locked in it. I close my eyes and see my eyelids from the inside: a bright-red Martian haze with formless rainbow-colored spots. I was probably playing with toy soldiers or something, but that's all disappeared: what I remember is just the bright warm, but not hot, light embracing me on the floor. Now, if you will, for me that image is filled with almost religious significance: the sun and I. The sun hasn't changed, and even the floorboards are still in the same place, but the openness of that child to the new—demanding no explanations—has gone. Metaphorically speaking, it is not for me any longer to lie in that circle of sun, not for me to lie with those thoughts, those fairy-tale castles drawn in orange clouds on the inner surface of my eyelids.

Fox: Why don't we meet in town? Like real people.

Gogol: How so?

Fox: Let's arrange for a classic date. A quiet walk, macchiato at a café.

Gogol: Hmm, that hadn't occurred to me. You remember, though, that they might be following us. You remember how you were afraid that they were listening to us. They'll recognize us immediately: either the surveillance cameras will pick us up or my flatfoots will pass on that I have a new contact. If they don't already know.

Fox: Let's think about how we can elude them. I want to walk down the street, nuzzling your shoulder. For it to be raining, cold and warm at the same time.

Gogol: We need to think about this. No matter what we think up, though, the likelihood that we can go strolling all over town unnoticed is rather small . . . You remember how quickly that red-haired bison in the Hawaiian shirt at the parade rehearsal got on our tail? The very idea is madness. But we could mark out a route and stroll along it with an hour's difference between us. First you, then me. Then we could meet here and discuss . . . Although that kind of behavior also could be suspicious. We could go for a walk like this: you go on Saturday at eight in the evening, and I'll go on Sunday at eight in the evening. Our eyes will encounter the same things: passersby, car lights, streetlamps, air, the wind . . . It will be as if we were together.

Fox: I don't want as if. Let's risk it. You and I. The same air, the same wind, and the same passersby for two.

Gogol: But what about being followed!

Fox: You said yourself that it was all paranoia. Even if it's not . . . To hell with it all . . .

Gogol: You stopped being afraid.

Fox: More than that. I'm staying with you today.

Gogol: For long?

Fox: Forever. Until morning. I'm not afraid now. That means that no one can hear us here, and no one will find me anywhere in any of my marvelous cages.

GOGOL: I want to hug you like this with our arms linked together. See, no one can tear you away from me. You're out of danger. You're my catch. A salmon fallen into the paws of a nasty grizzly bear.

FOX: The main thing is that he not paw me. Or at least not paw me to death.

GOGOL: Brilliant idea!

FOX: Stop! Ouch, you're going to leave marks. Bandar-log!

GOGOL: A Bandar-log inside a log. Not a Russian Bandar-log. A Bandar-log in a fog. Bandar-log paws you like a dog.

FOX: I'm going to pull your tail off, clumsy bear.

GOGOL: She-human, let go of what you were going to tear off, because for us bears this is our principal organ!

FOX: Enough already!

GOGOL: What does that patch of light on the wallpaper look like to you?

FOX: Like the letter *n*.

GOGOL: How unpoetic!

FOX: Hitler's mustache.

GOGOL: What a set of references you have! You might have said, "Charlie Chaplin's mustache." It would have been the same thing in visual terms, but at least sounded a bit more acceptable.

FOX: What do you see in that patch of light?

GOGOL: Oh, two enormous cliffs, like in the paintings of the German neo-romantics. They're all pitted with swallows' nests, entwined with fidgety flocks of sharp-winged birds that resemble check marks in a notebook. On the cliffs stand two neo-Gothic, white-sandstone castles. In one of the castles lives a young, sickly prince elector; in the other a maiden with eyes as dark as the waters of the Rhine. Between them lies an abyss, but once a year, on Saint Wilhelm's Day, this dark-blue violet-flowered wallpaper appears between them and turns into an invisible bridge emitting sheaves of sparks. But it appears only if Schiller's poem has been recited in time—the one about . . .

FOX: The violets on the wallpaper are pink, not dark blue.

GOGOL: You're wrong! You couldn't find darker blue violets in all the Bavarian Alps!

FOX: They're pink, like all the wallpaper.

GOGOL: Our wallpaper is dark blue. When we did this for the first time, I thought, how symbolic: all great deeds get done in stunningly tacky interiors.

Fox: Let's turn on the light.

Gogol: There. The floor lamp makes it even harder to figure out. They're sort of brownish. Let's try the ceiling fixture.

Fox: Salad-green?

Gogol: We're both wrong.

Fox: No, what about salad-green?

Gogol: Correct. And when was the last time we saw this room with any light!

Fox: When we looked at the wallpaper, you mean?

Gogol: Come to my claws, and I will lullaby you in this room with the salad-green wallpaper, and I'll take you to a kingdom where each of us has a castle on a cliff, but we'll live together in a hut near the river.

Fox: It's damp, I'll bet.

In the morning Gogol woke at 0835, proceeded to the kitchen (Microphone 3), where at first he banged around in the cupboards, by the sound of it, in the process of looking for some object. Then he crumpled paper. Moving into the range of Microphone 1, he whispered something to Fox, who appears to have been sound asleep. Point-source enhancement using the Echo-3 system allowed us to discern: "Let this violet napkin be the first thing my princess sees upon awakening." Fox, emerging from her sleep, spoke no words and left, locking the door with her key.

MINISTRY OF STATE SECURITY

Inventory of Household Refuse Produced at
Surveillance site: Private residence, 16 Serafimovich Street, Apt. 7

The present inventory is standard format and is appended to the case file in accordance with Directive 10-18: "Rules for Processing Trash Discarded from Sites Placed Under Operational Surveillance." It has been included in volume III of the case record to facilitate operational officers' ability to construct the most complete picture possible of the surveillance objects' daily routine and household habits.

Inventory compiled by Ermolaichik

The trash was taken out as both surveillance subjects, Fox and Gogol, left the apartment on 7 October. To capsulate the trash they used a standard nontransparent plastic bag with enhanced holding capacity and a draw-string of yellow celluloid. The trash was deposited in the container by Gogol while Fox started her Lexus SUV and U-turned in the lot.

At the top of the bag lay the box from a large-sized Four Seasons pizza from the Il Patio Pizza restaurant on Independence Avenue, and a receipt for 35,000 rubles, which included the price of delivery. The box contained two uneaten pieces bearing elements of seafood (shrimp and oysters) and olives. Three other pieces bore traces of having had the topping eaten off from the middle. The outer crust (dried dough) was left untouched. The diameter of the bites would lead us to posit that the described nibbling had been done by Fox (expert analysis was not conducted). At the same level of refuse an emptied bottle of Château Margaux red wine (France) was found, together with three used condoms wrapped in a thick wad of toilet paper. Two of the condoms contained traces of semen belonging to Gogol (analysis). There were also three banana peels and approximately 4 oz. of orange peelings.

Next the trash was laid out on uncut sheets of the free want-ad news-paper *All or Nothing*. The date and general nature of the newspaper made it possible to establish that the newspaper marks a second reverse-chronological layer of refuse, which contained two used condoms with Gogol's semen wrapped in a thick wad of toilet paper, two empty and crushed Unique soft drink bottles, and the wrapper from an approxi-mately 12 oz. box of Leonidas Belgian chocolates bought at the special diplomatic grocery store, 37 Zakharev Street. This layer also contained two used tickets to the October movie theater, an empty potato chip bag, and a birch-bark French Camembert cheese box. Also discovered in this layer was an open package of eating utensils used for consuming cheese—so-called skewers, made in Switzerland. Two skewers missing from the package were found inside the potato chip bag. The remain-ing eighteen skewers were still usable but for incomprehensible reasons had been tossed in the trash. Also found were approximately 5 oz. of potato peelings, an empty Maggi instant soup envelope, two Stimorol chewing gum wrappers, the skeletonized remains of two chicken legs, and fragments of the bones of the right wing and middle torso (ribs and backbone) of a chicken from which the meat had been chewed off. The chicken bears traces of curry sauce and was subjected to heat processing in an oven. At present a determination cannot be made as to which of the two surveillance objects ate which parts of the chicken. Consequently, no determination of their dietary preferences can at present be advanced.

The bottom of the refuse rendered a long, 12 in. tightly rolled package sealed with adhesive tape to prevent accidental opening or the penetration of smells. The package contained fifteen white roses (Netherlands), the stems of which had been snapped in two places—at the bottom and approximately 10 in. from the blossom. The blossoms were not damaged and all faced one direction. All the thorns had been trimmed from the roses, presumably at time of purchase. The package bore Fox's fingerprints, and dactyloscopic analysis revealed that the stems and flowers also bore Fox's fragmented prints. Neither Gogol's fingerprints nor fragments of his prints were found on the stems, the leaves, or the blossoms.

All items listed in the inventory not pertaining directly to the case as material evidence have been destroyed. The skewers were claimed for temporary storage by Major Timofei Dybets.

MINISTRY OF STATE SECURITY

Protocol: Audio Documentation
Surveillance site: Private residence, 16 Serafimovich Street, Apt. 7

11 October
Senior Operations Officer B. L. Vostrokhvostov

At 1800 the surveillance objects penetrated the surveillance site simultaneously, using a key to open the door. For some time afterward they chased after each other back and forth, squealing, between Microphone 1 and Microphone 2. Subsequently they stabilized themselves at Microphone 1 with the goal of engaging in acts of a sexual nature (50 minutes). After that they initiated the semblance of a conversation that was at first difficult to understand.

Fox: You are my country. Anatolia. Right here, where the blanket is, you are washed by the Aegean Sea. There, by the pillow—by the Adriatic. The Black Sea and Mediterranean are also here somewhere. You have been trodden by the feet of the Hittites and the sandals of the Phrygians. Somewhere here. My country. I will populate you with myself, Anatolia, and will live only in you. Camels, and Mauritian-style palaces, and sandy shores, and I have come to conquer you. Like the *Amundsen.* The ice-breaker.

GOGOL: Ooh, that tickles.

FOX: Somewhere over here Alexander the Great sought the fountain of eternal youth. To the southwest of Anatolia lay Lydia. Bear, I'll shave all your scraggly forests if I find out that Lydia lay here to the southwest. Did she? Well?

GOGOL: Come on! There were never any Lydias there.

FOX: That means that those damned ancient historians are lying. And did Croesus, the king of Lydia, live here? Here, on your ribs?

GOGOL: Croesus did live there, I can't deny it. But he was an Anatolian ruler: there was never even the scent of any Lydian rulers here. Then came the Persians and dethroned him. Their king was called Cyrus the Great. Can you imagine a ruler these days named Cyrus? What a hard time he must have had!

FOX: He would enjoy great popularity among the people. Every third man these days is named Cyrus. Was Croesus really that wealthy?

GOGOL: Not wealthier than Anatoly.

FOX: How's that?

GOGOL: I am the richest man on earth. I have everything I need— Elisaveta and an open packet of tea in the kitchen. Speaking of tea, by the way . . .

FOX: Croesus didn't have tea?

GOGOL: Croesus didn't have happiness. But I do.

FOX: When did you realize that you were Croesus?

GOGOL: When you came into my life.

[*Gogol sings to the melody of* "My Years and Days Are My Riches," *shifting the stress in Lisa's name to the last syllable.*]

GOGOL: "My Elisaveta is my riches."

FOX: I'm not talking about that.

GOGOL: But I am.

FOX: But still: was there a time when you realized that you had become what you'd wanted to be?

GOGOL: Once. I was wandering through the little stores at the Vienna airport on a layover to Bonn for some seminar. A writer "from over there": "Do they really let you write?" "Do you really have access to the Internet and can have a computer at home?" And other idiotic questions you don't know how to answer . . . So, I was strolling through the airport in that state of dislocation you experience in the international airports of cities you've never visited. I drank three Wiener mélanges and dropped into the bookstore, the only one there, relatively large, and with a salesclerk who resembled a mannequin.

Fox: A mannequin?

GOGOL: You know, your statistically average European intellectual. And so, I'm wandering among the varicolored book jackets, recognizing Dostoevsky, Nabokov (spelled Nabokoff), Kundera, Irving, Fitzgerald, and seasonal authors like Dan Brown. I felt as if I were dress shopping, as if each book wore a label [*indecipherable: send to decoding section*]: YSL, Zara, MNG . . .

Fox: Right, a women's novel written in the Zara style. A fashionable novel in the MNG style.

GOGOL: A Davidoff detective novel. Postmodern Absolut vodka. Then— whoa!—there among all the other dresses is an Anatoly Nevinsky. That's impossible. But it's my book. With a photograph of the Palace of the Republic. A narrow red italic font. And a deadly translation: *Prose.* In the original it's called *Pros.* A collection of prose fiction about a society where everyone votes pro: you know, "for." Either the translator didn't get it or couldn't figure out how to package it in English. So I'm standing there, looking at myself on the shelf, unrecognizable, glossy, and that airport, and the price tag—twenty-five euros—and my head starts to spin. That is, I knew, of course, that translations were coming out, and my agent had been putting money on my bank card, but to see it for real—that was something else! I had never thought about writing for someone. I almost broke out in tears, blubbering something to the salesclerk about how the book was mine, mine! Of course, he didn't believe me, so I stuck my ticket under his nose . . . Like a kid. Your phone is ringing.

Fox: Fuck.

GOGOL: What's up?

Fox: It's him calling. That's his ring tone.

GOGOL: So? Don't pick up.

Fox: I can't.

GOGOL: Not in my presence. Don't pick up.

Fox: You don't get it. I can't not pick up.

GOGOL: Destroy it. Throw it against the wall. Don't!

Fox: Hello, Nicky? Of course, I can. Right. Got it. OK. I'll be there soon. Love you.

Gogol: What was that all about?

Fox: I have to leave, immediately. Right away.

Gogol: What did you mean by "be there soon"? What are you doing? You . . . "Love you"? What the? . . .

Fox: Calm down! Enough!

Gogol: You're going to see him now? How? We just? . . . No.

Fox: Yes.

Gogol: No!

Fox: Yes. Yes.

Gogol: How? Well?

Fox: If I don't show up immediately, he might make a connection between my refusal and my cosmetologist, and God knows what that would mean for us.

Gogol: But you can be sick, can't you? Well?

Fox: You don't get it. We're not playing hooky. This is very serious. Serious. Our fantasies are over. Now back to real life.

[*Microphone 2*]

Fox: A very cruel life. Let me go already. Listen, you're being childish. You remember who he is? Come to your senses. Drink some water.

[*Surveillance object Fox departs the surveillance site. For some time after surveillance object Gogol mumbles incoherently to himself.*]

Gogol: How? He's going to touch her. She's mine. It can't be. He can't see how beautiful she is. All he sees in her are . . . ass, legs to be spread even wider, her flexibility . . . He's a beast. He's . . . Stick it in even deeper . . . He . . . She needs to be hugged. To flitter on your palm. To be cultivated, like a flower. Is she really going to let him . . . But it's impossible if there's no love. It will be painful for her. She'll make up some kind of theory about how it's better that way. For us. But I can't do that . . . I . . . And where are they? At the apartment? Let's assume she'll go there just to talk, to calm his suspicions, but he starts to embrace her right in the entranceway or farther inside, on that carpet or on the table, and she'll say that she has a headache, then he'll start petting her, and she'll get the urge, but her panties are still . . .

But what if she turns away . . . ? Says that she can't do it anymore, that she doesn't love him anymore . . . ? That would open up a huge, huge question. He just won't let her go . . . Although she might become frightened for me and say to herself: to hell with him, it's just bodies, but that little bud of hers, it's so small . . . No, it's unbearable even thinking about it . . . She's already there; they're already talking. Maybe it's even worse. Maybe they're not even talking. This is intolerable. I can't bear it. I should call her. I'll call her. She said that I mustn't, that the call would be traced, but fuck them, this is . . . It's possible that right this minute she's pulling her hair out, thinking: should I let him or not, then I call and remind her that there's us. There's our meadow, our rainbow. There's her Anatolia. Well? She's not picking up. Shit! She turned it off. Shit! I can't . . . That means they're screwing now, right? "At the present time the number you are calling cannot be reached." Shit, you bet that number can be reached, and how! I can't stay here. I, shi . . . I'm going there. Maybe I can see something from below. I'll start shouting, I'll . . . Fuck him! Let him kill me. Let him pull out his cannon and blast a shell into my fucking head. At least then she'll figure out that you can't associate with cannibals, you can't . . .

Surveillance object Gogol departed the premises of the surveillance site.

MINISTRY OF STATE SECURITY

Protocol: Audio Documentation
Surveillance site: Private residence, 16 Serafimovich Street, Apt. 7

14 October
Senior Operations Officer E. P. Tsupik

Potentially, in light of the nature of the information revealed below, the present protocol may be subject to excision from the case materials and classified as top secret.

The surveillance objects appeared at the surveillance site at 1500 and opened the door with a key. They immediately went into the kitchen and initiated a conversation.

GOGOL: OK, now that for sure no one can hear us, we can talk. But let's turn off our phones. And remove the batteries.

FOX: Why in the world did you call? From your phone? Don't you have any brains? It's the same as walking out into the street and shouting for all to hear: "We're having an affair!" Well?

GOGOL: Listen, don't. Put yourself in my shoes. I spent another hour and a half under your windows at the Marx Street apartment trying to catch a glimpse of you. I thought that I could see shadows behind the drapes. And I . . . In short, well, I went upstairs, rang the bell, and shouted, and knocked, and the neighbors came out and threatened to call the police. In short . . . Now I want to know what happened there. What happened between you. Minute by minute.

FOX: We were at the house in Sokol, not at the apartment on Marx Street. But if we had been on Marx Street . . . Listen, you almost killed the two of us. You've got to get a grip on yourself.

GOGOL: I imagined the two of you together . . . I just couldn't. I hurt so much.

FOX: I got there . . .

GOGOL: Did you sleep together?

FOX: I got there, but he didn't come out to meet me, as he usually does, didn't come out onto the porch . . . I sat in the car, and the words pounded in my head: "It's over, it's over, it's over." Then, I realized later, I turned on the emergency flashers for some reason. I thought that if I went upstairs, he would meet me, sitting in his armchair, totally calm. That he would start retelling me one of our conversations, word for word. Or show me a video . . .

GOGOL: And so?

FOX: It was very, very quiet, and I kept thinking about what he was going to say, and how he was going to yell: you see, I'd never seen him yelling or even annoyed . . .

GOGOL: And so? So he'd yell, so what? What's so awful?

FOX: I walked into the empty hallway and went up the stairs, and the staircase, usually very squeaky, didn't squeak, as if the sound had been turned off at the movies. I floated up the stairs, above them, paralyzed . . . The feeling was not like when you were a kid and ate chocolate before dinner and your grandmother found out and called you in to explain. It was as if I had broken a vase that could never be put back together. Or had had an abortion: the feeling of not being able to undo what had happened . . . I walked in. He was standing at the window . . . I said, "hello." He turned to face me, as if he were part of a display on a rotating pedestal in some museum. He looked at me. I immediately sensed his mood . . . He seemed frozen. Not like, say, the hands of a clock that's stopped, but like a giant red pine that's just been cut at the roots and is about to begin its eternal flight downward, snagging other, living, trees in its hair. It stands there, frozen, stands there for the last fraction of a second, still resembling a tree, but already having stopped breathing, already different from the other trees around it . . . That was what he was like. He smiled at me as if from some other dimension where he also existed. They had been showing a film, a comedy, and he had been watching it in the living room; he needed to smile, otherwise the viewers around him would have suspected something. So he smiled and said tenderly, that his son . . .

GOGOL: His son Roman?

FOX: That his son had been picked up at Heathrow with heroin. He was so wired he hadn't a clue that you can't pack goods with you to the airport. When Roman came to, they explained to him that his father had paid his bail and made an arrangement with his colleagues, and that he, Roman, would not be sent to prison, although the dose he had been carrying was almost industrial . . . When he found out about his father's intercession, he lodged an official claim that Muraviov, Nikolai M., was not his father, but the last cannibal of Europe, and that Muraviov, Nikolai M., could go fuck himself.

GOGOL: Listen, enough of the sob story! Did you screw? Tell me that, and you can keep going.

FOX: Admit it, Anatoly, you're an idiot, right? That's all you think about? We screwed or we didn't screw. You think that it's all physical? If we had sex, I was unfaithful, if we didn't, then everything's OK? You're supposed to be sensitive, subtle . . . Why can't you understand?

GOGOL: It hurts to think that you had physical contact. Of any kind. A kiss on the cheek. A hug . . . It hurts, understand?

FOX: He told me and then sat down at the piano. Slowly, very slowly, as if trying not to miss the bench. He started to play, and that was the most terrifying. He played Mozart's Piano Concerto no. 24. The larger part of the concerto is written in a minor key, but the second section, the larghetto, is in this extremely drawn-out, lazy major key hidden inside the wrappings of two quick, sad recitatives. The larghetto is my favorite Mozart piece, and he knew that, and he . . . Once when I turned on the television, he . . . started to play, and that sparkling interlude, that thematic impasse that Mozart loves to stuff into his truly difficult pieces, sounded during the weather report. It worked . . . He made a present of that Mozart to me, and ever since, all evening weather reports run to the accompaniment of the Concerto no. 24 . . .

GOGOL: You've gone off the subject. Very painfully off the subject.

FOX: He began to play the larghetto. And it . . . You had to hear it . . . It was so . . . like sunlight through the leaves of trees in June. Like a morning at a summer house: distant children's laughter coming from the neighbor's yard, the sound of water pouring out of a hose into a plastic basin, gooseberries, a window laced with last year's spiderweb . . . music to illustrate yin and yang, total balance, the whisper of waves . . . like a huge street banner with three-foot letters: EVERYTHING WILL BE ALL RIGHT.

GOGOL: Well, well . . . You've gone off on another tangent.

FOX: Right . . . With his back to me he started playing it like . . . Like late Beethoven. Three times faster, with unexpected crescendos that he inserted himself, pounding on the keys in places where they're supposed to be stroked as if pushing hair back from your face . . . The music hissed and dispersed into bubbles, as if during a storm in the Crimea, and it was . . . Black. Imagine a black, repulsive Mozart who had lost his hearing and for that reason was pulling at the last sounds to have sounded in his head, and composing them into . . . A death agony. For every required note his fingers played two or three sounds, as if Richter were playing and his fingers suddenly began to tremble . . . It was . . . Divine. And very painful . . . The man . . . No man has ever deserved such pain . . . Especially one who knows how to feel . . . Someone who so acutely . . .

GOGOL: OK. So he played. What happened next? Did you sleep together or not?

FOX: Listen, don't you get it? His playing was the most important thing. It . . . contained so much pain . . .

GOGOL: That doesn't interest me. I have no interest in what Nikolai Muraviov thinks about his son having gone off the deep end as a result of chronic overindulgence. I couldn't care less.

FOX: Intercourse is more important than pain for you? Why are you talking that way? You're not like that! You realize that it's possible that the two of us have injured another living being . . . I . . . When he finished playing, I touched him on the shoulder.

GOGOL: You touched him on your own initiative? That is, you went up to him and touched him?

FOX: It was as if his shoulder had acquired several new corners, as if he had been broken. I imagined his body all in triangles, as if drawn by the cubists.

GOGOL: Why did you come into contact with him? For our sake: why did you come into contact with him?!!

FOX: That's it.

GOGOL: What's it? That's where it all ended? You left?

FOX: Yes. I left. He didn't see me to my car. He and I haven't spoken since.

GOGOL: Is he going to call you again?

FOX: I don't know.

GOGOL: What if he telephones now? Will you go running to him?

FOX: Yes.

GOGOL: But . . . What about me? Lisa, why are you crying?

FOX: He doesn't deserve this.

GOGOL: Hey, this is me, your bear! Your bear cub! Come on, let's go, let's go . . . Anatolia, remember? Hittites, Phrygians, Croesus . . . You remember? My sweet . . .

FOX: Don't. Not tonight.

GOGOL: All right, come to me and my clumsy paws. I'll warm you up . . . Hey, why are you shaking . . . My poor little girl . . . Don't be afraid . . . No one here is going to . . . We're safe here . . .

Two and a half hours later Fox departed the surveillance site, and no further conversations were recorded; most likely, surveillance object Gogol had fallen asleep.

MINISTRY OF STATE SECURITY

SECTION FIVE

EXTERNAL CONTROL AND SURVEILLANCE COMMAND

ROUTE MAP FOR SURVEILLANCE OBJECTS FOX AND GOGOL

17 October

Compiled by the Field Operations Squad

Major M. N. Prokopiuk, Head

Cause to initiate field operations was warranted by Gogol's strange behavior. Exiting the stairwell of his registered residence (Zakharev Street) at

1900, he entered his personal BMW 6 automobile, license plate number 6428 MI-7, and set off for the department store On Niamiha on Niamiha Street. He was dressed in a gray raincoat, light-blue shirt, red necktie, and dark trousers. He carried a red oversized Samsonite laptop bag.

Having parked in the lot, he proceeded to the Rock House Café, where he ordered himself a black coffee (Americano) with two packs of sugar. It needs to be noted that the Rock House Café is located underground, which excludes the possibility of visual monitoring through storefront windows.

Having paid for the coffee at the bar, he opened his laptop and pretended to be preparing to work, by all appearances to mislead the field intelligence agents he imagined to be following him. Having sat that way for about 5 minutes, he closed the laptop and headed to the men's room, taking the bag with him. He emerged from the toilet wearing a leather jacket, a sweatshirt, and khaki pants. Then, once again with intent to elude surveillance, he positioned himself among a group of foreigners leaving the café, but he was immediately picked up when additional field agents were summoned.

Breaking away from the group of foreigners at the McDonald's restaurant, he immediately hailed a cab, in which he proceeded as far as the Victory Square metro station, exiting the cab at the Kristall store. Slipping inside the store, he rendezvoused with Fox. Fox was dressed in a long black raincoat, a dark-blue scarf, and dark low-heeled boots. Fox was not under visual surveillance, therefore no information is available as to how or whence she had arrived.

From Victory Square they proceeded down toward the house-museum of the First Congress of the RSDLP [The Russian Social Democratic Labor Party], where Gogol spoke at length, and Fox laughed. They proceeded further along the avenue—looking at the Svislach—in the direction of the Ministry of Defense complex. Here Fox took Gogol by the hand, but they walked at a distance from each other, leaving open the possibility of breaking their grasp at any moment. Gogol behaved nervously, constantly recoiling at passing cars and repeatedly attempting to relocate Fox further from the street. Fox, on the contrary, displayed no signs of uneasiness and conducted herself casually. Having gone as far as October Square, for the next 17 minutes they stood near the large plasma screen broadcasting the evening news. Standing with his back to the screen, Gogol pretended to be translating the news into sign language, his hand gestures having nothing in common with the real language of the deaf. As he did this he employed insulting, obscene gestures, particularly when the screen projected government news about current affairs in the country (consider the possibility of initiating administrative procedures). Their loud behavior and laughter (Fox) attracted a group of curiosity-seekers as well as the attention of a special forces patrol squad. The squad checked the documents of the disorderly Fox and Gogol and attempted to record their passport data, but were radioed by a group of field officers to desist so as not to negatively affect the course of the operation.

The surveillance objects proceeded further, toward the white church, observing the sunset over the lower town and the Trinity district for a considerable length of time. Gogol placed his hands on Fox's waist as she stood with her back to him (at the time both were facing the sunset). Gogol was approached by Evgeny Petrovich Mekeniuk, an instructor in philosophy at Belarus State University, as the latter walked from the No. 53 trolleybus stop. They greeted each other with handshakes and spoke for 2 minutes and 40 seconds. After this Mekeniuk continued in the direction of the park with the old city hall, where he was detained, ostensibly for a document check, and searched at the police post inside the Oktyabrskaya metro station. No objects of interest to Section Five of the MGB were found on him, suggesting that his meeting with Gogol had not been planned and that no transfer of secret information occurred during the handshake.

Holding hands, the surveillance objects proceeded further, in the direction of the embankment of the Svislach River, moving along the waterfront back in the direction of Victory Square. Stopping approximately 1,100 ft. short of the Zhuravinka entertainment complex, they began to kiss, and Gogol raised the hood on his sweatshirt, likely with the intent of avoiding recognition. Their kissing lasted 12 minutes, after which they headed down Yanka Kupala Street toward the entrance to Gorky Park. The only amusement working at the time was the shooting range. Here Gogol fired twelve shots into a paper target using a Tula air gun. Ballistics analysis of the target, discarded in a wastebasket 160 ft. down the path to the left, revealed that Gogol suffers from shortsightedness, overcompensates vertically high of the gunsight, and has a tremor (determined through shot placement analysis). Potentially, he may have self-confidence issues. Analysis of the results of his efforts at the shooting range indicates that he has no shooting skills whatsoever. After the shooting range, Fox wrapped her shawl around Gogol's forearm. They walked as far as the abandoned planetarium building and made an unsuccessful attempt to penetrate it, but the lock is made of tempered steel and protected from filing or breakage by a .3 in. shackle. With impunity, they approached the 50 ft. tower where a telescope had been installed during Soviet times, but later dismantled. The doors to the tower were also equipped with a cam lock, but the lower decorative plywood panel flew off when touched. Crouching, the subjects crawled into the tower. (Consider criminal charges for trespassing.) Once at the top, they spent 40 minutes on the telescope observation platform. Gogol opened the liplike shutters of the dome manually, with the help of a crank mechanism. Judging by the echo recorded through a microphone directed from below, Gogol and Fox engaged in conversations of a delusional nature. Gogol talked about and pointed out to Fox the planets and constellations, then talked some more about the Milky Way and his understanding of the Big Bang theory. He had no means by which to illustrate what he said: the telescope had been dismantled, and the sky was overcast with heavy clouds. Most of the time Fox laughed. Then they implemented kissing each other. Before descending, Gogol reclosed the shutters of the planetarium tower dome. Detailed inspection of the premises afterward revealed dried human feces in the southern corner, behind the telescope platform: they had obviously been produced not by Fox or Gogol, but several years prior.

Having walked through the park, holding each other by their extremities, they stopped at the Doverie-94 store cafeteria, where they each ordered a milk shake and black tea with sugar and lemon. They engaged in the consumption of their order in a distant corner of the premises, their backs turned to the video cameras. After that they undertook an attempt to proceed by foot through the eastern train station toward the apartment on Serafimovich Street; however, by all appearances, they began to fear being identified and, with intent to confuse, spent some time feeding the ducks a loaf of bread on the river adjoining Pulikhav Street.

Subsequently, they boarded an empty old-style No. 1 streetcar whose route crosses Kazlov Street into the Zialiony Lug section of town. Once in the streetcar, they opened the window and waved greetings at people driving by. They exited the streetcar across the street from the TsUM department store. By all appearances, their condition was freezing, and to warm up they raced past the monument to the violin player all the way to the Potsdam restaurant (Gogol won with a 7-second margin). They walked again as far as the bridge across the Svislach, where they parted, taking cabs. Gogol set off for his legal residence; Fox did not wait to see him off. Before parting, Gogol extracted from his pocket a children's bottle of soap bubbles, and they took turns blowing bubbles while leaning across the protective railing. One of the bubbles flew across the river and burst against a willow.

MINISTRY OF STATE SECURITY

To: Command K
From: Chancellery of Minister of State Security
N. M. Muraviov
Memorandum

Determine and, by 2000, 18 October, deliver to the chancellery information about the untraced channel of communications between the two objects currently under surveillance, Fox and Gogol, by which they scheduled their rendezvous in the Kristall store on 17 October, bypassing mobile telephone communications and audio monitoring. Intrusions into Fox's private life are strictly forbidden; use Gogol as the starting point and proceed from there.

    Similarly, deliver a strict reprimand to the operations officer in Command K who has been tracking Fox's and Gogol's communication through the World Wide Web Internet.

MINISTRY OF STATE SECURITY

OPERATIONS BRIEFING

Following a request from the chancellery of the Minister of State Security, N. M. Muraviov, within a maximally abbreviated period of time, an investigation was conducted into electronic mailboxes in the World Wide Web Internet accessed at any time from IP addresses linked to surveillance object Gogol. We report that as concerns the appearance of new usernames in his contact lists or messages sent to or received from the addresses of new contacts, no changes have occurred. Correspondence has been moderately intensive and essentially related to professional matters. A letter from Gogol dated 10 October and sent to the address of darius_kem@gmail.com—registered to A. L. Semchik (file number 28746454890745), currently on temporary study abroad in the U.S.— makes reference to actions set forth in the Criminal Code under "defamation of the Motherland and government officials"; however, this has no direct relation to the Fox-Gogol pair and, therefore, has been tabled temporarily to await further investigation.

Gogol has refrained from sending web text messages to any new numbers, and has not made use of IP telephony.

At the same time it has been established that on 1 September a new contact (334-112-6543-853) appeared in his list of contacts for instant ICQ messaging. All messages from this contact have been of an exclusively commercial nature, with no replies from Gogol and, for that reason, this contact had been excluded from tracking. Work in the archives of ICQ accounts affiliated with Gogol made it possible to restore the content of messages beginning 1 September: "100% PENIS ENLARGEMENT. BUY VIAGRA IN SUANX PIAUR, HONG KONG, 10297 SALAY STREET—BEAR'S LAIR 20674. ULTIMATE SALES 2 SEPT." Contrary to practice, the above-cited message came not from abroad, but from an IP address inside the country, which instigated further investigation. It was discovered that the message is unique and was not sent as part of a bulk mailing through email, ICQ, or any other clients for instant messaging. The IP address from which entry to the Internet was implemented belongs to the Beltelecom public access point at the Frunzenskaya metro station, which is not equipped with surveillance cameras. Owing to the amount of time that had passed in the meantime, interrogation of the female clerks at the access point did not result in a description of the person who had sent the message.

Similarly curious is the counterfeit spam message's date, 2 September, the same day the discounts on the advertised product were to be used. As the case materials reflect, the surveillance objects rendezvoused on 2 September. The British phrase "bear's lair" present in the address of the advertised store is a direct reference to the concept of a "den," commonly used by the surveillance objects in their household communication and subsequently appearing in audio-documentation protocols. Similar encodings have arrived at Gogol's instant messaging notification service, in no particular systematized pattern. That is, for the most part, the surveillance objects rendezvoused without traceable prior agreement through the World Wide Web Internet.

As for the meeting at the Kristall store at 1900 on 17 October, that afternoon a message from number 334-112-6543-853 arrived on Gogol's service with the following content: "NEW HOLLYWOOD BLOCKBUSTER *THE CRYSTAL OF FATE* WITH HIGH SCREEN QUALITY AND MULTIVOICED DUBBING AVAILABLE TOMORROW! LATEST NEW WORLD CINEMA RELEASES AVAILABLE AT AFFORDABLE PRICES AT THE STORE ON VICTORY SQUARE."

No film with the title *The Crystal of Fate* has been released by Hollywood filmmakers in the discernible past. The absence of a name or address for the store where the recipient of the "spam mailing" could buy the "new releases" should, by all means, have been a red flag for an attentive operations officer in Command K, but the contact, we reiterate, had been removed from monitoring. We bear obvious and complete blame for failure to provide field agents with up-to-date detailed information from Command K on their route. All guilty parties will be subjected to administrative censure, up to and including separation from the service. In the future all activity from ICQ number 334-112-6543-853 will be scrupulously tracked and decoded.

MGB

SECTION FIVE

COMMAND K

COLONEL SUKHOVEI, HEAD

MINISTRY OF STATE SECURITY

Protocol: Audio Documentation
Surveillance site: Private residence, 16 Serafimovich Street, Apt. 7

18 October
Second Lieutenant S. P. Akhremchik

At 1930 the surveillance objects began to issue sounds indicating their presence at the surveillance site. They proceeded to the kitchen, where they engaged in the consumption of food and discussion of its taste merits. Subsequently they proceeded to Microphone 1 (the living room–bedroom) where, as the saying goes, they made love to each other for nearly an hour. After that they had the following conversation:

Fox: My little one. You're so sad. So frighteningly sad. You've never been this way before. What happened?

Gogol: Nothing. Let's not.

Fox: What is it? Everything is fine.

Gogol: Haven't you ever thought that the beauty that we have, the beauty no one knows except us, is doomed? That it's . . . It's like a child with a congenital heart defect: it grows, it has fun, but it doesn't know.

Fox: My darling, everything's going to be fine. We'll get married.

Gogol: Don't say what you don't believe. Absolutely for certain nothing is going to be fine. Look, any change in the situation—how can I put this?—in the direction of bringing us closer together, of making things better for us, will spell our demise. And there's no ruling out that our demise would not be just symbolical, but for real, physical.

Fox: My dear.

Gogol: Hold on. The main thing is that in our current (frozen, hothouse) state the status quo can be maintained for only a not-very-prolonged period of time. Then, once again, everything will be over: they'll whip us. One of us could be killed or put away somewhere. Or we ourselves might decide that survival, just staying alive, is better than remaining together. We're doomed either way.

Fox: I can try to talk to him.

Gogol: If everything were only that simple, you know yourself, you would have talked to him long ago. Talked. But you can't, and that's one of our many, many dead ends.

Fox: We can leave the country.

Gogol: Ha, ha, ha.

Fox: One at a time, as if going on vacation somewhere safe. Where our safety would be guaranteed. To the U.S.?

Gogol: I told you about Trotsky, didn't I? Please note that all he did was write nasty things about Stalin. Our degree of heat intensity is different. Oh, how we're tied to our Stalin. Like members of the family. And you say, let's leave.

Fox: It's possible . . .

Gogol: That's it. Enough. Nothing is possible.

[*After a pause of 7 minutes*]

Gogol: Why is it that every beautiful love story contains the potential to be not realized in real life? Romeo and Juliet, the Montagues and the

Capulets. Essentially, precisely that's what makes love love: the absolute impossibility of its conversion into the everyday. Sixty years they lived together and died on one and the same day: that, essentially, is also a kind of relationship, but not ours, not ours.

Fox: Silly. Relationships evolve. From romantic love grows familial love.

Gogol: That's not us, Lisa, not us . . . We will love each other, like Romeo and Juliet, until death do us part, and both you and I know what that death looks like. But I'm not afraid. There is no way we can live outside each other. I could swear to forget you, for your sake, for the sake of your remaining alive. I could move to Moscow and become a television host, find a wife and have a family of two children. But the sad fact is that we both know how all that would end: that you would come running to me, and I to you.

Fox: Listen. I'll talk to him. I'll talk to him very respectfully. I'll explain that there's nothing to punish us for. That you and I are ill. Ill with each other. That we tried to cure ourselves, but nothing came of it. That we ask only for one thing: that we be left in peace, that he not touch the two of us. We'll move into your place on Zakharev Street. Or, better yet, we'll buy a tiny apartment, our own den. We'll do an insane remodeling job, the kind only an interior designer can do. For example, I've been thinking about a green floor. Flooring, I mean.

Gogol: That's yesterday. I insist on a transparent floor, filled with water, and with tiny goldfish underfoot. Like at the palace at Kosava. Nineteenth century. Day before yesterday instead of yesterday.

Fox: We'll remodel. There'll be a nursery in the kitchen. No. Better in the corridor. We can live in here. In the summer we'll take trips to my grandmother's in Kobryn.

Gogol: My mother has a dacha, don't forget. With peonies and hydrangeas, I think.

Fox: I'll get a job as a French teacher. Or become an office diva. In the evenings we'll watch movies on our laptops, and you'll always fall asleep during the melodramas. And snore, shameful bear.

Gogol: And you'll hate war movies, while I'll hoard them by the dozen.

Fox: We'll have our books, and read them in bed, side by side, and constantly read each other excerpts, and hush each other: "Don't interrupt my reading!"

Gogol: The baby's crying: your turn to pick him up.

Fox: Uh-huh, right away, I'm going.

GOGOL: This entire wonderful world, my Lisa, this touching and straight-and-narrow little paradise, will never come to be. The tragedy lies in that we are not the kind of Adam and Eve, in curlers and sweatpants, who would agree to inhabit it.

FOX: Adam. I won't part with a single atom of you.

GOGOL: Tell me, Lisa. What would happen to all your real and unreal estate, your houses and villas, if you were not to exist? Physically not exist? I mean, is there any threat that if he were to sense you had cooled to him he might decide to ensure his capital investments by means of removing the legal owner?

FOX: I signed a pile of documents in a bunch of languages, including, it seems, Latin. I think that among those papers there very easily could have been a deed of gift in his name, valid in the event of my incapacitation or death. But listen, do you really think that, were something to happen, the fate of that property would be decided by legal means? Wake up! You remember who we're talking about? He can deprive anyone of anything rightfully acquired, accumulated, or saved, and no one will make a peep, just the opposite, they'll thank their lucky stars to get off so lightly! In my case, as you understand, all of it, to put it mildly, kind of doesn't belong to me.

GOGOL: That's clear.

FOX: What's clear?

GOGOL: That you can't be killed for the sake of your wealth, and that I wouldn't get anything anyway, even if you were to leave a will.

FOX: Fool. Hand me my underpants.

GOGOL: What's wrong? Why are you leaving?

FOX: I have to today. I can't stay: it's dangerous.

GOGOL: You're going to him?

FOX: Don't talk nonsense.

GOGOL: Do you go to him every night? After us?

FOX: Nevinsky, channel your fantasies into short stories, not suspicion. You're better at them.

[Entrance Hall (Microphone 2)]

GOGOL: Sweetheart, I beg you, stay at least for tea.

FOX: I have to go.

GOGOL: I'm going to break your watch.

FOX: Enough. Ciao.

In fulfillment of orders from the special operations planning team we submit the following psychological portrait of surveillance object Gogol.

Dept. of Psychological Profiling
MGB School of Criminology
20 October

Study of the audio documentation on Gogol allows us to conclude that he possesses a choleric temperament with melancholic tendencies. His psychic system can be characterized as erratic, with a tendency for rapid mood changes. In addition, and this is supported by cryptographic analysis of his handwriting, his personality is such that he readily submits to suggestion and to the influence of others. Based on Gogol's personality traits, the person to "win him over" optimally should be psychologically self-assured and sanguine, as well as physically taller and more corpulent. He is more tractable in the evening than in the morning, and mornings generally is inclined to be irritable without cause.

There are latent inclinations of alcoholism. If introduced to a social circle of regular users of narcotic substances, he could become addicted to drugs.

He is easily aroused, but his behavior in crisis situations is unpredictable and could be influenced by as little as the number of hours he had slept the night before. He is cowardly, but this aspect of his personality is not dominant and to rely on its activation in an extreme situation would be unjustified. A high potential for aggression underlies his extreme irascibility. In states of anger he is capable of totally losing control of himself, although not to the point of loss of memory.

His texts permit us to conclude that their author operates on an imperative of diffidence toward reality and toward the primacy of any form of representation (including the representation of others' convictions) over the objective, material world. He is religious, but he determines the contours of his religiosity (q.v. M. Mueshörer's "prophet self-identification syndrome").

In combat conditions he would be entirely unfit for missions requiring lengthy, painstaking pursuit or repetitive, monotonous activities. He is better suited to work requiring quick wit and creativity.

Should investigative procedures related to him be brought to a conclusion, he will be inclined—given the proper approach—to cooperate. People of his temperament rarely become criminals, but if they do, are never effectively able to maintain secrecy about their actions and readily submit to provocation.

Destructive moods and thoughts of suicide are not characteristic of the object, and any attempt to instill same in him would prove effective only if he could be convinced of the correctness, usefulness, and positive value of suicide as the only rational and moral alternative to the senselessness of human existence. That is, a lengthy, well-orchestrated conversation would be required on, among other things, providence and religiosity, with the aim of releasing the subject from those paradigms of his worldview that forbid suicide and relegate it to the category of reprehensible behaviors. The conversation must be conducted by a "subject of trust"; otherwise the process of suggestion is certain to be discovered, interpreted, and blocked by him.

He is inclined toward the arts and creative endeavor in general. He possesses leadership qualities, although these have been insufficiently developed owing to his lack of confidence in himself. He considers himself to have a superb sense of humor, which he is prone to abuse. He pays attention to public opinion and listens to people's reactions. His relationship with surveillance object Fox may be qualified as "romantic" love.

Colonel L. P. Vinogradov, M.D.

MINISTRY OF STATE SECURITY

Protocol: Audio Documentation
Surveillance site: Private residence, 16 Serafimovich Street, Apt. 7

21 October
Operations Officer S. Krivostykh

The surveillance objects appeared at the surveillance site at 1924, Gogol saying, "It smells like home here. Of us. My apartment doesn't smell this cozy." For a while they pointlessly discussed various smells of coziness, their composition (the inhaling and exhaling of people who love each other, the smell of their skin, etc.), then switched to each other's smells, which resulted in their movement to Microphone 1, where they proceeded to sniff each other, including their private parts. The outcome—physical contact—was immediately established between them: Fox shouted loudly and indecently; Gogol wheezed. Achieving climax, they initiated a discussion of explicit topics.

GOGOL: Whenever it happens that forcefully, there's a moment, about a second long, when I seem to cease to exist. The sum of my sensations surpasses the capabilities of my physical body. As if, in addition to five sense organs, I had acquired five thousand more receptors. The sweetest of all states is communicated to each and every one of them all at the same time. Life, but more than in the simple, vulgar sense of the word. But maybe that's what life really is.

FOX: You never . . .

GOGOL: It's as if for a second I brush up against absolute bliss. Then it's taken from me. Why show it to me in the first place? What's the point?

FOX: Listen. How do you think we'll wind up? It can't possibly be, can it, that a person grows, spreads his wings, acquires wisdom, does good and commits evil, and then—wham! Nonexistence and emptiness. What was the sense of living then?

GOGOL: I don't think that all the religions of the world are misguided. That after someone else's hand closes our eyes there won't be anything. At the same time it's naive to expect some sort of Christian paradise or Buddhist reincarnation. Charon and the ferryman.

FOX: Well. What is there then?

GOGOL: What's there is nothing. In a certain sense. In another sense, everything. After all, eternity and absolute nothing are synonymous. Probably more synonymous than eternity and those seventy years some are lucky enough to inhale and exhale and blink their eyes. To experience what we experienced just now. Life is a squiggle in our eternally momentary nonexistence. We weren't, then suddenly our nonbeing acquired a different shape that breathes, and loves, and sins. Seventy years of this other-being-ness, then everything goes back to where it was before. To eternity. To momentariness. To the moment when the brain is no longer supplied with blood, but the neurons keep firing, still sending images to you.

FOX: Then why bother living?

GOGOL: Perhaps life—that brief, but, most important, finite misunderstanding—is what predetermines the images to come before you for the rest of eternity. You live. You live well. You finish living. You're already hardly here. All the things that you've done come crashing down on you. All the smiles. All the looks into the window of your car as it whisked you through the city at night. All the glimmer of advertisements. All the tears shed because of you. All the dances to which you had ever moved your body. All the melodies you had ever heard. All the deception, underhandedness, and cowardliness you're ashamed of. Then comes absolute nothing. That's eternity. That's precisely what we're destined to nonexist with, forever. Always. In this sense all the religions of the world are right. Life after death is predetermined by your actions leading up to it. By everything that you ever did. Heaven and hell exist. But there are no judges. There's you and your concepts of good and evil, your God, if you will. And you abide in eternal bliss. Or in eternal torment.

Fox: [*Transcriber's notation: undecipherable*] "For in that sleep of death what dreams may come? / When we must shuffle off this mortal coil . . ." Do you think they had good dreams?

Gogol: Who?

Fox: Romeo and Juliet.

Gogol: Unlikely. Suicide is a mortal sin in their religion. If they were Japanese, their dreams would have been a lot better.

Fox: Pity. I have a pistol. We could think about good things. Hold each other by the hand. If things got extreme.

Gogol: Never.

Fox: Never.

Gogol: The powers-that-be will change.

Fox: That's a laugh.

Gogol: Everything can change. But there's only one eternity. Rather, we're the only ones it has. No one is going to make any more like us. The pistol really is only if things get extreme. But I'm not going to shoot it at myself. The main thing is to get as close up as possible. I'm a worthless shot.

[*Pause: 10 minutes*]

Fox: What are you thinking about?

Gogol: Nothing, really.

Fox: But?

Gogol: I was simply looking at that patch of light on the wall shaped like pi.

Fox: I'm not asking what you're looking at. I'm asking what you're thinking about as you look.

Gogol: Nothing.

Fox: It's impossible to think about nothing. Even if you attempt to think about nothing, you'll be thinking about thinking about nothing. And that's not your style. You're more a spontaneous Nietzschean than a spontaneous Castanedan. Burly bear. They say bears can't fly. But you're in danger of taking a gigantic flying leap off this bed.

Gogol: Just don't get offended, OK?

Fox: Well?

Gogol: I was just thinking. In theory. Look. There's Anatoly Nevinsky. A writer no one can do shit to. Because he's more popular than Sierakowski. Sierakowski's the guy who disappeared, remember? So. The writer Anatoly Nevinsky cannot be put in prison insofar as he'll continue to write there and become even more well known. He can't be killed insofar as that would only triple his print runs. He can't be made to disappear as that would decuple his print runs. Then this girl shows up at his side, and he falls madly in love with her.

Fox: I understand.

Gogol: Don't look at me like that. You just almost proposed point-blank that I take poison. Both as a writer, and as a Romeo.

Fox: I hope you're joking.

Gogol: Yes. That is, I'm joking—mostly. But, you know, I wouldn't be a fully accomplished paranoiac if I didn't entertain the possibility that you were at my side not just by chance. Listen: I'm telling you this in order to preserve our intimacy. Because when you repress things like this, it's like stuffing your relationship with cotton.

Fox: Yes, I understand.

Gogol: No, you don't understand.

Fox: I understand. You think that I'm an MGB agent and that my assignment is to neutralize you. As a writer. And as a Romeo.

Gogol: Listen. I stopped writing because of . . . Because of us. I'm totally absorbed by our foolishness. That is, all these cars and houses make an impression. It has to be some sort of special project, an expensive special project, an expensive special operation.

Fox: My assignment is to strip you of your ability to write by making you fall in love with me and by demonstrating to you the impossibility of our having any future. Or to make you jealous and force you to attack

Muraviov with a pistol so his security guards can have the pleasure of cutting you down with their machine guns.

GOGOL: All the more probable given that there's already a pistol.

FOX: While Muraviov has never, of course, heard of me; I'm just your usual no-one-knows-anything-about-me major in the elimination squad. He'll be surprised to hear that you've been taken out because the short-barreled Kalashnikovs they carry are mostly to induce fear: they love to roll down the tinted windows of their security vehicles and casually stick them out the window, you know, like a Colombian drug lord out for a drive with his goons. At their massive drinking parties—on MGB day, for example, when even the goons get to drink—they hideously stuff themselves and shoot off rounds into the sky: thank goodness, those drinking bouts take place far from where decent people live . . .

GOGOL: They'll turn me into hamburger before I can even raise my pistol.

FOX: You know what, Nevinsky? I'm not even going to try to talk you out of that. I'm not going to remind you how you found me that night; I didn't find you. I'm not going to mention that I'm the one who's supposed to be afraid of you and not vice versa. I'm the one, after all, who has the real estate abroad and the unlimited credit card, and you're the one who could write a fabulous story for some magazine like *Newsweek*. I'm not going to appeal to logic to prove to you that I'm not an agent of the MGB. For the simple reason that I know what paranoia is. For every one of my arguments your paranoia will obligingly find ten counterarguments. Of course, they planted me on you. Of course, they planned it specially, they anticipated your route that evening, they cleared it of all other girls, and planted me there, drinking a latte macchiato. Oh, go to hell! Sit here and paranoia yourself! Maybe that will help you start writing.

Surveillance object Fox departed the site; 7 minutes later Gogol ran out after her. It was not possible to establish by means of audio monitoring at the site whether they met up out on the street.

Protocol: Audio Documentation
Surveillance site: Private residence, 16 Serafimovich Street, Apt. 7

25 October
Name and rank of recording officer not indicated
[Ascertain]

Gogol opened the apartment with his key at 1700 to begin waiting for Fox. Judging by the sounds from the kitchen, he cooked something, then cleaned up, then read. Fox appeared at 1800. Having made a din with the dishes during their consumption of food, they proceeded to the bathroom, a dead zone for the audio-monitoring system, spending 1 hour and 47 minutes there. During this time the sounds emerging from the bathroom included splashing water, muffled voices in conversation, and sounds indirectly suggesting that the surveillance objects had given themselves over to conjoint bathing. They then relocated to Microphone 1.

GOGOL: Your shoulder fits entirely into my armpit.

Fox: Without any gaps.

GOGOL: Direct proof that we were created for each other. You and I are two halves of one body torn apart and separated to test whether we would find each other.

Fox: Four-legged?

GOGOL: Hadn't you heard? People used to be four-legged and two-headed.

Fox: And reproduced through gemmation.

GOGOL: You're my main part. You contain all my organs. Without you I'd die.

Fox: And which organs are those? All your organs are huge, clumsy, and hairy.

GOGOL: My heart. My heart is inside you. And yours inside me.

Fox: More than anything else I'm afraid that I'm going to have to pay. Happiness like this doesn't just happen. I'm afraid that later on there'll be such unhappiness I won't survive it.

GOGOL: Before this we had unhappiness. The unhappiness of life without us. I'm your reward for having waited.

Fox: What stands in the way of your writing?

Gogol: That's a good way to put it: something stands in the way. A passive, subjectless way to put it. It's raining. Or snowing. And that gets in the way. Neither rain, nor snow, nor writing depends on me . . . But something really is keeping me from writing . . . You know the key thing that I've figured out about writing is that all texts are written with words. Don't laugh. OK, sure, it sounds like a no-brainer, but it's a lot more serious than you might think. Look. Sometimes, when you try to say something global, you turn to language as an intermediary, but the language is the principal component of the message.

Fox: McLuhan. The medium is the message. You've already said that.

Gogol: Keep listening. Try describing the interior of our apartment as it appears in the daylight, when we're not present, as just a room, and you'll inevitably come up against the obstacle that the usual words designating colors, light, and space say nothing. For example, you can't say that this wallpaper is just any color. If you do, you'll lead yourself into a dead end, into a conglomeration of lies. It's not a color; it's a shade of color. Literature is written by language. The author is the operator, the *scripteur,* as Barthes would say.

Fox: Oh! Barthes!

Gogol: Like that rain falling outside—do you hear it? In a text you can't write, "Rain was falling outside the window."

Fox: Outside the window the rain trickled like a woman's tears.

Gogol: Outside the window the rain trickled like an old woman's tears.

Fox: Outside the window the rain trickled like the tears of an elderly philosophy professor now barely strong enough to lift herself out of bed.

Gogol: Outside the window fell a Boldino rain.

Fox: Oh, but without that gypsy! Outside the window the rain fell like a failed writer.

Gogol: Describe us right now. Everything that's going on here.

Fox: They lay curled in a ball on the unmade bed, at the edge of which their discarded blanket chilled like an iceberg. It was exceptionally quiet, so quiet they could play their favorite game of breathing together, breathing in tandem, then she decided to be naughty and held her breath for a second, which threw off his rhythm, forcing him to chase after her like a clumsy bear, and they, both of them, found it amusing that they could hear the distant canned sounds of the train station, which in a sleepy female voice promised the departure of yet another train to distant parts. For them their unlit, rain-ruffled little room held more adventure and happiness than any other place on earth. Now you.

GOGOL: Coruscating from the headlights of passing cars, raindrops provided the sole light source in their tiny room, comprised of wallpaper of an indistinct shade and, anyway, invisible in the darkness, a bed, a chiffonier that looked like a bed stood vertically on end, so had they the capability of walking on the ceiling and along the walls they would surely have attempted to cover it with sheets, blankets, and pillows. Essentially, there was no visual proof that the room itself existed, least of all the crystal phosphorescent drops on the window. The only thing you could speak of with absolute certainty was that the two of them were with each other. Where they were, were they anywhere, or, just the opposite, did wherever they were exist only to the extent that they were with each other—these were questions more worthy of the violets, invisible to the eye, on the nonexistent wallpaper.

FOX: Try "nonexistence wallpapered."

GOGOL: On wallpapered nonexistence. See? I can't write because I can't find the words. The words don't want to flow through my fingers to the keyboard, and to do the writing for language would be too time-consuming and humiliating an endeavor. With zero, moreover, effect. I think that MGB agent Elisaveta Supranovich laced my meat-dumpling bouillon with some special concoction made from the pulverized books of the late Milorad Pavić and minced photographs of Michel Houellebecq, and the elixir has destroyed the neuronal connections between my fingers and brain, thereby annihilating my ability to transmit thought to keyboard. By the way, speaking of neuronal connections: you haven't seen the cheese skewers, have you? I bought some camembert, but can't find the skewers.

FOX: We probably just used them all up.

GOGOL: No way! Last time we used only a couple of them. Where are the rest?

FOX: What is it?

GOGOL: That wretched feeling again that there's someone else here.

FOX: Don't worry, silly! As if they have nothing better to do than swipe cheese skewers!

GOGOL: All right, to hell with them . . .

Fox: If you want to start worrying about our . . . circumstances, how do you camouflage your constant visits here? Still performing those clothes-changing tricks?

Gogol: No. I made a bunch of calls on the most bugged phones I could find and said that I had registered for Spanish classes at Sol. *Patria o muerte,* Che Guevara, *No pasarán.* Sol is right around the corner, on Labor Street. I even went there for real and paid money that I could have, by the way, spent on sweetened condensed milk. That's in case they start checking, but checking not too hard, not too meticulously—at least I'll be on the class rosters. But if they seriously decide to nail me, then, of course, no tricks will help. That's the whole thing: we don't know whether they're tailing me or not. You can't see them. Maybe they don't even exist.

Fox: Uh-huh.

Gogol: Elisaveta? . . . Elisaveta?

The surveillance objects spent the night at the surveillance site; in the morning Fox left first, at 0900.

Protocol: Audio Documentation
Surveillance site: Private residence, 16 Serafimovich Street, Apt. 7

1 November
Intern G. M. Tsyrkun

The surveillance objects appeared at 1800, opening the door with a key. Gogol said, "We have here a typical drama from the age of classicism. Unity of time, place, and action. Each act with the same sets and at the same time." To which Fox replied, "How many meanings the word 'act' has!" Then added that Gogol's "understanding of the unity of time is not Aristotelian." After that the subjects made their way to Microphone 3, continuing to jest.

Gogol: We turn on the light in the tiny kitchen, which seems to consist of only a window, but we don't touch the ugly yellow-glass light fixture that hangs from the ceiling like a spider ready to bite us on the hand were we to take a stretch. No, we turn on the little night-light in the range hood broken long ago. With its pummeled but kindly eye it cuts through the dark, immediately making us want to move closer to each other, because there's not enough light for two, just for one Elisavetanatolia. Go ahead: your turn.

Fox: The light immediately reveals the principal element of the kitchen, its main piece of furniture—the window opening out onto the view.

Gogol: There is no view. It's too dark.

Fox: The view of the pathetic playground, of the little courtyard in front of the tiny patriarchal bathhouse that appears still to be heated with wood. We soar above all this like a lighthouse beam illuminating a stormy ocean of green with the yellow eye of a range hood that died long ago of asphyxiation. We are on the captain's bridge, in the radio-control tower; we are the flight controllers of the world. Turn on the light.

Gogol: See? Why should I write anything after all that?

[*The lighting of candles turns into a kind of horseplay with
kissing noises. The objects arrive at Microphone 1, where they have
"the s-word." After that, having made several incomprehensible
remarks about the nature of the sensations they had experienced
and with no bearing on Section Five's field of interests,
they discuss a certain man.*]

Gogol: Tell me. I really didn't want to start up on this. I'm not even sure that I ought to right now. But still. Tell me. Did you talk to him? You . . . You promised, remember? That you would talk to him. That talking might alleviate the problem. So?

Fox: Darling. Don't. Don't let him into our bed. You shouldn't.

Gogol: I understand everything, Lisa. Everything. You didn't talk to him?

[*Fox emits a sound impossible to reproduce using letters.*]

Gogol: Tell me. Tell me why is it that each time when we start talking about him the expression on your face changes?

Fox: It's very unpleasant for me.

Gogol: Darling, but why in just that way? Your expression doesn't change in a way that says you find him unpleasant.

Fox: Well, what do you want? Well, think about it for yourself!

Gogol: So? Do you love him?

Fox: I don't know how to answer that question. For you. Here.

Gogol: Tell me.

Fox: Maybe I won't?

GOGOL: It's so simple: say no. Dear Lisa. It's so simple! Why won't you answer "no"? Hmm?

[*For a while the monitors produce silence. Then Gogol's footsteps are heard on Microphone 3 (kitchen). Ten minutes later Fox moves to Microphone 3. The conversation resumes.*]

FOX: What are you doing?

GOGOL: Have you ever wondered why this ceramic shoe lies next to those three boxes of matches? It's an ashtray, don't you think?

FOX: More likely a vase.

GOGOL: This shoe-vase full of burned matches? You never wondered? I'll tell you why it's here. Because the woman who owns this apartment is very thrifty. Example: one of the burners on the stove has been lit, and she needs to light another. She doesn't take another match. She pulls a burned match out of the pile in the boot. She lights it on the ignited burner. Like that. Then she looks at the flame for a while. Then she turns on the gas under the second burner, and voila! Thrift and flame, all at once!

FOX: Where is this going?

GOGOL: It's going, dear Elisaveta, to why the matches are lying here. Waiting to be used. They'd really like to burn. Or be thrown out. But they're kept here in this ashtray. Or vase.

FOX: Love is a very complicated word.

GOGOL: "No" is a very simple word. Just two letters. Two.

After that a door slams on Microphone 2: one of them has left. Twenty minutes later the other leaves. No further audio activity was recorded at the surveillance site.

MINISTRY OF STATE SECURITY

Protocol: Audio Documentation
Surveillance site: Private residence, 16 Serafimovich Street, Apt. 7

8 November
Audiotape transcribed by Senior Operations Officer M. G. Tsarikov

Surveillance object Gogol appeared at the apartment at 1100, opening the door with his key. Until 1800 he deported himself quietly, but paced from microphone to microphone. The audio picture allows us to surmise that at 1400 he fried an omelet, and the remainder of the time he gave himself over to reading print matter of the book variety. At approximately 1800 his movements acquired an increasing impatience: first he began to mutter the same words over and over, then to talk to himself. Some phrases he rattled off like tongue twisters; others he drew out slowly. A transcript of pure text, without chronometry, cannot provide a full representation of his monologue, which lasted 5 hours, until 2300, when he departed the surveillance site. At 2007 he went out for 15 minutes, possibly to make a phone call from a telephone booth outside [not recorded].

GOGOL: Lisa. Lisa-the-Fox. Elisaveta. Lizonka. Lizka! Liese. Lizik? Ma chérie. What in the world does he call her? What does he call her? With those thin lips of his. Parting them ever so slightly. How genteel! He probably smiles dreamily, "Leesa." "Nicky," she says. "Bonjour, Nicky." Nicky, shit. Nicky, Nacky, Ticky, Tocky. Wednesday. We meet on Wednesdays. And on Saturdays. Always on Saturdays. On Wednesdays, if we can. Today is Wednesday. You're going to come, right? You understood how I felt when I looked in your eyes and saw a Nikolai in each. In his crimson beret, damn it. You can sense that I'm here, and you know that I'm waiting for you. Can you hear that I'm talking to you? As if! I could go to any part of the city, crawl into the foulest squat hole in Loshytsa, for example. Crawl into it. And mumble to myself, "Dear Lisa, I am very lonely. It smells like cats down here, and I can see Cassiopeia through the roof. Come to me!" You would come, as you came not long ago to the bridge over the Niamiha. We hadn't agreed to meet, but I couldn't take it anymore. It was raining. The entire city was saturated with you. I talked to myself as I walked down the street. You heard me and came. You and I stood before the wall of that waterfall, and the place smelled like cats— no not like cats, like urine, because that place for so long has been not a bridge but a public toilet. Only lunatics in love, like us, could seek refuge from the rain there. You said that you had been sitting at the Hole in the Ground restaurant in Trinity. That suddenly you had been struck by the urge to go out for a walk in the rain. So you left, forgetting your umbrella. When you arrived at the bridge, you turned to go down the stairs, soaked as a homeless cat. I dried your hair with my breath. We knew then that we would never lose each other. That we would always hear each other's call. I'm calling you now. Come, please. Come and bring your "no" with you. Start by saying "no" right at the threshold. A beautiful, unambiguous "no." You've thought about it for a long time. You didn't want to answer immediately. What if I had tricked you? "No." "No," and "no." Forgive me for having made you wait: I know that you have been here since noon. Listen, I need a "no" from you, too. What about this: I'll say no, and you'll just be silent. I know that you don't love him. Silly Lisa, now I know what love is. If you loved him, I wouldn't exist. You see? Let's do it this way: I'll say no, and you'll ring the doorbell. And that will mean that I've got it all right. Let's do it? Listen, don't get miffed at me!

[*Kitchen (Microphone 3)*]

Water's dripping somewhere. Is that the faucet leaking? I'll have to poke around in it this afternoon. Or leave everything as is. Plop again. Shit, first it's not dripping, then all of a sudden it drips twice in a row. If it drips now, she'll come. It dripped! See, it heard! It dripped! Or did I just imagine it did? Got to turn on the big light. Oops, it dripped! But I wasn't trying to make a wish on it! Fuck it! What am I doing?

Lisa, just tell me what you want me to do to make you come? What? Do you want me to promise that it will never happen again? "What" won't happen? That I won't throw any more fits? Was that really a . . . Wow, excellent! Agreed. No more fits. I understand. Good. Now come on, ring the doorbell. Well? Damn!

Is it so hard for her to drive over here? It's obvious, totally understandable that I'm here! After a conversation like that . . . Although . . . I'm the one who left. I was the first to leave. That was no way to leave.

She might be at her palace in Tarasova. At her palace in Sokol. In the mansion in Raubichi. In one of her apartments in town. She could be speeding through the night somewhere on her way to Braslav, where she also has a residence. She's not thinking about me, and she can't hear me. She . . . she may be listening to the piano now, wiping away tears over a talented, soul-rending performance, from the concentration of human pain that pours itself out into a melody in a minor key. Why don't I know French? Why don't I play the piano? Why is it that when I feel down, all I can do is just howl, h-ow-ow-owl, and h-ow-ow-owl. That's so unmelodic. Damn it, real pain is never melodic. You're with him, yes? I shouldn't get in your way with my whispering? You're sleeping with him? Stroking his pedigree face? He's looking somewhere out into the distance, upward, right through you, and you're thinking about what kind of chin he has: no, not quite strong-willed, just a handsome chin that suggests thin musical fingers. You look at me like that sometimes, and I, to be honest, think . . . Think what? I'm afraid, afraid that I'm repeating one of his poses, one of his turns, and you're looking not at me, but at him. Ah, how I would play! A *Kreutzer Sonata* of some sort! You would weep. You would love me. I don't know how to do anything except scribble, and even that I can't do. What is it that I want? You love him by right. I'm an addendum, an emergency backup airport, a match in an ashtray. Second fiddle in a *Kreutzer Sonata* written for one.

That's cool. No big deal. A sex-friend. That's what people do these days. She never told me that she loved me. And you can understand why. She probably doesn't get enough tenderness. While I . . . It's my problem that I ran like crazy, baring my soul. It's cool. No big deal. Chill. Let it be. I'll love you quietly, so no one notices. Listen, enough already, huh? I'm going to lose it! Come already, huh? We're not going to talk about all this. I'll make you some black tea. Brew it too strong, and you'll scold me, but you'll really like it. We'll sit together and look at the blackness in the depths of the window, and contemplate the brake lights of the passing cars, and imagine that they're fireflies. I'll hug you, scoop you up as a bear would, under his arm, although what the hell kind of bear am I! Come? Come, huh? Dear, please? Lisa? My dear.

Surveillance object Gogol left without making contact with Fox, who did not make an appearance at the surveillance site.

MINISTRY OF STATE SECURITY

Protocol: Audio Documentation
Surveillance site: Private residence, 16 Serafimovich Street, Apt. 7

11 November
Operations Officer Second Lieutenant M. P. Sirakozha

Gogol and Fox appeared at the surveillance site at 1809 and opened the door with a key. While opening the door, Fox continued some thought she had:

Fox: I couldn't come, because I drove to my grandmother's in Kobryn, and only an inattentive burly bear like Anatoly Nevinsky would be unable to pick up on that.

GOGOL: Oh. Don't.

FOX: What?

GOGOL: Don't lie, Elisaveta. You shouldn't lie. To me.

[*After that the surveillance objects were silent for a while. Then on Microphone 1 came sounds of the bedroom variety and in part resembling those of a struggle. A lot of wheezing, fast breathing, and moans that sounded as if from pain. After 17 minutes the bedroom sounds were over and the surveillance objects again fell silent for several minutes. Conversation was initiated by Fox.*]

FOX: Don't you dare do that with me. You hear? Never dare do that with me.

GOGOL: But you were liking it. You didn't stop me. Maybe you're afraid to admit to yourself that you enjoy it precisely that way?

FOX: If you want to do it that way, get yourself a prostitute. Just don't do it with me.

[*After a pause of 8 minutes, over the course of which the surveillance objects emitted only heavy breathing, Fox renewed the conversation, but changed the subject to another partner of hers.*]

FOX: I was a third-year student at the Linguistics University: French, English, Spanish, Baudelaire, Verlaine, Rimbaud, Lautréamont. The smoke of opium on the page, words that whimsically curled and intertwined like rings of smoke, and thick clouds of smoke on all floors of the dorm: a combination that could have turned anyone into a Baudelaire. We memorized them all by heart, quoted them to each other, and choked with laughter when reading Soviet literary historians. There was one, a certain G. K. Kosikov. Whenever we got together for a party, we'd greet each other with a phrase from one of his articles, "Baudelaire Between the Rapture of Life and the Horror of Life." We would pat each other on the shoulder, and one person would ask, "But how do you liberate the imagination? How do you achieve the supernatural state of the soul?" The other would answer, again quoting Kosikov, "Narcotics? Cosmetics? Fashion? Dandyism?" and recite Baudelaire's famous phrase about how wine sharpens a person's senses and strengthens his character. Under Kosikov's banner we would crawl out for wine. There were French people everywhere. A French flag on the wall. Homework assignments to write something in French in Baudelaire's manner, and I composed a poem after his "L'Étranger" about clouds floating past the dorm roofs, fantastic pilgrim clouds, clouds that took the place of father, mother, and sister. Clouds that had never known family.

Then one day our happy-go-lucky university was informed that we were to be visited by the head of the MGB, Comrade Muraviov. We all, of course, nodded understandingly to each other as if to say we're the freest of all: we think in French, we write poems in English, and we can blow this country. They're going to try to brainwash us so we'll line up and stand at attention with the rest of our happy family of nations. For a week they aired the dorm of smoke clouds. Men in plainclothes spent three whole days walking around the classrooms and summonsing the more strident boys, the ones who liked to march down the streets with a drum and chant "The enemy is the state." On the appointed day we were all gathered in the main auditorium, held (just for good measure) for an hour and a half without fresh air, and, to knock us down a peg, not allowed out to use the toilet.

GOGOL: That's a tactic of theirs described in detail in their textbooks and referred to as "Subduing Emotional Outbreaks by Engaging the 'Call of Nature.'" Even if you want to call Muraviov a cannibal, after an hour and a half of waiting only one thing is going to be of any interest to you: to have it all end as soon as possible, get some air, and take a leak. Let someone else call him a cannibal.

FOX: Then in comes one of the Chaldeans constantly at his side to announce with great fanfare: "Ladies and Gentlemen! Minister of State Security Nikolai Mikhailovich Muraviov!" And they lead him in. With unbelievable pomp, of course, and an escort of security men in black. Then came the most interesting part. You understand that all of those gathered to greet him considered him shit. Every last one. And you couldn't say that he talked for a long time. And you couldn't say that he spoke well. That was the biggest mystery: no one could remember his speech, only his intonations and those attentive eyes of his. The papers, of course, published a transcript, but it's all just gibberish: about joining the Bologna agreement and the percent of the GDP spent on educational needs. And it seemed to everyone . . . that he sort of talked about childhood. And something else. That he told anecdotes, and therefore everyone laughed until they cried. I later asked him what he had wanted to say to us . . . But he just waved me off, as if to say, "I don't remember." When he finished his speech, everyone was in love with him. Everyone. Both the

girls and the guys. If anyone after that told a joke about him, there would
be this pause . . . really awkward, and the joke-teller would then apologize
for having said something stupid. The consensus was that he had been
very humane with us, kind. How could you make fun of him? What?

GOGOL: No, no, I didn't say a word.

FOX: It seemed to me that you . . .

GOGOL: You imagined it. I'm listening attentively.

FOX: I sat in the seventh row. All through his speech I had the feeling
that he was looking only at me, that he never took his eyes off me. That the
entirety of his heart-to-heart speech was directed only at me. Of course,
I was happy, then the girls said that they all had thought the same thing.

Three days later I walked into my dorm room—we lived one to a room
in blocks of three rooms with a common shower and toilet.

GOGOL: I know what the dorms are like.

FOX: So I get to my room and on the bed stand (the one I'd sat at
while writing about the clouds) is an enormous bouquet of white roses.
He . . . He always gave me white roses. Always the same shade: a little bit
cold, not the color of tea, more like emerald. As soon as I entered the block
I smelled the incredibly dense, even somewhat marine-like fragrance of
roses. A fragrance so overpowering that my head began to swim, like my
Baudelairesque cloud over the dorm . . . Right, so I opened my room, and
I saw this bouquet . . . It . . . It even made me shiver. It was a bit frighten-
ing, like seeing a hanged man. Something wafted from them . . .

GOGOL: Keep going!

FOX: At first, I wasn't frightened: the door to my room didn't lock, the
keys to the block were kept by the door guard downstairs, and another
copy kept by the floor manager. I immediately thought that Valka—this
one guy—had done it. He was a quiet kind of guy from the third floor.
I don't think I even tried to figure it out and just allowed myself to float
with these flowers on the wave of their fragrance. At night I had incredible dreams . . . My girlfriends, of course, immediately got all worked up:
Who? What? When? Which is why, probably, I was so calm, because they
were all so worked up. I thought about it within the context of the dorm.
Like "Valka's still a loser, and his hair is still greasy, and he's still got dan-
druff." That same evening the two of us ran into each other, and I looked
at him, very attentively, but he just turned his belfry the other way. Sending roses was OK, but talking made him sweat? In short, I didn't even
touch them; it seemed sort of weird to. Like touching Valka's dandruffy

146

hair. As if they'd leave greasy stains on my hands. So he sent me a bouquet of flowers? No big deal.

Anyway, exactly three days later—the flowers hadn't even begun to wilt, only the fragrance had abated a bit—I was standing in the shower. I had a lecture in forty minutes, and the bus ride took thirty. I was late already, and upset. All around there wasn't a sound, not even a draft. (Our block was at the end of the corridor, and the door to the balcony was always open because people went out there to smoke. Every time the door to the block opened, a draft swept in across the floor . . .) But there was nothing. Then, through the steam, through the smell of my shower gel— came another, very strong, marine-like wave of fragrance. I got out of the shower and opened the door to my room. Shit! A fresh bouquet stood on the table. The same kind of roses—snow-white with a touch of emerald. I clenched my teeth, quickly got dressed, and went to class. In the evening I went over to Valka's, mad and ready to stuff that bouquet . . . But he just bulged his eyes over the top of his glasses, cracked the door of his room open, and there behind him was a head. With a cold cream mask and what looked like cucumbers on her forehead. "Let me introduce you. This is my fiancée, Dina, from the medical institute." In short, Valka was no longer a suspect. I ran down to the door guard: "Who took the key to our block?" The door guard was a regular Brunhilde, as big around as an ancient oak they could have hanged the Decembrists from. She raised her plucked eyebrows and lit into me with a wave of cussing, threatening me that if I was going to take studs up to my room in violation of the rules, then come to her with complaints, she'd . . . ! In short, I was sure that the door guard hadn't given anyone the keys. The floor manager's reaction was the same. In the room to the right of mine in the block lived a young couple with a five-month-old baby. They couldn't care less about anything and they had no reason to lie, and, besides, they didn't know how. The room to the left was empty: no one had lived there the last six months or so. In short, three days later, there was yet another bouquet when I came home. This time I started crying, and the police were called in, but they just sort of stood around joking, asked a few questions, and didn't bother investigating.

GOGOL: Of course! They take orders from the MGB. The militia is a subsidiary organization. The lowest in the pecking order.

Fox: Do you really think they knew?! They have nothing else to do except be on the lookout for some guy in the dorm with a crush? In short, there I was, one on one with the bouquet. That's when I got scared. You understand: it finally dawned on me that I was totally exposed. Some psychopath was stalking me, even when I was shaving my legs or putting on eye makeup. Or reading in the nude.

GOGOL: So? The majority of people in this country over the age of twenty-five feel precisely the same way.

FOX: You don't understand. This was also extremely personal. Someone needed me. Me and nobody else. Someone knew my schedule, when I woke, when I went to the shower, and how much time I spent in there. Very soon after, I landed in bed with an unbelievably nasty chest cold. I didn't leave my room for five days. The bouquets were changed when I dozed off, as fever transported me into crimson, pulsating delirium. In short, I left whoever it was a note right alongside the vase. Something like "Stop this. You're scaring me. Don't spy on me. Tell me what you want from me." I thought that once I had an answer from him—something on the order of "I want to slice your body into forty pieces, fry it in vegetable oil, and gobble it down during a full moon"—I'd go back to the police, and those underage junior sergeants would stop making fun of me and get to work. His reaction was very elegant. I found no more flowers on my table. But they started to appear everywhere else. On downspouts, when I was out walking. I would find them in my boots when leaving some crowded party, when everyone went into the entrance hall to get dressed. I got on a crowded trolleybus and found a bouquet lying on one of the seats—for me. There were never any notes attached to them. Not a single word. He told me later that he had intended to court me like that forever, from the shadows, unobtrusively. He said that it would have been enough for him. I was the first to request we meet.

GOGOL: Why are you telling me all this?

FOX: In order for you to understand, my sad, silly bear: people are never 100 percent bad. Unfortunately, they're not 100 percent good either. Each of us has some good inside us. And beauty. And a ton of other qualities. I guess I'm just trying to explain to you why I couldn't answer "no" to your question.

GOGOL: Then why are you with me? Why aren't you looking for more of the good in him?

FOX: That question is the answer. The answer, my dear. The answer. An answer capable of dispelling all the chimeras beleaguering you. I am with you. With you, you hear? With you, and that's it!

Judging by sounds that resembled someone gulping back a stuffy nose and muffled frequent "coughs" like those a person makes when shivering outside in the cold, surveillance object Gogol was sobbing. After a while Fox joined him in emitting analogous sounds. Seventeen minutes later all the sounds dissipated, and the surveillance objects fell asleep (snoring, wheezing). One of them rose at 0345 and began to dress, wakened the other, and for a while the two of them made kissing sounds, then indulged in a bedroom scene they maintained for 35 minutes. After that they rested for 7 minutes, then continued dressing, which this time they successfully completed. Passing to Microphone 2, they departed the surveillance site, locking the door with a key.

MINISTRY OF STATE SECURITY

Protocol: Audio Documentation
Surveillance site: Private residence, 16 Serafimovich Street, Apt. 7

14 November
Operations Group Officer Major A. Semukha

After entering the apartment (having opened the door with a key), the surveillance objects spent a long time moving about the rooms in silence. After entering the range of Microphone 3 (the kitchen), they made a racket with metal pots, then, judging by the sounds, opened the window with considerable difficulty, almost breaking it in the process. The first to engage in the act of speech was Gogol. Audio monitoring was hampered owing to the fact that their voices were directed in the opposite direction, out the window into the courtyard.

GOGOL: You know, it's all the same to me, "no" or "yes." It's all the same to me how you're going to respond in the future. What's more, I'm not going to bother to ask you. It's just that when you're not with me, I can't breathe. As if there's less air. We're standing here side by side, looking down, and November this year is so cold. Your side warms my side, and I have no desire at all to talk. Words should be abolished. Everything would be so simple, if they didn't exist . . . In our kitchen you and I are in our den. Leaning out this window, we peer into the dark of the night. And everything has already been said. Lisa. That says it all.

FOX: [*Inaudible*]

GOGOL: I know you feel the same way. When we're together, everything is good. When we're apart, when we're waiting for our next Saturday or next Wednesday, everything is out of place. The whole world is out of place. But now everything is where it should be. There's no need to speak. I can describe in minute detail how my perception changes just before one of our meetings. About three hours before there's more air to breathe. I begin to feel happy. Then, when I'm already on my way to meet you, everything acquires meaning. The puddles. The cars. The people, whose faces become so beautiful. Then the game starts: I attempt to determine where we'll meet. Today, for example, I immediately figured out that I should wait for you in the archway, but sometimes you're standing not where you're supposed to, or you come too early. You see, that's why I always arrive early. I'm afraid that if you have to wait for me, you'll take offense and leave. I go home and wait for you here. You show up. There's no need to say anything anymore. Neither "no," nor "yes." What's more: it's all the same to me if you have someone else. It seems to me that you'll come out from under it, that it will pass. Because now we're the way we are. Because we're side by side, looking down, leaning out the window.

FOX: [*Inaudible*]

GOGOL: If you love someone, I will love him, too. The thing is, Lisa, we can never part. It's happened. It's too late! Don't you feel that? We even breathe together.

[*The surveillance objects locked the window and proceeded to Microphone 1. Coitus extended over a period of 55 minutes. Then the conversation was renewed.*]

FOX: Set a time and a place.

GOGOL: Let's meet where we blew bubbles. [*Note: location has been identified as the bridge across the Svislach on Independence Avenue—Section Five, External Control and Surveillance Division.*]

FOX: Let's meet by the screen where they almost hauled us in. [*Note: location identified as October Square—Section Five, External Control and Surveillance Division.*]

GOGOL: How about the place where we looked through the telescope? [*Note: location identified as Gorky Park planetarium—Section Five, External Control and Surveillance Division.*]

FOX: Are you happy now?

GOGOL: Yes.

Fox: And what is happiness?

Gogol: I think that it's a property imminently inherent in every being. But in predetermined quantities. No matter how much life might beat you down or bring you joy, your level of happiness will always be the same.

Fox: You mean, if we go our separate ways now, burly bear would be just as happy?

Gogol: The fact is, Elisaveta, that you, like happiness, are also imminently inherent in my being.

Fox: Can you remember a situation when your life was total shit, but you were still happy?

Gogol: I have to think. Right. For example: my first book had just come out, strange, with a letter *b*. [*Proofreader's note: The audio fragment was incorrectly decoded; the correct reading is "My first book had just come out*—The Country Whose Name Begins with *B*.] I was immediately asked to leave the school. Just because. As a kind of prophylactic: the book hadn't been banned and was in all the bookstores, waiting to be bought. But it contained a couple of observations . . . In short, owing to a stupid coincidence, I found myself deprived of the classroom portraits of Gogol, Tolstoy, and Dostoevsky that had been so dear to my heart. Teaching had been so good, honest! A classroom filled with light, the high school girls—hey, no hitting!—and the feeling that life was just beginning, that the ingenuousness of their perception was rubbing off on me. We would analyze books I had read hundreds of years ago, and those books took on relevance, like blockbusters released just yesterday. And then . . . No students, and no work. I couldn't get a job at any other school because I'd been blacklisted.

I found work at a parking lot out in one of the industrial districts. I remember how in the evening the mighty towers of the power plant across the road would cover the lot with their shadows. For days on end I sat at an oilcloth-covered table. Our booth had a tiny television with prickly needles for an antenna and a padded bench that was totally flat but suited me just fine because, while sleeping there was cozy enough, I slept only in bursts. The job was no honeymoon. When a car drove up to the gate, I had to push a button. The same when someone drove out. According to instructions, we were supposed to bend down, look the driver in the eye, and compare his face to his pass, but I quickly blew that off: no one stole cars anymore; the MGB had instituted a little law and order. And so, no sooner would I fall asleep and get all warmed up

151

and warm up the bench, and just as the streetlights outside the window had begun to metamorphose into something from a fairy tale and totally phantasmagoric, than someone would honk their horn from outside the gate. That meant that they had already flashed their headlights and now, having lost patience entirely, were leaning on the horn. We had to open the gate for them immediately, so I jumped out of bed, groped around, not remembering where the switch was, and it was dark, with nothing but a desk lamp that you also had to figure out how to turn on. Where just seconds ago there had been stars sculpted from streetlamps, there were no lights. Finally, though, I felt the gate button, then waited until they drove in. I was still plastered in sleep, but we couldn't lie down: we had to wait until the driver got out, walked around the car, looked at it, adjusted something on it, the bastard, opened the trunk, took some sort of bag out of it, moseyed over to our birdhouse, and tossed his pass in the window. Now I could sleep. I stuck the pass somewhere and raced to catch up on my sleep, while the stars had already melted, the stars were now just streetlamps, and the bench pad was cold and damp, as if the guy on the shift before had spilled beer on it . . . No sooner would I sink back into that world, warm it up, and tuck it under myself, than someone else would honk, and once again I'd drag myself off the bench pad onto the wooden, sand-crusted floor, and start palming the wall, looking for the hidden gate button. I was on for twenty-four hours, then slept it off at home. But even at home every honk of a car horn outside my window would send me falling out of bed to palm the wall where there was none—the wall was on the right-hand side, the sofa stood in a different place, and I recognized the gloom of my own place, crawled back into bed, covered myself up, and fell back asleep.

Fox: Were you happy?

Gogol. Never had life been so good. I often remember my evenings at the lot, how I had developed a passion for soccer—although I'd always hated it and despise it now. But there I used to watch soccer, even cheer for a team, the one with the gray-striped socks. Make some hot mush for the dog—a giant sheepdog that was sweet as a kitten . . . After that it was sausage for me. After that Uncle Seryozha showed up. He worked the other shift: he had trouble at home—his daughter, I think it was, had kicked him out of the house because he got in her way . . . He used to drop by in the evening to shoot the breeze (he called me professor), and what conversations we used to have! He was as wise as Socrates. I remember how when he heard my story about being fired from the school, he broke out laughing and said that only now had I become a real writer. I was pumping out my second book at that point, thirty pages a day . . . We used to watch soccer together. The BBC came there to see me, to make a film about me. Uncle Seryozha even got interviewed: he made some sort of speech about how the times were such that the only job a decent person could get was as a watchman. In the mornings I made myself strong coffee in a military-surplus pewter cup on a propane stove. It was so delicious! Ah! He'd come out, leaning on the banisters that had been welded together out of rails, the sun would emerge from behind the concrete-panel apartment buildings far off on a hill, and I had the sense that I understood everything about life. Everything. Over there in those buildings people were waking up. Getting dressed. Drinking tea for breakfast. Heading off to work. While I could sit and read Borges and retell him to Uncle Seryozha in the evening.

FOX: Oh, that's interesting! Retell Borges. How do you do that?

GOGOL: One day this guy finds this thing under the stairs in his house. How can I explain this, Uncle Seryozha? It's like all the things in the world are collected in that one thing. You look inside it and you immediately see everything. That steam plant of ours, the automotive suspension plant, the mines in Sologorsk, and everyone who works there. Here you're supposed to ask how he had enough eyes to see it all.

FOX: So, son, how did he have enough eyes to see it all?

GOGOL: "Son" isn't one of Uncle Seryozha's words. Better "Tolyan."

FOX: You're talkin' some pretty weird stuff! What people won't think up! So, Tolyan, how'd this guy have enough eyes to see it all?

GOGOL: He would sort of switch from one thing to the next. He saw horses against the sunrise on the shore of the Caspian Sea; he saw the decaying remains of his beloved in the ground; he saw Earth from all angles. He could have gone a whole year and not got up, just looking. Here you're supposed to ask, "So what'd he do with that thing?"

FOX: And what'd he decide to do with that thing? Sell it to buy himself hooch?

GOGOL: Elisaveta. You have very distorted ideas about simple people. If a man works as a watchman at a parking lot, it doesn't mean that he's . . . primitive. He doesn't reduce everything to just "buying hooch." It's a lot more complex. Uncle Seryozha, by the way, knew how to take pleasure in beauty more genuinely than you do.

Fox: So what'da hell d'he do with dat ting? Figure out a way to make use of it for people? Make some sort of car out of it? Or television?

Gogol: That, Uncle Seryozha, is how one of Borges's contemporaries, the Soviet writer Andrei Platonov, would have thought. But we're talking about Borges. The critical twist in his plots is always something a regular person, sort of like you and me, could bust his brain on but never be able to predict where he's gonna take the plot. The story ends with the house with the thing being demolished. And the poet who had used it to describe distant parts of the world in his poem breaks down. But, again, Borges wouldn't be Borges, but Kuprin, if he left it at that. It ends with the thing found in the demolished house turning out to be a fake. The real one was in a mosque in Cairo, hidden away in one of the pillars. How's that for postmodern?

Fox: Well, I'll be damned! So what's the difference between the real one and the fake?

Gogol: That's not the point!

Fox: Then, Tolyan, what is the point?

Gogol: The point, Uncle Seryozha, is that the story is about love. It ends with the hero trying to remember whether he'd seen that thing for real or whether he'd just imagined it. Then he switches to his dead beloved and realizes that he's forgetting, irretrievably forgetting, the features of her face.

Fox: Each of us is an aleph. Each of us contains all the facial features of all the people on earth. Is there a lot of Uncle Seryozha in me?

Gogol: There's precious little Uncle Seryozha in you. Very little. You're not at all alike.

Fox: Every human being is an aleph. I see your face in every passerby.

Gogol: I know which passerby you're talking about, but it might just be that you're the aleph. That you're capable of finding anyone you want in me. That's why the big question is whether you need me at all.

Fox: Remember what I told you? I am with you, you hear? When we're together, there is air to breathe.

Twelve minutes later the surveillance objects left the surveillance site.

Protocol: Audio Documentation
Surveillance site: Private residence, 16 Serafimovich Street, Apt. 7

18 November
Resolution: In light of the nature of the problems discussed at the rendez-
vous described herein, this protocol is to be removed from the case file
and designated top secret.
Section Five
Audio-Documentation Command
Colonel Sokolov, Head

At 1907 the surveillance objects penetrated the apartment simultaneously, having opened the door with a key.

GOGOL: Well, where are you dragging me? Let me at least take off my
coat! Hang my hat on the antlers. Huh, if we were to be overheard by
someone who didn't know that the coatrack looked like deer antlers—not
looked like, but really was deer antlers—they might think that "hang my
hat on the antlers" meant to put it on my head, and not to take it off. Why
the kitchen? Uh, I'd prefer to be dragged over there: look how the bedroom has opened its jaws! The bedroom has opened its jaws, and I want
to fall on the pillows! Lisa! Come fall on the pillows with me! Well! Why
are you so serious? Has something happened?

FOX: Sit down and stop joking. I think that you're feeling wonderful,
but I have something to talk to you about, and precisely for that reason
you're making jokes, because you're afraid. Don't be afraid. Everything is
in our hands.

GOGOL: At least I can put on the teakettle. Will you have some tea? Tea
served from the paws of a bear . . .

FOX: Sit down and listen. I've been preparing myself for this . . . For a
long time . . . And I still don't know where to start . . . At the last moment
each time I would tell myself: when I get there, I'm going to look at him,
and I'll immediately figure it all out. I'll figure out what to do. And I look.
And I don't know. I am not going to cry, because I've already cried myself
out over everything there is to cry about. So. Now I need to tell you.

[*Gogol is silent. Fox pours tea.*]

Fox: That great master of nuance, Ryūnosuke Akutagawa, has a short story where the hero, a profligate Buddhist monk–alcoholic, tells of the three fundamental circles of hell: the hell of distance, the hell of closeness, and the hell of loneliness. "Beneath the world where all living things breathe, hell stretches for five hundred *ri*," I think is how it goes. Underneath the earth there are only two circles of hell: the hell of distance and the hell of closeness. The hell of loneliness, as Akutagawa writes, "is in the ethereal spheres above the mountains, the fields, and the forests"; that is, at any moment a person's happiness can turn into eternal torture and suffering. Right. Here Akutagawa ends, and I begin. I have a vague suspicion that all the hells a person might encounter begin right here, on this earth. All of them, not just the hell of loneliness. The hell of loneliness is punishment for our transgressions. Why await the punishment in the afterlife, when all punishment is right here? Try to love two people, and there's your hell. But hell is not a tormenting recollection of something already committed that occurs to you just before the end, as you said, but here, in the real world, in everyday life. No matter what you do, you make someone hurt. One of the two. Ah, screw all these literary associations! What kind of bizarre habit is it to build your most serious conversations on literature?

It seems to me that this conversation is going to be our last, Anatoly. Give me your palm. Like that. Look me straight in the eye. I told you that I was with you and would stay with you forever. Now it's up to you to decide for how long. Here. Under my heart. Right here there is another living creature. Guilty of nothing, sacred. In the grand scheme of things I have no relation to it; it's been decided for me that it should come into being inside me, that I'm to be its vessel.

Gogol: You're pregnant! Wow! So what are all the tears about! That's! . . . We'll leave the country! We'll save it!

Fox: Stop, stop, stop. If only it were all that simple.

Gogol: A boy or a girl?

Fox: I don't know. It's too early to tell.

Gogol: That's wonderful! There are three of us! Three, love!

Fox: I'm telling you, it's not that simple!

Gogol: What's not that simple? We're having a baby! A little child!

Fox: There aren't three of us, but four.

Gogol: What?

FOX: That. There aren't three of us. From the very beginning there weren't two of us, but three. And now there are four.

GOGOL: What are you getting at? Whoa! I'm going to be a father!

FOX: Come to your senses, OK! Who told you that you were going to be a father? Who?

[*Gogol says nothing for 4 minutes, 20 seconds;*
Fox pours him some tea.]

GOGOL: What does that mean? How's that? You? . . .

[*Fox says nothing.*]

GOGOL: You were sleeping with him all this time? Yes? With me and with him? That's it, isn't it?

FOX: Two lumps of sugar?

GOGOL: You were trying to keep us out of danger, right? You were afraid that he would suspect something and knock me off, right? So, therefore, you went to bed with him? Or what? I don't understand! Lisa, I don't understand! I don't understand how you could . . . with me and with him. How could you? The very idea that you touched him on the shoulder when he told you about his son almost sent me off the deep end! But you and he were . . .

[*Gogol begins to shout.*]

For the life of me, I just don't get it! Why didn't you tell me? So what now? Look what you've done now!

FOX: It seems to me that it would be easier for us to have this conversation if there were leaves on the trees. Those black silhouettes against the light of the streetlamps? They're so barbed. Just looking at them makes you want to die. If only it were July now, and the leaves were rustling, and it were possible to talk and go for a walk, and there were bugs, and gnats, and life all around . . . We would walk arm in arm, and everything would be all right.

[*Gogol says nothing.*]

I didn't tell you everything about the time we met when . . . when he played . . . Rather, you wouldn't let me tell it all. You see . . . he's the same kind of man as you, only twenty years older. Can you imagine someone taking me away from you, and you're twenty years older? With no hope whatsoever? . . . Whether you're the Minister of State Security or a janitor, how could you live with that? I saw that he knew everything. He knew everything about us from the very beginning. He felt it. I saw it in every stroke of his hand . . . Well, I felt sorry for him. I stroked his hair. I felt the pain that this creature, this bundle of nerves, had undergone. And I, I was the only one to blame. For him I was . . . his hope for turning over a new leaf. A hidden, kind, beautiful world that existed parallel to his everyday existence replete with the roaring of beasts. With his alcoholic wife and drug addict son. He believed in me as the light of his life. To betray such faith would be a greater crime than murder. I stroked his hair, and he sobbed over his Mozart. Then when you and I happened . . . I thought about you. I understood what hell is. People like you and I are incapable of committing adultery. He immediately sensed you in me, in my entire being, and became stiff as wood again. He didn't come down to see me to my car.

GOGOL: Did you see him after that?

FOX: No. He stopped calling me.

GOGOL: You're sure that the baby is his, and not . . . not ours . . . ?

FOX: In terms of timing, it's his. Your favorite word. Ovulation.

GOGOL: And what now?

FOX: I wanted to ask you what's next. I don't know what's next. I'm tired and confused.

[*Twelve minutes later*]

Here's what we'll do. I'm going to wash the cup and put it to dry. I'm going to go into the entrance hall and put on my coat. I'm going to open the door. I am going to turn back and look at you. All the time I'm doing this you have the opportunity to ask me to come back. If you ask me, Anatoly, I will come back here, to the kitchen, and we will resume drinking tea and thinking about what to do with all this. If you think that I don't understand what the danger is for me that I have Nikolai Muraviov's illegitimate child under my heart, then you're mistaken. Mistaken. I understand it all perfectly well. So. If you don't tell me to come back, Anatoly, I'm going to close the door, and after that we will never see each other again. You understood all that?

No auditory response was registered. After that there were sounds of activity in the kitchen (the sound of water, the ring of a cup), a person's footsteps toward Microphone 2, the rustle of a raincoat being put on, a 30-second pause of total silence, and the click of a closing door. Judging by the audio signal from the surveillance site, Gogol did not see Fox to the door. After sitting in the kitchen for 40 minutes, he got up, walked to the entrance hall, and, forgetting to put on his coat, walked out without locking the apartment with his key.

MINISTRY OF STATE SECURITY

SECTION FIVE

COMMENTARY FROM THE AUDIO-DOCUMENTATION DIVISION

On 19, 20, 21, 22, 23, 24, 25, 26, 27, 28 November surveillance object Gogol appeared at the surveillance site—Private Residence, 16 Serafimovich Street, Apt. 7—but spent the time there alone. Each visit commenced at 1200 and concluded at 2300. The nature of his nervous peregrinations about the site and of his continuous conversations with himself suggests that he anxiously awaited the arrival of surveillance object Fox, but to no avail. Of particular note were his obsessive, repetitive requests addressed in the informal "you" to a certain subject not present at the surveillance site to "cancel" certain "conditions." Thus, on 26 November, for 2 hours Gogol paced from microphone to microphone, repeating, "That was unfair. Love, that was unfair. I hadn't had a chance to understand anything. I didn't even see you to the door. You shouldn't have proposed that. We needed to talk it all through. You should have given me some time to think. That was unfair," etc. We would characterize the psychoemotional state of surveillance object Gogol as overwhelmed, with all the symptoms of deep depression of a destructive nature. On 28 November, while peregrinating through the apartment as if searching it, he repeatedly emitted psychotic expressions, such as: "I'm asking you to come back." "You hear?" "I'm asking you." "Come back," etc.

Surveillance object Fox did not appear, call, or contact Gogol by any audio-monitorable means on any of these days, leading us to conclude that either the relationship between them had ruptured owing to a personal disagreement, or that all reliable channels of communication between them by which they might have agreed on an assignation had been severed, or that something had happened to Fox to preclude her appearance at the surveillance site. On 29 November Gogol did not appear at the

159

site, and from 1 December, in connection with the end of the rental period for which the owner had been paid, the apartment was leased to 2 female students from the Institute of Physical Education (M. K. Reborian, originally from the city of Glybokae) and Iu. M. Sramniuk (from Gomel) for temporary occupancy (3 months).

MINISTRY OF STATE SECURITY
TO MINISTER OF STATE SECURITY
N. M. MURAVIOV
RECOMMENDATION FOR DECORATION AND BONUSES

For their painstaking labor monitoring field-operations site Private Residence, 16 Serafimovich Street, Apt. 7, we recommend Senior Operations Officer E. P. Tsupik for decoration and early promotion, and L. L. Skrygan and P. D. Movseisiuk for Luch wristwatches. Senior Operations Officer E. P. Tsupik also is recommended for transfer to the Section Five Clandestine Division, and Senior Lieutenant A. M. Gevorkian for demotion and transfer from the Section Five Audio-Documentation Division to the MGB State Property Protection Service. Following complete and exhaustive documentation on the site, all forms of monitoring have been withdrawn.

29 November
Ministry of State Security
Section Five
Audio-Documentation Command
Colonel Sokolov, Head

PART THREE

1

WHAT CAN I TELL YOU about those first days without you? I remember a door closing: not loud, but in the way that signals final farewells—delicate and quiet, as if the metal were afraid to intrude too much on our memories. It wasn't a slam, but a click resembling a whisper. You had left, right? Why was I in the kitchen and not in the entrance hall at that moment? It seems I was already talking to you at that moment, or did that begin later?

It was as if everything had turned into a comic strip. Or a movie shot with strobe lighting. As if each third frame in the video of my life had been excised by some invisible editor. As if I were watching myself from the side, in total darkness, and brightly flickering spotlights illuminated first hands raised in dance, then hair frozen in midair, then a jump. To this very moment I continue to exist in that ambiguous, bobbing light, in those disconnected, jerking movements. As if after that click of the door in farewell the light penetrating my consciousness through the gun slits of my eyes dimmed slightly, as if an internal shutter had narrowed. The days grew gloomier, while the nights, on the contrary, lighter: they had lost the blackness that had once given them color. Everything real had faded, but perhaps it's the insomnia, the insomnia.

I saw myself as if from behind, as if in a music video, with a melody even—an intolerable, compulsive melody—that swelled and faded, a kind of compulsive glam sung in a shrill male voice. Something like UPA-PA, UPA-PA, UPA-PA, UPA-PA, I GOT YOU, BABY, UPA-PA. I jumped and rocked to it—sometimes too fast, sometimes too slowly. When you were there, the light was bright and steady. You disappeared, and only the flashing spotlights and discotheque masquerade remained.

I got up . . . stool I w . . . nt to . . . 'oor I ope . . . d . . . doo' I tried . . . to catch a . . . axi but they wouldn't sto . . . I wen . . . on the str . . . tl . . . ghts leading me 'long They st . . .d as . . . p . . . rk pat . . . I wal . . . ed 'long the p . . . th Up 'head . . . was d . . . rk.

Sort of like that, I guess.

I was soaked through and, it seems, frozen, because I wasn't wearing a coat or hat, only my dark-blue sweater with the words BEAR BEARS BEAR on the front—a present from you. It seems we had been talking, but I'm not sure that you were with me at that point. I remember the steam coming from my mouth and thinking that November was a cold month; I remember the frozen puddles underfoot and thinking about what happens to fish when they freeze, then about the headlights of the minibus taxi that had stopped, although I hadn't waved it down. Perhaps I had been walking on the pavement?

I gave someone some money, Lisa! I'm sure I gave someone some money, and that is one of my strangest memories of that evening. Whom and for what would I pay in that condition? Not even that: what need did I have at that point for things that could be bought with money? You have to agree: it was some sort of delusion or deception. But I very distinctly remember a woman in a kind of coachman's coat haughtily accepting a ball of crumpled bills from me and with true coachman's disgust returning it to me, after having unstuck several bills from it. I remember her face with her large features and flat nose, which would have been well complemented by a bushy, gray-streaked beard with a piece of cabbage stuck in it. I remember her violet lips; I remember that we were engulfed in a murky light, and it was precisely that murky light, Elisaveta, that led me to conclude that I was probably inside a minibus. In minibuses people are supposed to pay.

It seems it was precisely in the minibus that I found within myself the ability to string certain primitive brain impulses into chains of causes and effects. (The woman with the violet lips and the flat nose was interesting in and of herself, but I had given her something. Yes, I had given her money, which meant that I could ride, ride, r-i-i-i-de farther, to the flicker of the streetlamps outside the bright windows.) The ability some might mistakenly qualify as thought. But were those processes taking place inside me thought? I remembered that you and I had parted, and that my thinking had been too slow at the moment when you were waiting for "one, two, three—come back, come back to me, let me hug you, come back!" I hadn't been able to. I rode and watched the flicker of the streetlamps outside the windows—rather, no—at that point I had been in the kitchen, now I was in a minibus. Or remembering myself riding in a minibus, or eating, no, riding. In my opinion my slowness to react had been natural, wouldn't you say? Look at me now, and you would understand, right? How else could I have reacted? At that point I was thinking in strobe-light flashes, as if at a discotheque, under bright lights. It was my slowness to react, my actions, that led to our falling-out, our breaking up, our burning out, and burning up. Lisa, we had been singed, and had burned out! We had singed our wings and fallen from grace! But there's still a chance. That is, having saddled your fast-fast horse, or rocket (nowadays it's hard to tell the difference), you arrived at some far-reaching conclusions as a result of my failure, my dumbfoundedness in the kitchen, but I will find you and bring you back.

I want to tell you in complete seriousness that I didn't call to you to come back because I hadn't managed to comprehend anything, nothing at all. I remember shouting at you, then I remember you, I remember the puddle of love for him that you spilled out before me from your contemplations on hell—love and hell and loneliness, and Akutagawa—a multi-layered concoction, a latte macchiato. And the baby! The baby! When I recovered my wits about how to answer you, you were gone, you had already clicked the door shut.

But I'll bring you back, Elisaveta. There in the minibus I realized immediately what I had to do. I needed to get to the train station. Because if you wanted to run away, to disappear, then the only way to do that was by way of the train station. What's the train station got to do with it? Are you kidding? Come on, Lisa, let's figure two factors into the mix. First, not that much time had passed since the moment I had been too slow to react and my hesitation had elicited that quiet, delicate clicking of the door that to this day keeps me up at night. I had to hurry. And I hurried. With the same intensity and, alas, with the same results as when I had been too slow to react. Second, Lisa. Second, I relied entirely on instinct to tell me what to do next. And my instincts told me that if you had gone to a station, it had to have been the train station. I swear to you that if you had left me by way of a station, it would have had to have been the train station, and only the train station . . .

You understand, of course, that what I was doing was new for us. When you used to call me, I came. Up until then we had always moved in each other's direction. But now I called you and heard only your more rapid breathing, saw only the hem of a raincoat fluttering in the distance, and wasn't even certain that it was you. Ah, if only you weren't running away, Lisa! Ah, if only you called me! Or at least just stopped for a while to look back!

The station greeted me with an abundance of glass reflections. I saw throngs of people, and it seemed that I was saved. I followed my own logic, which at the time seemed ironclad: I looked for you in the crowds. Few people were out on the streets at night. But at the station there were many. Hence, the greater the probability that one of them, say, that girl over there, behind the brawny guy with the Rollaboard in the shadows of the café, or on the escalator—that one of them, one of the figures generated arbitrarily by my consciousness in this conglomeration of nocturnal human beings—would turn out to be you.

I floated on the waves of my joy and peered into people's faces. I jogged the perimeter of all three floors—there are three of them, right?—but I couldn't find you, Lisa! My sense of perception reeled. Then I realized that the probability of finding you did not depend on the number of arbitrary walk-ons on the set. You had left. You were hiding. Hiding from me, Lisa! I needed to look for you as if you didn't want me to find you. I was at the train station because people came here to leave town.

Tickets for international routes can be bought only by showing a passport. I don't know how the floodlight illuminating my dimmed consciousness spotted that idea in the torrent churning inside my head. I think at that moment I was trying to convince you, Lisa, that you can't love one person and sleep with another. So, if you were sleeping with me, that meant you . . . But to hell with that! I rushed to the ticket counters. My God, how . . . My God, how hopelessly I lied, Lisa! What a pile of utter bunk I dumped on the oval, curly head of the cashier after having waited my turn in line! That there'd been a plane crash in Alushta, that communications were down, that in three months we were getting married. That I thought a baby was involved. Clearly, the state I was in at the moment, my agitated distraction written in big letters across my tousled forehead (I had no hat, Lisa! My hat and coat had disappeared somewhere), inclined the middle-aged cashier to put herself in my shoes. The counter was closed, and I was escorted to the station manager, where I retold my story in all its disconnected confusion, tracing a pattern that I couldn't reproduce now even if I read it off paper but at that point I easily kept straight in my head and effortlessly embellished with new details. They served me tea—in one of those metal glass-holders with a long packet of sugar with a train on the wrapper that to this day still rustles and leaks in my pants pocket. They jubilantly informed me that no woman with the name Elisaveta Supranovich had boarded any train within the last three hours, which in my story, in the Gothic rosette of my lies, meant, it seems, something good. In short, I matter-of-factly thanked the station manager, who had expected me—at the very least—to fall on my knees and raise a prayer to the Almighty, bowed with composure to the ticket agent with the big hair and the huge tits, and next remember myself standing in front of the suburban train schedule. Here—admit it—I miscalculated. What I should have done back there in the station manager's narrow, fluorescent-lit office was immediately exclude the train station as an option. But I continued not to hear you as you ran from me, and that, and that, Lisa, was my principal error. I find the business of scouting, sleuthing, stalking to be profoundly vile.

In the time between that click of the door behind you and my arrival at the station only one suburban train—to Orsha—had departed. Orsha meant Saint Petersburg, I reasoned. It was in Orsha, next to the highway, that all the hitchhikers began their treks to Petersburg. If you got as far as Russia, you could lie low in some Minusinsk or other, and no one—not I or they . . . I realized that I needed to rush to Orsha. I figured that at ninety miles an hour—I wouldn't, of course, agree to less—I would arrive at the station at the same time as you. I would meet you as you got off the train, we would embrace, and I would call you, call to you—or do anything else I needed at the count of three—and after that we would be together again. In Minusinsk, or somewhere on the Ob–Yenisei Canal.

The station's panes of glass reflected me multiple times over as I careened down the escalator, stopping only once. On the second floor of the station a girl in a short gray faux-leopard jacket, with wind-burned hands, filtering coffee for someone out of an espresso machine, suddenly struck me as resembling you. I got off the escalator and went to stand in a long (two people!) line, discovering to my amazement that there were herring sandwiches, *chiburreki,* and cabbage-filled pies in this world. I looked at her hands, and the thought occurred to me that your hands had been unbearably cold when you left me, and they very likely could have broken out in chilblains within the few hours that separated us. Essentially, I didn't exclude the possibility that she was you (even when presented with an obvious dissimilarity) until I stood just opposite her and looked her in the eyes, and she asked me, "Good evening?" Immediately, and for many years hence, I realized that I would never search for you among girls selling *chiburreki* in cafés. It was so unlike you.

I returned to the flying carpet of the escalator, but her question "Good evening?" had set off a series of bad questions in my head. First of all, what had led me to decide that you had gone to Russia? Why, if I had decided that, had I beaten it into my head that you had left from the railroad station, when all you had to do was get off in Uruchie, flag down a passing car, and in ten hours you would be in Moscow? The questions themselves weren't earth-shattering, but their occurrence put me on my guard. I jumped the rails of instinct, having realized that all my hysteria had nothing to do with instinct, that just as before I hadn't a damn idea where and why you had run off or how long you were going to hide from me there. It was a moment of utter helplessness intensified by an awareness that the hands on the station clock were approaching midnight, and the convergence of those two vectors—one long and the other a bit shorter—bode something incredibly fatal: if allowed to converge, we would never meet again, and they were getting closer, and closer, and . . .

The station's windowpanes directly in front of me reflected the two giant towers of the city's gates. I even turned around to figure out how the devil such a huge structure could be behind me where the waiting room was supposed to be. Instead of the towers I saw the escalator, the girl with the mechanical coffee-extraction apparatus, and several chance people in whom it was downright stupid to expect I'd recognize you. Realizing that the towers of the gates were not reflected but were located outside the windows where I stood, I glimpsed my own reflection somewhere on the level of the sixth floor, which positively confounded me.

And then a revelation occurred. I suddenly sensed quite acutely that you had never thought of leaving the city, that you were here, and very close by. Lisa, I knew that you were in the snow-white living room on Marx Street! I sensed your presence there, as if you were calling me—shrilly, shrilly, shrilly—and I ran, ran and stumbled, because after a mistake like that I had no right to take a taxi. Elisaveta . . . To this day I don't know how to describe that sensation. Perhaps you can help me? As if you felt . . . as if you hurt, not as I hurt now in this semidarkness where I rave with my memories, but with acute, throbbing, punctuated physical pain. As if you were screaming, Lisa. To this day I am unable to comprehend what was happening. After all, I wasn't imagining it. It was you, for certain. I know the warm aftertaste of our bond, of conversations we've had while each of us was at a different corner of the city but later retold to each other with accuracy down to the interjections. Why were you screaming? Were you waiting for me there, and when I didn't show up, you screamed and left? You screamed because the hands of the clock converged and we still were not together?

How I ran, Lisa! As if I didn't have a heart that could stop, didn't have lungs that could burst. The fact was—you were melting. I felt how your breathing, which had become quite distinct, was fading in my consciousness, and that if it faded away entirely, I wouldn't know where to run or where to continue looking for you. Café signs and ads with attractive women—with eyes so syrupy I imagined they were sirens intent on luring me from my path to you—flashed by. I ran even faster. Near the square opposite MGB headquarters I was almost struck by a police car: rolling across the hood, I dashed off, leaving them perplexed as to how to assess their own offense.

The chairs in our café were set on the tables and looked like the death-stiffened legs of cute bugs, but I drove the image out of my mind. I didn't recognize our courtyard. Flying in, I surveyed the empty, evenly cracked brick walls and ran out again, but after verifying my location against the impartial No. 39 house number, I returned. I thundered up the stairwell. I pressed the snout of the doorbell flat against the plane of the wall, and it screeched plaintively until I placed my hand against the door. At that moment, I realized that behind the door you, Lisa, were no more. The space behind the door was icy and empty, like the house of a dog that had just died. I saw not a trace of you there. I found it difficult to believe even that you had ever lived in that apartment. Instinct told me that yes, yes, you had—you had, until the station clock hands had converged into a single fatal straight line, into a single vector pointed austerely upward: 0000. You had not waited until I arrived. You had disappeared somehow all at once from all the places I could see and feel. You weren't anywhere anymore.

No, I didn't pound on the doors as you might now fear. I conducted myself respectably, like a deflated balloon. On spaghetti legs I plodded down the stairs, finding the space between them either too great, requiring strenuous effort on my part to overcome the gaping emptiness, or too small, my foot meeting the head of a stair where there should have been a space, causing me to give it my sole, and descending the stairs was so torturously difficult, more difficult than speeding like a black cat across the center of town from the train station to Karl Marx Street. Apparently, my frantic sprint up and ominous descent down the stairs provided the pensioners in that stairwell a topic for discussion at dominoes for many weeks.

I don't remember what I did after that, Lisa. The realization that we would not meet anytime soon left me at a loss. I think I strolled around in some park. I was still constructing grandiose plans, like making the rounds of all your apartments and mansions, and I was setting out to do just that, when halfway to the next planned address I was paralyzed by your silence. I'll tell you why I didn't continue my search that night. When I had touched the door and felt the absolute emptiness behind it, when the sound of your breathing faded from my ears, I suddenly understood what you had meant by "we will never see each other again." We might live in the same city. We might drink coffee at neighboring tables. But your breathing would not be for me. Your eyes would cut through me just as mine had recently cut through the glass at the train station, not seeing the glass, seeing only the towers of the city gates beyond. You would look through me and see his towers and love them.

Toward morning, which just didn't want to come, I found myself at home at my white table with the chocolate end. I was explaining to you that the child couldn't not be ours because you didn't love Muraviov. I argued that, convinced that I was still in the kitchen at our den. I went over to the sofa, closed my eyes, then opened them again, gazing into the Gothic blackness of the invisible ceiling. Perhaps I slept, but perhaps not. Next I heard the sound of cars, it grew lighter outside: a new morning had dawned, and you were silent.

Then I understood that everything depended on me, Lisa! I had ceased to exist for you, but I could convince you that I existed. Persuade you not to look through me. I began to write letters to you, delivering them to the feet of your white living room, where I had heard you for the last time. I inserted the envelope into a narrow crack, bent it, and pushed it through. It disappeared into the door's belly, and I imagined how its ear showed slightly on the other side, and you fished it out at the other end with your fingers and helped me by pulling it, and for a while I even heard you giggle. I rang the bell—pardon me for that. You didn't open the door, Lisa. You didn't open the door because you weren't there. I set a date for us to meet and begged you to forgive me.

Having pushed the thin strip of the envelope into the crack in the door, I left for our den: it seemed very important to get there before noon, although you never showed up there before four or five. Again I had begun to fear that I would miss you. I waited motionlessly for you, sometimes even forgetting to turn on the light. You see, I was convinced that you were in the city. That if I did a good job waiting for you . . . really a good job . . . that you weren't coming because I was doing a bad job of waiting—that's why. I waited selflessly. I waited for you according to all the rules. I waited for you imploringly. I waited with bated breath. If you only knew how many times I heard your footsteps on the stairs! How many times that treacherous door that had quietly clicked shut that one time opened just as quietly, just as delicately, but only now so joyfully! Unlocked, clicked, and swung wide open, an indistinct rustling coming from the direction of the coatrack. I was all ears! Imploringly I held my breath. I needed only to believe. To believe that it was you: after all, you had never been vindictive! You took your first indistinct step down the corridor, and there the vision disintegrated. You never, Lisa, never came closer. Why? The number of days I hadn't slept was more than five, six, seven . . . Who counted! But I heard only, heard only that first step . . . and . . . This is gloomy, but I'll say it just the same. Don't take offense, OK? Never once did I hear your breathing. The sound of you clearing your throat . . . nothing. Only a muffled rap on the door, a click that more resembled a dream, and the rustling of feet in silk stockings, my favorite milk-white silk stockings, against the boards of the floor. Of course, I would quickly give up just sitting like that and waiting. Having hardly caught the first sounds, I would dash into the corridor, madly, my wheezing and stomping smothering the magic that fed my hopes. I found nothing, Lisa! Only the light silk scarf you had left on the coatrack. Since then, every evening, I rehang it on another branch of the antlers, trying to convince myself . . . To have something to believe in . . .

You know what else? . . . The evening after you left . . . I was sitting in the kitchen and lit a candle, our silly "post-solar clock": at the time I still didn't fear burning it down entirely. I hadn't yet realized that when it was used up, there would be no new clock. I sat, staring into the flame, and I was very cold, because your present, the sweater with the BEAR BEARS BEAR, had disappeared somewhere. Opposite me stood the chair on which you had sat when you asked me to take you by the hand, when you started that conversation with the click of the door at the end. Drawn by some strange assuredness, I stood up . . . I went over to it, I put my palm on its spine, and distinctly—distinctly, Lisa!—distinctly felt your warmth.

Everything around me was icy cold, I was cold: you yourself know what the heat there was like. But the back of the chair and the surface of the table where your elbows had been—they were warm, conserving your heat. The next evening this didn't happen again, and I was sad, as I'm sad now, when I'm compelled to admit a certain something to you.

Starting tomorrow, I won't go to our den anymore, Lisa. Today is November 28, and you know perfectly well that we rented it until December 1. Soon other people will be going there. I sense that I won't see you there anymore, and I pray to God that you will come to me somewhere else, even to the gray gloom that surrounds my sofa as I talk to you, as always, Lisa. I won't trouble you anymore today. You need to rest: after all, I'm constantly bothering you with my stories. Sleep tight, my dear girl. I will guard your sleep, rocking you in the armchair of my clumsy bear paws.

[2]

IT WAS, IT SEEMS, December 1 or 2. Keeping track of their time had been very simple before: their Wednesday was the hour hand, their Saturday the minute hand, and all events of the week fit within this interval of three or four—depending on the turn of events in relation to the split between the hands—days. Now, when the den, the very space that had contained their time and their clock hands, was gone, having been inherited by new tenants, he felt powerless before the wasteland of winter's whitish time gauged by nothing. All pursuits (even the most trivial) in which he might have submerged himself had disappeared. He walked and walked endlessly around the city, finding something shameless in idle walks on weekdays when people's faces were focused, their movements abrupt, and there were so many automobile horns everywhere. He was far from certain, however, that today was a weekday and not some major day off.

In the window of their café he caught his reflection: lanky and seemingly bound many times over with cord. ("And whatever had she seen in me that was bearlike?") He shuddered: the same had happened yesterday, or had it been the day before, or, had he just imagined it very vividly while lying on his sofa at night? Imagined it so as to decide what he would do, how he would react, if it happened. But now he saw, saw with his own eyes, that there was an empty latte macchiato mug standing on their table, standing opposite the end where she had always sat, standing in the exact same way, having slipped from the black marble block in the center of the table onto the snow-white wooden trim, its long coffee spoon, which resembled the chrome detailing on an automobile, tossed on the saucer in exactly the same careless way. No one bused the mug from the table. Why didn't anyone take it away? Was it a sign? She's telling him that she still comes to the café? What kind of strange, indecipherable game was this? In the meantime, a gaunt waiter appeared at the table with her unfinished latte macchiato and solemnly placed a tiny chessboard near the glass, the check protruding and intended, naturally, for him, Anatoly. Anatoly was already running for the door, running to intercept this sign from her, splashing through a puddle, then in the doorway bumping into some fop with a scarlet scarf wrapped over his corduroy jacket, when a thoroughly imperturbable young woman in coffee-colored stripes picked up the check sticking its tongue out of the chessboard and placed her money on Elisaveta's message for Anatoly. Once again his heart leapt, then skipped a beat, then resumed beating with indifferent regularity. Simply some striped girl had drunk her macchiato here, picked up the check, and paid it. There were no messages from *her*, and, just as before, she was not there.

His wet shoe—where had the water come from?—squishing, he walked on, past the residence, past the azure (as in Beardsley drawings) park on "Panikovsky Square," past the tank that stretched its frozen trunk toward the sun, along the cobblestones, down, down in the direction of the park. Just at that moment the first snow began to fall. ("The first snow is falling, Lisa! The first snow! It's a sign, right? We're going to meet today?") The snow was fine and prickly, tolerable only for the sake of the white beauty it lent the asphalt. He stopped on the bridge near the circle to look at how the river coped with the snow: the snow melted before it reached the water, and this also meant something for him and Elisaveta, but he couldn't figure out exactly what. Enough snow to make a snowball had accumulated in the folds of his coat, and he did make one, with his bare hands—it was easier that way. After holding the lumpy ball in his palm for a while, he dropped it to the ground for lack of anyone to throw it at. In the phantasmal light their little boat resembled the watermark on his snow-white paper that morning: white with light-blue trim, the boat was submerged in whiteness just as Anatoly had wanted to submerge himself in some sort of insignificant business so that time would pass more quickly, so that time, essentially, would pass. On the granite curb opposite him a female figure in a dark coat stood looking at the watermark of the little boat, as if attempting to ascertain the authenticity, the genuineness of this reality.

He did not allow himself to run over to the woman because that striped girl, of course, had been punishment for his excessive haste. Elisaveta did not like it when he hurried and, therefore, she would appear to him today on and off at all their spots, testing his endurance and expecting a truly measured reaction. He would approach her in precisely that way, respectably, slightly sloshing the moisture in his shoe—that was nothing, it could happen to anyone! Ultimately, she had nicknamed him "bear" not for the qualities that he possessed, but for the ones, likely, she wanted to see in him. That was what he would live up, would live up to. Meanwhile, the brown figure, the dark silhouette, moseyed down the park path, but moseyed quickly. What other explanation could, could you, Anatoly, find, except that this was another attempt to run away: after all, the weather outside was not the sort that inclined one to take slow walks. But was it she? Unfortunately, he had never seen her in winter clothing. He didn't know whether she had a coat like that or how she walked in the snow. In that respect the snow could be a bad sign, since it marked the approach of the ice age, where there was no room for the two of them, but it—the snow—also provided hope that spring would come and, if she did not appear before then, he would find her in the melted city, find her, and this time never let her go.

The phantom up ahead already had a good two-hundred-yard lead, and Anatoly could barely make it out in the distance, as if the little figure were an image on a black-and-white television with a lot of static and a speck of static had covered it over entirely. Then the snow suddenly stopped pouring flour down his collar and started coming down very slowly, fluffy as if on New Year's Eve. Now there was no making anything out, even at a distance of thirty feet. Anatoly continued to make his way, not hurrying, because he could still make out her tracks. As he followed her, the routes she might take next occurred to him in clusters: the untraceable (the metro, taxis); the traceable (along the Svislach toward the Niamiha); and those that offered the prospect of a rendezvous (the Kristall shop on

Victory Square! Please, please go to the Kristall shop on Victory Square!). Meanwhile, the depth and contrast of her tracks began to fade—like disappearing ink on paper—turning first into light white indentations in the crusty snow that were possible to make out only by walking bent toward the ground like a monkey while (to hell with all those vows not to hurry!) plowing full steam ahead not to fall behind—and then finally turned into an even white surface. The phantom disappeared into the snow-impregnated air. She was no longer there. He could still move forward as he tried to assure himself that he saw tracks. And he did move forward, of course, hobbling, and already beginning to shiver with hopelessness. Nothing, nothing was visible to the eye.

Left without tracks, he didn't know where to go, so he walked and thought about how strange it was: usually tracks were an effect, but for him they were a cause. Those tracks had been the cause of his tracks, and if someone now were to plod after him, his tracks would be the cause for that person's tracks, but then all these chains of tracks had turned into blind paths because the phantom had faded. No, he corrected himself, "phantom" is a bad word. Simply another woman—a woman he didn't know—had been walking ahead of him, and her tracks had been covered over with snow until they disappeared entirely, and it was a good thing, in fact, that he had not caught up with her and thereby had managed to avoid yet one more misunderstanding. In the meantime, the snow issued forth newer watermarks in the light: a streetlight with a white ball instead of a lamp slowly floated past, a gazebo seemingly sculpted from snow suddenly appeared right on his path. None of this had any meaning; he needed a new sign from her in order to continue breathing, to keep going. Finding no sign in his surroundings, he found one in his head—the bridge, the bridge on the Niamiha where he had once so happily waited for her, and she had come, and so what if he had waited for her there at least a dozen times since she had dissolved into thin air, he would go to the bridge, and she, of course, was already shaking the snow out of her mane and huffing in the twilight, while there he was, walking around in circles who knows where, the idiot, not having figured out immediately that he was supposed to run to the bridge. Apathy was replaced by a painful, already (alas!) familiar joy with a bitter aftertaste at the bottom. At first he walked quickly, then, having slipped once, slid ahead, flushed, jacket open, the array of sounds he made doing nothing (alas! alas!) to overcome the hopeless silence in his head. He was in luck today: someone really was waiting for him under the bridge, and as soon as the black cave opened out into the light at the end of tunnel, he caught sight of a lone person standing just as immobile as the woman in the coat who had contemplated their boat before dissolving into nowhere. He flew under the bridge and headed straight toward the figure—stumbling as he attempted to slide but not finding the required smoothness underfoot, tripping with quick, resounding steps that boomed inside this concrete sack—when suddenly something strange happened to the figure. That is, he already saw, of course, that it was not Lisa (it was too tall and too broad), but he hadn't expected this either. The silhouette all of a sudden split into two: starting at the head, it formed two faces, two noses, two necks, two bodies, three—no, four—hands. It was just two lovers kissing, but the din he'd raised had startled them, as if they were two schoolboys smoking in a corner of the school yard. He found himself alone in the solemn darkness of the space under the bridge: it was like being in a movie theater with a semicircular screen of falling snow, while he and Lisa sat in the warmth and touched each other's frozen palms.

"Look at the snow, Lisa," he said trustingly. Someone answered.

The quiet, melodious sound echoed from somewhere off to the side, on the right, from precisely the spot Lisa had just been. It was his phone, his phone, damn it! Unraveling the layers of his scarf, undoing some strings and a what-is-this-doing-here button, he had enough time to think that the telephone call, received in response to his phrase "Look at the snow, Lisa," was a very good sign. He was still riding the inertia of this thought as the voice in the phone—male, unfortunately, and completely unfamiliar— spoke.

"Rovich, investigator from the Prosecutor's Office of the Ministry of State Security," the phone continued, not noticing that a large fragment of what it had said had fallen unheard. Anatoly volleyed the last fragment back with a hoarse "Huh?"

"I said, hello, Anatoly Petrovich! Can you hear me?" Anatoly Petrovich— that's him, he, Nevinsky, of course, the one who had just been thinking about Lisa. "Yes, I hear you," answered Anatoly. "I hear you," he said, this time with more confidence, because now he really could hear and was listening.

"This is Evgeny Petrovich Tsupik, an investigator from the Prosecutor's Office of the Ministry of State Security. Section Five, eh-hem," the phone added for some reason, somewhat constrained.

Anatoly was silent, not knowing what to say in this situation, whether to say anything at all.

"I am a big fan of yours." The voice in the phone sounded friendly and ingratiating. The statement had been intended to extract an answer, which it did.

"And to what do I owe the attention of Section Five?" Anatoly tested using a confident voice.

"You and I need to meet, Anatoly Petrovich. Could you be at my office at the Central District Prosecutor's Office at 0900 tomorrow morning? Forty-three Pulikhav Street. Someone will meet you at the door and see you through security."

"Are you summoning me to an interrogation?" Anatoly inquired with interest.

"For a conversation. Let's call it a conversation," the voice in the phone insisted enthusiastically.

"Nevertheless," he attempted to collect himself. "Nevertheless. Why . . . What's happened?"

"You really can't guess?" his interlocutor hinted, but Anatoly still did not understand. "We have to talk to you about a certain affair our enemies on the Internet are jabbering about. But we won't do this over the phone, will we? Did you jot down the address? Forty-three Pulikhav Street. Don't be late!" The last phrase had a different ring to it, the kind of voice accustomed to saying, "In the event you do not appear, you will be brought compulsorily, under escort." The masterly touch lay in that this grating metallic note hung in the air for all of a second and could easily have passed as distortion from a bad connection.

Anatoly could not think about tone of voice now; he had to remember the address, and he had so many questions, and not all that long ago Lisa had been at his side, and now they were summoning him to the MGB for who knows what. He leaned against the wall and took a few deep breaths. He pulled out his phone. He studied it. He remembered the thought that had induced him to pull out his phone. Yes, of course! He dialed.

"Dan?"

"Tolya! Say, brother, wuzz up?"

"Dan. Can you tell me what our enemies on the Internet are jabbering about?"

"Whoa, dude, flavor of the month. About the mysterious disappearance of some chick named Elisaveta Supranovich."

"Uh-huh," Anatoly said more slowly, more for himself than for Dan. "Uh-huh."

"Well, like the regime's latest bloody crime. *Charter's* reporting that her tragic disappearance is the two hundred twenty-sixth in a series of missing-persons cases in the country, etc., etc. They're hinting, naturally, but not too *bardzo*. They say 'career officers' at the MGB—'patriots of the people' they call themselves—leaked the skinny. That is, in short, that the MGB sent up the balloon. Nobody lower than assistant head of the information directorate. Whenever anyone lower down leaks dope, it's usually signed just 'officers of the MGB.'"

"So why would the MGB want to flash this case?" Anatoly hopelessly tried to figure out what he should do now, but he had to say something, had to . . .

"Connect the dots, dude. It means some operational necessity arose."

"Got it, Dan." Anatoly made up his mind. "Dan, it looks like I'm in trouble."

"Big trouble?" the phone laughed.

"Trouble with the MGB, Dan."

"Then it's big." The phone got serious.

"Dan, I need help. Probably I need something like a consultation. How to act during an interrogation. I've been called in for an interrogation. Tomorrow."

The phone whistled, which could mean either something immensely cheerful or something entirely uncheerful.

"Eighteen hundred. The Dukhmiany Bar near GUM. Be there, and I'll send a guy over to prep you," the phone offered.

"Thanks, Dan." He had to elongate "Dan" to give himself time to figure out that "1800" wasn't the price of services, but one of Dan's usual linguistic eccentricities. Right, right, 1800, six in the evening, eighteen zero zero.

"Got it. How will we recognize each other?"

After a short pause Dan said, "Grow up," and ended the call. Right. What a question. How will an MGB officer recognize him: really, really stupid.

The festive word *dukhmiany* can be translated as "redolent." It can also be translated as "fragrant," but in this case "redolent" was more appropriate. The Dukhmiany Bar was one of those establishments that mainly resemble a gated archway, and the people who frequented it had the same faces as those who slip into archways to take a leak. At one time there had been a gateway—a cozy little dead end for those suffering from the urge—but it had been walled off, a few tables set out along with a bar, and the sequence of cause and effect was thereby reversed. To the chance onlooker out on the street the goings-on there, in the dark, crowded reaches of the bar, would likely seem no more decent than taking a leak in a dark courtyard. People here got loaded hastily and shamefully, shot by shot, practically without talking. The Dukhmiany was set off from its surroundings by a plastic curtain, the kind behind which butchers at the market dress pork. It seemed, if you were to wait long enough, dressed slabs of meat crowned with a pig's head grinning like a Buddha and with an oversize tongue hanging out would come crawling out of the Dukhmiany right into the elegant center of the city. At one time the curtain had been transparent with coquettish latticework that suggested the gates of a castle—originally the bar had been designed as a place for the brutal drinking bouts of medieval times minus the romantic aureole that surrounded them in computer role-playing games and children's books about princesses. It was a tavern that catered to trolls, and trolls crept here from all over the city, making it completely unsuitable for people. Inside, the bar was crowded. The counter burned with the implanted teeth of beer bottles and the fool's gold of chips bags. That was it.

Anatoly looked around timidly, as he moved for the third time from the head of the line back to the end. To be inside the premises and not stand in line seemed impossible: even the people sitting at tables with full mugs seemed to be standing in line. He had, as it were, already picked up on a certain meditativeness of ritual in his peregrinations and experienced the assuring touch of routine: he just stood and did nothing, not having to run anywhere, not having to search, not having to think tortuously or remember. Everything happened of its own accord, and he needed only to stay behind the black curly-wool back of the head in front of him, and when it was replaced by the black curly wool of the barman's face, smile guiltily, step back, and return to the end of the line near the exit. Of course, he phoned Dan again. Of course, his cell phone was silent. Finding himself at the sticky bar for the fourth time and already having turned away to concede his place to someone thirstier than he was, Anatoly found someone standing alongside him.

"Get a beer for me and yourself and go sit at that table," the someone said flatly.

Anatoly set in front of his interlocutor a cellulose mug into which the barman had decanted beer from bottles that so reminded him (to the point of revulsion) of the slimy bladder of a medium-sized animal that he frankly was glad not to have followed the man's instructions, having ordered himself green tea instead of beer.

"Victor Ivanovich," said the man in the same monotone as before. "A great admirer of your talent." Anatoly was about to smirk, but the man's next phrase stopped him. "Now pour out that tea, get yourself a beer, and quit fucking around."

Not having time even to think, Anatoly daintily poured the tea into a trash can, tossing his plastic cup into it as well. Feeling his spine helplessly dampening with fear, he thrice regretted having asked Dan for the favor. Of course, it was better not to meet with people from the MGB. Not at interrogations, not on the street, and not for consultations. Under no circumstances. He was a fool for getting himself into this. Possibly he had made it much worse for himself, and for Lisa, Lisa.

Cautiously setting his mug on the table, he politely seated himself alongside, sensing that his trousers were not entirely touching the bench, and his legs were taut and ready at any moment to spring across the table toward the exit, where he could break into a run, although this comrade probably had a gun.

"To our acquaintance," Victor Ivanovich toasted.

Anatoly understood that now he would have to drink the liquid, and drink he did. The beer had the aftertaste of Duchess pear soda and was so sweet it could easily have been distributed at morning snack time in kindergartens as *kissel.* His interlocutor was a swarthy balding man of indeterminable age. "He could just as well be forty as twenty-five," Anatoly described him to Elisaveta, catching himself at the thought that women were usually described that way in books. Victor Ivanovich's ears protruded too aggressively from his skull and were sharp as a vampire's, resembling a kind of assault body part to be used in some strange form of physiognomic warfare. The man was very pale, and his face was covered with a five-o'clock shadow that resembled coarse ground pepper. "Guys like that have to shave twice a day just in order not . . . Just in order not to look like that," Anatoly thought to himself with revulsion. The beard on a corpse must look exactly like that. His jacket was woolen with what seemed to be gray-black accents that, in combination with that impossible face, looked as if part of the black pepper from his face had fallen onto his jacket, as if this creature had shaved in his jacket and not shaken out the bits of stubble, which had then spread to his shoulders and fallen onto his collar where the insignia of the MGB—a shield, a sword, and a snake—shone like a used bullet casing. Anatoly would have bent closer to look at it, but that would have been impolite.

The comrade took a deep breath and leaned against the back of the bench. His teeth turned out to be terrible, which for some reason terrified Anatoly even more. All around them the crowd jostled, spoke loudly, and laughed. People drank beer while standing in line for more beer. Any one of them could turn out to be Victor Ivanovich's colleague. If his name really was Victor Ivanovich.

Anatoly decided to take advantage of the pause in the conversation to formulate his case, which he already had lost any desire to formulate at all.

"You see, Victor Ivanovich, I have been summoned to the MGB tomorrow for an interrogation," he began.

"Interrogation?" his interlocutor cut him short. "Are you sure?"

"No. They called it a conversation."

"Ah-ha. That's very important. And?"

"In the course of that . . . conversation I might be asked things about a person who they seem to think was kidnapped, but really wasn't . . . I can probably speak frankly with you, since you were sent by Dan? This person is just hiding. And I am afraid of giving away information I shouldn't . . ."

"Do you know anything about Elisaveta Supranovich's whereabouts?" The man known as Victor Ivanovich swelled professionally and even became somewhat taller.

"I don't know anything at all! I only know that I don't want them to find her because of my carelessness. The thing is she . . . She's so vulnerable. But I might . . . Accidentally."

"Listen here, OK," his interlocutor began, after spitting on the floor. "Your case is shit. Of course, I don't know all the details and haven't looked into the operational situation . . . It just looks like they've outplayed you. Outplayed you both. She thought that she could make a clean getaway . . . You thought that she had split to the other side and didn't go to the cops. But they outplayed you, get it? They were five moves ahead of you, chewed you up and spit you out. The girl, of course . . . Too bad."

It couldn't be said that Anatoly understood very much of what had been said. His head was drilled by the thought of whether in principle he had made a mistake opening up to this guy, although he hadn't quite opened up, just sort of cracked the door, and that guy had those teeth, a tic in his left cheek, and a face covered with pepper . . . Outplayed us . . . Outplayed us . . .

"Listen up, huh!" Victor Ivanovich was asking something.

"Yes, yes."

"Look me in the eye," he growled. And Anatoly stopped following the movement of his fingers on the table.

" 'Who's your dick?' I asked."

It took Anatoly some time to figure out the question. Right, of course, "dick." Investigator.

"Tupid. Poopid . . . Tsupik. My investigator is Tsupik." Anatoly could barely get it out.

"He's shit, not a dick," Victor Ivanovich concluded. "That means you won't get hammered. He's new in the Prosecutor's Office. Not too long ago he was an operations officer. He still doesn't know how to put the screws on, but he's got a good nose for operations. If you suddenly decide to withhold anything, think hard about how you'll do it. Take something before you go there. Valerian drops. He'll be two steps ahead of you, even he. I'm not talking about if you get skewered by a real pro. Remember this name. Zverev. Zve-rev. Repeat after me."

"Zve-rev," Anatoly obediently repeated the two syllables.

"If you hear that name . . . run . . . If you have the chance, leave the country. He'll hit you with everything in the book, extreme measures. He's a beast. As for Tsupik, Tsupik's nothing. Although with guys like you . . . Listen, can you stop wiggling your eyebrows, bitch? Can you stick your hands under the table and chain them there? Think about this: you write those books of yours, then they read them. You're ABC for any dick. He scratched the back of his head: he's thinking. He raised his eyebrows: he's scared. Fuckin' inscrutable, are you? Decided to withhold information from the investigation, huh? You haven't even figured out for yourself that you're trying to hide something!"

Victor Ivanovich switched so quickly from blatantly insulting to confidential that Anatoly's suspicion abated, and he listened attentively to the new information.

"Listen," his interlocutor continued. "As soon as you get there, ask what case they called you in on and in what capacity. If they called you in, there has to be a case. How's it been classified? Missing persons? Murder?"

At the word "murder" someone inside Anatoly screamed and collapsed.

"Have they called you in as a witness or as a suspect? If you're a suspect, kiss your ass good-bye: no crossing the border, and pack some warm socks for a trip in the other direction. But the advantage is you don't have to answer questions. None. If you're a witness, be careful what you say and, most important, read before you sign, got it? Read, I'm telling you, word for word, anything you're going to sign. Fuck, why do you keep eyeballing the table when I'm talking to you? You can say anything you want. They might record it or even film it. But the case file, when they put you on trial . . ."

("Put me on trial," the phrase echoed in Anatoly's head.)

" . . . put you on trial, will contain only the protocol you either signed or didn't sign. If they slip you obvious lies, don't sign it. Or sign it only after you've written out all your objections. And the main thing. But it won't do shit to help, if you keep doing that with your eyebrows. Fuck, can't you shave them or something? You'll lose points in the beauty contest, but at least they won't give you away. Now, if you want to play stupid, don't say 'I don't know.' If you know and say you don't know and that shows up in the transcript, it's an automatic five years for perjury. So you look him in the eye and say, 'I don't remember.' It's possible not to remember even what you said the day before. But it's not possible not to know what you know for certain. It's a question of style, like your scribbling, but it can save you from the bench and get you back to the good life. Especially when you're up for a third term, and you know all our tricks. Would you quit raising your eyebrows again! I'm a dick, a dick. Therefore, this juice I'm selling you is worth its weight in gold. Say hi to Dan. And finish your beer. I hope we never see each other again. Ever. Pray for that!"

Victor Ivanovich spat on the floor again and gave a short nod, but he was already looking beyond Anatoly, already getting up, already entirely engrossed in some other thought. Burying his insignia and placing his black hat on those impossible ears, he disappeared behind the backs of the crowd, flapping his raincoat like a vampire, and at that precise moment Anatoly finally remembered who the severe MGB inspector reminded him of. He hadn't gone out the door, but through the wall: he walked straight into and disappeared behind it. Ah, right, it was just a curtain, a curtain. For certain not a door, but a curtain. A curtain, behold! Behold a threshold.

"Extreme measures," "the bench," "murder"—the new words palpitated in his brain like spiders. This had so little connection with their world that he felt like breaking out in loud laughter to shake the delusion, and, it seems, he did break out laughing, causing someone's shoulder to the right to shudder. But what was most terrifying was that—whether of his own will, or by his own initiative, or just by way of the natural course of events—those words were now in such close proximity to him that they were precisely the words he needed when explaining himself to the investigator. Set his own poisonous spiders loose on the spiders of the investigator's question, "What were you doing on the evening of 18 November?" The problem was that his spider supplies were a bit wanting. He was playing this game for the first time and sensed that sooner or later he could get deflected into an ordinary, frank conversation, without venoms and antidotes, without fight rounds and safe mode. What, essentially, did he have as backup? That pepper-dusted vampire hadn't helped him a bit. He hadn't stuck a tarantula in a jar into his pocket, hadn't presented him with a string of dried bird-eating spiders that could be reconstituted with a secret spell (e.g., "Article 124 of the Code of Criminal Procedure states . . ."). Or maybe not? He had helped a great deal, a very great deal, and triple thanks, Dan, and, by the way, he ought to call him. The comrade had helped him figure out what the conversation would be like. Of course, Anatoly was going to prep. He would collect himself. He would memorize his only combat tactic: "I don't remember. I don't remember anything at all." Apparently, though, he needed to say it as if he really didn't remember, because as soon as the investigator figured out that he'd been prepped, he'd start "skewering" him, whatever that meant. In the case of the MGB it could mean an awful, awful lot.

But here's the catch. How to say "I don't remember" to the question "Did you know Elisaveta Supranovich?" Only two answers were possible: "Yes, I did" and "No, I didn't." The fact that he'd been summoned meant that he knew her, he knew her, damn it, he knew her, and they knew that he knew her. (That damn paranoid "they" again!) And even that . . . Victor Ivanovich had got down to business straight off . . . "And didn't go to the cops . . ." How did they know everything? How much did they know? Had they bugged the phone? Followed us on the street? Though that wouldn't have given them much information . . . and five years for perjury. "Five years," he said to himself, having caught sight of his own eyes two feet ahead. Oh, right, he had left the Dukhmiany. He was standing at the long counter of the confection section at the TsUM department store, where Stalin-era milkmaids overhead gently fanned sheaves of grain. "Ah, my dear little milkmaids! Did you, with your sheaves of grain, really not know anything about the interrogations, the prisons, the labor camps?" The little milkmaids' cheeks grew rosy, the cows bellowed, and in the background the bright sun shone like the radiant future, Stalin's sun. He sipped his coffee.

Why had they started a search for her? How had they found out that she was on the run? From enemies on the Internet, as Poopik had put it? But they were the ones to leak it to the Internet in order to say to me tomorrow—in response to my question about why they had suddenly rushed to search for ordinary citizen Elisaveta Supranovich—in order for them to raise their eyebrows in disbelief (I wonder whether dicks have facial expressions? Or do they not, like that guy?), in short, in order for them not to raise anything in disbelief and say, "Well, old man, what other alternatives do we have? They're looking for her on the Internet, everyone's hot and bothered, everyone's calling and asking 'Where's Elisaveta?' Therefore we don't need to search for her at all?" Come to think of it, she could have fled the country using the same forged passport the MGB had issued her. Anatoly had looked for her at the train station, but he hadn't checked the surname Supranovich at the airport. Anyway, all these checks would have been senseless, because she probably had as many passports as apartments and houses. But unlike Anatoly, at the MGB they knew perfectly well about all her passports and all her addresses.

"When and where did you last see Elisaveta Supranovich?" How was he supposed to answer to this question? Not say "never" and "nowhere"? Say, "I don't remember"? It had been two weeks ago! How could he answer "I don't remember"? No, he should say when, the exact date and time, but leave where somewhat vague. He couldn't surrender their "den" to those bastards. They would turn it upside down; they'd sink themselves boot-deep in it. He couldn't. Couldn't. They used to meet somewhere in town . . . No, that's a lie. Five years, five years: they hadn't met in town; they'd met at the apartment. He waited for her on the landing between floors. That meant he remembers when, but he doesn't remember where? And look unsure, like, I'm in a state of shock. And he was—no need pretending here. Now just insert the keys into the slots on the locks, turn them just so, pressing lightly. Take off your coat, hang the keys on the nail. Excellent. As if he wasn't going to the MGB tomorrow. Set the alarm clock a bit earlier, as if he were going to fall into the deep sleep of a legendary warrior, and "Hello, sofa! My head hurts, sofa. My poor head is pounding from all this."

There was one other thing. What did "outplayed you two" mean? Victor Ivanovich the Terrible had repeated the phrase several times, several times, and it had sounded so ominous and at the same time was so in-comprehensible . . . He had been attempting to communicate something important, but had not wanted to give it away. After all, he was probably under oath, Victor Ivanovich, and who was he, Anatoly, that MGB inves-tigators need risk their careers and share service secrets because of him? Especially since the MGB shared only those secrets they needed to share for operational purposes.

"Outplayed" was it? Or maybe he'd meant "overplayed"? "Overplayed" could refer to a bad actor, who, for example, needs to depict a night before an interrogation at the MGB. The fool paces about the stage, creaking the floorboards, pacing and nervously drinking tea from a faceted table glass. But, my long-haired friend, the night before an interrogation at the MGB is when you lie still as a mouse on your sofa. When there is only a half-inhalation or a half-exhalation of life left in you. When you are entirely engrossed in your thoughts, and not up to pacing all over the place. The whole interrogation is in your head, and there, on the inside, you have already been told that there is incontestable proof that you lied. You turn cold. You sweat, although you still have not seen the evidence and the course of your conversation with the interrogator over the last half-hour has grown out of your answer to the question "first name, last name, legal address." That is overplaying. Were the fool to be called in for an interrogation with serious allegations hanging over his head, then he would play it for real. Oh, how he would play it! He would lie on his sofa and mumble, like Anatoly, although Anatoly, it seems, was mumbling to himself, to himself . . .

One problem, though, is that "overplayed" doesn't really work in the passive, and Victor Ivanovich—forget about his pepper—had meant the word in the sense that they'd been outsmarted. "Outplayed" held the most sinister of connotations . . . none of them comforting. In chess, you're "outplayed" when you mount a subtle attack: at the far right of the board the defense has a gap. Two moves hence and you can move your queen over there. The king will have nowhere to go, nowhere to go except into the line of attack of your queen. Therefore you need to defend the queen with this here bishop. Two more moves, two more moves, and it will all be over. You look up, trying not to gloat at your opponent. And you discover that you had been checkmated five minutes earlier. You had been outplayed. Outplayed. Outplayed.

[3]

"CURTAINS, RUSTLED BY THE WIND," that's how it went, wasn't it, Lisa? "Rustled by the wind," duh-duh–duh-DUH, "make it possible for the wind to exist." "A chill breathes through them—the first, still premature, whisper of autumn." You had a shimmer of sun on the side of the coffeepot, your conversations with a glass of juice in which I was hidden, and a light rustle across the wood floor. That was morning. Of course, I remember. Of course, I remember, Lisa.

There's the patch of light on the coffeepot—bright as the sun itself. But it's not the sun; it's the kitchen light. It's still dark, Lisa, still dark, because it's a morning in December, and the sun has been exiled until spring, and all patches of light need to be man-made. No, of course, I didn't make myself coffee in the coffeepot—such aristocratism would be inappropriate, given that I would hardly be able to taste the coffee, even if I chewed the beans. I just threw a handful of grounds in a cup and scalded the fuzzy mound with hard-boiling water, and in revenge the entire mound floated to the surface and is now getting caught between my teeth. Oh, yes, Lisa, when you were recollecting your morning you said something else, about a kind of stylized dream that seemed to be from Carroll's *Alice,* although here I'm filling in the blanks for you: probably that was just shorthand—a "Carrollesque dream," or "Carrollesque garden," because you dreamed not about the garden itself but about a tiny door leading into it, but all that has been lost already under a pile of words, and I am imagining something completely different from what you had in mind. As for my dreams, Lisa, it's all very simple, with no need for Carroll or C. S. Lewis: I had no dreams, if I slept at all. Now I'll turn off the vigilantly shrieking alarm that foolishly thinks it can rouse me! Although I had to set it, had to set it.

I have no glass of juice: in these twilight times of mine the refrigerator fills itself up, mostly with *pelmeni* meat dumplings. Right now I'm full, full of reflections of you. I opened the window, Lisa, to see whether the wind would rustle the curtain. No, Lisa, the curtain stood stiff with horror. For that reason there is no breath of coolness; what there is is the fatal cold of a December night that probably chuckles when I refer to it as morning. If you think that my insomnia has led to something productive, you're mistaken. I haven't thought up any crafty devices to lead the interrogator by the nose; more likely I'll work myself into such a state of anxiety that immediately upon arriving I might as well set my nose at the interrogator's feet and propose that I lead myself by the nose for him for the entire interrogation. The refrigerator just growled and shuddered; that seems to be a signal for me to go. I have the suspicion that the refrigerator is in cahoots with them all: there's something vaguely reminiscent of a career MGB agent about it, but I'm joking, joking, darling.

I had thought, of course, about getting into the warm, respectable comfort of my car, and just now, walking past it, I smiled in delight at its fender, glistening—like a Vermeer canvas, but (and this is one of those things that occurred to me last night) I wouldn't dare drive there in my BMW, in my Frau. That would be overconfident beyond the pale, and not as a demonstration of my *dolce vita*. You see, dear Lisa, I have no idea when they'll release me from the "conversation" or whether they'll release me at all. You've likely read about people who dropped into the MGB to pick up relatives after an interrogation and wound up disappearing for years. I hate to think that my car could wind up in a special lot for those summoned for interrogations, be drifted over with snow, and by the time the tenth spring arrived, the tenth spring from now, a tree would have grown right through it, and I wouldn't be able to do anything about it. People are responsible for the beings and things they domesticate. It would be the same as leaving for an interrogation without first feeding a kitten. The keys and documents are below the mirror in the hallway; my mother knows.

In the spaces between the buildings the sky was black, and the streetlights like disproportionately large stars in this sky. We all should have been punished long ago for stars no longer visible in our cities. How can a person go to an interrogation and not see stars? Is that any way to run the world?

Once beyond the courtyard I discovered small groups of people dressed in fur coats and trudging toward the streetcar stop, indifferent to the sky and the stars after having created this reality and filling it with posts, streetlights, and high-rise buildings. The MGB is just finishing what they began. What we began. No, they.

Inside the streetcar it was cozy and almost warm. Its windows, illuminated with a warm yellow light from within, smacked of a Coca-Cola Christmas ad. The streetcar was jammed with Santa Clauses riding to work without yet having donned their costumes, and the crowdedness created a bit of warmth. We inhaled and exhaled. A half-hour remained before the interrogation. The streetcar accomplished the improbable: it transported me out of a December night into a December morning. When I got off at the Park stop, near the frozen river—which looked like an industrial canal for supplying a reactor's coolant loops or, worse, like a sewer for chemical waste—the sky was no longer black but azure-blue with a dawn that burst forth onto Pulikhav Street through the infantry and artillery of daybreak. That is, were I on my way to our place for an assignation, Lisa, it would have been a dawn. But dawn is too inspirational, too optimistic a word. I'll use the same cautious term they use in weather reports and call the armed struggle for the sky taking place behind the clouds and the bright-orange streaks in the east a sunrise. I needed to head in the direction of this heavenly battle, and how beautiful the city—its streetlights, streetcars, lampposts, and the high-rises—now seemed in its inability to tame the blazing heavens, which appeared to be avenging the stars. Yes, yes, sunrise in the city—with its cruel sun that lacerates the eyes of the insomniac—is vengeance on us all for not respecting the stars . . . Oh, is this gloomy building the place? No. I was just frightened, Lisa. Why am I so afraid of this appointment? After all, I am guilty of nothing (that's no defense) and no threat to them (that's a defense). What's my existence, my scribbling to them?

The farther I went from the streetcar stop cozily nested in the belly of our Gorky Park, the more distressing the cityscape grew. To the right stretched an endless wall, behind which the skeleton of an industrial structure with punched-out eyes and a roof gone off the deep end rose with hysterical screams (architecture as music in stone?). All the buildings accompanying me on the right seemed to have some special function: they didn't look at me; they weren't just standing with their backs turned toward me, as happens in certain elite neighborhoods; they were escorting me under guard to the building of the Central Region's Prosecutor's Office of Section Five of the MGB. Their windows all burned with the same identical greenish light, as if scanning me, and it occurred to me that each of them was equipped with a camera and dozens of heat sensors and various other detectors to record the expression on my face and the quickness of my step and thereby to evaluate my psychoemotional state, my predisposition to lie, and my guilt. It was paranoia. Paranoia. Just my paranoia.

Unable to bear it, I brushed myself off the narrow sidewalk leading along the service buildings and turned toward the river that supplied the coolant loops of the abandoned factory and walked along the frozen river with occasional thaw holes in its middle that reflected reddish-orange flashes of the heavenly battle. I somehow recognized the high-rise I needed immediately, as if I had been there before. I had thought that the Prosecutor's Office would be encompassed by a ten-foot fence, like a prison, but once again those were my foolish fantasies. It was ordinary Soviet architecture. Resembling a polyclinic with a certain whimsical green tile lining the space under the windows. I should have driven here in my Frau.

With steps whose every muscular movement brought visible relief, I approached the building, discovering unexpected indications that my feet and hands were freezing, but that was nothing: in a building like this one they might even treat me to tea. The entrances turned out to be armed with protective metal barriers, but that was understandable, it was like that everywhere—antiterrorist measures. Or just in case some criminals attempted to liberate their buddies. This was understandable. The metal barriers were set out as a labyrinth, which forced you to turn several times and walk in the direction opposite the exit, then—sideways, sideways—before you arrived at the entrance with its sixteen-foot wooden doors. Of course, there were cameras—two cameras, one on the right, the other on the left—but that too was normal, since this building was not entirely a civilian structure; on the whole, Lisa, I had nothing to fear.

I pulled the heavy door, not entirely eager to submit, and stepped into absolute darkness, allowing the door to slam shut with the sound of live bait shot from a fishing slingshot as it hits a sand embankment. The premises were illuminated by a single 60-watt bulb, which was why I didn't shudder immediately: my eyes needed time to get accustomed to the initially incoherent (Oh, God!) darkness and to make out a second sixteen-foot armored door with studs like those on a World War I tank: by the looks of it, this door led to the MGB Prosecutor's Office.

I stood in the narrow five-foot space between the decorative simulacrum of a door that seemed to have been designed not to frighten outsiders and the gloomy metal door that led to the MGB, that had last been painted long ago but, judging by the bubbled layers of paint that hung from it, used to be painted often. I cast my eyes along the metal surface, looking for a bell, but, of course, there was none: a doorbell would have made this armored colossus accessible, controllable, from the side where those to be interrogated stood. I stood and sensed how precipitously I was losing size, but the door still didn't open. Then—I don't know after how many seconds—I decided to turn around, and shuddered once again. To the right, in the wall of the giant door frame, was a reinforced glass window with little holes arranged in a whimsical little circle. All this time a pair of unbearably attentive eyes had been watching me through the window from underneath a shiny visor. Frightened, I noticed none of his other features, or perhaps, my dear Lisa, he didn't have any! I hurriedly approached the eyes and the visor—what an enormous door it was— taking two, three, four steps to travel the width of its right panel, leaned toward the holes in the thick glass, and stated: "I'm here for an interrogation. At nine."

The eyes asked point-blank, "Investigator?" I needed to have spent all that time inside that building, in front of the huge, old, terrifying door in order to comprehend that he'd asked a question. But comprehension did little to help. I needed to provide a last name that had not at all stuck in my head. It had stuck, but with long ears, a dark, childish part of the hair, a mustache, and other insults drawn on its face and concomitant with its short pronunciation. "Poopik?" "Tupid?" What the hell was his name? I was not eager to try these variations aloud in the presence of the attentive eyes underneath the visor.

"Nevinsky, Nevinsky. I am at nine A.M. I don't remember who my investigator is."

The eyes slowly, drawlingly, pronounced the name. I understood that the voice behind the glass was amplified many times over: even the visor cap's breathing could be heard. The little holes were there so I would approach the window more closely and bend toward it so that he could study my face.

"How can you not know who your investigator is?" the voice asked. I had the feeling that that same evening those eyes would tell his officer friends about me as an anecdote. "Get this: I processed a pass for this nerd today who didn't even know the name of his investigator." I was at a loss how to answer, Lisa. He put the question in such a way, as if the investigator were my guardian angel or lover. I fumbled for an idea with my lips, but he had already softened. It was obvious that he knew perfectly well who my investigator was and hinted through the hidden speakers right in my ear, "Tsupik. Tsupik is your investigator. Do not forget that again. Now . . ." (It took him a while to find a euphemism for the word "armed convoy.") "your escort will be right out. Wait here."

The huge door set into motion, slowing caving inward. Just at that moment a shrill alarm went off. At first I didn't understand that the alarm was signaling that the door was opening. In this building, Lisa, it's such an event when a door opens that they sound an alarm to give everyone a heads-up, even if the door was opening not to let me out, but, just the opposite, to suck me in. Beyond the door the light was so bright, so starkly bright that it hurt my eyes. The escort waited for me just at the entrance, left arm at his side, right arm bent and on his belt. Ah, right, he was wearing a holster. A holster with a pistol. If anything happened, he was ready to shoot in my direction. Was it unfastened? It looked like it wasn't. I allowed my face to grimace in perplexity, but neither his pose nor the expression on his face changed, and another thought occurred to me: how many of those who'd come before me had expressed the same surprise. If suddenly I turned out to be someone close to him—a coworker or just a cop who'd brought in a criminal and was amazed by his deportment, his hand on his holster—he would have brushed it all off with a grimace of repulsion for his own seriousness: "We have orders."

The door took a monstrously long time to open. Not waiting until it had swung wide enough for me to walk straight in, I—"What's your hurry?"—squeezed through it sideways, and having squeezed through, I found myself at a table covered with sheet metal, with simple instructions printed in red on the sign above it: BEFORE LYING ITEMS ON THE TABLE, INFORM THE CONVOY OFFICER OF ANY WEAPONS, SHARP OBJECTS, OR FLAMMABLE LIQUIDS IN YOUR POCKETS OR PURSE. I had the urge to correct and expound on the "lying," but was stopped once again by thoughts of how many "intellectuals" before me had attempted to bring the capriciousness of language to the attention of the organs; that for the most part in Section Five they interrogated precisely the kind who got worked up over "lay" and "lie" (perhaps it had been written as "lying" deliberately?) and that this demonstration of illiteracy was something you, nerd, could do diddly-squat to fix; that now you were the one who had to follow the rules for armed escorts and interrogations; and that it was precisely "lie" and not "lay," and if you started pontificating, you'd be given an explanation so competent as to who was an "intellectual" and who wasn't that you'd lose all desire to talk about language again, even before the desire appeared. This was a kind of torture, an additional form of psychomanipulation. But that was my paranoia again, my eternal paranoia.

"You know, it would be better to write 'lay' instead of 'lie'; otherwise it's not entirely correct," I couldn't resist saying. And I pulled from my pockets some crumpled sheets of paper, a metro token stuck inside them, and a straight pin.

"Understood. We'll correct it tomorrow." The officer saluted, after having arrived at some sort of conclusion about me. "Follow me. You don't need to lie anything from your pockets on the table because your status is different: no pat-down required."

He allowed himself to take three steps forward before I collected what I had pulled out of my pockets. I ran after him, trying not to step on the multiple shadows he cast under the merciless fluorescent lights. Arriving at a turn in the corridor, we found ourselves in front of a door, this one modern, made out of thick glass and steel-reinforced plastic. He placed his finger on a scanner and uttered a short phrase, and I thought about how all employees here must have identical fingerprints to simplify recognition. We ascended half a floor up the staircase, found ourselves in front of another door, and once again he scanned his finger and uttered an audio command. The length of the spaces one could pass before reaching the next post fell within the shooting range of a Makarov—not very long. That intolerably bright light: they ought to receive occupational hazard bonuses. We took a turn to the right past a walled-off staircase—by which we could have traversed in one minute the distance it had taken us ten minutes to walk—and then went down a narrow corridor to another narrow staircase that must have been installed when they converted the building for the MGB. Security checkpoints were everywhere. This went on for an unbearably long time, and I was already beginning to think about the investigator and prep myself for the interrogation, and it was like picking an abscess: why were they doing this to me, Lisa?

We reached the end of the corridor and stopped in front of a solid door painted, like the rest of the corridor, light salad-green. The escort took the intercom off his belt, stopped its hissing with a professional flick to switch on the receiver, then uttered a single word: "delivered." (That was me; I had been delivered.) No response was required, and he immediately placed the intercom back on his belt, hastily, by all appearances sensing the inappropriateness of the entire procedure: here he was talking to someone in the presence of the person he was conveying, the subject with whom he had avoided all pronouns and nouns, using only impersonal commands.

The door sounded a bell—not the rasping metallic sound of a drill, but an even, synthesized tone, though that didn't make it any less unpleasant. Once disarmed, the door allowed the guard to open it. Allowing me to pass first, the officer latched the door behind me: when doors here close, they don't rattle! They're already docile! Once again I found myself in the space between two doors: behind me was the solid, heavy door to the corridor; in front of me a sentimentally yellowish door made of varnished Soviet particle board with a window of frosted glass the color of milk and decorated with stamped geometric designs. There was also a new nameplate: E. P. TSUPIK. It had the look of a school principal's door, and now I was the schoolboy troublemaker. Well, here goes—I walked in!

The space behind the door did not live up to my expectations. After such a long reception and that corridor, I had assumed that I would see an office appointed in the style of design-minimalism: a desk with a dim lamp, a comfortable chair for the investigator, and an iron stool with no back and fastened to the floor for me. Nothing more. Nothing with which I, a dangerous subject under interrogation by the MGB, could crack the fragile skull of the investigator. But this office looked like a combination of residential apartment and an engineer's cubicle at some design institute. An engineer who spent too much time in that cubicle and therefore likely considered it more home than the place where he slept with his borscht- and pickle-reeking wife. In this space there seemed to be more light, and the very quality of the light was different. Oh, yes, the space adjoined a window, one that wasn't crisscrossed with bars: apparently this floor of the building was high enough that the person who risked a step out the window would have to be resolved to commit suicide, to which the prosecution would not object. The walls were lined with bookcases filled with thick tomes, and I wondered which of the classics investigators at the MGB now read. No, those were only mouse-colored binders with an endless number of case materials, and my case must be here somewhere, close by, close at hand.

Behind the desk in a welcoming pose (smiling, even!) sat a man of medium height with a large head and eyes that seemed to have too much space between them—an exact copy of the person depicted in the photograph on his desk that seemed a bit too, if you will, deliberately half-turned into the space of the office and not, intimately, at him. The photograph also contained two children, meaning that it had been taken by his wife, who was present in the photograph exclusively as the angle of view of her husband and children. The desk was covered with a sheet of glass with various graphs, lines, and charts beneath it. There were also documents on top of the glass, and an old computer with a yellowed (like paper) plastic monitor. The computer, Lisa, was more pathetic than anything else.

Once again I was struck by the urge to tell you, my dear, that they are all normal people, that this fellow was an average guy, and that in principle his job was ordinary too, and he didn't look like a vampire or a deity—but I'll refrain for the moment. I looked unabashedly about the room, noting on my second glance around the inventory numbers traced with a thick brush on the bookcases and the absence of a portrait of Dzerzhinsky or Muraviov, whom in my fantasies I had allowed to occupy a central position in the place where I would be interrogated. The man's smile waited patiently, and I returned my gaze to him, discovering that his hair was a light straw color and his eyes appeared bottomless owing to irises that seemed to have faded from constant exposure to the window's sun, just as had his monitor, and the shirt he wore, which was old and manufactured in some country that long ago had ceased to exist, like Czechoslovakia. The unreality and immateriality of these things left their traces on his entire image, lending relevance to what had been lost, like the U.S.S.R.

"Hello, hello." He rose to meet me after I had taken several more steps into the depths of the office, his greeting signifying unequivocally that I was now here, yes, here. I had unequivocally arrived. "Those security measures of ours didn't frighten you, did they?"

I seconded his tone of voice, responding in similar spirit that it wasn't every day you entered the same doors as those who had been arrested, but he corrected me:

"Uh, no. Here I am going to have to disappoint you: those in custody or under arrest are delivered by way of the inner courtyard. There's a fence there, and so forth." But I was still examining the long line of chairs in front of him and deciding which of them I was supposed to sit in. "Have a seat, please," he offered finally, just as in the movies—yes, yes, not "sit down," but "have a seat." I think it had really occurred to them that there was a huge, superstitious difference between the two.

I sat down, and once again he said nothing, repositioning some papers, which went on for so long it seemed as if he were proposing that I be the first to speak or that he was studying me surreptitiously, while I, remembering the advice of the peppered guy, asked:

"Before we begin our conversation, I would like to ask you . . ." Here I acted a bit too much like a free citizen, designating a long polite pause for him to insert his "name and patronymic," but I couldn't address him as "comrade investigator," as a prisoner would. That was all you and I needed, Lisa. He returned my politeness and volunteered in the same tone of voice:

"Evgeny Petrovich. Both of our fathers were Pyotrs."

"So, I wanted to ask you, Evgeny Petrovich, in what capacity have I been invited to your office? As a witness, a suspect, the accused?"

"My dear Anatoly Petrovich, why the formalities! Why make a mountain out of a molehill? What accused? If you were the accused, my good fellow, you would have arrived here not on your own two feet, but under armed escort, in handcuffs. I've called you in to have a perfectly normal conversation . . . As an admirer of the arts, if you wish. Well?"

This turn was not to my liking. He was trying to establish some kind of contact, to build a relationship, when everything within these walls was supposed to be unambiguously impersonal: "walk down the hall, sit down, answer." Why would the MGB want to establish a relationship with me? If they want to learn something about you, Lisa, let them ask! But if this is just a conversation, I might forget something extremely important and harm myself, you, us . . .

"All the same, Evgeny Petrovich, I would like to clarify for myself one important point. In light of the fact that my status relevant to the case you are conducting will not be formally determined soon . . ." I wove this web of complex terminology, hoping to pass as informed, prepared for a five-hour conversation, and knowledgeable as to how not to divulge information during it, of how not to incriminate myself. "So, in light of the fact that you prefer not to inform me of my status, might you apprise me, at least, of the article under which procedures have been initiated and the case is being investigated."

"So, Anatoly"—the investigator grew attentive and a bit sad—"I see that you found it necessary to consult with someone in anticipation of our meeting. Do you know what that leads me to conclude? Tell me, why would an ordinary person called in for a conversation undertake measures to defend himself? A person who has confidence in himself and who experiences no sense of guilt? Well, think about it. That is, Anatoly, for some reason you decided to play it safe and ran to . . . What? You called a lawyer? Perhaps you've also already given an interview about having been summoned by the MGB, and about having your fingers crushed in a doorjamb?"

"I didn't call anyone and didn't give any interviews," I bridled. "I didn't give any, because I didn't see any reason to. As for guilt or innocence, you yourself understand how anyone on their way to an interrogation at the MGB can hardly be certain of anything. You've done a lot to ensure it's that way."

"Oh, you shouldn't be repeating all those myths about us," the investigator scoffed. "You're a sensible person. But, let me repeat, this fretfulness of yours leads me as a professional to wonder."

"Listen," I was carried away. For some reason I couldn't just let him tell me his thoughts and get on with the interrogation. "Listen. Here we are, the two of us, having a conversation, as you would say, and if I say anything wrong, you're going to enter that into a transcript, then call me in again, only this time in handcuffs. Because a transcript is the basis for . . ."

"You, my good fellow, just don't want to hear what I'm saying. Why are you so unwilling to trust me?" The fact of the matter is, Lisa, he really did look insulted! Well, if not insulted, at least ruffled, and I was really beginning to feel ashamed. "I'm telling you: this is a friendly conversation. That's all! And I'm . . . I'm, by the way, not going to compile any transcripts! None at all! We're speaking off the record."

"I won't have to sign anything?"

"Nothing! We'll have our conversation, and you'll go home to finish drinking your coffee." (I hadn't finished my coffee, Lisa!)

"All right. I understand, Evgeny Petrovich. I will answer your questions honestly. Off the record."

"Good. What was the nature of your relationship with Elisaveta Supranovich?"

And here—perhaps he did so on purpose, Lisa—I was at a loss. The fact was, my sweet, he spoke of you in the past tense. While I was contemplating that grammatical nuance, the time came for me to answer that horrible question hanging in the air . . .

"Well, our relationship was warm and amicable."

I know, Lisa, that you're going to object that perhaps I shouldn't have said anything to him about us, but we could have been seen, seen, and it was better not to lie to him outright. I gave a superb answer: short and unassailable. "Warm and amicable." Who would contest that our relationship had been "warm and amicable"? No one!

"When and where did you become acquainted?" he responded immediately.

"We became acquainted . . . in the spring of this year. At the Chess Café on Karl Marx Street. By chance."

"How often did you meet after that?"

"Well . . . We met . . . regularly."

"Was your relationship of a romantic nature?"

How was I supposed to answer that question? How broad was their definition of "romantic"? Did they mean sleeping together or sheepish transfixion at the door of your bedroom, with a bouquet of roses?

"I don't know," I rushed to answer, at the same time contemplating the silliness of the term. "Of a romantic nature? As when you go to the movies holding hands? We didn't go to the movies. I request that you make special note of that in your . . . report. Not once."

"Why are you being so rude to me?" The investigator, disappointed, set aside a document that had turned up under his hand at that moment so bitter for him. The document, which had despaired to crawl under a pile of others like it, bent upward and then expired.

"Excuse me, please, Evgeny Petrovich. The truth is it sounds silly— 'romantic nature' . . . Like something off a condom wrapper or in a high school principal's speech just before the prom . . ."

"All right, Anatoly, let me put it this way: did you enter into intimate contact? Let me rule out any future verbal loopholes: did you, as they say nowadays, have sex with citizen Elisaveta Supranovich?"

I was the one who had driven me into a corner. I could have answered something about "romantic relations," then wiggled out of it any way I wanted, saying that had I understood "relationships of a romantic nature" to exclude sex . . . in short . . . What was I to say? Right, this:

"Is it possible for me not to answer that question?"

"It is," the investigator answered, even more disappointed.

Well, the whole scene . . . was like one friend asking another: "So did you screw her?" As though the second guy, the high-minded one, wasn't telling, but of course he hadn't screwed her, because if he had screwed her, he would have described it in full detail already. Maybe that's how he understood it? Or did he know something? The problem was that I didn't know what he knew, and I couldn't very well ask, and it wasn't enough that he might know a lot, he might ask a direct question about what he didn't know. And God forbid I lie about something he knew!

"Well, Anatoly. I have the feeling that our conversation is going nowhere. Can you just tell me, then, when and where you last saw each other?"

"But why have you started looking for her, Evgeny Petrovich? If we're going to have a conversation, it goes in two directions, and I get to ask you some questions, too, yes?"

The investigator reflected. That is, you and I understand who gave the orders to search for you. But he couldn't tell me "Nikolai Mikhailovich, personally." The situation had been reversed: I knew what he, the snake, was attempting to conceal.

"The girl has disappeared," he began.

"Who says she's disappeared?" I refused to let him relax. "What if she suddenly left on vacation to Nice?"

"Without telling anyone?"

"Who would she tell?"

"Well, you, for example, Anatoly." The investigator's eyes flashed slyly, and I realized that I wasn't the only one having fun. "Did she tell you where she might leave for?"

Perhaps they had called me in just to ask this question.

"No, Evgeny Petrovich, she did not inform me that she was planning to go anywhere."

I think that I told him a bit of an untruth: you had said that you were going to disappear, but "disappear" and "go away" are not one and the same thing, right?

"I have no idea where she is now. And I'd like to know who told you that she has disappeared? Maybe he knows." I cast off all reserve.

"The missing Elisaveta Supranovich has a grandmother in Kobryn whom she called no less than twice a week. Besides her grandmother she has several girlfriends. All of these people have brought it to the attention of the proper investigative authorities that all lines of communication with Elisaveta Supranovich have been severed and that no one has seen her for a long time. We could not possibly not react. What's more, the foreign mass media received a lead . . ."

"That you yourselves planted," I exploded. "Admit it! If we're having a heart-to-heart conversation!"

"This is the first I've heard of the MGB collaborating with antigovernment publications abroad," he parried professionally. "But the fact that even they started talking about this disappearance left us no option but to investigate. We opened a case."

"Missing persons or murder?" I put the question prompted by the vampire.

"Dear, dear Anatoly Petrovich! In forensic science no determination of murder can be made until a body has been found. A body hasn't been found!"

When he called you a "body" it made me sick, and I meekly held my silence.

"When and under what circumstances did you last see citizen Supranovich?"

"November 18," I responded, perhaps a bit too hastily.

"That is, on the evening of her disappearance," he said slowly.

"Are you sure the disappearance occurred on November 18?"

"An aggregate of factors, Anatoly Petrovich, permits the investigation to presume that the disappearance occurred on 18 November at around midnight," he stated matter-of-factly. "Precisely where and when did you and Elisaveta Supranovich meet on 18 November?"

"In the evening."

"At what time?"

"In the evening."

"Be more precise!"

"Well"—I decided to surrender (after all, our conversation was off the record)—"at approximately 2000."

"That allows me to conclude that you, esteemed Anatoly, were the last person to see citizen Supranovich. Where did your meeting occur?"

The question I was so afraid of.

"Well . . . I don't remember . . . I don't remember, Evgeny Petrovich." Not even I would have believed me, Lisa! It sounded so pathetic. I expected further questioning and even threats.

The investigator lowered his head and cleared his throat.

"All right," he said. "All right."

The protective magic offered by the peppered vampire had worked. Apparently, "I don't remember" was a form of protection.

"I can't force you to remember all that," the investigator said contemplatively. "Modern medicine is not aware of any drugs that refresh memory. Usually in such circumstances a person is placed under arrest for six to eight weeks, which gives him adequate time to recall all the nuances of the case he's been called in to discuss."

His intonation had changed: I heard his complete readiness to arrest me. More important, I saw not a single reason to prevent him from doing so. I was here, on his territory. My car was parked at home.

"But I am not going to arrest you. I'll simply suggest that you reflect more on the following. Just sit here for a while and think. You are the last person who saw Elisaveta alive. After that she disappeared. And for some reason you are refusing to inform the investigation of the place where your last meeting occurred. Is that normal? Is that not supposed to lead me as an investigator to certain suspicions?"

Here, my sweet, the protective film that had prevented me from arguing with this person who continued to use the past tense when referring to you ripped. As if I supposed that you had heard it all and pursed your lips when I hadn't corrected him.

"What makes you think that Elisaveta Supranovich has, as you put it, 'ceased to exist'? What kind of language is that? Is that what you call professional? After all, you yourself said, no body—no murder, and there's no Elisaveta . . ."

"If you were listening to me attentively, I never used the word 'murder.' Although as it seems to me as a, believe me, rather experienced operations specialist, the scene found by the investigative team at the apartment on Marx Street gives us cause to believe that Elisaveta Supranovich is no longer among the living."

No, Lisa, I still felt that they could be playing with me, but enormous hammers had started pounding in my ears, blood began to pulse in my eyes. (I wonder whether he could read me as well as that beer-guzzling physiognomist?)

"What was there?" I asked, my voice hoarse.

"In investigative language it's known as 'evidence of a struggle': overturned furniture, broken dishes. Blood that—it saddens me to speak about this, Anatoly Petrovich—was positively identified through comparison with data in her medical records as Elisaveta Supranovich's. Do you want to see the photographs?"

I shook my head like a madman. Don't. Now you need to calm down and continue the conversation in a . . . calm tone of voice. No longer among the living? What the fuck had he cooked up, Lisa? What's he . . . Huh? The office began to swim, but I kept my bearings. Calmly, Lisa. Under your heart, as you put it, you had the child of the Minister of State Security Muraviov. You were afraid of being followed. You wanted to cover your tracks. Overturned furniture, of course. Of course, a blot from a pricked finger (immediately, I hope, disinfected with perfume). Yes, yes, it all fits. But why was I starting to talk about this aloud? What kind of fool was I? I was trying to prove to him that you were alive!

" . . . possible to allow that Elisaveta didn't want anyone to know that she was on the run, that is correct," all of that said by my voice, the voice of the person who wanted to conceal precisely this, Lisa! Forgive me! I simply wanted to make a convincing case that you were alive. "Instead of disappearing quietly, she overturned the furniture in the apartment and planted evidence of a struggle. And, well . . . She dripped some blood from her finger."

The investigator looked up, by all appearances to demonstrate his contempt for my idiocy, but my version was more to my liking, much more . . .

"Anatoly," he said, pulling out a stack of documents. "It wasn't just blood. Other bodily fluids and tissue fragments were discovered at the scene of the crime."

"And what kind of bodily fluids does a person have?" someone asked for me.

Evgeny Petrovich smirked as if he had just told his friends a joke in the presence of a foreigner, and the foreigner hadn't understood, while all his friends had been laughing for some time already.

"Well, in our particular case . . ." His hands unsealed the packet of documents. "We're referring to the contents of her intestines, silly as that sounds, which spilled out as a result of disembowelment that resulted, possibly, from multiple stab wounds, but that's not very professional of me: I am presupposing what I can't know (the packet of documents was unsealed and one of the photographs slipped out face up in the direction of my eyes). What's more, even if you could explain to me how Elisaveta managed to squeeze so much blood from her finger, it wouldn't answer the question why, in order to stage her own disappearance, she punctured her gall bladder, as evidenced, once again, by the picture of the crime scene."

The photograph turned in my direction, finally, and my eyes saw what he had been describing. Oh. There. Fuck. I can't. I'll talk. A bit disconnectedly. Lisa. Fuck. Photographed there. There was the living room. The white living room with the grand piano. One of the chairs was overturned, and the floor, and the rug, or animal skin—I don't remember what was there, fuck. Right in the middle like the stain of the Black Sea on a map of the world . . . excessive, enormous, and frightening, Lisa, a pool of blood . . . there . . . He says the blood is yours, fuck, how much was left in you . . . What's this? . . . And those fluids . . . Indeed, it might have been staged, but where did so much of your blood come from? And the room, the same one, I examined it as if through a magnifying glass. Right, he was showing me different photographs, including one of just the floor shot close up using macrophotography.

"At the same time, it cannot be asserted beyond doubt that the pieces of intestinal tissue and bile belonged to Elisaveta Supranovich: she had no tissue samples taken when she was alive, and only an autopsy will provide the definitive answer. When the body is found."

His voice was saying something, but I was thinking. Lisa, there is so little air!

"I want to make an official statement," I stated, already looking at myself as if from the outside. What else could I do? I didn't know. "I want to bring to the attention of the investigation the fact that Elisaveta Supranovich had, as you put it . . . a romantic relationship with Minister of State Security Nikolai Muraviov." (Forgive me! Forgive me! Forgive me!) "Therefore, should it be proven that Elisaveta Supranovich was murdered . . . Muraviov . . . and his ministry . . . To which you also . . ."

"Slander, my esteemed Anatoly Petrovich, is a crime punishable by law. Think about that."

"Right, yes, excuse me. I have no proof for the court. Then let me put it another way. I request that the investigation, if it cannot answer the question at least ask itself. At least. Please. I am asking, without . . . the question of . . . Just give it some thought, Evgeny Petrovich: how could an ordinary girl . . . unemployed as I understand? Right. An ordinary unemployed girl own five- or six- or devil-knows-how-many-room apartments in the capital, mansions in Tarasova and Sokol, and real estate in Italy, France, and Belgium? Where did she get so many cars? Hmm?"

"Listen, my dear fellow: Elisaveta's property status has no relevance to the case. It has been established, for example, that no valuables were removed from the apartment, and for that reason we are not inquiring into how much she had of what. Probably, the court itself will not inquire. You and I are having a conversation about where you were on the night of the kidnapping, and you're telling me about mansions!"

Got it. That is, it's stupid to complain to mama about mama. Well, that's clear. They'll see what they want to see, but I don't believe that you're dead, Lisa! We were outplayed. That's what was meant by "outplayed." He's asking something again.

"What kind of letters did you write to her?"

Ah-ha! He knows about the letters? Though, of course, if they found out immediately that you had disappeared, then the apartment, without doubt, had been under observation—Oh, God! Had I revealed too much in those letters?

"Perhaps, you might remember now where you and Elisaveta Supranovich met on the evening of her disappearance?"

I didn't react at all, it seems, but he had already moved on to something new. Judging by his fricatives and lancitives, the something new was important.

" . . . attention to the situation you've found yourself in, Anatoly. I am not calling on you to cooperate with the investigation. By all appearances that would be naive on my part. In your situation, to collaborate . . ."

He was talking as if he suspected me in connection with your disappearance, Lisa!

"Just consider what we're left to think about you. You met with Elisaveta that night. The neighbors at 16 Serafimovich Street, in apartments 11 and 13, heard some activity in your kitchen around eight in the evening."

(He knows so much!)

"They heard Elisaveta say something to you, and you shouted at her, Anatoly. The neighbors will testify to that in court. Further—I am not going to beat around the bush, because you don't want to talk to me anyway, so at least give it the proper amount of thought—further, they say that they heard a door slam and a woman's high heels running down the stairs, and that shortly after Elisaveta left, you followed. We don't know where you were in the space of time between 2000 and 0000, but we're working on that, and soon that information, too, will be incontestable: the cameras at the train station provide interesting results . . . So, we know that—thanks to video monitoring devices, again—that you were in the proximity of the building on Karl Marx Street that night at approximately 0020, just at the time when—as blood coagulation tests have shown—when Elisaveta's encounter with an unidentified kidnapper (we won't call it a murder for now) occurred. We do not know where you were after that, just as we do not know what you did with the body. That's the situation. It's all simple and straightforward. Like a conversation between two friends."

I was stunned, of course. I just sat there, silent, repeatedly gulping down my saliva. I had too much saliva in my throat, and I was attempting to swallow it all down, but there was too intolerably, inhumanly, much, and it wouldn't go down . . .

"But"—here Evgeny Petrovich raised one finger to attract my convulsive attention—"I will do this. I will let you go, Anatoly Petrovich. I will release you and will not even ask you to sign a guarantee note that you will not leave the country. You may go wherever you please."

I balked at his summation. It was illogical. From everything he had said it followed that I should be locked away right then and there. Did this person really believe me? What kind of idiotic game was this?

In the meantime, Evgeny Petrovich had submerged the button on his old intercom and ordered affably: "Escort."

"Well, you see? And you thought so poorly of all of us." The investigator grinned as he rose. "We had a wonderful conversation, you told me nothing, and I revealed the entire case to you." Rustling could be heard outside the door. "That's all. You can go. I want to emphasize once again, Anatoly Petrovich, that I am not requiring you to sign a guarantee note that you will not leave the country. You are a free person and can travel freely to any place that comes into your head. For the time being, I am not requiring an oath. And for the time being you are free, naturally."

This, of course, was the devil's work, Lisa! If they were certain that I killed you, then why were they releasing me? Why had he mentioned the guarantee note a second time?

"I can go now?" I asked to make sure.

"Go, go," the investigator urged me, with a gesture toward the door. "Think hard about everything I told you and make a decision. Good-bye."

I couldn't have killed you, Lisa. But the way they put it, it was precisely

I who had done it, but I . . . I never struck you; it was you who beat your bear and pushed him off the bed. I vaguely remember what I did at the station that evening and why I suddenly ran to the apartment on Marx Street—an awareness, vague forebodings . . . I had mistaken the coffee girl for you; I had intended to speed to Orsha in my car. Total nonsense. What had forced me to run to your place? I had had the sense that you were calling me, and I had run, as fast as my legs would carry me, but how could I explain that to the investigator? How should I answer their questions, if they arise, and they will arise, oh, they will arise!

What did I do after I felt that you were no longer in that icy snow-white living room after I left Marx & Spencer Street? My eyes have preserved the memory of a park, streetlamps, and park paths . . . What did I do there? How can I prove to them that I didn't hide—forgive me, Lisa—let's assume your body was there—how could I have carried you down from a third floor more like the fifth? How could I have carried you, unnoticed, across the center of town? Where did they get those crazy ideas?

"Thank you, I can just leave? Good-bye, I wish you well"—although I'm not certain those steadfast eyes in the weapon port could be wished well, that the well wouldn't kill them, wouldn't spell the victory of good over evil. But (alas!) it is not proper to wish anyone anything bad, not proper. If we, Lisa, really had . . . fought in that snow-white living room, I would have been soaked with your blood, but I didn't discover any traces of blood on myself when I woke! Murder—that's an immense shock; if you've committed it. You'd remember what took place for a long time after. I would have remembered. But where did they come up with those crazy ideas? I? You? Killed? And buried your corpse somewhere, like a hard-core criminal? Well? I, with only enough skill to pound a computer keyboard? Buried . . . a corpse . . . I didn't even have a shovel, comrade investigator. Could you, Anatoly Petrovich, have dumped citizen Supranovich in a sewer somewhere so that now she's covered over with snow? But where is the blood? Where were the traces of soil under my fingernails that morning? I rolled her in a carpet, did I?

I remember my first morning without you, Lisa, I remember that I was like a robot, that essentially from that day forward I walked about constantly in a somnambulistic state, but that was all because I had lost you. I had become angry with you when you said that you were pregnant by Muraviov. I hated you, Lisa. But it never would have occurred to me to strike you. I've never hurt anyone except myself. No, it's all delirium,

delirium carefully inculcated in me by the MGB. They want me to come to them with a confession, to admit to a murder I didn't commit. But why didn't they make me sign the guarantee not to leave? He, that Poopik fellow, had said that I could go wherever I wanted, but why would I want to leave? After all, you disappeared here. I will stay here. I don't believe that I killed you. I love you. Let them all fuck themselves.

[4]

HE UNDERSTOOD what was obstructing his recall—a certain plastic melody coming from the bedroom, a thin, tentative little voice that lacked, if you will, a couple of notes. It wasn't so much the melody that kept him from concentrating, but a certain strained quality that lent the music a primitive fourth-grade-music-school quality. A robot—thoroughly repulsed by his own work but fated, despite this, to crank out the required number of not entirely mutually concordant notes over and over to the same preprogrammed beat—would have played like that, producing a melody of sorts, but strained, strained, and how with that music could he remember where his father's damned (not damned, but beloved) knife had disappeared to? Yes, yes, the light had again gone out precisely when Anatoly was in the final stages of some activity that required light— something sentimental—although he couldn't now remember what. The light had to be restored so it would be there when Anatoly next took it into his head to engage in the same activity. But the knife had vanished. He tried sticking an ordinary table knife into the fissure of the fuse box (noting as he did the frication of the phrase "fissure of the fuse box"), but the knife, as predicted by family legend, merely bent itself out of shape, its blade twisted sideways, and although Anatoly spent a long time trying to straighten it back into shape, he did not entirely succeed. He searched the entire apartment, but his father's two-millimeter-thick, wooden-handled knife didn't turn up, perhaps because bathroom cabinets illuminated by a sole wind-flickered candle surrender very little information. In the end the fuse box opened with the help of an ordinary fork handle, but he needed to remember now where his father's knife had gone and not wander about the apartment like a geriatric count scouring his ancestral estate for his young wife. Remember where, when, and under what circumstances, but that strained, heaving—as if climbing uphill—music from the bedroom kept getting in the way, damn it.

"Hello?" Anatoly said into the receiver.

"Tol, hi. It's Dan." His voice was serious. Dan with a serious voice? "Tol, I did what you asked me to. It's all beginning to come together, Tol. Meet me in fifteen minutes at the Niamiha fountain."

That meant he had to pour himself into his coat and head out. Fifteen minutes. Hmm.

"My Frau doesn't look good in the daylight," he decided in his head as he got in behind the wheel and remembered how enigmatic and even solemn the car looked in the dark. Yes, yes, BMWs are nocturnal automobiles. He tried to distract himself with more nonsense as he cut a series of sharp turns and headed for the avenue. But his consumerist positivism quickly waned. It was apparent from the protracted delay he took pulling away from the stoplight when a girl at the wheel of an SUV turned up alongside him. In addition to that, at the intersection near the Trinity district he decided that he was a passenger, and it took a while for him to realize that the horns blaring behind him were not intended for the driver of the minibus he was riding in, and that he—he—needed to wake up, come to his senses, and keep his eyes on the road. In all other respects his driving style was the same as always.

After parking the car, he took as a sign of imminent release from his depression the extent to which the car stood in geometric proximity to the white line designating the boundaries of its parking space; he was so elated that for a while he couldn't remember why he had driven to the store, and he was already running down a mental list of possible household purchases. Oh, right, Dan! Dan was about to tell him something important. Something of such value that . . .

"At the Niamiha fountain" was his and Dan's toponymic shorthand for a summer café so approximating the Dukhmiany Bar in its backstreet quality that as proof it no longer closed down for the winter. Dan certainly knew how to designate meeting places. But he had his own reasons, his own reasons. In light of *what precisely* he wanted to communicate he needed to be certain that the place was safe for the gloomiest of conversations.

The snow-drifted plastic tent bedecked with a local beer sign was located on the second level of a shopping complex built back in the days of the Evil

Empire alongside a coquettish—coquettish for a country that once had produced more atomic bombs than men's suit styles—winding staircase to the first level. Alongside the café's tent was a balustrade made of metallic plates already tinged with rust. In the summer the place was crowded, but in the winter, when the entirety of the second floor was blanketed with snow, the only people with any reason to come here would be the groundskeepers who spent the whole day clearing the snow and hoped to warm up with a refreshing libation. It was, indeed, groundskeepers with kind red faces and wearing orange uniforms with runic acronyms on the back who were the tent's only visitors when, not entirely confidently, Anatoly opened the door.

The café had no heat except vodka and a hot plate on which to fry pancakes, and for this reason the woman behind the bar and only waitress was difficult not only to remember, but even to catch a glimpse of under sweater, scarf, and fur hat pulled down to her eyes.

Dan, of course, didn't show up—not after fifteen minutes, and not after half an hour. Anatoly ordered himself green tea—a portion of quickly cooling boiled water in a plastic cup that came with a folded packet you were supposed to unfold, disembowel, and dip into the water. The teabag immediately filled his cup with swamp ooze that reeked of fish, or was it campfire? He was amazed that the tea wasn't half-bad. He also realized that the balustrade looking out over the fountain could be seen through the tent's Plexiglas window, and standing on the balustrade were a he and a she, embracing and looking downward, he shyly withdrawing while she clung and clung to him, both of them laughing and in love. (If only he could catch a glimpse of their faces!) And that tea was burning his cheeks, how hot his cheeks were from the thin, salty rivulets streaming from his eyes to the corners of his lips. No, damn it, damn it, hurry up and wipe them away with the back of your freezing hand!

Dan burst into the café with typical Dan energy. A short coat, a sweatshirt hood, and two tiny earbuds that swung pendulously from his neck and through which electronic "pump house" sounded like a chirring grasshopper. As if after a quick run, he collapsed sideways onto the bench opposite Anatoly and quickly looked under the table. Dan had never had habits like that before, and Anatoly, raising his eyebrows, was already pulling the battery out of his cell phone.

"I'm gonna get myself a beer." Dan jumped to his feet again. "You want one?"

Anatoly nodded toward the tea, whose remains, clumped around the squeezed tea bag, were already crusted with ice.

"What's with the piousness? Doing penance? Not a drop? Hey, maybe a beer anyway?" Dan was already sitting down with an overflowing, dripping plastic mug.

Anatoly grimaced and without having entirely thought it through, blurted out some commentary:

"Come on, man . . . It's not even Salivaria beer. The sort of sweet one. I understand that the malt is local, that there are no alternatives in this country, and brewers get put behind bars, but why do I have to pour that 'food security' down my throat? And why are you all so hooked on beer? Why don't you also tell me that you're a great admirer of my talent . . ."

"Tol, I'm a great admirer of your talent." Dan apparently had picked up on a certain shade of Anatoly's intonation to which he should have taken offense, but hadn't entirely figured out what stood behind the tone or why he should be offended. "Otherwise I wouldn't risk my ass. What's the problem?"

"Yeah . . . I got offered a beer in approximately the same circumstances."

"Ah, right. How did it go?"

"All right. It went all right, Dan."

"Did that Ivanich guy tell you what to do about the transcript? Read carefully whatever you put your autograph on?"

"Dan. There was no transcript."

"Now you're talking nonsense." Dan was so convinced he was right that he didn't bother to listen to Anatoly's response, but he turned off his player anyway, thinking that when Anatoly started to answer, he would remember how it had really been and correct himself.

"Dan, I realize that it sounds strange, but there was no transcript."

"Dude, these guys don't work without transcripts. For them a transcript is the fundamental form of record-keeping. If there's a transcript of the interrogation, conversation, or inquiry, then the interrogation, conversation, inquiry took place. No transcript means that instead of doing what he was supposed to, the dick went to a soccer game. Quit talking out of your ass."

"Dan, that's the whole point: I was warned. Over a glass of beer, by the way. But there was no transcript!"

"I need another toke on that one," Dan pushed his dreads into the hood of his sweatshirt. "It doesn't jell. Then what the hell did he call you in for? Did you spill anything?"

"No, I didn't say much at all. More like he talked a lot. Too much even."

"Listen, spare me the semantics! 'Too much.' He said as much as the office told him to say. Let's turn to something else. I don't want to go into details, but I'll tell you one thing so you can scope the situation for yourself. So what was the gist of everything he said? What stuck in your head after the conversation? The main thing?"

"That they suspect me of committing a heinous crime."

"Well that's normal, Tol! That's how you always feel after a conversation with the MGB! But what was special? What was significant besides that?"

"That they didn't force me to sign a guarantee that I wouldn't leave the country?"

"I'm not asking you. I'm more suggesting that you give it some thought."

"Yes," Anatoly said to himself, "I'll give it some thought. I'll think about why they called me in just to inform me that they weren't issuing an arrest warrant. And that I could go anywhere I wanted. While I can still go. For the time being. Which means, immediately. That's it. They called me in to suggest that I leave the country. How interesting!"

"How are things in general?" Dan looked at him closely. He was a good guy, Dan. "Tol, I don't want to frighten you, but you look lousy. They didn't shoot you up with anything?"

Anatoly shook his head and spilled, like beer: The person who lent meaning to my inhalations and exhalations, the girl who called my body "her country," "her country, Anatolia," has been killed; she's no longer among the living; she doesn't answer when I talk to her, and they suspect me of committing the murder—me—and we had a nasty talk the night before it happened, and the neighbors are ready to testify in court that they heard it. So, Dan, my friend, how would you expect me to look?

Naturally, he said this all to himself, to himself. Dan was a good guy. He was solid as a rock. He'd done a lot to help him. He was on his side. And because he had to answer something, this, it seems, is what he said:

"Dan, listen, doesn't it bother you that you drink beer, just as they do? When I met . . . with that Ivanovich, he went heavy on the beer . . . Is this institution-wide?"

"Tol, man, beer is a solar drink, Jah* in a world of water. Just look at how it smiles at us when held up to the light. As for Nalivaria there's not a country in the world with as sweet and at the same time bitter, foamless

---

* In the Rastafarian movement Jah is the name of God.

beer! It's a kick in the balls of globalization. I mean the globalization of taste. Everywhere, from Jakarta to Mexico City, the taste of beer is pretty much the same; only ours is so unique it brings tears to your eyes. No, my man, when it comes to beer I am a patriot."

Anatoly still wanted to ask whether Dan had ever seen corpses at the scene of some incident; whether he'd ever gone with an investigation group to the scene of a crime to better understand the particular nature of working for the MGB; whether he'd ever conducted an interrogation, or shot a weapon, but all these questions were not so much insulting as they were incorrect and hurtful. He admitted:

"To be honest, Dan, my sleep of late has been terrible. And so has everything else. You understand what an interrogation at the MGB is. But, thanks for everything, friend . . . You're not like them, even if you do work for them."

"To the point, Tol, to the point." Dan turned serious—something Anatoly had just said was not entirely to his liking. "Tomorrow at seven at the philharmonic there's going to be a gala concert. Until this morning no one suspected anything, and tickets were available everywhere—at box offices and ticket agencies—as they should be. Well, this morning word came down that Muraviov was going to the concert. Ticket sales, of course, have been canceled, and all tickets for the two rows in front and two rows behind the one where Muraviov will be sitting have been recalled."

"What for?"

"Those rows are for his bodyguards. It's always that way. Padding. 'Always Ultra' is what they call it. Muraviov's row is for state functionaries: members of the cabinet, the President, the Speaker of the House, and other riffraff. Naturally, I can't get you a seat in that row or in the bodyguards' rows. And in general it would be better to seat you ten rows behind Muraviov so as not to raise suspicions. Sorry, but you'll be right near the exit. No one, not even television, has any info that Muraviov is going to tomorrow's concert, so people are scalping tickets as usual. Now, closer to the topic. Tol, under no circumstances should you attempt to approach him before the beginning of the concert. You'll be stopped in your tracks, and if you look suspicious, they'll lock you up. They don't mess around. You arrive, sit down in your seat, and stay there like a moth on a woolen coat. In connection with the honored guest's presence the program has been shortened from two to one part because it's hard to manage security during intermissions. Two old-fart virtuosos from Soviet times—people's artists, laureates of state awards—are going to play. When they finish playing, the audience will call them back for an encore, as always happens at those stuffy events. But anal says that they're going to split immediately: into their cabs and back to their respective domiciles.

"Who says?" Anatoly was surprised.

"Anal. The analytical section. According to their field prognosis—and anal, believe me, never makes mistakes—the old farts want to protect their reputations. The ones awarded state prizes by the Party are all vain. They think they're all Richters, the fuckers! They'll be afraid that Muraviov will want to climb onto the stage to hug them, after which they won't even get invited to play at the Jurmala festival. Like von Karajan and Hitler. Some handshakes never wash off. Of course, nobody gives a shit about these Karajans, especially after anal's prognosis . . .

"Here we come straight to your plan of action. When you see that the concert is over and the geezers have left the stage, start edging your way toward the exit. Of course, they'll immediately cut you off: there will be snipers in the balcony, and the hall is under observation from backstage. But there'll be a lot like you; it's normal not to want to stick around for an encore. At some point everyone will rise to their feet and start shouting 'encore': you'll have two or three minutes before that. As a rule it gets pretty difficult to move around almost immediately, so try to be in the aisle by that time."

"Which one?"

"Hold on, I'm getting to that. After letting the audience yell 'encore' for five minutes, representatives from youth and veterans' organizations (the first three rows in front of the stage) will start chanting 'Mur-ah-viov' instead of 'encore,' calling him to come on stage. Gradually the chant will be picked up by the rest of the audience, and you should join in too, otherwise they'll notice and surround you. At this point all the exits will be closed, as both a security measure and to guarantee that no one leaves while he's playing. Muraviov will go up on stage. He'll play several pieces, something not too long, because he doesn't like to play for long in public. People will not be sent back to their seats for this period of time. From here on there are two possible scenarios. The first is if there's a 'code red,' an Achtung, or the security chief gets a bug up his ass for some reason, or without reason, more likely, Muraviov will slip backstage and be led out through the back exit. This might happen for several reasons, like, well, he thinks he played poorly. Or he imagines negative vibes from the audience . . . In short, if he splits, don't get upset. Lie low and wait for my next call. The second scenario is more favorable. Muraviov comes out to speak with the people. Basically, the conversation will be short as he passes through the crowd, listening to their praise. His heavies, Tol, will have determined that the safest evacuation route is by way of the central exit. It's the widest; in case of panic or a stampede Muraviov wouldn't get trampled. From where you're standing it's an equally zippy move either to the left or to the center, so, as soon as everything is over, remember: leg it toward the middle, to the center aisle. And wait for him there. If you're lucky, you'll wind up an arm's length away."

Dan flicked his finger at a glossy square of paper lying on the table right in front of him; spinning like a top, the square landed right in front of Anatoly. STATE PHILHARMONIC SOCIETY it read. Indicating that the conversation was over, Dan finished off his beer in several large gulps and had already begun to get up, when he suddenly remembered and sat down again.

"One more thing, Tol. I don't know what you've got planned: that's your business. Only God forbid you try to smuggle a weapon inside. Or, if you manage to smuggle something in, you try to pull it out. There's a ton of undercover agents planted in the crowd, and every half-yard of the hall is covered by a barrel with optical monitoring that's checked constantly. If you so much as stick your hand inside your jacket or make a quick move, you're a corpse. They'll load you with so much lead your coffin will be too heavy to lift. These people are accustomed to shooting other people; for them it doesn't matter . . . You, Osama bin Laden, their own mother . . . One other thing. If you intend to do something stupid, they'll detain you, interrogate you, and, possibly, break all your fingers. So, remember: you bought the ticket from a scalper the day before the concert. You haven't seen me and received no instructions."

"Dan," Anatoly grimaced in reproach.

"That's it. Ciao. Wait for ten minutes, then leave. Break a femur." Dan winked to Anatoly, pulled the hood of his sweatshirt over his head, and waving across the café, dissolved into a closed door. "Thanks, Dan," Anatoly shouted belatedly through the doors. "Thanks a lot," he repeated, not quite sure that he was grateful.

He looked out the Plexiglas window. Plexiglas. Acrylicized glass. Crying-eyes-icized glass. A window of crying eyes. But no, the couple over there, unfortunately, had left. Or maybe not. But of course they weren't there, luckily, luckily, luckily.

He had already donned his raincoat, already buttoned and belted it, already opened the door, when the telephone rang back in the kitchen, but just then he wasn't up to farewell speeches, no matter who was calling, and he crossed the threshold and was just about to close the door while the telephone continued to moan—it really needed help—and thoughts of Lisa suddenly flashed to mind (as if she could call him on his home phone), and without removing his shoes, he stamped over and picked up the receiver, unable to say anything because of the disquiet that had suddenly overcome him. What if instead of "hello" he heard the sound of her laughter! Wouldn't that be sweet! But no, it was that mocking, sniggering question again:

"Hello. Is this the Nurmambekov apartment?"

He made a torturous attempt to respond in the right way. Anatoly simply repeated:

"Hello. Hello?"

The mocking baritone at the other end scoffed, reveling in his role as spy:

"Vanechka, kitten! How are you? Does your throat hurt?" These words would have been more appropriate for a seventy-year-old grandmother who had spent her life working as a kindergarten teacher, not this voice.

"Are you pooping OK?" the joker intensified his mockery, his voice already distorted by laughter.

Listen, my friend, the car is already on its way, already on its way to your phone booth, which they'll dust for fingerprints and cell samples on the receiver you placed against your ear. What in the world does he want?

"Auntie Alia called again today." He moved on to business, and the rhythm of his speech changed to swift and broken. Anatoly tuned in and listened, and listened. "As I was saying, Auntie Alia asked me to tell you that you should leave immediately for New York. You got that, Vanechka? New York. On the next plane. Uncle Tazik is ill. There's a flight in three hours. If you miss it, Uncle Tazik will die, and we'll all be very sad."

Anatoly hung up, not waiting for the voice to finish. He forbade himself to think about this. Don't think. Don't think! Why should he leave the country? He can't leave. Sorry, Grizzly, he can't. He also forbade himself to think about why everyone, from the investigator to his former friend, was telling him to hightail it out of the country.

From his house to the concert hall was about a twenty-minute walk: taking his Frau was absurd, no matter how tantalizingly her distended nostrils peeked out from under a snowdrift. That mental pinprick again: devil knows where he'd greet the dawn, given his plans for the evening, so his Frau was better off flashing her nostrils under the light of the cozy streetlamp that over the years had become a kind of home furnishing. The snow, which had fallen while it was still light outside, had stopped, and fairy-tale snowdrifts awaited the departure of fairy-tale carriages, the black ironwork hedge rails in the park reminding him of those times when society had still been (wonderfully!) class-based, and parks had been carefully protected from the citizens who now slept in them, scarves spread out on the snow and foot hooked over foot.

Along the right side of the tiny street, through the enormous gate that opened out into the city center, he counted eighteen parked and snow-covered automobiles, but couldn't remember whether this meant that she was alive or that she no longer existed: once again he had forgotten what he had wished for when he started counting, odd or even. For him her death was a horrible feeling inside, a restless quiet. He would tell himself "she's dead," and nothing would happen, but later an icy nonexistence signifying his own death, which would also come someday, surfaced from somewhere below. It seemed like this was the only way to determine where she was now, and—if she was no longer—to imagine that he, too, no longer existed. The most terrifying time to play this game was at night, lying on his back, when his now open, now closed eyes relayed one and the same gloom, indifferent to everything, and he really wasn't sure that he wasn't dead.

Walking out onto the avenue, Anatoly stopped in his tracks for a second, frantically turning his head in various directions: everything was decorated in holiday lights and wreaths; everything shimmered with waterfalls of lights; people were preparing to celebrate something Decemberish, but for him all celebrations were canceled until Elisaveta was found. Burying his head in the raised collar of his overcoat, he marched off morosely, sensing that deep inside him a kind of holiday spirit had surfaced in an inappropriate wave: a chance memory of a children's Christmas party. He resisted it until he felt that without Lisa even the most sincere merrymaking would always contain a note of sadness, like a tree ornament given as a present by someone who had moved away long ago but whom you still loved so much it would be better to accidentally break it. The crowd flowed forward, bellowing, intoxicated, singing, and engulfing—like foamy water over cliffs—the featureless figures in black posted at intervals of seventy steps, which meant that Dan had been right, right.

The posted figures were all dressed differently: some wore long over-coats, while others wore thick jackets, some wore caps, others fur hats, and still others' heads were uncovered. What united them was the black color of their clothing, their tall height, and their total immobility. No, of course, much more united them and distinguished them from the crowd. Headphones with winding cords extending from one ear to somewhere behind the back, short haircuts, the expressions on their faces, the protu-berances on the left side of their chests (were even these men "packing"?), the gaze with which they studied every passerby, the gaze of eyes better not to look into, better not to raise one's head toward. But he raised his head, and he looked, and though it lasted but a second, the "black guy" reacted immediately, having identified something suspicious in Anatoly's look. He raised his sleeve and tensely spoke something into his wrist. If they were to arrest him now . . . No, they weren't going to detain him be-cause for the moment they had no grounds: he was your average freaked-out city-dweller, of which there are so many on the eve of your holidays. But the next one met him with a turn of the head and a steadfast gaze: it would be best if he were to drop in for a coffee somewhere and come back this way later, when the excitement of the chase had subsided a bit. But time, time! He was afraid that after Muraviov's cortege arrived at the concert hall, the entrance would be cordoned off even for those whose tickets had not been recalled.

Someone in the crowd ran by, drunk, hot, crazed, and obviously pre-senting a threat only to his own person and his nose on the smooth ice coating the sidewalk. But they already had him in their sights. They were already running after him. A spark of nervousness ran down the chain, and it seemed that they had forgotten Anatoly. The square in front of the concert hall was captured in a double ring, and the entire avenue had been closed to traffic. He'd been right to go on foot. In order to cross into the secured area you needed only to show these people a ticket—by the way, where was his ticket? Once again, a bit too furiously, he started pulling his pockets inside out and patting down his trousers; once again, they took note of him, and a couple of particularly black silhouettes had already broken rank and were headed toward him, when the ticket turned up in the pocket with which he had started his search, and he showed them the slightly crumpled ticket, and grinned such a pathetic, frightened smile that both of them withdrew to their posts in the ring. A classical music lover. Typical in all his psychopathological glory. The shoulder to whose head he had extended his ticket slid aside, and—just as had the door at the Prosecutor's Office—left him just enough room to squeeze through sideways. Apparently, a certain protocol existed for admitting regular citizens, regardless of where: they had to enter sideways.

He managed to pass about fifty yards without a pat-down, then slipped into the crowd backed up on the stairs at the main entrance. The faces above the black shoulders had already encountered his crooked grins. Lanky, thin, and nervous, he had become the object of their ridicule. What names were these towering shaved hulks calling him? Were they even capable of joking? At this point he had to remove all metal objects from his pockets and step through the metal detector; he prayed it wouldn't go off. The metal detector noticed nothing. Good. Very good.

"Ticket number, seat," asked the man checking those who had passed though security. Hearing Anatoly's answer, he nodded toward the door he needed and nodded to the fellow standing at that door to make sure that Anatoly entered there and nowhere else. When Anatoly was a punch-length away, the fellow, looking him right in the eye—for the umpteenth time that evening—said: "Do not get up from your seat and make no attempts to leave. When it's all over, you'll be allowed to exit."

Anatoly spent a bit more time looking for the numbers on the rows of seats and making sure, when he found his, that the numbers matched those on his ticket, trying as he did not to look too lunatic, because he was being tracked by eyes everywhere. He had only to pass twice from one end of the row to the other, and a polite man in black appeared at his side and showed him where to sit. The man walked to the end of the row and stopped at the spot where the row opened out into the aisle, and—Anatoly had not expected this—similar men, polite and dressed in black, were standing alongside every row, and there were many, many, many of them. He allowed himself two more glances around: to the right, at the dress circle (although they couldn't be seen, there were undoubtedly people with rifles up there), to the back, and toward the exit. The last glance told him that from his row to the doors—which, were he to pass through them, he'd never see Muraviov—was a distance of about ten yards, so he had to be careful when choosing the moment to get caught in the crowd. The foot soldier, the comrade guarding Anatoly's row, would probably hasten him along if he passed from the space of his row into the aisle before the chaos he needed for cover had begun.

He needed to keep these nuances in his head, but his head was full of only, "How do you like these plush burgundy seats, Lisa? Don't they strike you as having been made from the skins of slaughtered teddy bears?" In response—he had already learned how to answer for her—came a joke about which parts of flailed teddy bears had been used to produce the wall of plush, followed by his creeping, secret smile on that same account. Surveying the few rows of ordinary music-lovers sitting around him, he noted an abundance of tailcoats: from behind they all looked like Muraviov's bodyguards, the pomp of tailcoats distinguishable from the threat of uniforms only by the feebleness of the black silhouettes. There were also ladies dressed in evening gowns that revealed their withered shoulders, former beauties discernible only by their correct posture and the bearing with which they held their heads. Next to him a husband complained to his wife about how the evening had been spoiled, but he spoke in whispers, whispers, his eyes darting this way and that so as not to direct—God forbid—the funnel of the hand that covered his mouth in the wrong direction. Slowly, even here in march step, two rows of men made their way toward four empty rows in the middle. They wore sweaters and suits of exaggeratedly frivolous colors and vests, all designed to camouflage the black birthmark each of them had on the back of his neck. Their task was to create the appearance of ordinary, joyous citizens surrounding the minister, just in case Muraviov suddenly waved to the cameras. Lined up in front of their seats, they sat down in unison, apparently having received the command to do so.

It grew quiet; now even the disgruntled were too afraid to whisper. Only one row still remained empty—the stretch of burgundy plush right in the center of the hall—and Anatoly took in with his eyes the church-style chandelier and the reddish luster of the organ, which lent the concert hall the semblance of a minimalist Catholic church in Western Europe; the only thing missing was a crucifix over the orchestra pit. He looked about, camouflaging his interest in the hall's remarkable architectural features and trying not to miss him, to see him first, and to get a sense of his entire being before his face assumed its usual expression for the television cameras. From somewhere off to the side a procession floated slowly into the hall; at its center, looking straight ahead and intensely engrossed in thought, so resembling and not resembling his photographs and television persona, was Muraviov. His entrance was not announced, but the hall broke into applause, starting somewhere up front and soon picked up by the back rows, and even Anatoly, thinking that in all cases he was unusual, unusual, applauded the stealthy figure, the bronze face with its passionless and even, perhaps, fastidious mouth, the corners of which arched downward, like Beethoven's. "Yes, yes," thought Anatoly, "as if Beethoven had taken up politics, cut off his long hair, and assumed a dignified air, while at the same time remaining the same raucous eccentric. What kind of voice did he have?" thought Anatoly. "She probably loved him for his voice. What's it like?" His eyes simultaneously switched to secondary details: the tailcoat, the white penguin-like chest and bow tie— just a tad more voluminous than a minister's should be. "Hmm, right," Anatoly thought. "The crimson beret is for another target group." So how to figure out which of them she loved? No, "loves"—no past tense! And, most important, which of his "selves" he himself considered the real one? The delegation lined up, then sat down like an avalanche, all at the same time, but not on command: no one dared sit down before Muraviov.

The houselights began to dim, just as the brightness of the moon intensifies as twilight turns to night, and the principal actor on stage turned out to be the organ, illuminated from below, with chairs set out like fence pilings beneath it. Like ghosts, the musicians filled the stage, where their instruments awaited them. From the depths of the hall two shriveled men appeared, eliciting a respectful "oh" in the rows of those few who had known the soloists when they still basked in the glory of their Melodiya recordings. Anatoly immediately nicknamed them Bobkins and Dobkins. The old men's faces exuded the radiant expression of naïveté that distinguishes people who have given their entire lives to sheet music in a country that hardly resembled a melody for flute and harpsichord. Peering attentively into their glowing, bashful faces that seemed to appeal to the audience (Ah, enough! Ah! Let us get on with burying our noses in the sheet music and evolving into a melody!), Anatoly concluded that they were decent men, that the acme of their careers had come in Lord knows what times, and that neither G-sharp nor F-flat were guilty of anything.

The program announcer, who resembled an Italian-American mafioso with a maudlin facial expression, spoke about the imminent "tussle" between the two outstanding maestros, the names of Bach and Chopin figuring in his speech more often than anything else. The musicians approaching the stage under the antiaircraft floodlights were certainly neither Bach nor Chopin; they must be intending to play Bach and Chopin. Once Anatoly's eyes grew accustomed to the darkness, Muraviov's head was perfectly visible: the nape, the forehead, the eyebrows, and even his lips. On and off the minister turned and looked back over his left shoulder, constantly, it seemed, searching with his hypnotic gaze for someone sitting right next to Anatoly. Anatoly wasn't worried. The palms of his hands were sweaty simply because the hall was so stuffy.

The conductor (who resembled Beethoven in terms of hairstyle) waved his baton, and the enormous loom of the orchestra began to weave the complex lace of a Bach melody that was light as a child's morning recess. The melody ticked like a tiny clock whose tempo would first slow down, then speed up, and—here one could understand why—Anatoly relatively quickly began thinking about how good it would be if all the clocks of the world would go backward, so that their barbaric, broken evening could be glued back together again with an apology. In the meantime, Dobkins, who had cropped up behind a harpsichord at the back of the stage, joined in the cyclic and regular weaving of the loom. His first warm chords—whose tremulousness resembled the play of sunlight on a spiderweb strung across a path into a forest—were met with applause.

Muraviov was visibly tense and leaned forward, listening raptly to the maestro's playing. The melody resounded with new force, although the harpsichord merely repeated everything that had already been said by the orchestra. Bach as performed by Dobkins beamed and gushed; it buzzed like a leisurely bumblebee and streamed with June rain, and it was so inexpressibly wonderful that you wanted to break into applause and smile, which many of those sitting around him did. Then Bach diminished and faded like the last Gothic cross, like a glint of light in a stained-glass window, and Chopin began. He was like his name. His music bubbled with the foam of champagne spilling from a bottle, surging and flowing from side to side across the stage. The thought came to Anatoly that there was something unhealthy about civilization going directly from Bach to Chopin. With the help of a piano located at the other end of the stage, opposite Dobkins, Bobkins helped Chopin lose his mind, rise up, fall, stand on his head, play the fool, weep, and take pills. He played furiously, thrashing at the keyboard, and the piano periodically moaned from dissonances, sudden accelerations, and insane decelerations, but this music with the power of a Force-5 storm at sea appealed much less to Anatoly, who, on the inside, was just like it.

He desired the appeasement of Bach, who entered in the rays of a setting sun on an unpainted wooden floor, a sofa alongside grandfather's radio receiver at the summer house, midday at a lake when you doze off, catching zzz's instead of fish, then more summer rain, then the complex melody of water dripping on leaves, then the sight of the sky as it opens up above as you plop yourself into the uncut grass. The harpsichord sounded flittingly; he wanted to catch it between his palms, to put it in a flask and carry it with him, releasing it when his spirits were at their lowest. Then came Chopin again, this time a bit calmer, gracious even as it danced, extended its tiny foot, curtsied, and twirled as it should, in step. And yet each note contained a kind of rupture, not always expressed, but ready to slide into hysterics. The audience liked it and applauded Bobkins and shouted for an encore, while Muraviov sat very still, no longer turning his head this way and that, entirely absorbed in another musician's performance and making mental notes, probably, of its strengths and weaknesses, its technical virtuosity, and the exaggerated carelessness that supplemented and revived emotions jotted on paper in miserly musical symbols.

On stage the two virtuosos had attempted to prove something, either about themselves, or about their instruments, similar yet so different, or about Bach and Chopin, or about the epochs in which the former and the latter had written their melodies, and Lisa probably would have liked Chopin more, and she would have told him that Bach was for beginners, that Bach was too simple and saccharine, while the flute solo coming from the stage and accompanied by the harpsichord was so intricate it made you realize that the human soul was not the thing we were accustomed to think it was. The melody lifted the soul from the listener, dipped it in icy flowing water, rinsed away the clumps of dirt in its cracks and crannies, in its embellishments and clogged lace, leaving only something intricate, light, and upward-bound. Lisa was already pulling at his sleeve and telling him something about Chopin that was imperceptible to his ursine ear, and their neighbor to the right had already begun to look askance at this strange young man talking to himself, forcing Anatoly to pretend that he was humming, or counting beats, or doing devil knows what else that might require him to move his lips.

The lights—revived and growing brighter above—announced that there would be no more of the light of Bach's music. The announcer said something from the stage: apparently they were conducting a vote by applause, and it was still too early for Anatoly to stand up because he would have been the only one standing. Then the winner, Bobkins, after being awarded bouquets of flowers for his performance, left the stage, while the dishonored Dobkins, whose calm light had not been to the audience's liking, bowed, the orchestra bowed, and the curtain closed and settled, as the first quiet calls for an encore began to sound, and the first of those wanting to leave had stood up, and there turned out to be many, very many of them. The foot soldiers gestured to them to return to their seats. Apparently, the order to "release" had not yet been given, but the human masses, like the wave that had risen in Chopin's music, were already a melody demanding to be developed and not inclined to tolerate a stop. The calls for an encore diminished, more people expressed their practical desire to quit this event of state, his neighbors in front rose to their feet, and Anatoly, having assessed his chances of getting caught in the aisle and not between rows where he wouldn't be able to get out . . . wouldn't be able to get out . . . realized that his time had come. In the meantime, the human rumble crescendoed and acquired the organized form of repeating sounds, and the front rows were already chanting "Muraviov," and Anatoly joined in with a loud, confident cry, all the time making his way, pushing his way, detouring his way forward, proposing with an insistent smile that they rise, push back their seats, and let him pass, and the chanting turned into a roar, and movement began in the row for state dignitaries, everyone rising and half of the cabinet of ministers clearing the row, allowing a slow, erect figure to pass. The bodyguards contained those already standing in the aisle, clearing a path, and Anatoly made his last lunge, forcefully, but with extremely polite demeanor (can't attract attention!), yanking by the collar a three-hundred-pound listener who was blocking the space between the rows. The latter turned around abruptly, flashed his eyes, and was even ready to take a swipe at him, then, by all appearances, he found something about Anatoly fitting the nature of the event, obediently retreated, and even sat back down in his seat, although everyone else was standing, while Anatoly, pretending just in case to be desperately in need of the facilities, squeezed his way into the aisle, where he came to a dead halt.

Muraviov was already on stage. All movement toward the exit stopped. The doors, it looked like, really had been closed. With their shoulders the bodyguards cleared a small rivulet between those standing and guarded it with locked elbows, just in case the maestro suddenly decided to beat a swift retreat from the stage.

Muraviov said something in a low voice to the conductor rushing toward him.

"Wolfgang Amadeus Mozart," declared the announcer in a voice that cracked from excitement. "Concerto no. 24 for Piano and Orchestra. This work . . . uh . . . is a rare phenomenon in the keyboard legacy of the great composer, written in the minor key . . ."

Somehow, perhaps just by raising his eyebrows, Muraviov had informed the announcer that any further reflections on the topic were superfluous.

"At the piano," now more frightened than ever, the announcer declared, "Mikholai Nikhailovich Muraviov."

The announcer clearly did not know the pianist's name and patronymic—which had been whispered to him a second before he came out on stage, but apparently not in enough time for him to commit them to memory—and he bungled it shamelessly, with unpredictable (for the time being) consequences. On unsteady legs he quit the stage to collapse in a faint somewhere backstage.

The conductor issued quick instructions to the orchestra. Muraviov floated to the piano, settled himself at the keyboard, and seemed to have lost all interest in his surroundings. With three forceful strokes the string section began. The sounds seemed not so sad as tragic. Muraviov listened to the orchestra, rocking back and forth as if in a trance. His eyes were closed. Anatoly could already feel that the performance would be more than just Mozart's Concerto no. 24. The minister's fingers floated toward the keyboard; they lay on it, shaking slightly, as if he were practicing his entry. Just then the orchestra deferred to the piano; it sounded in a shriek ending with a wail. The minister radically slowed the tempo: the notes in the piano score in this section were few, and he forced every one of them to sound with force. Anatoly had never heard an interpretation like this. It was amateurish, of course, particularly after the athletic pirouettes of the two virtuosos of keyboard technique. But precisely in this amateur voice against the background of the orchestra lay its sincerity. As if a heartrending operatic aria were being performed not against a false aluminum-foil backdrop, but at night, in the mountains, each nuance intoned and delivered only for its own sake. After a few strokes of the keys Anatoly understood and felt everything.

Muraviov played about lying with open eyes at night and talking to her. But she wasn't there. About walking to the center of town with its lights and wreaths and people playing in the snow. Understand? People throwing snowballs! How could that be ontologically possible, any of it, when her hand was not alongside yours, not in your hand? Without transitioning, he played about how her curls used to shake when she teasingly ran away from him; the way she dreamily rolled back her eyes before uttering another piece of nonsense. About sitting with the phone the length of an extended arm away, screen side up, just in case *you don't hear the ring.* But she had no way to call, and the phone never rang. About writing her letters and knowing that she would read them, and she did read them, at the same moment he, Anatoly, wrote them, as she stood alongside him, looking over his shoulder and reading them, perhaps running her transparent hand through his hair and giggling and watching what he was concocting to let her know, to designate a meeting. Or, again without a transition, of how monstrously painful it had been for her at that moment, how savage it had been when you touched her belly, and it was slippery, and hot, and none of it could be undone. About that dark-red tongue of blood on the snow-white floor. Then, again without transitioning, about how she licked the macchiato spoon before placing it on the saucer, or how you walked to the little boat, and for one second the combination of light, shadow, smells, and the angle from which the trees opened up overhead gave birth to the same feelings as when she was with you, and you wanted to capture that sensation and fill yourself with it forever, and you even understood more or less how to do this: simply lose your mind, stop the train of your thoughts, and live right here, with her, no matter how they might try to restore your dimmed wits. Or, after a brief, brilliant surge in a major key, about how you look at children, strangers' children, look at them and want to howl, your eyes turning into lakes that can no longer be contained to hold back heavy tears, each with a triple dose of grief. The music makes you writhe. You place your face in your hands, as if attempting to poke out your eyes, and from somewhere in your gut, like some stranger's terrifying laughter, come sobs you cannot control. He played all of this about her, while people all around looked at each other, and the bodyguards knowingly looked the other way: the men had been touched by their chief's music.

Anatoly could hardly have said how long this lasted. As if Muraviov had been telling him about her, unhurriedly, and him alone. Yes. A pause. A pause. The orchestra pointed its bows belligerently upward. Was that all? But no, something quiet and slow sounded from the stage. Lisa was speaking, of course. The larghetto. The movement where the major key was hidden inside a wrapper of two fast, sorrowful recitatives. Her favorite Mozart piece. Of course, Lisa.

Here there wasn't a word in the past tense. Muraviov was saying something to her alone, and it wasn't for Anatoly's ears to hear. It seemed that he was professing his love for her, and this was neither painful nor terrible: now all men could profess their love for her, and Anatoly, jealous Anatoly, would no longer be jealous. Another intimate passage picked up by the orchestra (how could the orchestra even think of interfering in this lyrical exchange?), and Anatoly understood that he must immediately cork his ears, that he had no right, that Lisa would have been offended, but the melody was picking up speed and fluttering, tenderly and slowly, not raising a single splash, towards the cliff where it would turn into a component of the weather forecast, and if only Anatoly knew how to play, he would have played it exactly the same way . . . Then, suddenly, the melody screeched with a false note and halted. The orchestra maintained the background for a few more measures, then disintegrated into a cacophony of instruments, and also fell silent. Muraviov sat there, his back turned to the audience. There was a tense pause. The lights began to go on, but, by all appearances, the bodyguards had issued the order to turn them down again. The pianist got up from his instrument, closed it carefully, like a casket made of precious stones, and staring at the floor, headed off toward the steps leading down from the stage. Feeling his heart had started to beat with berserk speed, Anatoly realized that the minister would pass through the concert hall, not because he wanted to interact with the audience, but because at that moment he was not up to security considerations or the brilliance of his image: he walked out of the concert hall as he had when he had been a normal member of the audience, which meant for Anatoly one step, one more step closer.

They shouted bravo to him, mawkishly and insincerely in the front rows occupied by a special clack, and sincerely, in amazement, in the middle, where the connoisseurs sat. Someone tossed white carnations in his direction, and the bouquet struck him in the shoulder and dropped dead at his feet. The maestro didn't even raise his eyes, while the grateful listener had already been seized, crushed, and dragged off somewhere, his raised hand, fingers splayed, bobbing through the crowd. For Anatoly—three, two, one step to go. Of course, the main thing was to find the right intonation. Intonation and appropriate volume.

"Nikolai Mikhailovich," he called to him quietly, just loudly enough to be audible, and only with difficulty. Another step forward toward the exit, head cast down, not turning around, and, that meant, past him. "I am Anatoly Nevinsky." A slight pause, but then another step forward with no intention of stopping. Then, finally, rather loudly, "Elisaveta Supranovich."

The figure stopped in its tracks, causing a small furor among his bodyguards. The minister turned around slowly, as if in a dream, running his eyes across the faces, but, as could be expected, not finding anyone he knew.

"Anatoly Nevinsky. Elisaveta Supranovich," Anatoly repeated the successful spell once again, and Muraviov discovered who it was coming from. He thought for exactly one second, looking at Anatoly.

"In the car," he said, more likely to one of the foot soldiers standing alongside him than to the person he was inviting. Turning away, he continued walking toward the exit at the same pace and in the same state of contemplation as before.

Anatoly was pulled from the crowd by strong but rather courteous hands and set on the path of the narrow cleared rivulet in the aisle. Of course, he was supposed to follow this solemn figure. Once out in the foyer, he attempted to catch up with the minister to say something more to him—what, he didn't know yet, because his entire complicated plan, beginning with Dan's call, had ended right there with his first words to Muraviov. Someone from behind stopped him: a hand that barely fit on his shoulder set him straight forward and indicated with a few jerks that he was to follow, not walk alongside.

On the square in front of the concert hall, right on the sidewalk, an endlessly long black limousine with a state flag instead of license plates pulled up like an alien spaceship. Alongside stood cars obviously armored for protective purposes, threat and challenge tangible even in their shape: in the black hoists, in the predatory radiator screens that resembled snarling jaws, and in the solid-cast wheel disks, which resembled the runes of some bellicose, now extinct people. The bodyguard walking at Muraviov's side took a few quick steps forward and opened the door of the limousine with obvious effort. Not altering his pace or his step, Muraviov got into the car without even bending over to pass through the door. Anatoly hesitated for a second, not knowing whether he was allowed to go where the Minister of State Security had just passed, but the bodyguard, apparently already having violated procedure by holding the door open for so long, made an impatient gesture, and Anatoly was pushed from behind.

Inside the car it was hardly as spacious as its exterior dimensions suggested, and by all appearances, a large part of the chassis was taken up by the protective armor. The bodyguard slammed the door, which inserted itself into grooves with a weapon-like rumble that ran through the entire interior. The escort cars turned on their blue flashers, and the cortege took off, quickly picking up speed. Anatoly raised his head toward his interlocutor. There was no light at all, the only illumination coming from the lights outside the window. It might have been possible to turn on a light, but there were so many buttons lazily inlaid into the leather interior, each of the buttons capable of signaling the beginning of a nuclear war, that Anatoly resisted the urge. One half of his face framed by the contours of the window and the other drowned in darkness, Muraviov looked at him in the twilight, calmly and carefully, and under this gaze it was impossible to look away.

"Why did you desire a meeting with me?" Muraviov finally asked, as if Anatoly had submitted an official request to his chancellery.

Filling his lungs with air, of which there immediately seemed not enough, Anatoly answered:

"I wanted to ask . . . I . . . to learn more precisely from you . . . What happened to Elisaveta Supranovich?"

The question hung in midair. Apparently, Anatoly needed to explain how he knew that name, but how?

"She and I . . . We were close . . ." It was not easy to maintain the tone set by Muraviov's first question—not even by the whole question, just the archaic construction "desire a meeting."

"What happened to Elisaveta Supranovich?" The minister restated the question in amazement.

"Yes. What happened to Elisaveta Supranovich?" Anatoly had wanted to put the question another way, something like "Where has Elisaveta Supranovich gone?" but he found an optimistic formulation of the question, like "Where has she gone?" entirely inappropriate, while the pessimistic "Where is her body?" too obviously suggested that the other man had personally contributed to that formulation.

Muraviov pondered the question, looking now at the city flickering by outside the tinted windows, now at his own reflection against the background of that city, now at the reflection of Anatoly, who, naturally, stared at Muraviov.

"You don't know?" he answered at last.

Anatoly wanted to respond that even if he hadn't known, he would have understood everything from the way Muraviov had played that night, that it was all monstrous, and, essentially, he had no more questions, but he needed somehow to ask him about her. After all, he was the minister of the MGB. He knew everything, but how . . .

"Who did it?" Anatoly once again formulated the question broadly, observing the taboo on that fateful word they seemed to have established between them.

"That's the question," Muraviov reacted faster than the last time. "That's the question, Anatoly. Knowing that she was murdered . . ." He had decided not to observe the taboo. "Knowing in full . . . detail . . . in such detail . . . that . . ." His voice grew hoarse. He stopped talking, and it seemed as if he would never speak again, but he continued: "Knowing in full detail how the murder took place . . . her murder . . . how Lisa was killed . . . Our analysts explained it to me in great detail, with charts . . ."

Here Anatoly should have thought it amusing that those analysts were referred to as "anals," which he knew because Dan had told him. He did find it amusing, on some other, hysterical level, but he was sufficiently composed not to smile.

"So, knowing all this from descriptions of the crime scene—the overturned furniture, the evidence of a struggle, et cetera . . . I have yet to hear a single credible version of who did this or why."

Anatoly listened very attentively. If he analyzed it, this phrase should tell him whether the MGB had been involved in this devilry. He listened attentively, with all his might, to Muraviov's intonation and memorized every intonational nuance, all four inhalations and exhalations that Muraviov made as he uttered the phrase, but he still could not determine whether Muraviov was telling the truth. Rather, he could not believe that Muraviov was telling the truth. Because that was precisely how it looked—as if he were telling the truth. And this was very bad for him, Anatoly, because it meant . . .

"Even your version," the minister continued thoughtfully, "and by that I mean the one whereby the murder was committed by you, leaves me with many questions. What were your motives? Where is the murder weapon? Why didn't you leave any tracks? Where did the body go? The crime seems to have been committed by a complete nitwit. But it is possible that everything was done precisely so that it would seem that way to me. The nitwit has not been found yet."

Once again they rode in silence. Anatoly thought about how at that speed they had only a few more minutes before arriving at the minister's residence. He had to hurry. It was not fact that Muraviov would propose he share dinner with him. Anatoly made up his mind.

"Tell . . . Tell me, can you not exclude the possibility . . . that . . . well . . . that someone killed her . . . Well, that is, to hell . . . I'll say it! I thought that she was killed on your orders, Nikolai Mikhailovich."

Muraviov shuddered, not like a criminal captured in a place he had thought safe, but like a person stunned by a slap in the face.

"My orders? What are you? . . . Why do you think that? What kind of a relationship do you think we had? You think that I was jealous, do you?" Muraviov's face twitched nervously several times. "I sincerely wished you happiness when she told me, then . . . that evening, that she was carrying your child, that you were planning to start a family, and that she asked for only one thing, that I not touch the two of you." His face took on a sort of capricious expression. "I told her then . . . I told her a lot about life. She and I had not had a heart-to-heart talk for a long time. And that was our last conversation."

"You said the child was mine?" Anatoly interrupted Muraviov. Muraviov, not accustomed to interruptions, continued speaking:

"It was so sincere . . . She said that she would be happy with you, that you would have . . ."

Anatoly stopped him.

"Nikolai Mikhailovich, the night she and I quarreled, she told me that the child was yours, that she was carrying your child under her heart. That was why we . . ."

Muraviov started even more. He was amazed. How to determine to what extent his amazement was genuine?

"My child? What kind of silly fantasy? . . . Listen. Let me tell you about Lisa. I played for her, you understand? She was my audience. I played the piano for her when I was sad. We would meet, and I would play for her. Of course, she fantasized. She said that we would marry, I would get a divorce, give up my post as minister—in precisely that order, by the way . . . There was never anything ambiguous about our relationship, although she often wept when I played for her. We never . . . I am not going to try to convince you of anything: that's not how I do things. As for her fantasies, forgive me, but I am fifty-five years old. What divorce? What retirement? She herself, it seemed, was joking. I knew that sooner or later she would find herself . . . someone like you . . . I sincerely wished . . . my little girl happiness. I registered several houses and cars to her so she would not grieve: I'm not immortal, after all. Then you appeared . . . We had . . . a conversation, exactly the kind I had imagined we would. I told her about my son, and she told me about you and said that she loved you very much. I wished you both happiness and promised that I would play for you both at your wedding, but that, to be totally honest, was a lie."

Anatoly felt that the car was driving too fast, that his brain couldn't keep up with the speed, although some clarity was beginning to emerge, and the clarity nauseated him.

"Wait a minute! All that is not true. I am beginning to remember. She never told me that she loved me. But you . . . I think," his voice was not keeping up with his thoughts, and his thoughts were attempting to catch something even faster and more important, and the race was torturous. "She loved you all the time when she and I were together. Of course, only you! She needed me as an extension of you to make ambiguities possible."

Something unusual was happening to Muraviov. It seemed as if Anatoly had inserted a note of dissonance in the plan Muraviov had conceived and already carried out.

"What are you talking about?" he screamed. "She and I talked about music, exchanged jokes, some letters, tokens of . . ."

"It doesn't hold water, Nikolai Mikhailovich! She told me about your tenderness and your caresses. She told me about the roses. Do you really think that after all that a girl is going to listen to you play and not think that it's intended for her? She loved you. You didn't see that? It makes me bitter that I wasn't able to replace you entirely. In many ways the child really was yours . . ."

Muraviov grabbed the telephone receiver on a long spiral cord from the door handle and shouted to it, "Here!" The cortege came to a sharp stop without approaching the curb, and the stupid mug of the escort vehicle appeared for a brief moment in the rear window, illuminating the inside of the limousine with the glow of its flashers. Muraviov looked off to the side. Anatoly didn't understand. He couldn't figure out what was happening and why everything that had been so painful for him suddenly had become inexplicably painful for the man she had loved. The massive door slid open, and a bodyguard appeared in the aperture. Muraviov nodded to him, and the bodyguard placed his leg, bent at the knee, on the seat, and crawled inside after Anatoly, from which Anatoly inferred that the conversation was over and that he had to leave. Everything here was done by hand, even the invitation and removal of interlocutors. There was something primitive in this, but at the moment Anatoly needed to think not about that. He turned toward Muraviov, who was pressed in the corner of his seat, and leaned over.

"May the Lord protect you," the minister said under his hand, hiding his mouth and a large portion of his face. Could people like the minister . of state security actually cry?

The cortege tore off like a herd of horses, engines roaring, and one of the escort vehicles sped past Anatoly with only a quarter-inch between it and his hip. He jumped back, right under the wheels of another that didn't even think to turn its steering wheel, and only a miracle saved him from being hit, while the face behind the automatic barrel hee-hawed inside.

He stood there in the middle of the deserted six-lane avenue, the cortege's flashers and the black pancake of the limousine having already turned into tree ornaments on the horizon. A police officer from the widely spaced cordon along the road turned to him politely—he had seen from whose car he had emerged:

"Please leave the roadway. It's about to be opened for traffic. Can I take you somewhere?"

Anatoly shook his head in confusion, walked to the sidewalk, and wandered off, continuing to ask in the slow silence that had fallen, Who did you love, Lisa? Why did you lie to me about the child, and did you lie? He loved you, and everything he said about the absence of ambiguity in your relationship was unexpectedly poor by comparison with how sincerely he had spoken of your murder. He loved you more than life, Lisa, and thought that you loved him the same way, which was why he registered his wealth in your name. You found me in order to love him even more, in a vital, material, youthful, and foolish way, but he regarded this love as betrayal and ordered that you be exterminated, with the baby, which, of course, had been conceived with him. But now, now, having heard of your love for him not from you, whom he might not believe, but from me, he understood it all, and that was why he began to weep. He understood that he had murdered the woman for whose sake he had lived, that he had murdered his last hope of being human. His beastly present had invaded the human dreams for the future to which he allowed himself to succumb when he played for you. He understood that I was he, his own projection into a younger man's body, that I had never really existed, that to be jealous of her with me was tantamount to being jealous of her with his own reflection, but you can't be brought back. And the main thing is that he had repeated this version to himself many times, he had tried to convince himself of it; all those months he spent trying to believe that he should not be jealous, yet he still issued the order. But why did he so sincerely deny that he was involved in your death? Had he really succeeded in convincing himself that he hadn't ordered the hit? Or had it all been done for him by his ambitious underlings? Some idiot from security to whom he had once poured out his heart and who had taken his words as an order?

His simpleminded version, Lisa, about the pianist and his listener doesn't hold up! It crumbles into pieces! It's as if the contents of our conversations were put in a blender, then poured on his head, and that he, having confused everything and everyone, concocted his idea, convinced himself of it, and attempted to convince me, not understanding that I, I! had participated in the conversations that they had bugged for him.

Our dreams of having a family and your promise to talk to him came after your meeting in Sokol, where he played for you and complained about his son. He himself said it was there you had asked him to leave us in peace, not to touch the two of us—those had been precisely your words, precisely how you had put it then, under the light of the floor lamp, but you could not have said it that way in your conversation with him; instead you would have said something like leave "Anatoly and me" in peace, leave "him and me" in peace. It was language, comrade Muraviov, that caught you red-handed! Saddest of all—I know you too well, Lisa, my dear, fragile Lisa, my nonconfrontational, lazy Lisa, to believe that you would have initiated such a conversation for the sake of our little paradise.

By the same token, I know you well enough to understand all your unpredictability and to concede that both his version and mine are possible. You could have spoken with him and extracted guarantees of our safety, then dreamed about this with me as if it were something unattainable, then told me that the child was his, to test me and leave if I chased you out, because, if I loved you, I would accept you with another man's child, and if I did, then you would tell me that the child was mine, and we would name him . . . Ecclesiastes, for example. You could have convinced me that you loved him just to play with me, to drive me mad with your irresponsibility, then, just when I was on the verge, grab me by the hand and bring me back from madness, embrace me, ask for forgiveness, and smother me with kisses. You could have said the same to him—that you loved me—simply so that his and my feelings for you would be real. It could be that you really did listen to him play, and loved me, and did not utter the "no" I needed to hear from you simply because you feared that his ears were listening to us . . .

With you, Lisa, anything was possible. I don't know what's worse: to believe their ridiculous version that you loved me and that it was I, insane with jealousy, who killed you or that you loved him, and he killed you out of jealousy of me, not having realized that in the labyrinth of your fanciful soul I was his double?

But even if it's so, if I am the reflection, then allow me on the basis of my rights as a reflection, Lisa, to believe that at some point in your informal "you's" directed at me, a substitution occurred: addressing him through me, you suddenly saw me in him. You realized that I, even as his reflection, was also myself. Remaining a nothing, just one more episode in his life, which you wanted to live with him, I was myself, the same "myself" you loved. And even if ultimately your love was for him, it was also your love for me—in him.

5

I DON'T KNOW HOW LONG I wandered the labyrinths of our conversations, first assuring myself that we had loved each other, then that we had not—all of it in the present tense, to which I really no longer had any right. It was the middle of the night, and I explained to myself once and for all the reason I couldn't fall asleep: you had been my reason for waking up in the morning; when you disappeared, so did my reason for waking up, which meant, therefore, that I no longer had any reason to fall asleep. I was doomed to insomnia.

Various combinations of three components—love, a child, and murder—wove themselves into complex fanciful patterns. I had already concocted an explanation of how it could have happened that you loved me, and the child was mine, but your murder was not real, staged instead as some sort of complex (perhaps already forgotten) provocation. The most interesting of these fanciful patterns were, perhaps, those in which one of the three elements was inverted. No love became love. Your murder at the hands of state security forces had been devised but not enacted or carried off. Most complex of all was the child, which, to support some versions, became first Muraviov's, then, after having been conceived, mine, at which point the entire string of patterns died in its tracks and, laughing at its own unlikelihood, disintegrated into a pile of tiny crystals. These crystals of hope, which kept me from falling asleep, would then reconstitute themselves as ever more fantastic patterns, all beginning with the words "All right, let's assume that you . . ." and, as they wove themselves further, gave birth to new dramatis personae: remorseful hit men stunned by your beauty had run off with you, while their section, fearing the wrath of the highly placed person who had ordered the hit, invented all that nonsense about the spot on the floor and evidence of a struggle. I invented a janitor's wife who had rushed to warn you that they had come for you and, as a result, had died on the spot after having been held captive by them. You, you, of course, were waiting for me, alive. It was like writing: I invented plot after plot, ending after ending. But there was nothing about this creativity that needed to be written down. It required of me only that I construct ever craftier combinations that turned brutal outcomes into a different child, into a happy ending with a kiss against a sunset backdrop. I convinced myself that if I applied all my multidirectional imagination and imbued the plot with all the fantasy allotted for the totality of all my future works, the tiny crystals of hope would reconstitute themselves as the desired artifact illuminated by a pale urban moon, and you would appear right on my doorstep, which would be revived by your nocturnal ring of the doorbell.

I would think all this while on my sofa, still hoping to fall asleep. Sometimes it happened that I did fall asleep, and a few hours of darkness outside the window would lapse. But not tonight: my happy-ending game was too interesting, so I poured boiling water over a pinch of fragrant black tea from a tin and paced the kitchen like a Dostoevsky hero, then went into the main room and turned on the television, the flicker of half-naked bodies on the music channel creating a rhythmic tension that made me want to set my plot to soul music, in English.

And so, Lisa, the blood, bile, and "intestinal tissue," as the friendly inspector had put it, had been obtained for you by one of your doctor girlfriends, perhaps even in exchange for monetary remuneration—not that I would want to think poorly of your doctor girlfriends. The chair had been overturned, blood spilled (and incorrectly identified in analysis as yours based solely on type!), and bile sprayed all over, while you yourself had hitchhiked to some distant Russian city. At the moment I had been scratching at your apartment door, you were still there and you heard everything, but remained silent out of principle, because I had not lived up to your expectations and, basically, turned out to be a total asshole unwilling to accept you with someone else's baby under your heart. You said to yourself: I'll wait to see how far my bear will go to track me down. And, when you were told—the question is by whom? Let's say some good person at the MGB!—that I had met with Muraviov and spoken with him in such a way that he had tossed me out of his limousine as it was still moving, you realized that your bear was worthy of forgiveness. You bought some pensioner's twenty-year-old Lada hibernating in his garage until summer, and you drove all night down the potholed roads of the Smolensk region. At this moment you're about to ring the doorbell, and we will embrace and kiss—sooner against the backdrop of a sunrise than a sunset—and sail off into the wonderful, foggy unknown to await the birth of our baby, whom, at your insistence, we will call Ecclesiastes. At home we'll call him Éclair, or by the diminutive Clucker.

The doorbell did not ring, and I was beginning to unravel the next version—number what?—of our happy ending, when movement, a bit too much for four in the morning, could be heard in the courtyard. There were cars out there, people speaking in muffled voices, doors slamming, rasping walkie-talkies, and all of it poured into my stairwell. The doorbell screamed (for an eternity) as someone's finger pressed and refused to release the button for the entire minute it took me to throw on some decent clothes and rush to acknowledge my presence at home with shouts of "Who's there?" although it was already dreadfully apparent who it was. "MGB. Open up!" came a voice from behind the door.

The landing barely accommodated all my visitors. There were a dozen policemen in black leather jackets with visor caps pulled down over their eyes. There were plainclothesmen in dark wool coats and suits of all shades of gray. There was even my neighbor from downstairs, mustached Sasha, in a white sleeveless borscht-spotted undershirt and padded running pants. From behind the police officers' backs came Investigator Poopik, the one who had interrogated me not long ago and now began to talk a blue streak.

"Hello. Tsupik. And why aren't we asleep? We drove up and saw the lights were on. What's up? Can't sleep? Or did someone tip you off?" he asked cheerfully and amicably.

I couldn't find what to answer to this question and grimaced as if to say, "To what do I owe the visit?"

"Anatoly Petrovich, we have a search warrant signed by the prosecutor of the Central Region authorizing a search of your premises," the investigator said. "A search and, why hide it, your arrest, based on the results of the search. You won't stand in the way of the investigative group's work?"

I kept thinking about what role my good-natured friend Sasha in the spotted undershirt and striped pants had in the investigative group, but, apparently, some part of my being was thoroughly prepared for the search and said, "You may begin your work. The apartment is at your disposal."

I kept wanting to ask Sasha, "*Et tu, Brute?*" but decided not to. Sasha let them all pass into my apartment while he remained standing on the landing. When I approached him, he said, "They woke me up. Said I needed to be a witness. What the hell is going on here? I gotta get up at 6:30 to go to work. How long is this gonna take?" I shrugged. It would have been difficult to say, "I'm really sorry, but I don't know how long it's going to take. They suspect me of murder. Remember how you and I got out of hand playing dominoes last summer?"

The uniformed police and plainclothesmen spread out to different rooms and exhaustively knifed, moved, overturned, probed, turned inside out, and bent things originally put in their places by my father. Their actions contained something of my father's interest in the nature of those things, but the gears of the alarm clock, for example, interested the detectives not because they were trying to figure out how it was made, but because they wanted to know what it might be hiding. Dad could take apart and reassemble a VAZ-2107; these guys knew only how to take things apart, scattering the pieces all over the floor. A six-and-a-half-foot hulk in a police uniform was removing books, one by one, from the bookcase, quickly flipping the pages as he held them not right in front of his face, but in front of his eyes, then tossing them on the floor. They were not placed, not laid, but tossed in such a way that the spines shattered and the pages ripped and fell out. Unable to endure this, I squatted down and started moving the books, like wounded warriors from the field of battle, to the side, smoothing out the crumpled pages and placing one volume atop the next in even piles: the collected works of Saltykov-Shchedrin, Chekhov, our family's pride and joy, the pages still not cut, while the policeman glared at me, not missing a beat in his work, as if I were a dying man attempting to haul a box of nickel silver tableware to the life hereafter. I wanted to explain to him that books were not the same as nickel silver, that you must not treat them that way. That even if I were buried six feet under, the books could be deposited in a library—in the MGB's own. That this same policeman could have himself a good laugh reading the acerbic Shchedrin. But all I could say was:

"Why?"

He seemed to be flinging them just so I would ask, and with obvious pleasure and upon the first request, responded:

"If as a result of the search your personal things are harmed in any way, you can sue for compensation." Flinging the next volume (Walter Scott's *Ivanhoe*) like a flat stone across water into a distant corner, where it smashed against the wall, he added, "After doing your time, of course."

Several of the men smirked: you could tell this wasn't their first search that night, and the number of jokes they could crack was limited. A few searches back they might have echoed their colleague's chuckle, but now, at five in the morning, they were conserving energy.

"So why does Section Five always conduct searches at night?" I asked two terribly squeaky leather jackets dissecting my stereo speakers.

"There's a lot of fieldwork to do during the day." The bass speaker was split open with a penknife, the resined reed paper that not so long ago had been capable of being a violin, a flute, or a bass guitar hung downward like the hand of a corpse.

"Perhaps I can help you?" I offered the two men ripping off the back cover of the television, cracking the plastic because they had overlooked one of the screws.

"Vasily, do your job." One of them, most likely senior in rank to Vasily, nodded in my direction.

Standing on my stepladder and examining the glass cover of the ceiling fixture and so intent on his task that he had lowered the plate that covered the ceiling wires, Vasily climbed down, brushed his hands against his pants to dust off the whitewash, and ordered me to follow him. He took me out to the kitchen, where he asked me to place everything in my pockets on the kitchen table, then probed the seams of my clothing, and turned my pockets inside out, while I watched this thickset man with his crew cut and his unexpectedly hooked nose, and marveled at his ability to do all these things with my body without looking me in the eye.

He twirled and turned me as if I were a present and he a professional gift wrapper, his hands already adept at trimming, wrapping, gluing, measuring lengths of paper, cutting, fastening, and making a bow, while all the time thinking his own thoughts and never communicating in any way with the present. His son had to be enrolled in boxing class. His wife wanted a new car. He was dying to go fishing, but wasn't so much the fool to go ice fishing. Raise your arms. On the other hand, the good thing about ice fishing was that once you cut a hole through the ice, the fish pushed themselves out, in the direction of the light. Bend your leg here. You just sit and haul them out one after the next, literally. And, if you're with the guys, next comes the campfire, and three long hits of hooch. Unzip your fly.

"Found it!" voices yelled from the bedroom.

Stomping heavily, as if they owned the place, they ran to the bedroom. (It goes without saying that they "worked" without having removed their shoes. Wherever they went to do their "work," no one was going to stand on ceremony. Even at home they removed their shoes only with a certain amazement, reminding themselves that at home they were not to knock books off the shelves—not to rip open, break, or gut things—that they needed to be careful, when all the time their hands itched with the urges of their profession. Oh, how tempting it would be to take the porcelain dog—a housewarming gift from the mother-in-law—off the *secrétaire* and smash its head against the kitchen table to discover, with great professional delight, a note inside from a lover, or some piece of mother-in-law slander against the husband, or something else.

"Witnesses!" came another shout from the bedroom. The detective patting me down, still thinking his own thoughts, quietly reported to the corridor: "He's clean."

Confident that in the bedroom they had found some inanity like a forgotten can with coffee they mistakenly took for hashish, slightly rolling my eyes and ready to smirk, to hasten their admission of having made a mistake and missed the mark, I set off for the bedroom. Lots of them had already gathered there, and Sasha's face slid downward as he looked at me differently, his mustache that minutes ago had soared upward now had landed and folded its wings.

"Write," someone pulled him toward a transcript. "Here. Legibly. 'During search of the armoire in the bedroom, the third shelf revealed a dark-blue sweater spattered with reddish-brown spots, presumably blood.'" The visual informing these strange words that had no place in my apartment was my dark-blue sweater, the one that had disappeared on the night of our quarrel, the one with the words BEAR BEARS BEAR across the chest. It lay untouched, folded so the words were not visible, right there on the third shelf of the armoire, where I would never have put it consciously or unconsciously—what is it doing here?—because this shelf was for dirty underwear, not for knits. It was, indeed, when you looked closer, covered with reddish-brown stains—large and reddish-black, like bear fur. But, damn it, blood is red, and this substance was reddish-brown, and I had never seen it before, never seen it before . . .

"I didn't do it, I didn't do it," I rushed to tell Sasha and the second witness, a policeman. "Can you enter in the protocol that I did not put it there, that the accused refuses to admit that he put it there, that the sweater was planted?"

"You can explain that to the investigator during the interrogation," said Tsupik, who had turned up at my right. I noted immediately, of course, his shift from the respectful formal plural "you," with which he had addressed me so far, to the belittling singular form.

A man with thin rubber gloves—not even rubber, almost cellophane and threatening at any moment to fly off his hands—slowly unwrapped the evidence on a special plastic surface. He was followed by a photographer with a large flash. Two policemen had already lit up cigarettes and were flicking ashes on the floor, sensing that now they could do this, that now, if they wanted, they could piss on the carpet. They discussed the oddness of the spots, as if the sweater had been dipped in a puddle of coagulating blood, or placed up against a corpse with intent to stain it. I heard all this, but it would do me little good now.

"Do you recognize this object?" Tsupik asked, returning to the formal plural "you" for the transcript, which only further underscored my status as determined by the grammatical number of the pronouns used to address me. Henceforth I would be addressed in the plural only during legal proceedings. All rise, the court is in session. Sit down. Are you aware of the consequences of providing the court false testimony? Very well. Now sit down and keep quiet.

"Yes. It's my sweater; I used to wear it. That night it disappeared; I couldn't find it." Explanations were unnecessary; they simply checked a box next to "yes." The words "this object was stolen from the apartment by the MGB, stained with blood, and planted"—alongside which, at my insistence, another check mark could have been added—were not included.

"Petrov, keep an eye on the client," Tsupik ordered a thin policeman with a youthful face who reached readily for the handcuffs on his belt. The investigator shook his head to indicate that I was not yet so much their client that they could cuff me. Rather, I was one-hundred-percent their client, but they might need my hands for something, and there was no way I could possibly run away.

I went from room to room, watching as they leafed through the diary I had kept while still at the university and where I would occasionally jot down thoughts about *Ulysses*. "Ulysses-who-pisses," they joked and turned to me for an explanation of who "Who-pisses" was. Like a fool, I answered about Joyce and, to my misfortune, used the word "Dublin." With the inavertability of a steamroller they started in on the joke about "Dublin' over with laughter." They made short work of shredding the bound newspapers (now banned) stored in the ceiling cabinets, hinting that these were problematic—as if I could have greater problems than those I had already—while they themselves pored over front pages with photographs of Muraviov holding a machine gun at firing practice or of others from their organization (who had since left the country) describing how they had executed missing members of the opposition. I myself no longer believed these articles, but they crowded over and eyeballed these novelties accusing their organization of things that were not scribbled on some wall in handwriting that quivered from fear (for example, "The MGB are fags!"), but printed in block letters that seemed to guarantee the authenticity and gravity of the information. For them these newspapers were like a pornographic magazine found under their parents' bed. These newspapers had been destroyed long ago, online archives hacked and erased, and nowadays few had access to the special collections where another two or three stacks of these newspapers still could be found. Off to the side a policeman was reading aloud my juvenile poetry. They had found the school notebook that not even I had been able to find, although I had searched for it, wanting to resurrect all my singsong, poorly rhymed, abstruse (as only a fifteen-year-old teenager's could be) experiments with prosody. They laughed aloud: "There on the ceiling of life having passed, he searched for the cobweb of days," which they rhymed with "And gave himself over, while flat on his back, to crap from his genital phase." Tsupik stood among them, his sternness gone for the moment. He listened, his faded eyes twinkling, and couldn't hold back a grin. He found this funny. Dimples appeared on his cheeks. When he caught my eyes, though, he diverted his gaze. The search had turned into a kind of cultural event for him, like a Iosif Kobzon concert or Evgeny Petrosian stand-up routine; those were the limits of his emotions right then.

"Found it!" A voice shouted from the toilet.

Off they stomped again, taking Sasha—who had been standing in the corridor, turning his head this way and that, like an owl—with them. Later, the poetry lovers and those bent over the newspapers would claim that they had been examining documents, when in fact they had been collecting information about their own beloved ministry.

Near the tool cabinet in the toilet stood a young uniformed officer with intelligent facial features. (For some reason he struck me as the kind who might spend his evenings writing about "the cobweb of days" for some female commercial high school graduate.) He literally trembled with excitement. Evidently, for the first time he HIMSELF had found something important! Evidence! And what was it? Exercising my rights as who knows what, owner or suspect, I made my way to the front, and they let me pass. Once again there was something comical—or was it my brain, Lisa, feverishly searching for something comical in this increasingly gloomy dead-end situation? Whatever. But there was something ridiculous in this crowd of people in police caps, with standard-issue weapons, and detective faces hovering over a gaping toilet. "Who's next?" I was tempted to ask in retaliation for all their idiotic jokes, but didn't. At the top of the toolbox the teenager had apparently extracted from the cabinet lay Dad's handmade two-millimeter knife with the wooden handle professionally joined to the metal blade. All the detail of Dad's craftsmanship, however, was hidden under a reddish-brown, sticky goo (more black than red). I understood distinctly that no matter how it had wound up here—I had been looking for it several days ago and remembered seeing with my own eyes that it wasn't here. But how could I prove that! Where had it been? And when had it reappeared? Like the sweater, it lay in plain view. Did they really think that the killer would keep these two main pieces of evidence of his crime out in the open, unlaundered and unwashed? Right . . . No matter how it had landed here, it was the same knife with which someone had slashed your body, Lisa. This went beyond the sweater found on the shelf in the armoire. This object contained the energy of the life that had been taken from you. I looked at it and sensed that you had been killed with it. Having come in contact with this piece of metal made by my father, my jack-of-all-trades father who years ago had sharpened it so it never again required sharpening, you could exist no more. Who had thought up how to do this so brutally? If they had decided to deprive you of your life, why had they not used one of their own instruments of execution with which they had already killed so many? Why had they used my father's knife, which was guilty of nothing? How could anyone have cut and slashed you open (my God!) with this two-millimeter-thick piece of metal designed for industrial purposes? With its blackened, and in some places even rusted, jagged blade? . . . the cruelty . . . I can't, I can't . . . I sat down on the floor alongside the toilet and lost my sight. Probably because I had covered my eyes with something. They curtly asked me something. It seems I said "yes." But the voice I had heard, that voice, was now dictating:

"'A handmade knife . . .' Write smaller, damn it, there are only three lines! Where are you going to squeeze the rest? Cramp it in between the lines . . . 'Handmade, with a wooden handle. Steel, wood, the blade approximately ten inches in length. Covered with reddish-brown stains. Presumably, the murder weapon.' Give him some water."

Someone kicked me in the ribs with his boot: I was sitting on my haunches, leaning against the wall at the entrance to the toilet, my face buried between my knees, which I embraced with both arms. I bent over and raised my head, and the boot asked me, "Want some water?" I shook my head, shook it and continued to shake it for a long time, for another reason, you know why. Lisa, it's important that you know that I didn't kill you! This is some sort of vaudeville. It's possible for a person to have doubts about where he was the night before, or the night before that, especially after such a shock, after searching for you, but when I saw that piece of metal, I understood, first of all, that I would never have dared even to point it in your direction, never, under any circumstances. Second, no matter what state I had been in, I would never have tossed it in the tool case, and they're saying now that the bloodstains were no less than two weeks old when it was placed here. No, I'm not going to listen to them, Lisa. I saw what you were murdered with. I can imagine the sound the blade made as it entered your body—crunching and plunging. My God! I must sign everything right away, confess right here and now that I killed you, and let them sentence me to the maximum and kill me immediately, right here, next to the toilet, so I won't have to learn any more details. I can't bear it. I don't want to know all this. I don't even know how to address you, Lisa! I saw the instrument that took your life, and I felt, felt everything, my dear, my little one . . .

"I want to make a confession. I want to make a confession, sign . . ." I think I said that aloud, because Tsupik turned up alongside me. Bending toward me, he said in a conciliatory voice, "You'll speak with the investigator first, then sign." They stomped about for quite a while after, but without their earlier fervor. I was informed that in the interests of the MGB my notebook of verse would be confiscated, but that it would not be included in my case materials because it might be of use as material evidence in some other case, all of this said as they laughed: it was OK for them to laugh now!

Once, as I was raising my head, one of the investigators in plainclothes came into view: he was examining an elegant Indian cane with a shoehorn at the end; it had been inherited from a relative, a former officer in the White Army. It was because of this relative that I read Bunin with such pride, with the feeling I had real, blood ties to the entire story, the entirety of 1917. He held this elegant object with its yellowed ivory horn covered with tiny cracks, and quietly asked his colleague something, part of which I heard: "What do you think?" The other fellow answered just as quickly, "Fuck it, you want to risk getting sacked?" They both knew that I was watching, that it was forbidden, absolutely forbidden to haul that thing home, so the first one ostentatiously, with a triumphant smile, broke the antique, then broke it again just above the shoehorn, then looked through the reed, first against the light, then at me, informing me as he looked: "I had to check that you hadn't hidden any narcotics in this thing." With those words he tossed the crippled object to his feet. Immediately someone else stepped on it.

With a heavy heart I thought about how long it would take to clean up the apartment and that I needed to call my mother, and asked if I could, but was told, "No!" I dropped my head back on my knees and was overcome by an untimely (I couldn't show them how I felt!) shiver. At a certain moment the rustle of clothing signaled someone's presence alongside me. I raised my head and saw Tsupik, who sat with his back to his colleagues and was looking right at me. It seemed he knew that I wasn't the killer, he believed me, not them . . not himself. Not the MGB. He was about to say something crude to me that would nonetheless let me know that not everything was lost, and I even smiled at him to say that this was all the devil's work. He did speak, and you know what he whispered? "Why didn't you leave, Anatoly? I told you to! Why didn't you leave?" Why hadn't I left? Because I needed to look for you, Lisa? Because I was sure that I hadn't killed you: despite my paranoid doubts I was certain of that and saw no reason to hide and thereby cast any shadow of doubt on myself: if he left, he must be guilty. I answered, "I didn't kill her," but he just waved me off, got up, and turned his back to me, and it seemed that he and I would find common ground. I would tell him everything that had happened, and he, though ready to condemn me, would let me know who had done it. He had a conscience, Lisa. Or he hadn't been an investigator long enough. Following the trajectory of Tsupik's movements with my eyes, I caught sight of Sasha watching me surreptitiously; he seemed to be tortured by a mass of questions that for him were purely philosophical, about how a person could knock somebody off yet not change in the least. You couldn't tell by Tolyan's face, bearing, or the expression in his eyes that he had slashed someone. With a handmade knife! If that don't beat all! No, the world is truly full of riddles! He'd have to sort this one out over a bottle with the boys. It occurred to me that thanks to me Sasha was undergoing one of those few epiphanies that simple people like him—who don't do a lot of reading, who watch only serial dramas on television, and who cull their wisdom solely from real-life experience and for that reason are truly wise, like the ancient Chinese or the Greeks—are destined to undergo. I smiled at Sasha, and he seemed to want to smile back, his mustache seemed to move, but then he stopped and turned away. And shook his head. I needed to adjust to my new status as murder suspect. Which, for all intents and purposes, was equivalent to that of murderer.

"Get your things," Tsupik said, approaching me. "I think there's no need to explain why you have to come with us." I nodded. I tried to remember what I'd been told about arrest and things to take. For some reason my head filled with idiotic dried bread crusts that one was supposed to have dried in advance, but I hadn't, therefore . . . Of course, warm things. I put on several sweaters, having first made sure there were no drops of your blood on them, Lisa, underclothes, on top of them trousers, high lace-up

fur-lined boots, an overcoat, hat, and something else. They led me out of
my own apartment. How strange: guests leading the host. A voice came
from behind: "Don't rush, turn the key twice to lock it, or someone will
break in and the MGB will get blamed again." In a closed, leather, broad-
shouldered, and stamping circle they led me out into the courtyard.

Petrov, who had been entrusted to keep an eye on the client, led me to
the UAZ police car, intending to seat me in its tiny section for arrestees
behind a caricatured grating, and I already imagined my gaze through
the bars, my last "forgive me" to my Frau half-buried in a snowdrift. But
Tsupik stopped him in his tracks: "He'll ride with me." The agents divided
up into various cars, someone was already turning one of the cars around
to head out, and Tsupik approached an old Volga (remarkable solely for
its tinted windows) and invited me to get in on the passenger's side. Inside, the car smelled of gasoline and Soviet imitation leather. He turned
on the radio: a sleepy DJ was announcing something in an intimate voice.
We took off, drove out onto the avenue, and headed off toward the center
of town.

"I arranged it that during the inquiry you'll be kept in the American
sector. That's the inner prison of the MGB in the main building."

I noted that when we were alone, Tsupik once again addressed me with
the formal plural, confirming my sense of his sense of my innocence, and
I was grateful to him for that "you."

"The confinement conditions are a bit better there, and there's heat in
the cells. Suspects are kept in isolation, especially those like you. But that's
only until your hearing, so don't be in any rush. Do you know what confinement conditions are?" He turned up the radio's volume. "You can't
talk to anyone in the cells." He looked me in the eyes and had a meaning-
ful expression on his face that made him look like the French comic Louis
de Funès. He wanted to add something else, it seemed, about why they
had come in the middle of the night and about what he thought about my
case, but at the last moment he turned away and watched the road.

Having arrived at the ornate Stalin-era palace of the MGB, which was
illuminated from all sides, we turned onto Komsomolskaya Street and
braked just opposite a cul-de-sac at the entrance to the Dzerzhinsky Club.
Cul-de-sac—Tsupik's back. The cul-de-sac ended in a decorative gate
painted the same color as the building. The investigator flashed his lights,
and the gate opened.

"I didn't know there was a door here," I couldn't resist saying.

"Nobody knows. Until they're delivered here." We drove into the gate and inside the courtyard was a whole city block of buildings occupied by the MGB. A man with a mirror on a long handle came out immediately and checked underneath the car. Then he knocked on the driver's-side window. Tsupik rolled down the window and said simply "One." The man made a notation in his list (how many notations had he made over the course of that one night?) and stepped aside.

Maneuvering slowly between the buildings, of which there were many, we drove through another gate in a sixteen-foot wall topped with barbed wire and pulled up to a round structure with barred windows. For some reason I felt like a tourist visiting architectural monuments long ago obliterated from maps of the city. On maps this area was a gray half-mile-square space that the MGB represented as a single structure, its headquarters. Aircraft flying over the city detoured around the center of the city so that no one, God forbid, might take a photograph of this secret prison. And here I was standing right in front of it. As a prisoner.

Tsupik got out of the car, as did I, after discovering that I was at the far end of a gunsight aimed at me from a platform above. I also discovered that the sky was covered over with barbed wire, that the gate had already closed behind the car, and that a gray-painted tin door with a narrow slit led inside. The investigator proceeded somewhere within and picked up a file of documents. When I tried to follow him, the armed escort shouted at me, "Where are you going? Halt! Face the wall." Then they led me into a tiny room with a wooden floor, bars replacing two of its walls. Tsupik marched quickly in the direction of the exit. I thought that he would return: he hadn't said good-bye. But they had already called me over and led me away. Yes, of course, who was I now, that he should say good-bye to . . .

I handed over all my things, including the keys to my Frau and the keys to my apartment and asked once again about a call to my mother and was once again refused. They took most of my "articles of clothing" (as they called them) after finding a strap and shoelaces, which were forbidden because I might want to hang myself in my cell to avoid their form of justice. Too many emotions were running through me, but I no longer felt each of them individually as sharply as I had when they started the search. I noted for myself: I'm being photographed; I'm being fingerprinted; I'm being taken down a circular corridor painted that same green color familiar to all former Soviet citizens because since primary school all our lives it had surrounded us: in clinics, at the draft board, inside government offices, at passport registration points. Here was where it originated! We were all prepared for it at any moment; it did not surprise us as much as it would those who might wind up here twenty years from now, with no memory of that sticky, nauseating green.

"Halt. Face the wall!" They removed my handcuffs (when had they managed to put them on?) and opened the thundering, heavy door that led to my cell, whose number I sternly forced myself to note and remember: this was important. This was almost like fate! But it flew from my mind immediately: I started thinking, and next thing . . .

Bright electric lighting, a bed on metal springs, a small hidden "muzzle"— as they referred to those white-painted hole-punched metal sheets over the tiny windows—and the dense green (of course) color of the wall, only—one, two, three, four, five—steps in length. Oh, and the intolerably stinking plastic tank near the door. Why was it there? Right behind the door? Ah, that's a toilet, a toilet, because it's impossible to do your business when you're being watched, and here in the corner was a dead space, if you leaned back against the wall just this way. On the floor, two inches from the wall, a white line traced the cell's perimeter. What for? It looked like the chalk circle in the film *Viy*. I was within the white circle. Nothing would hurt me. Taking a couple steps, I sat on the bed. I would have sat there for half an hour. An hour, maybe. Then gone, Lisa, to stand under our bridge. You remember the game called the "happy ending" of the novel? I had concocted a dozen endings: according to each of them you would be waiting for me after having returned to the city. But I was here, in quarters I could not leave of my own accord. I needed to go to the bridge. I would take up my post there, and everything inside me would calm down immediately. Even if you never came, I would find peace. I'd sit here for half an hour, then head off to the bridge. To the bridge. Take a stroll: it wasn't far, just a fifteen-minute walk. Down Komsomolskaya Street. Turn off toward the Niamiha . . . past the streetcar stop, and down the stairs, and there you would be waiting for me, Lisa . . . The escort's steps stopped at my door, and the metal observation window slid open.

"What the hell is this?"

Perplexed, I raised my head. What was this remark supposed to mean? That I had violated some rule while simply sitting on my bed? Expressing polite bewilderment, polite, very polite, I remained seated. The door rumbled open, and the escort, blackjack in hand, stepped forward and stood right in front of me: a sadist's pale face, teeth hidden in rage.

"You out of your fuckin' mind?"

He lit into me with his blackjack, not paying particular attention where. My cheek was in his line of attack, but I covered it with my hand, at the same time opening up my rib cage to take it in the diaphragm and slide off the bed, breathing, breathing—whether my sight would be restored depended on my breathing. I doubled over in pain, as he continued to shout and rage:

"Out of your fuckin' mind, are ya? Decided to buck the system, did you? Just checked in and already causin' trouble." His boot, barely emerging from the twilight, struck me at the stem of my neck, and it hurt, hurt, hurt . . . I turned over on my back and stuck out my arms in front of me, rasping pathetically, like a child, "Don't hit me! Don't hit me! Don't hit me!" When I saw that he wasn't going to hit me again, I pleaded, "What did I do? What did I do?"

He had already cooled off, already understood that I didn't understand what I'd done, honestly didn't understand. Stepping over me with his rock-hard sole, he said:

"You fuckin' think you're at a sanitarian? Ya? You think you're here for a vacation?"

I couldn't help but make mental note of his confusion of "sanitarian" and "sanitarium," but he probably didn't know that a sanitarian was a person; if he did, he probably would have decided that a sanitarian works at a sanitarium, but that was the punster in me thinking, while my torn diaphragm and throbbing neck kept stammering against all linguistic will:

"I don't understand, don't understand, don't understand . . ."

His linguistic confusion had frightened my diaphragm and throbbing neck; it seemed to them that a person who confused forms like that could kick someone to death: he was beyond comprehension, made out of a different kind of dough, and physically must despise anyone who said "sanitarian" and meant "sanitarian."

"During the day inmates are to remain standing. No sitting. Crossing the white line and leaning against the wall also are not allowed. Got that, fag?"

He waved his blackjack through the air, but my frightened visage was no longer driving his sadistic instincts in the direction of more beatings, and his blackjack just whistled through the air.

"I understand . . . They hadn't told me . . . Didn't instruct me." That little word of theirs, "instruct," had a placating effect on him, as if it were a sign of my willingness to play on his linguistic field and to submit in terms of lexicon. Measuring me up with another look, and disappointed not to find even a distant suggestion of resistance in my face or pose, he headed to the exit, while I looked and looked at the window: outside, it was still dark, so what in the hell did they mean by daytime around here? He had followed my gaze and explained, now calmly:

"Daytime starts at 8:00 A.M., indicated to inmates by deadening the intensity of the lights." (The lights had already been "deadened"!) "And our punishment block isn't heated. Three days in the tank, and you're an invalid for life."

He left, as I continued to lie on the floor, taking advantage of the brief reprieve, but the floors in the cells weren't wooden, and the cement was frozen and damp, the dampness contributing to the stickiness of the green paint I had already noted on the walls.

It all turned out to be not that terrifying. I sat, sat on the edge of my bed, trying not to creak; both his steps in the corridor and the scraping of the observation window were perfectly audible, so I only needed to jump up in time as the steps neared, and they knew, probably, they knew that I was cheating (everyone cheated?). The entire system was designed solely so prisoners wouldn't sleep during the day.

Near midday, judging by how the whitish light outside the painted window had achieved its greatest intensity, several locks began to grind heavily and in sequence, followed by footsteps—lots of them. It was the changing of the "screw." The new screw was heavier on his feet, walked a lot less, and for the most part sat on his creaking chair about sixty feet down the hall: crea-ea-eak—he's getting up, crea-ea-eaakk, caaa-rrreak—he's sitting back down, creak-creak-creak—he's changing the position of his legs without getting up. On his watch you could sit and even lie down on the sly.

When it grew dark outside the window, they delivered the food: "Open the food slot. Any slops to dump? No? Then take your ration," which seemed no less tasteless than the food I'd eaten over the last few weeks, Lisa. A bit later, the lamp over the bed began to burn more brightly than it had, signaling that it was OK to lie down, and the one with the heavy steps and heavy breathing approached my door and said through the observation hole: "Arms on top of the blanket when you sleep." I lay down, continuing to shudder at every crea-ea-eak, caaa-rrreak, crea-ea-eak, but the reality of the cell was already floating away: outside the painted window I was walking through a snowstorm toward the bridge, humming to the beat of my steps. I could already see your silhouette, and you told me that from now on we would meet here, that that was how it had to be, and you and I spoke about Mozart and Bach, you told me about double harpsichords, and I kissed your fingers, discovering a barely visible birthmark on the first phalange of your index finger and said that it resembled the dot of an *i,* then showed you mine, which resembled yours, on my ring finger, and the two of us decided that our birthmarks comprised the two dots over a *ё,* and we formed the letter by intertwining our fingers, and just at the moment when I was about to kiss your lips, the door rumbled open, and a voice said:

"Nevinsky, interrogation."

I jumped from the bed and discovered that no, the door was closed, closed, closed. Only the food slot was open. I blinked my eyes, not understanding how I would squeeze through the slot to go to the interrogation. I had such a taste for strong green tea, that . . . He barked:

"Turn around and put your hands through the food slot toward me. You have to put on handcuffs, bonehead."

Fearing a beating, I hastily did everything I was told, and the cold steel snapped around my wrists, then the door opened. "Stand and face the wall," was repeated about every ten doors on our way up.

Lisa, I thought about Tsupik, that because of my comfortable accommodations in the "American sector," he would be required to drive to interrogations from his office, that the roads were covered with snow, and that there was probably a blizzard. When they led me into a small office illuminated with the same intense, physically warming yellow light, I wanted to ask him two things: was it true that you had a birthmark on your index finger, and was it really snowing, but both questions were silly, and I had already turned my attention to the office, which much more resembled the interrogation room of the MGB that I had imagined: a desk, a chair fastened to the floor, and a light above the desk. There was nothing which I, a dangerous suspect being interrogated by the Fifth Section of the MGB, could use to crack the fragile skull of the interrogator.

Tsupik was writing something on ruled paper and didn't raise his head when I entered—no, of course, when I was led in. They led me in and removed the handcuffs. I asked, by all appearances violating many, many taboos, if it was snowing outside, and he paused, raised his head, smiled, and said that a thaw was promised for tomorrow, but until my case went to court I wouldn't be allowed any walks. Then he finished writing and offered it to me to sign, and I, of course, signed it without reading, and he scolded me as if he were my father. Undertaking to make sense of the complex words on the paper, I couldn't understand a thing and asked him to explain it to me, indicating that I was helpless. He pushed the paper to the side and sadly (so it seemed) announced:

"It's a ruling to replace your investigator. My approach and my views of your role in this case, and of methods to be used in working with you, did not entirely satisfy the investigatory group. I've been taken off the case. I was obliged to inform you of that in writing. Now I'll bow out. Wait. Your new investigator will be introduced to you immediately."

He rose, a bit too hastily, so I didn't have time to thank him, to say that he had helped me a great deal, even with his simple plural "you"— perhaps that was precisely the reason he left so quickly—he didn't want all that. The door slammed behind him, and I remained in the two-foot circle of the red metallic desk lamp with an on-off switch that I all of a sudden wanted to flip, and stretched out my arm and flipped on, and its light turned out to be much brighter than the ceiling fixture. I directed it toward myself, closed my eyes, and was able to withstand only a few seconds. The new investigator looked at me as he stood in the doorway, dusted with pepper, and even his jacket was the same—gray with an un-bearable quantity of black flecks.

He walked over to the desk, watching me intently. He sat down. He turned the light away from me. He turned it off. He opened his mouth full of bad teeth, which in the near future I could expect to see often, very often, every night, because interrogations here are conducted at night, and during the day you're not allowed to sleep. He said:

"I'm your new investigator. My name is Zverev, Victor Ivanovich Zve-rev, remember?"

I nodded, nodded to him, and even was ready to repeat it again, as I had back then, when I had committed it to memory. After that I did what I had decided to do at the first interrogation, back when riding in Tsupik's Volga. I offered to confess to everything, to write a candid admission of guilt, and assume all guilt. I was ready. "The main thing," I asked, "please spare me all the investigatory procedures. I don't want to know how she was killed. I want to forget that she was killed. Let her live inside me, right here, all right?" I touched my chest. I promised to say everything that needed to be said in court. I promised to accept and acknowledge any verdict. He very attentively heard me out. He smiled. He lit a cigarette. I very vividly pictured him taking the transparent, elastic, plastic mug of beer and gulping it down without taking his eyes off me. He exhaled smoke in the direction of the desk, and its clouds engulfed us, in part making us one.

"You don't get it, Nevinsky," he said predatorily, and that terrified me, Lisa. He didn't beat me and so far had not even threatened to, but I was terrified. "A candid admission of guilt is called that not because it's the easiest way to get five years instead of the rope when you're totally fucked, like you are. A candid admission of guilt is called that because the suspect under interrogation admits the full extent of his guilt. Full, understand. He admits, damn it, what he did. The whole mess, bitch. And the state is not demonstrating its humanism when it reduces his punishment and allows him to live. In this country there'll never be any fuckin' leniency. No. The state demonstrates its cruelty by allowing someone who can't live any longer—who doesn't want to live, who is losing his mind from aware-ness of what he did—to live. Look me in the eye, damn it!"

That was because I was so terrified I had taken my eyes off that pos-sessed maniac, Lisa, and he really looked possessed.

"Your problem, Nevinsky," he continued, "is that you, bitch, invented a situation that was too clever. You, fucker, suspect everyone around—the MGB, the state, Minister Muraviov—of having committed what you yourself did. You think I didn't read your testimony? You concealed your mind, your memory of how you, fucker, stabbed a person, an innocent girl! A fragile, fucker, defenseless girl. You concealed this behind suspi-cion of people in the service. So, fucker, look me in the eye, bitch! So my task lies in helping you remember how you committed this murder. Step-by-step. Move by move. So your hands once again hear the crunch of ripping flesh. So you re-create how she screamed. So you remember how she writhed in pain as she slowly expired in a pool of blood. You're going to recall all this, in minute detail, and tell it to us. And that will be a candid admission of guilt and remorse for your actions. A real admission and real remorse."

That was his speech. After that he set to asking about details of our last meeting, insisting in particular that after leaving Serafimovich Street I had ridden not to the train station, but home, home, where I had spent a certain amount of time. I just couldn't figure out why he needed all this, then I remembered the knife, the knife—I had stopped there to get Dad's knife in order to go to your apartment and murder you with that knife. To be honest, I really wanted to fling him the bird and say, like Neo in *The Matrix,* "You can't scare me with this Gestapo crap. I know my rights. I want my phone call," but I was sure he was prepared for this and that his immediate response would be to wipe my mouth off my face, so I listened, and nodded, and the further, the . . .

I shall tell about my life here, my sister. I was given a room, situated, by my calculations, in the crypt of the central cathedral. Alas, we both know too well the reason they keep me under lock and key, just as we know that considering the act I committed, the best place for me would be among wild dogs or in a cesspool, but the mercy of God truly knows no bounds.

When things get particularly difficult for me, I imagine myself in an enormous, airy, Gothic cathedral woven from air and casting its wings up there above me, above the ceiling, above that eye-blinding, never dimming (neither day nor night) fucking white light that shouldn't fucking be here in this asshole of a crypt, like some sort of vestige, right. No, no, no cursing, stay calm. What's important are Faith and Equanimity, not to lapse, not to lapse right now, or everything will come crashing down from all sides . . . Think about the peaceful quiet of the cathedral there up above, the cathedral situated between me and heaven, the cathedral in whose foundation, for my own well-being, the brethren have locked me away.

There, behind the doors, where they took me only once, to bathe—of the entire procedure I remember only a white wall constructed, it seemed, of enormous polished tiles and icy water streaming from a rubber hose— there, behind the doors, is a corridor, and on and off one can hear the footsteps of pilgrims descending to bow before the sacred relics. Some of them wear iron-wrought boots.

Please don't think that I've imagined all this: in the heavenly cathedral between me and the clouds services are held, and at first I was surprised that I heard nothing, until once—at a very complicated moment for me, about which later, later—I distinctly heard the peal of distant bells calling us to vespers. That distant bell-ringing reproduced, I think, a fugue (Bach?) I had once heard somewhere, and I took joy in it as an acknowledgment of the cathedral and refutation of the word "prison" that had come from who knows where and made the inside of my head itch.

Several times I heard the services going on up above, the cautious sounds of an organ, and a choir intoning a melody by the group Enigma, and I wanted to sing along, but I couldn't do it in Latin.

My collaboration with Blessed Victor Ivanovich has been going on for about three weeks: I can judge by my beard, which was still just prickly when we began to prepare for confession and Communion and has grown into a tousle of hair that I can wrap around my finger as I pace about my cell, long enough for me to wrap an entire finger with a single strand, and I wonder what you will say when you fly back to see me again, sister. The last time you fluttered in and out too quickly, but there was so much shouting coming from the other side of the doors when I began to talk with you aloud. (I am not to interfere with the silent generation of those in wrought-iron boots.)

The effort that the Blessed Vicar has invested in his work with me is yielding its first fruits. I have remembered much of what my poor, confused mind had earlier denied. The Blessed One began by applying a series of logical arguments to prove to me that you never, of course, could have loved me, because my rival—whose name now is of no significance (we agreed to forget it and in the presence of other people, in court as well, to refer to him simply as "he," and this is important, very important, though I don't remember why)—was so superior to me.

He was worthy of your love because, as opposed to me, a commoner, he is an educated man, spiritual, and knew books as well as how to interpret them in different languages. You came to love him for his love of the arts, for his rich raiments, and his good manners, which, of course, I could not possibly possess. Here you see how far the Blessed One went to find the roots of my deeds. After all, he might have moved directly to the events of that night. But such is the difference between a channel of God's mercy and an ordinary murderer: he wants not to punish me, but to help me, me personally, to acknowledge and to repent, to confess and to cleanse myself. Saint Augustine in a discussion with Evodius maintained that free will is given to man by the Almighty. The Almighty endowed us with it, sister, so that you might decide for yourself whom to love and whom not. Attempting to win your love, I went against the free will given us by Him, and, thus, I went against God. When I did not succeed, I committed the mortal sin of murder, manipulating my own free will as freedom to act against God. This is where the brotherhood interceded, and they will undoubtedly help me repent in full measure.

255

I remember, certainly I remember, sister, how, clinging to my now readily apparent spurious innocence, I tried to convince myself that you loved me, and I you, and for that reason I could not have raised a hand against you. Blessed Victor Ivanovich helped me to understand, he, like any priest in collaboration with the Almighty and drawing his wisdom from the heavens, knew everything about us and even—you won't believe this!—recited word for word the contents of our conversations, helping me to interpret them correctly. There is one moment that now seems to me the fruit of my crippled fantasy. Back then I insisted on interpreting what had happened and attempted as well to convince the Blessed One that he could not know anything about us, that he was a stranger—Victor Ivanovich a stranger! Then he worked a miracle. He gestured with his hands, and the confessional resounded with the words of our conversation, our last conversation, muffled, but intelligible nonetheless. I heard myself shout at you, and, of course, there could remain no doubt that the Almighty had granted me this miracle in order to facilitate my remorse. My poor intellect still attempts to resist, to kick up—like a colt just having left the bosom of its mare—all sorts of self-justifications and still to suspect that other people had committed the murder for me.

Here, sister, I must once again lift my voice in praise for the Blessed One for having applied so much effort to lead me to a true confession. My senseless objections were finally worn down by the ceremony I had feared most and that laid the path to my surrender in this senseless, ridiculous struggle. The ceremony was called an investigatory experiment, and essentially it reconstructed, step-by-step, the actions I had perpetrated that night so fateful for our love. I remember how I resisted and raged. To me, poor fellow, it seemed that I would be murdering you again, and thereby relive the events that I had already been through, or not been through—at the time. Fool that I was, I thought they had arranged this, that they, sister, had murdered you! Victor Ivanovich could not force me to undergo the investigatory experiment: the brothers' charter does not provide for me to be submitted to the procedure without my full, humble consent, and he would speak with me for days on end, he would come to my cell. He and I would engage in discussions of astronomy, of the organization of the university, of Augustine, and of Him, who in his wisdom had created all this. As I now recall, more from a fear that my mind would grow even dimmer as a result of his stories, our discussions included quite frank conversations about how, for example, a person with knife wounds to the abdomen dies. I agreed to take Communion. The brotherhood brought me to the apartment on Marx Street, the same one where you parted with your life through the deeds of my sinful hands. By that time I already knew what to do and how to do it. They dressed me in the same garments I had worn on the night of the crime, placed my father's knife in my hands, and invoked with their prayers the silent golem of a girl who looked extremely like you. I already knew, already knew, how to do it, how it had happened.

I rang the bell, the door opened, and I took three steps across the carpet (you were walking alongside me, to my right), then I pulled the knife out of the pocket of my coat, and turning around to face you, I delivered stab wounds to your abdomen—no fewer than three, as they said, but I am yet to remember exactly how many. You fell, and I sat on a chair next to the coffee table and watched as you died, then . . . What happened next, what I did with your remains, the brothers, unfortunately, do not know, and my poor mind, confused by what occurred, is still of no aid to any of us here.

I remember, Lisa, how the knife entered the abdomen of that plastic doll molded to precisely your height. I remember how the knife ripped the skin, how you bent over and screamed. Right now I see your figure in the unlit room, I see how you are dying, not on the level of recollection, fantasy, or fear, but as a series of physical sensations, as the physical memory of my eyes and hands, and herein lies the great merit of this Communion, this investigatory experiment, this little procedure, as they called it.

I am now unable to separate myself from this murder. When Victor Ivanovich and I talk about it, I recall the room, and the clumsy handle of the knife in my hand, and the coldness of steel on the pad of my hand, near my little finger, where the wooden handle ended and the iron began. I do not know whether what I remember is the real murder or just the investigatory experiment, but that's not the point. The point lies in that from now on all these memories will remain palpable, tangible. I no longer will have to fantasize while talking with the brethren and making my confession.

After the investigatory experiment, my mind, confounded by what had happened, dulled, and, I admit, I lost control of myself. Of that time I remember only how I sat on this here bed, my legs tucked underneath me, and shuddered with strong tremors from fear, while tiny awful *presences* slithered out of the walls and danced about me, driving me to howl and to pound my head against the door. A doctor was summoned. He gave me injections, after which the sensation of horror did not pass, but was stifled, and the tremors I'm telling you about grew less intense, retreating to my spine and to my calf muscles, which shook constantly and sent shivers through the rest of my body. Then, no longer able to coexist with all this, I attempted an even greater sin, suicide, picking my wrist open with the edge of the metal bowl they brought my food in, which I had filed to a sharp edge against the wall. The shameful traces of the crime I had devised, the paint on the wall scraped off by the metal sharpened against it and the stones revealed beneath it, remain visible to this day, above the slops bucket, but I don't want to remember those dark times.

Whether due to the injections or—and how I want to believe this, sister—due to the confessions I made nightly to the Blessed Victor Ivanovich as a result of my own spiritual labors, the horror gradually receded, just as did the curse of amnesia reigning in my soul. All the things he told me I could recollect with ease and readiness, as if he were showing me pictures of people I knew and my task was to describe their personalities.

But let me tell you about our brotherhood. It is enclosed by a very high wall of gray sandstone belted by a moat that is dried up now, thanks to the peacefulness of the times. After crossing a bridge, you find yourself in a courtyard decorated with manicured fruit trees. They are cared for by the brother-provisioner, a good-natured chubby fellow who loves gardening and talks to the animals in the sheds. Sometimes, when waking up, I discover alongside my bed a saucer of honey or a chicken egg, warm and just taken from the chicken, still in feathers. The provisioner and I converse in half-whispers through the window, because the rules forbid talk among the brothers. He tells me the latest news, about the cow that just calved, the roof over the baptismal fonts that caved in from old age, and the restoration of the frescoes in the right nave of the cathedral.

In September the novices gather a wonderful harvest of crunchy green apples, and their smell wafts through the entire courtyard, blending with the smell of golden hay that carpets the ground. In small gusts the wind whips up smells of both putrefaction and life, and there is no sweeter time here than autumn, sister.

In the early winter when the snow has still not fallen, our cathedral shimmers with hoarfrost, and on moonlit nights it seems as if it is carved from ice. The brothers believe that on Christmas Eve a miracle occurs: for several seconds the enormous cathedral becomes transparent, and if you peer between the buttresses and flying buttresses, you can see the lights of the infirmary, the scriptorium, and the refectory, all situated behind an apse. How wonderful it is to come out of the dormitory on a fine but still freezing March day, and, after singing praise to the Almighty, to set off down the snow-dusted ground past the kitchen, the library . . .

Lisa, you and I both know that there is no kitchen and no library; no scriptorium or baptismal fonts, no refectory, no dormitory, no cathedral with frescoes and stained-glass windows, no enormous rosetta window; there is no brother-provisioner, there are no fruit trees, no green apples, no honey or bells; there are no sounds of an organ or of a choir. All of this is the illness of salvation. I am in prison, in the American sector, constantly shivering and stiff from cold, resuscitated only by the thunder of boots and the screams of those being interrogated. The interrogations, carrying slops down the corridor to the right, hands cuffed from behind, the contents of the bucket plopping and splashing onto my back, and these fucking lights. But, calm down, calm down, don't curse. Faith and Equanimity. Not to lapse, not to lapse, not to lapse . . .

The Blessed One has prepared me completely for my appearance before the Holy Court. I am certain that my testimony will be clear and not incoherent. I promised under no circumstances to contradict myself, for otherwise I shall cast umbrage on the holiness of the Vicar and on his ability to cure souls through conversations about the sins they have committed. He says that I am not entirely healed of the spiritual wounds I suffered in the process of making my confession, that traces remain in my appearance and my speech. I developed a terrible stutter, and my front teeth disappeared somewhere, leaving only sharp edges that cut my tongue. For that reason he will write down how I should answer the judges' questions, and I will read them off the page. He also said something about the two options the Holy Fathers might determine as punishment, but I'm not interested in hearing about that. After the murder I committed—on the grounds of sinful jealousy moreover—what difference does it make if the thread of my life is severed or if I live a bit longer and pray to the heavens for forgiveness?

The principal benefit of everything I have undergone in our brotherhood, it seems to me, is the remorse that now possesses all my being. I deprived a person, a person I loved, of her life. When I recall, Lisa, your hair pulled back in a neat Pioneer (as I called it) ponytail, my heart fills with such suffering that for a second I doubt that I could have murdered you, the most precious living being on earth, and once again I want to rip open my veins or howl, but in those moments I evoke the sensation of that handle in my hand—I don't remember whether that was during the real crime or the penitential reenactment—and I agree, yes, I agree with everything, I agree. I have cried all the tears I could cry over your death. Inside me I have closed all doors leading from recollections of the event to the assessment of it, for precisely through those doors—my two demons, madness and doubt, penetrate my being, and for that reason . . . Enough, enough about that.

Lisa, I want to share with you something miraculous, and this story will be the last time I appeal to you, for I must allow you to make your peace with the world, and I have no right to trouble you anymore in that place where you are now. The first time it happened was soon after I had stopped resisting and doubting what Victor Ivanovich was (as I used to say) "inculcating" in me. I accepted my guilt and lost my mind because of it. It was one of those terrible days when I was still just learning to cope with life with new memories, and I was pacing about my cell and repeating the words "killedkilledkilled" very, very quickly, and then I started sobbing, then paced some more, and from the depths of my chest emerged a moan, and, it's true, human speech does not have words to express certain emotions.

There in the holed tin sheet that covers the white-painted opaque window a tiny aperture emerged. It's possible that it's not even an aperture, but just a crack between the tin sheet and the double-barred window, the tin sheet with the holes serving to ventilate the cell, while another window frame, the one underneath it and also covered with opaque glass, prevents the penetration of any direct sunlight. Well, in this complex window system a gap the size of a needle eye appeared, but it never makes itself noticeable, even on the sunniest days when the window blossoms with a holy luminescence. Only on rare occasions, when the position of the sun, the angle of the window, and the bars of the grates and frames fall into a single line with my redemptive, microscopic, needle-eye aperture does a ray of light enter my cell. Beginning as a pinprick barely visible to the eye, it quickly grows into a triangle on the wall at the level of my chest as a rather noticeable elongated spot. (I guard it from the brethren, and when the miracle occurs during rounds, I stand so they won't notice.) The little spot remains on the wall not more than a minute, then it doesn't disappear, it evaporates slowly, like a real miracle of God. I place myself in its Light, which fills my being and blinds me through closed eyes over the course of my confession grown unaccustomed to sunlight, and it warms me, and it communicates to me something very, very important. It communicates to me, Lisa, my dear Lisa, the sound of your name, as the two hot streams traitorously trickling down my cheeks right now communicate to me in your voice, Lisa, that I will be forgiven in that place whence comes Your Light, for God is love, and I love You. I love You. I love You. Forgive me, and farewell.

TRANSLATOR'S NOTES

16   **Lavrenty Tsanava**   A protégé of NKVD-MGB chief Lavrenty Beria, Lavrenty Fomich Tsanava (Dzhandzhava, 1900–1955) was appointed to oversee the Belarusian branch of Soviet state security. Demoted in 1952 for "serious errors," he was arrested and imprisoned following Stalin's death, and took his own life in prison.

17   **a Repin painting**   Trained at the Saint Petersburg Academy of Arts, Ilya Repin (1844–1930) was a prolific painter and one of the founders of the Itinerant movement, which challenged the limitations of Academy painting by introducing subjects from contemporary life. Best remembered for his large realist canvases, such as *Barge Haulers on the Volga* (1871–73), Repin also painted portraits. In his assessment of the costuming of the dramatis personae in Marleen Gorris's 2000 film based on Vladimir Nabokov's novel *The Luzhin Defense,* Anatoly probably has in mind Repin's portraits.

22   **"Rastaman," "Jamaica," and "Babylon"**   Dan appears to be a Rastafarian and fan of Bob Marley. The song he hums is Marley's "Rastaman Chant."

25   **Better to do as Plutarch had**   A reference to historiography as practiced by the Roman historian Plutarch (46–120), reputed for having placed didactic purpose before factual accuracy.

29   **like Savrasov**   *The Rooks Have Arrived* (1871), by Russian Itinerant artist Aleksei Savrasov (1830–1897) and currently housed at the Moscow Tretiakov Gallery, depicts the beginning of spring with the arrival of rooks against a background of melting snow, a white church, and a blue sky.

32   **Alessandro di Mariano di Vanni Filipepi**   Early Renaissance Florentine painter Alessandro di Mariano di Vanni Filipepi (1445–1510) is better known as Sandro Botticelli.

35   **Chukcha Yagerdyshka (from Lipskerovo, it seems)**   The reference is to a character from Dmitry Lipskerov's 2001 novel *Rodichi* (*Kin*). Illiterate

and alcoholic, Yagerdyshka distinguishes himself by raising a white bear cub whose mother had been shot by hunters.

35 **"I remember the wonderful moment"** Russian readers of *Paranoia* recognize the reference to Aleksandr Pushkin's 1829 poem dedicated to Anna Kern, "Ya vas liubil" ("I loved you . . ."), one of many literary sources that inform the novel, thematically though not stylistically: Pushkin's poem is remarkable for its total absence of metaphor.

35 **a Gorky park** Parks "of rest and culture" named after Soviet-Russian writer Aleksei Peshkov (1868–1936), whose nom de plume was Maksim Gorky and who in Soviet times was touted as the father of socialist realism, can be found in most major cities in Belarus and other countries in the former U.S.S.R. For his pen name, Peshkov chose the adjective "*gorky*" (bitter or embittered) to signify his reaction to the human suffering about which he wrote. In an entirely different context, at Russian weddings, the short adjectival-adverbial form "*gorko!*" is periodically shouted by guests to the newlyweds to indicate that the guests need "sweetening," which is accomplished when the couple kisses. In this novel Martinovich frequently employs puns—some, like this one, virtually impossible to render without comment.

38 **the Library of Adventure and Fantasy series** A popular series of adventure and science fiction books for children and young adults, the Library of Adventure and Fantasy (Biblioteka prikliuchenii i nauchnoi fantastiki) ran from 1936 to 2004.

38 **like sailors on the *Cheliuskin*** A Soviet steamship commissioned to explore passage through the Northern Sea Route, the SS *Cheliuskin* became icebound and was then crushed by ice packs in the Chukchi Sea. The members of the crew, who survived by repeatedly rebuilding an airstrip on the ice in order to be rescued, were known as *cheliuskintsy* and are still regarded as national heroes and symbols of comradeship and perseverance.

42 **Magnasco's *Bacchanalian Scene*** The original *Bacchanalian Scene* by Italian painter Alessandro Magnasco (1667–1749) is housed in the State Hermitage Museum in Saint Petersburg.

44 **the familiar "you"** Russian, like a number of other Indo-European languages, has preserved use of the second-person plural (in Russian *vy*) as a respectful form of address to be used in all formal situations. The second-person singular (*ty*) is used among "consenting adults," as well as with family members, children, pets, and God.

47 **he had made up the comical Nurmambekovs** The Nurmambekovs may be Anatoly's invention, but Nurmambekov is a legitimate Kazakh surname.

56 **Sierakowski, Wróblewski, and Dąbrowski** All three men participated in the Polish liberation movement of the 1860s. Zygmunt Sierakowski was a

Russian-trained general who, on returning to Poland, went underground, participated in the uprising, and was hanged in 1863. Walery Antoni Wróblewski was a Russian-educated member of the Polish gentry who participated in the revolutionary movement at the same time as Sierakowski, but managed to avoid the death sentence by escaping to Paris. While in Saint Petersburg, Jarosław Dąbrowski collaborated with other Polish and Russian military in preparations for the January Uprising (1862). He was also involved in the plot to assassinate Alexander II in 1881, but managed to escape to France. At the time of the uprising the governor-general of the Vilnius Region was Mikhail Nikolaevich Muraviov-Vilensky (1796–1866). Muraviov opposed all attempts by the Polish gentry to liberalize tsarist policies and to resist Russification. (Muraviov himself had forbidden the use of Polish in public and attempted to close down Catholic churches.) Following the uprisings Muraviov, in the name of Tsar Alexander II, authorized the execution of more than one hundred and sentencing of nearly 2,500 participants to hard labor or exile in Siberia.

56   **July 2 . . . no "memorial day"**   In Belarus July 1 is Water-Transportation Workers' Day, and July 3 is National Independence Day.

58   **Alla Pugacheva**   Currently retired but never out of the spotlight, in the late 1960s Soviet-Russian pop music superstar, songwriter, composer, producer, and actress Alla Pugacheva (b. 1949) captured the hearts of millions of Soviet listeners (including no few "intellectuals") with lyrics drawn from a wide gamut of sources combined with melodies and singing styles ranging from her own and Russian folk to Edith Piaf and Peggy Lee.

62   **the stagnation period**   The "stagnation" (Russian: *zastoi*) refers to the period from 1965 to 1985 during which the planned economy of the Soviet Union and its satellite states gradually declined to zero growth. Economic stagnation was accompanied by massive shortages of consumer products, unrealistically low salaries, and political repression.

69   **Bay of Finland**   In December 1907 Vladimir Ilich Lenin fled Russia by crossing the ice of the Bay of Finland; ten years later, in 1917, he would return to lead the Bolsheviks in revolution. Lenin's trek across the ice was memorialized by Soviet artist Aleksandr Rylov (1870–1939) in his 1933 canvas *On Thin Ice.*

69   **The Chemical Brothers**   Tom Rowlands and Ed Simons are a British electronic music duo who came together in 1991 as the Chemical Brothers and are still performing together at the time of this publication. The song cited by Martinovich, "Believe," which featured guitarist Kele Okereke, was issued as a single from their 2005 album *Push the Button.* The music video is available on YouTube.

78   **the monastery in the village of Zhirovichi**   This village is the center for Russian Orthodoxy in Belarus, including the Holy Ascension Stavropegial

Monastery, the Minsk Spiritual Academy, the Minsk Spiritual Seminary, and the Regent's School.

84 **Ivan Melezh**   A World War II hero, Ivan Melezh (1921–1976) was very prolific and probably among the most decorated of Soviet-Belarusian writers. His socialist realist prose earned him numerous prizes and awards during the Soviet period, including the Lenin Prize (1972), the Yakub Kolas State Prize (posthumously, in 1976), and the order of the Red Banner of Labor (twice, in 1967 and 1971). Melezh is best remembered for his trilogy, *The Polesie Chronicles,* about life and political change in the Polesie area in the late 1920s and early 1930s. Anatoly questions the sincerity of Melezh's writing.

84 **Vasily Shukshin**   Vasily Shukshin (1929–1974) was an actor, filmmaker, and writer best remembered for short fiction and films about his contemporaries caught in the cultural differences between village and city life. Shukshin's prose is recognizably self-referential, which lent the writer immense creditability in the late 1960s and early 1970s, when Soviet censorship was particularly stringent. He is appropriately juxtaposed to Melezh.

95 **ABANDON ALL COATS**   The sign above the door plays with the final line in the inscription above the gates to hell in Dante's *Inferno* (Canto III, line 9): "Lasciate ogne speranza, voi ch'intrate" ("Abandon all hope, ye who enter here").

98 **Feliks Dzerzhinsky**   A professional revolutionary and member of the Russian Social Democratic Labor Party (RSDLP), Feliks Dzerzhinsky (1877–1926) was the first head of the Extraordinary Committee (Cheka), which subsequently evolved into the OGPU, NKVD, KGB, and in Russia the FSB. Dzerzhinsky is considered the father of the Soviet security forces, and typically his portrait hangs in all security offices. Tsupik is apparently so devoted to his profession that he has hung Dzerzhinsky's portrait over the fireplace at his home. Dzerzhinsky was born in the same district of present-day Belarus as Martinovich, near Ashmiany.

99 **reading Esenin**   Sergei Esenin (1895–1925), a romantic poet in the first quarter of the twentieth century, wrote lyrical nostalgic poems extolling life in the Russian countryside. His subjects as well as his reputation as a heavy drinker and troublemaker contributed to severe censorship of his work during the Stalin era. He and his work were "rehabilitated" during the Khrushchev Thaw of the 1950s.

99 **"You tenderly embrace the curves of your guitar"**   The first line of a song by the popular Russian bard Oleg Mityaev (b. 1956).

99 **a conversation about Serafimovich**   The apartment is located on a street named after Aleksandr Serafimovich (1863–1949), a prolific and decorated Soviet writer awarded the Stalin Prize in 1943. Not unlike Martinovich, Serafimovich began his career as a journalist.

99 **Saint Seraphim of Sarov**   The most renowned and beloved of Russian-born saints, Saint Seraphim of Sarov (Prokhor Moshnin, 1759?–1843) was a monk, hermit, and elder at the Sarov monastery in Central Russia. He was distinguished by his asceticism and humility.

102 **A butterfly versus a tank**   "The Butterfly and the Tank" (1938) is a short story by Ernest Hemingway based on the writer's experiences in Spain. The Dukhmiany Bar described by Martinovich on pages 178–79 bears a strong resemblance to Hemingway's bar in Madrid.

102 **the Grand Duchy of Lithuania**   Anatoly is likely alluding to Moscow prince Vasily III's annexation of Lithuanian territories following the famous battle of Orsha in 1514. During the battle Muscovy lost 30,000 men and Lithuania only 500. Despite the outcome, the Muscovites captured Lithuanian territories.

104 **the Ferris wheel**   The Kobryn Ferris wheel was dismantled in November 2011.

108 **Schiller's poem**   The legend and painting to which Anatoly is referring is unclear; the appropriate Schiller piece to read on Saint Wilhelm's Day might be *William Tell*.

109 **"this violet napkin"**   According to Slavic folk traditions of dream interpretation, if a woman sees a violet in her sleep it may be warning that she is in danger or that she might incite someone to do her physical harm.

110 **a receipt for 35,000 rubles**   The exchange rate at the time was approximately one U.S. dollar to 3,000 Belarusian rubles, so the pizza with delivery cost about $10.20.

112 **"My Years and Days Are My Riches"**   A Soviet hit song from the 1970s composed by Armenian Georgy Movsesian and performed by Georgian singer Vakhtang Kikabidze.

120 **the Kristall store**   The brand store for the Minsk Kristall Winery and Distillery, famous for its vodka.

121 **Yanka Kupala Street**   The street is named after Belarusian writer and translator Yanka Kupala (Ivan Lutsevich, 1882–1942), considered by many the national literary hero of Belarus. Lutsevich, whose lyrical verse extolled the beauty of the impoverished Belarus countryside, derived his nom de plume from the holiday of Ivan Kupala, a pre-Christian Slavic holiday celebrated on the eve of the birthday of Saint John the Baptist on the Russian Orthodox calendar, July 7.

122 **the monument to the violin player**   The sculpture referred to on Yakub Kolas Square is titled *Simon the Musician* (*Symon-muzykant*), its subject drawn from Belarusian writer Yakub Kolas's eponymous 1925 poem. Yakub Kolas (1882–1956) figures among the "fathers" of Belarusian literature, his favor among the powers-that-be reflected by the size of the square named after him compared to the relatively short street named after Yanka Kupala.

125 *The Crystal of Fate*   The "Hollywood blockbuster" to which the message refers may be an allusion to a real computer game titled *Final Fantasy Crystal Chronicles: Ring of Fates.*

127 **palace at Kosava**   This neo-Gothic castle, now in ruins, was built in the 1830s by Polish aristocrat Wandalin Pusłowski. The structure has twelve towers, one for each month, and windows allowing each room to be illuminated by sunlight two and a half days of the year. Following the 1863 Polish uprisings ownership of the estate transferred to Russian aristocrats.

132 **Do you think they had good dreams?**   In the Russian original of *Paranoia* the MGB agents transcribe Shakespeare's English inaccurately, and in a footnote Martinovich provides a Russian translation from Boris Pasternak's 1942 rendering of the play. Well known for his creative translations, Pasternak renders Shakespeare's lines: *Kakie sny v tom smertnom sne prisniatsia, / Kogda pokrov zemnogo chuvstva sniat?* (What dreams shall be dreamed in that deathly dream, / When the shroud of earthly feeling is removed?).

136 **a Boldino rain**   At his estate in Boldino, near the city of Nizhny Novgorod, Aleksandr Pushkin (1799–1837) spent one of the most productive periods of his life, the autumn of 1830. In the course of three months he completed his narrative poem *Evgeny Onegin,* wrote five short stories (his first attempts at prose) collected as *The Tales of Belkin,* his four "little" tragedies, and a large number of lyric poems. He returned to Boldino in the autumn of 1833, where he wrote one of his most famous lyric poems, "Autumn," about his favorite time of the year.

136 **like a failed writer**   Possibly Fox here refers to Pushkin's 1830 epigram, written at Boldino, on Faddei Bulgarin ("Epigramma na [Faddeia] Bulgarina"): "It's no disaster, Avdei Fliugarin, / That you weren't born a Russian baron, / That on Parnassus you're a gypsy, / That society knows you as a turncoat fink: / The problem is your novel stinks." Bulgarin worked undercover for the Third Section of Tsar Nicholas II's secret police and is considered to have informed authorities of plans for the Decembrist uprising of 1825.

144 **a certain G. K. Kosikov**   G. K. Kosikov, "Sh. Bodler: Mezhdu vostorgom zhizni i uzhasom zhizni" ("Charles Baudelaire: Between the Rapture of Life and the Horror of Life"), in Sh. Bodler, *Tsvety zla. Stikhotvoreniia v proze. Dnevniki. Zhan-Pol Sartr.* Compilation, introduction, commentary by G. K. Kosikov (Moscow: n. p., 1993), 5–40.

144 **Baudelaire's famous phrase**   A reference to a poem from Baudelaire's *Les fleurs du mal,* likely "La fontaine de sang": "Le vin rend l'œil plus clair et l'oreille plus fine!"

153 **One day this guy finds this thing under the stairs in his house.**   Anatoly retells Jorge Luis Borges's short story "The Aleph" (1945).

154   **Andrei Platonov**   Andrei Platonov (1899–1951) was a Soviet Russian writer, trained as an engineer and hydrologist, whose stylistically inventive modernist writing drew thematically from the lives of such "simple" people as Uncle Seryozha, hence Anatoly's comparison of their reactions to Borges's "Aleph." To support his family Platonov himself worked on and off as a janitor.

154   **Kuprin**   Alexander Kuprin (1870–1938) was a prolific Russian writer, the contemporary and colleague of Ivan Bunin, Anton Chekhov, and Maksim Gorky. Kuprin's work, like Gorky's, tended thematically toward the "lower depths" of Russian society. In his assessment of Kuprin's work the usually skeptical Anatoly appears to agree with Soviet literary historians' interpretation of Kuprin as a realist-positivist.

156   **as Akutagawa writes**   Ryūnosuke Akutagawa (1892–1927). Akutagawa's short story to which Fox refers, "Kodoku jigoku" ("The Hell of Loneliness"), has not been translated into English. (My gratitude to Kathryn Sparling.)

169   **the impartial No. 39 house number**   House No. 39 on Karl Marx Street is a corner building, identified as house No. 14 on Engels Street. Martinovich reversed the house numbers for the respective streets. The discrepancy in house numbers is not a figment of Nevinsky's overwrought imagination.

173   **"Panikovsky Square"**   Officially, this square is now known as Aliaksandrauski Square in honor of Alexander Nevsky. The square is the site of Minsk's first public fountain (erected 1874) at the center of which stands a sculpture titled *Boy with a Swan*, which has inspired the popular name of the square as "Panikovka" after Mikhail Panikovsky, a central character in Ilya Ilf and Evgeny Petrov's popular novel *The Golden Calf*, who steals a goose. The square is also reputed to be a central gathering place for Minsk's gay community; "the azure" may be a reference to gays ("blue" in Russian slang) who gather in this square.

178   ***Charter*'s reporting . . .**   The human rights organization Charter 97 operates a Belarusian online news site in opposition to the Lukashenko regime (http://charter97.org/).

220   **Bobkins and Dobkins**   The nicknames recall Bobchinsky and Dobchinsky from Nikolai Gogol's comedy *The Inspector General* (1836).

242   **like a Iosif Kobzon concert or Evgeny Petrosian stand-up routine**   Like Alla Pugacheva and Vakhtang Kikabidze, popular singer Iosif Kobzon (currently a member of the State Duma of the Russian Federation) and stand-up comedian Evgeny Petrosian are icons of Soviet stage and television who achieved their popularity in the Brezhnev stagnation period.

244   **I read Bunin with such pride**   Ivan Bunin (1870–1953) was a distinguished writer before he emigrated from Soviet Russia in 1919 to settle in France, where he turned his subject matter to the terror and destruction

of the Revolution of 1917 and the civil war that followed; the fate of the White Army, which opposed Soviet power; and the life of Russians in emigration. In 1933 Bunin was awarded the Nobel Prize for Literature.

247 **a photograph of this secret prison** At the time of publication of this translation, overhead photographs of the KGB complex in Minsk were accessible on Google Maps (search term: "KGB Minsk").

248 **the chalk circle in the film** *Viy* Martinovich here refers to the highly popular 1967 Mosfilm film based on Nikolai Gogol's 1835 eponymous tale.